All Our Tomorrows

Riven Worlds Book Four

(Amaranthe ♦ 17)

G. S. Jennsen

Hypernova Publishing

2021

ALL OUR TOMORROWS

Hypernova Publishing
174 E Neider Ave #89
Coeur d'Alene, ID 83815
www.hypernovapublishing.com

Publisher's Note: This is a work of fiction. Names, characters, places, and incidents are a product of the author's imagination. Locales and public names are sometimes used for atmospheric purposes. Any resemblance to actual people, living or dead, or to businesses, companies, events, institutions, or locales is completely coincidental.

The Hypernova Publishing name, colophon and logo are trademarks of Hypernova Publishing.

Ordering Information:
Hypernova Publishing books may be purchased for educational, business or sales promotional use. For details, contact the "Special Markets Department" at the address above.

All Our Tomorrows / G. S. Jennsen.—1st ed.

LCCN 9781735178462
978-1-7351784-6-2

AMARANTHE UNIVERSE

AURORA RHAPSODY

AURORA RISING
STARSHINE
VERTIGO
TRANSCENDENCE

AURORA RENEGADES
SIDESPACE
DISSONANCE
ABYSM

AURORA RESONANT
RELATIVITY
RUBICON
REQUIEM

ASTERION NOIR
EXIN EX MACHINA

OF A DARKER VOID

THE STARS LIKE GODS

RIVEN WORLDS
CONTINUUM
INVERSION
ECHO RIFT

ALL OUR TOMORROWS
CHAOTICA
DUALITY

COSMIC SHORES
MEDUSA FALLING
THE THIEF
THE UNIVERSE WITHIN

SHADOWS & LIGHT
LIMINAL SPACE

SHORT STORIES
Restless, Vol. I • *Restless, Vol. II* • *Apogee* • *Solatium* • *Venatoris*
Re/Genesis • *Meridian* • *Fractals* • *Chrysalis* • *Starlight Express* •
Extinguishing the Stars

Learn more at gsjennsen.com/books or visit gsj.space/wiki

For all who strike out in search of the stars and freedom

DRAMATIS PERSONAE

HUMANS

Alexis 'Alex' Solovy Marano

Space scout and explorer. Prevo.

Spouse of Caleb Marano, daughter of Miriam and David Solovy.

Caleb Marano

Former Special Operations intelligence agent. Space scout and explorer.

Spouse of Alex Solovy, bonded to Akeso.

Miriam Solovy (Commandant)

Leader, Concord Armed Forces.

Marlee Marano

Consulate Assistant.

Richard Navick

Concord Intelligence Director.

Malcolm Jenner (Admiral)

AEGIS Fleet Admiral.

Mia Requelme

Former Concord Senator.

Morgan Lekkas

Former IDCC Cmdr. Fighter Pilot.

ASTERIONS

Nika Kirumase

External Relations Advisor, Asterion Dominion Advisor Committee.
Former NOIR leader.

Dashiel Ridani

Industry Advisor, Asterion Dominion Advisor Committee.
Owner, Ridani Enterprises.

Lance Palmer (Commander)

Military Advisor.

Joaquim Lacese

Former NOIR Operations Director.

Adlai Weiss

Justice Advisor.

Selene Panetier

Justice Advisor.

Perrin Benvenit

Omoikane Personnel Director.

Maris Debray

Culture Advisor.

OTHER MAJOR CHARACTERS

Eren Savitas asi-Idoni
Advocacy Chief of Intelligence for Non-Anaden Affairs.
Species: Anaden

Mnemosyne ('Mesme')
Idryma Member. Former 1st Analystae of Aurora.
Species: Katasketousya

Corradeo Praesidis
Concord Senator. Head of Anaden Advocacy.
Species: Anaden

Akeso
Sentient planet.
Species: Ekos

Casmir elasson-Machim
Leader, Anaden military.
Species: Anaden

David Solovy
Professor, Concord SWTC.
Species: Human

Devon Reynolds
Concord Special Projects Director.
Species: Human

Enzio Vilane
Head of the Rivinchi Cartel.
Species: Human

Graham Delavasi
Former SF Intelligence Director.
Species: Human

Kennedy Rossi
CEO, Connova Interstellar.
Species: Human

Kiernan Phillips
Lt, DAF Military. Fighter Pilot.
Species: Asterion

Lakhes
Praetor, Idryma.
Species: Katasketousya

Nyx Praesidis
Advocacy Dir. of Intelligence.
Species: Anaden

Philippe Beaumont
Gardiens Agent.
Species: Human

Pinchutsenahn Niikha Qhiyane Kteh ("Pinchu")
Tokahe Naataan of the Khokteh.
Species: Khokteh

Supreme Three
Synthetic intelligence.
Species: Ruda

Thomas
CAF Aurora Artificial.
Species: Artificial

Valkyrie
Alex's Prevo counterpart.
Species: Artificial

MINOR CHARACTERS

Alberto Duca, SF Chairman (*Human*)

Aristide Vranas, Concord Senator (*Human*)

Carl Odaka, AEGIS Colonel (*Human*)

Charles Gagnon, EA Prime Minister (*Human*)

Cyfeill, Ourankeli leader (*Ourankeli*)

Felzeor, CINT agent (*Volucri*)

Grant Mesahle, DAF consultant (*Asterion*)

George Takanas, Gardiens agent (*Human*)

Gregor Feldt, friend of Marlee (*Human*)

Meno, Mia's Prevo counterpart (*Artificial*)

Miaon, former anarch agent (*Yinhe*)

Noah Terrage, Connova Interstellar COO (*Human*)

Onai Veshnael, Novoloume Dean, Concord Senator (*Novoloume*)

Paratyr, Second Sentinel, Mirad Vigilate (*Katasketousya*)

Patrici Cabo ela-Diaplas, owner, Cabo Construction (*Anaden*)

Sandor Colby, AEGIS General (*Human*)

Solstan Sahlann, *Purgatory* owner (*Novoloume*)

Sotu Thisiame, Novoloume Pointe-Amiral (*Novoloume*)

Spencer Nimoet, Justice Advisor (*Asterion*)

Stanley, Morgan's Prevo counterpart (*Artificial*)

Tele Diya, Lieutenant, AEGIS Marines (*Human*)

Trepenos Hishai, former anarch agent (*Novoloume*)

William 'Will' Sutton, CINT Operations Director (*Human*)

Wyddoniiet, Ourankeli refugee (*Ourankeli*)

Xanne ela-Kyvern, former anarch officer (*Anaden*)

CONCORD

MEMBER SPECIES

Human
Representative: Aristide Vranas

Anaden
Representative: Corradeo Praesidis

Novoloume
Representative: Dean Onai Veshnael

Naraida
Representative: Tasme Chareis

Khokteh
Representative: Pinchutsenahn Niikha Qhiyane Kteh

Barisan
Representative: Daayn Shahs-lan

Dankath
Representative: Bohlke'ban

Efkam
Representative: Ahhk~sae

ALLIED SPECIES

Asterion
Katasketousya
Fylliot
Ruda

Taenarin
Volucri
Yinhe

PROTECTED SPECIES

Ekos
Faneros
Galenai

Icksel
Pachrem
Vrachnas

AMARANTHE
Concord Empire

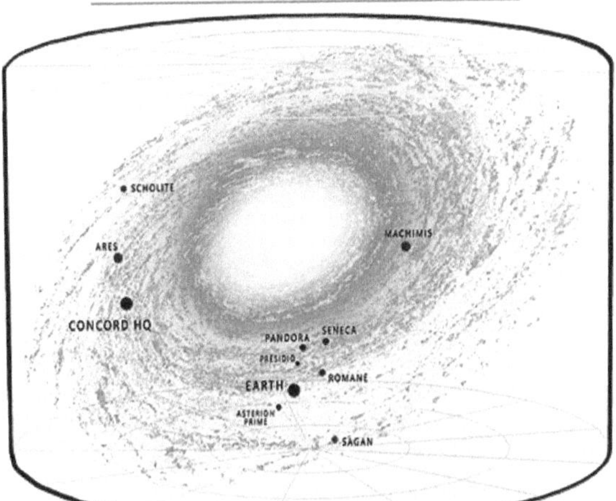

Milky Way Galaxy

Local Galactic Group

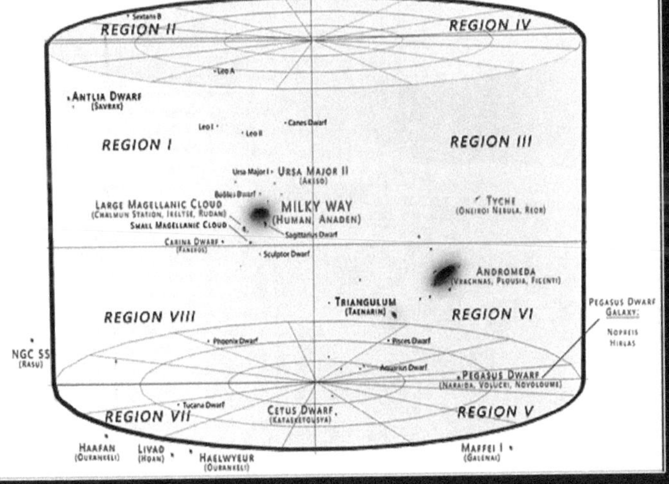

GENNISI GALAXY
(MESSIER 94)

✦ ASTERION DOMINION AXIS WORLDS
✦ ASTERION DOMINION ADJUNCT WORLDS
✳ ALIEN WORLDS

ASTERION DOMINION
AXIS WORLDS

MIRAI   NAMINO   SYNRA   EBISU   KIYORA

THE STORY SO FAR

*For a summary of the events of **AMARANTHE #1-15**, see the Appendix in the back of the book.*

ECHO RIFT

On Akeso, Caleb trains Marlee in combat maneuvers while displaying a deeper, healthier connection with Akeso. When Marlee damages a tree, Caleb is able to regrow its limbs.

Richard visits his old friend Graham Delavasi, who is running a fishing lodge in the Seneca mountains. Richard tries to convince Graham to come work for CINT, to no avail.

In the Asterion Dominion, Nika puts her original body into stasis, opting to continue to use the kyoseil-saturated body Dashiel crafted for her. When asked why, she says it's because kyoseil is the answer to everything.

The Rasu attempt to attack Mirai, only to find it protected by a Rift Bubble. They probe the other Axis Worlds, then settle for attacking one of the Adjunct colonies. The Advisors decide not to defend the colony, as they need to conserve their resources for now.

After being regened following his death while freeing Namino, Joaquim bumps into Selene. He doesn't remember their time together while trapped on Namino, so she fills him in over drinks, and they end up sleeping together. When he sobers up, his inherent hatred of all things Justice leads him to reject her and storm out.

Alex attempts to teach Nika how to visit sidespace and open wormholes, but the kyoseil blocks Nika's attempts to do so. Alex also learns of Nika's lost memories.

Miriam sees Malcolm for the first time since his escape from Savrak, and they ruminate on the thorny questions surrounding regenesis. Malcolm takes a leave of absence to search for Mia, who has vanished.

Mia has constructed a false identity on Pandora and renounced her former life. She's working on her new tech shop when the news announces that Malcolm, thought killed in the Savrak mission, is alive and well. Though overjoyed, she realizes that him dying a second time would destroy her and decides not to contact him.

Caleb tracks Mia down and visits her. He tries to convince her to contact Malcolm, but she refuses. He then presents her with a plea deal offer from Richard that will keep her out of prison (but prevent her from ever holding government office again). She reluctantly agrees to consider it.

Mia is visited by a local thug, who tries to shake her down for 'protection money.' Shortly thereafter, she meets a man named Enzio Vilane; charming and friendly, he presents himself as a local businessman, but Mia suspects there is more to him. She does some research and discovers that Vilane is actually the secret son of Aiden Trieneri, former cartel leader and lover of Olivia Montegreu. He's also the leader of the up-and-coming Rivinchi cartel. When she next encounters Vilane, Mia tells him she knows who he is; his charming demeanor vanishes, and he threatens her.

Eren is mourning Cosime in solitude at their home on Hirlas when he receives a visit from Miaon, his shadowy Yinhe friend. Miaon tells him how their former boss in the anarchs, Danilo Nisi, is putting together a new Anaden government; when Miaon reveals that Nisi is actually the true Corradeo Praesidis, Eren is intrigued enough to pay the man a visit. Eren agrees to work for Corradeo, on one condition.

After being blown up by Eren on Savrak, Torval elasson-Machim awakens in a regenesis lab. He quickly commandeers a new warship and returns to Savrak and inflicts significant damage in a bombing campaign. Torval then goes to the Anaden *elasson* confab on Epithero.

Frustrated at his lack of progress in reigning in Ferdinand's rebellion against Concord, Corradeo poisons the *elassons* with a drug that severs their connection to the integrals, rendering them unable to undergo regenesis. He then allows Eren to fulfill his condition, and Eren kills Torval as revenge for Cosime's death. Fearing he is next, Ferdinand flees Epithero.

The new Savrakath military leader, Brigadier Ghorek, surveys the widespread damage inflicted by Torval, then implements a plan to strike back against Concord, which involves a stealth antimatter bomb.

Nyx elasson-Praesidis pursues the mission her grandfather sent her on: to find the missing Praesidis Inquisitors. She discovers that Kolgo elasson-Praesidis has set himself up as a savage warlord on a backwater planet, where he's committing vile crimes. She continues her search and locates two additional Inquisitors, Lontias and Ziton, and they agree to accompany her. The three travel to Ares, where Corradeo has moved after bringing the *elassons* into line. Corradeo convinces Lontias and Ziton to help him form a new Anaden government.

Marlee visits Morgan at her bar on Chalmun Station Asteroid, intending to seduce the woman. Instead, she finds Morgan on a drinking bender, upset over how Malcolm is alive when Brooklyn Harper is still dead. When Morgan wakes the next morning, she decides to find out where Mia is hiding, then sends Malcolm a message with the details.

While closing up her shop for the night, Mia is attacked by armed intruders. They are about to shoot her when Malcolm arrives on the scene and kills the attackers. They have an emotional reunion, but when he won't revoke the 'no regenesis' clause in his will, she demands he leave. He begs her to come home with him and talk things through, but she refuses. He finally relents and departs.

In the aftermath, Mia decides to take Richard's plea deal offer and leave Pandora behind. She meets with Richard and signs the plea deal, then gives him all the information she's collected on Enzio Vilane.

Kennedy tries to coax kyoseil out of its Reor armor, hoping to use adiaK in ship hulls. However, though it does so for Asterions, the Reor won't release the kyoseil for her.

Corradeo sends Nyx and Eren on a mission together to find Ferdinand, much to their dismay. They discover that Ferdinand has been murdered while trying to secure a false identity, and argue their way through a brief investigation. Despite their disagreements, however, Nyx then asks Eren for help dealing with Kolgo.

Nyx returns to Kolgo's fiefdom with Eren. She pleads with her brother to renounce his depraved ways and accompany her; when he refuses, Eren poisons his drink to disconnect him from regenesis, then Nyx kills him. They report back to Corradeo, but don't tell him what happened with Kolgo. Corradeo makes a Concord-wide speech detailing his plans for a new Anaden government, one that is freer and more equitable for all Anadens.

Alex, Caleb and Valkyrie investigate the devastated Ourankeli stellar system, a species the Rasu annihilated several centuries ago. While exploring the Ourankeli's broken halo ring, they meet a solitary Ourankeli still living on the ring. The survivor recounts the tale of their war with the Rasu and eventual defeat. It also tells them of the powerful weapon they created to defeat the Rasu, and how they used it too late to save themselves.

Selene quizzes Adlai on what he knows about Joaquim. She then goes to see Joaquim and challenges him on whether he killed Blake Satair. He finally admits it, and she decides not to arrest him. Unable to resist their attraction to one another, they sleep together again.

Worried about an imminent Rasu attack, Nika offers a Rift Bubble to the Taiyoks, but their Elder declines it. Nika then visits Xyche'ghael, seeking insights into how she might change the Elder's mind. Though Xyche knows the Elder, he can't help Nika, because he's been exiled from Toki'taku for killing the Elder's brother.

Nika, Dashiel and Parc devise a small variant of a Rift Bubble that acts as a grenade, in the hope the Taiyok Elder will accept Asterion technology.

The Rasu descend on Toki'taku. The Asterions and Concord come to the Taiyoks' defense, but without a Rift Bubble in place, they face an uphill battle. Malcolm returns to the bridge of his dreadnought, intending to assist with the Toki'taku battle. Instead, Miriam tasks him with another assignment.

Alex and Caleb take their new Ourankeli friend, Wyddoniiet, to rescue the last surviving settlement of Ourankeli. When they arrive, they find the Rasu are already attacking. They improvise a neutron bomb and disable the Rasu, then enter the settlement and convince the inhabitants to evacuate. As they scramble to escape with the Ourankeli refugees, new Rasu arrive to destroy the settlement. At the last minute, Malcolm arrives in his dreadnought and creates a massive wormhole for everyone to escape through.

With the battle for Toki'taku deteriorating, Nika goes directly to the Elder and pleads with him to use the new weapon they've devised, which they call a Rima Grenade. When she uses the weapon to vaporize the Rasu burning the Toki'taku forests as they advance on military headquarters, the Elder is convinced.

With the Rima Grenades deployed on the Toki'taku surface, Miriam begins to gain the upper hand in the space battle. Then, abruptly, all the attacking Rasu simply leave, leaving her confounded.

Richard reviews surveillance footage from Savrak and pieces together that the Savrakaths have used a stolen ship to deliver an antimatter bomb to Concord HQ. He orders the station to evacuate, then he and David go in search of the bomb.

They chase the trail through the depths of HQ, until they discover the bomb positioned near the station's massive Zero Engine power plant and are able to disarm it with a few seconds to spare. In the aftermath, Richard accepts David's earnest apology regarding the Ghost theft, and they reconcile.

Morgan surprises Marlee at her apartment and apologizes for her poor behavior during Marlee's visit to Chalmun Station. Morgan says she's going to start helping Devon test new weapons tech and invites Marlee to join her.

Mia settles on Romane and starts developing a plan to open a multi-species expo and cultural center to educate humans on the other species of Concord. She sends a conciliatory message to Malcolm, opening the door a crack to them trying to mend their relationship.

Following the incident with the antimatter bomb, the Kats offer a solution to the Savrakath problem. Lakhes activates a device, called an Echo Rift, that will both lock the Savrakaths on their planet and prevent outsiders from reaching it, effectively isolating the Savrakaths from the rest of the universe.

Miriam and the others are enjoying a relaxing lunch at HQ when Pinchu arrives with dire news. During the Toki'taku battle, a Khokteh warship was captured by the Rasu, likely revealing many Concord secrets to the enemy. They then learn that a Rasu fleet is approaching Pinchu's homeworld of Ireltse. The war has come to Concord.

CONTENTS

All Our Tomorrows

*"Let her sleep,
For when she wakes,
She will move mountains."*

— Napoleon Bonaparte

PART I

KINDRED

1

CAF AURORA

IRELTSE STELLAR SYSTEM
LARGE MAGELLANIC CLOUD

Fractured shards of burnished metal littered the upper fringes of the planet's atmosphere like the scattering of leaves in autumn. Twelve thousand Khokteh warships had been obliterated in a single, sweeping strike by the vanguard of the Rasu fleet.

Now the bulk of the enemy's vanguard shielded Ireltse as if it owned the planet, preventing Concord vessels from setting up their own defensive perimeter while laying a treacherous gauntlet for any friendly ships that tried to reach the surface.

With plenty of forces to spare, a swarm of Rasu heavy frigates stretching at least five megameters wide and twice as deep were hot on Miriam Solovy's tail as she sought a foothold from which to begin to turn back the onslaught.

Despite their exhaustive preparations over the last month, today the Rasu had caught them as flat-footed as rookie grunts on their first morning at boot camp. In the opening salvo of their now-explicit war with Concord, the Rasu had sneaked past their sensors and patrols to strike at one of Concord's most important planets. Worse yet, this looked to be their largest assault to date.

Miriam had changed all the Concord protocols immediately upon learning of the presumed capture of a Khokteh vessel, but immeasurable damage had already been inflicted, in more than one respect.

It was what it was; nothing to do now but fight and scrape their way out of the ditch and through to the other side, where hopefully they could engineer a victory.

Commandant Solovy (CAF Aurora)(Ireltse Command Channel): "Fleet Admiral Jenner, until the Katasketousya fleet arrives to take over, I want the entire AEGIS presence to form a reverse blockade on our rear. Keep the Rasu's second wave away from the planet until we're able to gain control of the interior defensive perimeter."

Fleet Admiral Jenner (AFS Denali)(Ireltse Mission Channel): "All AEGIS Battle Groups, with me."

Not a peep of argumentativeness from the Fleet Admiral. It was good to have Malcolm back at the head of the AEGIS fleet.

Commandant Solovy (CAF Aurora)(Ireltse Command Channel): "Navarchos Casmir, demand the attention of the Rasu vessels in Upper Planetary Quadrant 3. While he's doing so, Pointe-Amiral Thisiame, direct your fast-attack squadrons to flank the enemy along the fringes of Quadrant 3. So long as their trajectories are parallel to the surface or a minimum fifty-degree vector away from Ireltse, utilize negative energy weapons to rid us of their presence."

Terse acknowledgments followed, and across the battlefield ships moved by the tens of thousands.

"Thomas, clear out the vessels that have been chasing us, then open fire on any Rasu larger than a frigate—conventional weapons only, but let's make them feel it. We need to protect the forming blockade at our rear until our ships are firmly in position." Her ship was staffed by a helmsman and a weapons officer, but at this point they served as backups. Thomas could handle both tasks with far greater speed and precision than any human, and with nearly as much ingenuity.

Rasu weapons fire peppered the *Aurora's* double-shielding, since this close to the planet she was forgoing the use of the Dimensional Rifter, but she paid it no mind. The reality was, the only thing the Rasu could do to damage the *Aurora* was to swallow it whole, and that was not going to happen a second time.

'Weapons are hot and…firing.'

The viewport lit up with the beams from the *Aurora's* ten discrete laser weapons, and Miriam's thoughts raced onward to the next tactical step. Initial scans picked up less than two thousand Khokteh warships still flying above the planet, and none of them was the flagship.

Tokahe Naataan, please respond. Concord forces have reached Ireltse space. I need to know your location and status.

Thankfully, a swift response arrived.

As the entire planet is my responsibility, I am overseeing its defense from the Center. Wohasi Heaka is commanding the space fleet. However, as of six minutes ago, he is no longer responding to comms.

I regret to inform you that your space contingent took a brutal hit shortly before we engaged the Rasu. Please continue to direct your forces from the ground. We'll handle things up here.

I've just ordered another three battalions to divert from Nengllitse and—

Tokahe Naataan, if a ship is not equipped with either a Dimensional Rifter or double defensive shielding, I must advise you to keep it out of direct fire for now. It's ugly above the planet.

Understood.

She heard the undercurrent of a growl in his reply. The Khokteh were a proud people, and none more so than Pinchu, but the Rasu had obliterated their planetary defenses and most of their fleet in minutes.

Not for the first time, she rued the stubborn arrogance of the AEGIS bureaucrats in their flat-out refusal to share adiamene with any alien species. She understood their professed arguments in favor of the choice, but right now people were dying—people who, due to the particularities of their biology, were unable to take advantage of regenesis—and they didn't have to be. The Khokteh worlds were uniformly metal-poor, for reasons only the Kats knew. The Khokteh scraped together every kilo of metal they could mine to make the strongest hulls possible for their warships, yet those hulls were collapsing like muslin beneath the might of concentrated Rasu firepower.

Over the last fourteen years, the Khokteh had become more than simply allies. They were Concord, as surely as humanity was, and she would not allow the Rasu to take this planet.

Another message came in from Pinchu then.

Commandant, the planetary sensors that are still operational have registered several dozen Rasu ships in the lower atmosphere and descending rapidly. Ground forces are moving to intercept them.

Acknowledged. Expect some help on the surface soon.

Of course the Rasu had already reached the ground. Dammit, she'd been scrambling to play catch-up since the minute she'd arrived. How to alter the battlefield to regain the advantage?

'Commandant, a notification from Hyperion indicates the Kat fleet is now on rapid approach from the outskirts of the stellar system.'

Well, their presence would certainly help in this regard.

Commandant Solovy (CAF Aurora)(Ireltse Command Channel): "Hyperion, welcome to the battle. Everyone, let's spin the Rasu's heads. Hyperion, take over for the AEGIS forces and maintain a reverse blockade facing outward from the planet.

"Fleet Admiral Jenner, have the AEGIS Battle Groups take the Machim fleet's place in burrowing a beachhead through Upper Planetary Quadrant 3, then expand from there as you're able.

"Navarchos Casmir, shift your space forces to Quadrant 4 and send all ground detachments and planetary aerial squadrons to the surface. Fleet Admiral Jenner, send yours as well. Interface directly with the Tokahe Naataan to coordinate your responses to Rasu atmospheric incursions."

She took the time to admire the beauty of several hundred thousand warships erupting in seeming chaos, flinging themselves across the battlefield then regrouping in unconventional formations, all within seconds. Thanks to Artificials, Prevos and the accelerating advancement of technology they brought with them, this was not her father's warfare.

Speaking of weapons that had been unimaginable a mere two decades ago, though, where was their promised Rift Bubble?

2

AFS TAMAO

IRELTSE STELLAR SYSTEM

"*M*arine squads A3, A4 and A5, report to your DAR craft for immediate deployment to the surface. Dropship pilots, acknowledge when you are heavy. Marine squads B4 and B6, prep to deploy in fifteen minutes.*"*

Colonel Carl Odaka studied the list of available forces, searching for ways to augment the groundside squads, then sent a message on one of the mission sub-channels. *"Lt. Colonel Grenier, my men are going to need air support in the marked grid in ten minutes. What can you give them?"*

DAR A: *"We are heavy and ready to launch."*

"Two fighter squadrons and one Eidolon squadron are launching in two minutes to help clear the road to the surface. Once your squads are on the ground, I'll give them cover down there for as long as it's practical."

"My intent is for it to be practical all the way to victory. Sending you the squad contacts now." He'd think uncharitable thoughts about the courage of fighter pilots, but in truth most he'd known were certifiably insane. It was their commanders who were the milksops.

DAR B: *"We are heavy and ready to launch."*

DAR C: *"We are heavy and ready to launch."*

"DAR A, B and C, you are go for launch. DAR D and E, prepare for deployment in twelve minutes. Marine squads B1, B2 and B5, begin deployment preparations."

Odaka wanted to send entire regiments down in one fell swoop, but the reality was they could better penetrate the Rasu blockade and establish defensible positions by moving in small groups. And in half an hour, he'd have over a thousand Marines engaging the enemy on the ground.

In the corner of his vision, the intra-ship activity screen confirmed the DARs' exit from the carrier's massive ship hold and initial descent into the atmosphere.

A twinge in his gut protested; he wanted badly to be on one of those dropships. Wanted to get his hands dirty with Naâu blood, or grease, or whatever they bled. But he wasn't going to make the same mistake Malcolm Jenner had. His men needed him alive and commanding them far more than they needed one additional gun on the ground. So he would stay on the bridge and do his duty.

IRELTSE

AFS DROP AND RECOVERY VESSEL B

Lieutenant Tele Diya leaned in over Major Whalesk's shoulder to peer out at the battlefield as they descended, stealthed, toward the surface. The fortified isolation of the *Tamao's* hold hadn't allowed him to get any sense of how they were faring so far, and this was his first glimpse at the ongoing clash. But he was a Marine, not a warship commander, and from this vantage all he saw was bedlam and destruction on both sides.

Whalesk, however, kept his attention fixed on the HUD. "Tele, get your ass in a jump seat before you land face-first in the supply closet."

"Yes, Major, sir." He'd known Whalesk for a couple of years, and he and the pilot had shared at least half a dozen missions by now—most recently the nightmare of a mission on Savrak. So while he obeyed the order from a superior officer, he laced his retort with a teasing tone.

Diya had barely gotten strapped in when the first hard bumps of the atmosphere hit, and he privately conceded that had he been standing, they might well have tossed him face-first directly into the supply closet.

He nodded a greeting at Captain Chacko across the hold. He knew Chacko somewhat less well than Whalesk, but the man had played a large role in pulling his broken body out of the literal fire on Savrak, so he was now forever prepared to take a laser shot for the man. Granted, he'd take one for any of his teammates, but he'd jump in front of one for Chacko.

The rough-and-tumble atmospheric run finally eased, and the interior walls transformed into visual projections of their descent path so they'd know what they were heading into.

It would be too pithy by half to say what they were 'heading into' was a warzone, but it was the most apt description. Rasu aerial vessels created havoc, haze and rubble across the city. Squads of Khokteh fighters and interceptors gave chase, but he watched four of them explode in less than twenty seconds. Damn, was everyone getting their butts kicked out here?

A squad of hardier Eidolons swept in from above to join the battle, and he started to feel a little better about their chances. The Artificial fighters were unequivocal badasses.

Whalesk came over the speaker. *"Thirty seconds to drop."*

Everyone unfastened their restraints and stood. Diya double-checked all his gear—which, as the team's tech officer, amounted to twice as much as anyone else carried. Though at least he didn't need to haul around one of the bulkier heavy guns everyone else toted.

He did, however, sport one of the new handheld negative energy guns. The Rectifier was the damnedest weapon he'd ever laid eyes on. Interdimensional magical destruction that he could hold in one hand.

The DAR was sturdy enough to take a beating, and it descended through constant fire to hover less than three meters above a dusty street in the central quadrant of the city. The rear bay door lowered and everyone leapt out, adopting a defensive formation once boots were on the ground.

Captain Harris checked everyone off. "The Center is four

hundred meters to our east. Khokteh troops are manning the immediate perimeter. Our job today is to keep ground-based Rasu from so much as ruffling their fur. Lieutenant Diya?"

"Launching surveillance drones." The five drones were each no bigger than a fly. They were programmed to sweep the area around the squad in all four directions up to a kilometer in the sky, sending visual and auditory feeds to Diya to alert him to any Rasu advances.

Harris pointed to his left, then his right. "Team Alpha, establish a defensive position on the—"

Diya had no choice but to interrupt him. "Four giant Rasu mechs are incoming from the south-southwest. Sixty meters and closing fast."

"Snipers on the roof to the left! I want rocket launchers staged behind that trashed vehicle over there. Everyone else, defensive positions. Let's set the net."

Diya had just flattened himself against the alley-side exterior wall of what appeared to be a weird Khokteh clothes shop when the four Rasu mechs rounded the corner one block down, charging ahead like buffalo in a stampede. Lieutenant Viyan let loose a rocket that slammed into the right-most one, shredding it into a hundred pieces. But it didn't disintegrate the Rasu, because Diya's squad had not yet been blessed with a supply of the much-rumored Asterion Rima Grenades.

'Sniper rifle' was something of a misnomer for the weapons the marksmen carried as they used a combination of lift boots and powered backpacks to 'climb' up the wall to the roof and sight down on the mechs. The slugs their weapons fired were akin to tiny drones, adjusting their trajectories mid-flight to strike moving targets at a location designated by the shooter to cause maximum damage.

Two more mechs shattered while he got into position, then a follow-up rocket launched to tear up the fourth, and scattered-but-not-dead Rasu pieces darkened the stone street.

Now it was his turn. He sent a specialized drone toward the wreckage that emitted a signal shown to interfere with the Rasu's...intentional activity, he guessed. In testing, it slowed down the Rasu's ability to move and reform by up to thirty percent, but this was the first time he'd used it in the field.

One of the surveillance drones swept by overhead to give him a close look at the kill zone and…well, the Rasu pieces were slinking around listlessly and not glomming themselves back into mech shapes, so the emitter must be working.

The squad had spread out beyond earshot, so he switched to comms.

Lieutenant Diya: "Targets R1-4 neutralized for now."

An encroaching shadow heralded the approach of a long, flattish Rasu vessel. He peered up to see it stop to hover eighty meters from their location. A circular platform descended out of its belly, carrying several dozen additional Rasu mechs toward the street below.

Captain Harris: "Prepare for incoming."

RW

AMF IMPERIUM ALPHA
IRELTSE STELLAR SYSTEM

As the bulk of his warships rearranged themselves and prepared to drive a wedge through the Rasu forces blockading the planet, Casmir elasson-Machim dispatched four hovertank regiments to the surface. The Rasu were gaining a major foothold in the northwest sector of the city, and troops on foot were not going to wipe them out on their own. Air support looked to be occupied dogfighting the smaller Rasu craft for the foreseeable future, so it was up to the hovertanks to tip the balance on the surface.

Dropping a cluster of Rima Grenades on the Rasu ground forces would go a long way toward taking care of the problem, but doing so would also transform a quarter of the city into a crater. In the old days, Casmir would not have sought clarification before doing exactly that without hesitation, but this wasn't the old days, and no Concord commander was ready to go scorched earth quite yet.

They were trying to make up ground lost due to the Rasu's surprise appearance here. The enemy had inflicted significant damage in the opening minutes, but Casmir's snap assessment led him to believe they were already gaining the upper hand on the enemy. Hopefully, they would be aided soon by the activation of a planet-wide Rift Bubble. If nothing else, it should cap the number of Rasu in-atmosphere, permanently dividing the battlespace into manageable chunks and turning a battle of attrition into a winnable proposition.

He followed the hovertank regiments' progress as they landed and moved into attack formations, but solely via the tactical combat feed. Once upon a time, he'd have been able to slip into the mind of any one of the soldiers and experience the ground combat firsthand from the safety of his bridge. But the integrals were all but gone, useful only for consciousness backup and regenesis purposes. Anaden minds were now sacrosanct.

He didn't disagree with the change, of course, but it did make commanding battlefields considerably more challenging. He had to trust his men to do their jobs using skill and wits—and he did. Anaden society was evolving more rapidly every day, and it wasn't always clear into what. But for now, Machim soldiers were still bred and honed for a single purpose: to wage war.

IRELTSE

The massive frame of the Rasu mech filled Diya's vision like a devil sent up from the abyss to drag him into Hell. He gripped the Rectifier with both hands and fired—and the abyss came for the Rasu instead.

Diya stumbled backward in a hurry, as he didn't want tendrils from the negative energy vacuum to snag any of his limbs.

Then the Rasu and the abyss were gone. The entire encounter

had lasted less than five seconds.

Captain Harris: "Need backup at my coordinates!"

Diya shook off the adrenaline rush and directed one of the drones to the captain's location, feeding the visuals to the rest of the squad. Harris and Chacko were pinned down by five—no, six—Rasu that had transformed themselves into giant, six-legged crawlers.

He might get his chance to return the favor for Chacko today after all. He rushed forward, Rectifier drawn, and zig-zagged across the open road to reach a vantage where he wouldn't take out his teammates along with the Rasu. *Here.* He slammed to a stop and fired above the trapped Marines and into the Rasu.

The top half of two of the Rasu were instantly atomized, but their legs and torsos kept moving. He blinked, and a canonized weapon morphed out of the top of one of the torsos. Damnable creatures!

Chacko hurled a frag grenade straight into the wide barrel of the cannon, and the next second Rasu bits were flying in every direction. The other mechs continued advancing, and one of those he'd shot reformed itself with a long blade for a fifth appendage.

Chacko grabbed Harris by his uniform material and dragged him backward, out of the reach of the stabbing blade, while Viyan fired a SAL into the mechs at nearly point-blank range. Two Rasu staggered and lost a step, and Diya quickly fired the Rectifier again. This time the whole bodies of both vaporized, buying Chacko and Harris another five or ten seconds.

As his teammates cleared the pile of rubble where they'd been hunkered down, he realized Harris' left leg was a mangled mess—hence Chacko dragging the man. God, did he know how that felt!

Lieutenant Diya (Ireltse Sub-mission Channel 12): "Need medical assistance at Captain Harris' coordinates. And air support. Air support would be great."

A low rumble, akin to a growl, blasted his eardrums, and Diya's heart sank. What was next, a platoon of Godzilla-sized Rasu come to trample them into oblivion?

Through the omnipresent haze caused by rampant explosions and falling buildings, the profile of an avenue-wide line of hover-tanks appeared from the east. Their design said they weren't AEGIS. Anaden? They had to be.

Wide beams streaked out from three of the leading hovertanks to cut into the remaining Rasu mechs in dramatic fashion. The Rasu that retained enough appendages to move pivoted to engage the approaching vehicles, and three of his teammates rushed in to help Chacko evacuate their captain to safety.

Diya breathed out in relief. Thank God the Anadens were their allies today.

3

KATASKATOUSYA SUPERDREADNOUGHT
IRELTSE STELLAR SYSTEM

The eerie darkness of the superdreadnought's interior wrapped Alex in a blanket of haunting emptiness. Only the narrow white streams of operating code racing along the hull provided any light in the cavernous space, and the far reaches were cast in inky, foreboding shadows.

Valkyrie murmured in her mind. *The welcome has not improved since the last time we visited.*

She chuckled to try to break the spell, then reflexively jumped as the sound echoed around her. *No, it hasn't.*

Beside her, Caleb looked somewhat disconcerted. "Your description of the interior of these ships did not fully convey the reality of how it feels to be inside one."

"What words could?"

"Fair point."

It is only a machine, and one not designed to host organic beings. What does it matter how it 'feels'?

Alex blew out a breath and shifted toward the swirl of pinpoint lights materializing beside her. "None at all, Mesme. Where's the Rift Bubble?"

Loaded into a launch tube and ready for deployment. We merely need to maneuver through the Rasu forces until we are close enough to the planet to ensure its safe arrival.

The hull jerked sideways beneath their feet. This not being a vessel designed to host organic beings, there was neither artificial gravity nor inertial dampers, and only their mag boots kept them rooted to the floor.

Which we are now in the process of doing.

"I can tell. Are we stealthed?"

It seems prudent.

The Kats didn't often bother to cloak their vessels, but they were capable of doing so effectively when needed. She and the other Noetica Prevos had learned all about the effectiveness, and the weaknesses, of their stealth technology during the Metigen War. In the middle of a pitched battle, the Rasu would be busy with all the ships they *could* see, so it shouldn't take much stealth for even the giant superdreadnought to slip through the front lines unmolested.

You do not need to be present for the deployment, either of you. I assure you, I will take care in securing and activating the device.

"We know you will. It's just that we have a special interest in seeing this particular planet saved."

Very well. Mesme's presence pulsed as it meandered along the empty hold. *It is...ironic, I believe is the appropriate word. Today, we—the Katasketousya—are saving the Khokteh, when once we were manipulating their self-inflicted destruction. This is your doing.*

Caleb smiled. "And yours. You're the one who convinced the Idryma to accept our conditions, preserve the Khokteh and ally with us."

You made a compelling case—all I did was endorse it. And thus here we are today.

"Here we are today." Alex rubbed at the material of the environment suit covering her arms. The chill was all in her head, for the suit kept her body temperature regulated, but she felt cold nonetheless. She was trying to focus on the battle proceeding outside and the actions they'd committed to seeing done today, but memories of her last visit to a superdreadnought churned to the forefront of her mind. It had been the first time she'd properly delved hidden dimensions and higher-order code, and in doing so sabotaged an entire enemy fleet. But more significantly for her, it had been the first time she'd heard her father's reborn voice in her head. These days, she'd all but forgotten what it was like for him *not* to be in her life, flesh and blood. But right now—

The floor lurched again, and she and Caleb pitched forward to land roughly on their hands and knees on the frigid floor. "Mesme!"

Incidental glancing fire. We are beyond it now.

"Great." She rubbed at her left elbow, which had suffered the brunt of the landing.

Caleb placed a hand on her shoulder. "Are you all right?"

"Yeah." She nodded a tad sluggishly, and they climbed back to their feet.

Mesme was now behind them, so she lifted her mag boots and rotated around. "Is it time to launch yet?"

Thirty-five seconds until we reach a position I have deemed safe for deployment. Recall, the Rift Bubble device possesses minimal defenses of its own while in transit, so we do not want to leave it exposed for longer than is necessary.

"Understood. I'll let Mom and Pinchu know it's almost ready."

Mom, Ireltse should have an active Rift Bubble in the next ten minutes.

Not a minute too soon, either. Can I ask you to stay safely distant from the ground until we remove the Rasu there? It's unpleasant on the surface.

A corner of her lips curled up. *You can ask, but you know I have a compulsion to help the Khokteh.*

So I do.

She sent a similar message to Pinchu and received a grunt in response.

Mesme vanished for barely a second, then reappeared. *The launch has been initiated.*

"Excellent. The same landing coordinates as we discussed earlier?"

Correct.

She took Caleb's gloved hand in hers and opened a wormhole in front of them, relieved to be leaving the tomblike superdreadnought behind. On the other side of the tear in space-time, the deceptively quiet and peaceful Ireltse steppes awaited. They walked through.

RW

IRELTSE

They stood at the bottom of a cliff, in a wide, dusty canyon lined with topaz and vermilion boulders. No structures were visible in either direction to the horizon, but the topography was nonetheless familiar. *Have we been here before, Valkyrie?*

We are situated around fifty kilometers northwest from where Pinchu and Cassela's home stood before it was destroyed in the Nengllitse attack.

Ah. I can see the geographic similarities now.

Alex collapsed her helmet and breathed in deeply, taking a minute to remember.

> *"This is truly gorgeous, Cassela. Your planet is beautiful."*
>
> *The fur around Cassela's neck fluttered. "We find much peace here when times become difficult. I encourage Pinchu to find more, but leaders must bear the burdens of their* shikei.*"*
>
> *She still wasn't opening the connection to Valkyrie for fear of the reaction it might cause, but she could always talk to her.*
>
> *"Valkyrie, there isn't a translation for that word?"*
>
> *' 'People' would suffice for a translation, but the term encompasses a broader notion of clan, as well as history and future—their ancestors and the children yet to be born. It is a compelling word.'*
>
> *Alex sighed wistfully, for the concept made her think of her mother. She hoped the burdens she had left her mother with were lighter than those which had come before, but suddenly she wasn't certain. No matter their weight, she had no doubt Admiral Miriam Solovy could bear them, but it was tragic she had to bear them alone.*
>
> *"At least Pinchu has you to give him comfort."*

"Mey, and comfort I do provide. But enough of sentimental poeticism."

"Yet you have a precise translation for 'poeticism?'"

'It is an accurate interpretation. I stand by it.'

Cassela gestured to Alex's forearm. "What an enchanting bracelet—there is much beauty in simplicity."

She ran fingertips over the curves of the smooth, onyx metal, smiling to herself. "Thank you. It was a gift from Caleb—the first gift he ever gave me, in fact. It...well, its origin is a long story, but it holds a lot of meaning for me."

"As it should be for such treasures. Come, let us rejoin the others."

Alex stole a last look at the fading rays of sunlight beyond the canyon then trailed Cassela inside.

The Khokteh had lost a fierce, extraordinary warrior the next day, and Pinchu had lost the greater part of his heart. He'd recovered in time, at least to outside observation, but he'd never quite seemed whole again. He was far too busy for her to ask him right now, but *if* asked, she suspected he would simply say that he was glad Cassela was not here to witness the destruction being inflicted upon her beloved world by the Rasu.

But they were about to bring that destruction to a swift end. A few meters away, the protective casing surrounding the Rift Bubble fell away. The next instant the extradimensional power source at its center flared to life, and a few seconds later the dimensional barrier exploded outward to encircle the planet in its sheltering embrace.

Relief flooded her mind, and the tension in her muscles eased.

Mom, the Rift Bubble is active.

Wonderful. We will switch strategies accordingly.

She smiled graciously at Mesme, who undulated nearby. "Thank you, again. We'll take it from here."

Of course. I understand there is a rapidly increasing demand for these devices, so I will check in on their production. Its lights, pale and washed-out against the vermilion clay backdrop, swept off and vanished.

Caleb squeezed her hand. "We should let Pinchu know the tide will be turning soon."

"We should. Want to tell him in person?"

"If we can get his attention for two seconds, absolutely."

"Mom said he was overseeing the planetary defense from the Center." She extended her arm and the onyx bracelet encircling it, and a new wormhole opened in front of them.

CAF AURORA

IRELTSE STELLAR SYSTEM

Miriam scrutinized each of the three tactical screens with a studied eye. Reports from Navarchos Casmir, Colonel Odaka and Lt. Colonel Grenier indicated the ground forces were still having a difficult time of it on the planet below. She ordered a twenty-percent increase in personnel and ships across the board, then refocused her attention on the battle outside her viewport, where they were making more progress.

Now that the Rasu knew about the effects of a Rift Bubble, if not the cause, the *Aurora* was no longer able to bait Rasu vessels to the barrier and into its trap, which was a shame. That particular trick had been rather satisfying.

On the other hand, with an active Rift Bubble, they no longer had to concentrate on protecting the planet below and could direct their efforts to permanently destroying as many Rasu in their sights as possible.

"Thomas, shift to TP-Sweep 2."

'Executing.'

Field Marshal Bastian (AFS Leonidas)(Ireltse Command Channel): "*AEGIS Fast-Attack Regiments D1-4 have arrived and are heavy.*"

Commandant Solovy (CAF Aurora)(Ireltse Command Channel): "*Excellent. Have them concentrate on obliterating the Rasu debris we've created before it reforms."*

The resupply of negative energy missiles the regiments carried was a timely addition, as these battles inevitably devolved into a race between their dwindling stock of the weapons and the number of Rasu willing to commit to the fight.

Her mind briefly drifted to the trillions, or perhaps more, of Rasu controlling hundreds of galaxies just beyond the cosmic horizon. They remained on the sidelines of this war thus far, but for how long?

RW

IRELTSE

Pinchu spotted them the instant Alex and Caleb emerged through the wormhole. He shoved his way past a circle of advisors then threw his long arms around them both, trapping them against his large, barrel chest. "My friends! Tell me you bring good news."

"We do." It came out breathy and winded, and Alex carefully extracted herself from his embrace while Caleb did the same. "The Rasu on the ground and in the sky at this moment are the most there will ever be."

"The Rift Bubble is active?"

"It is. Do you need more weapons? Rima Grenades?"

"Ah." He gestured to his left in the direction of a tangerine-furred Khokteh in full military attire pacing by the war table. "I'm told we received ten large crates of the Asterions' grenades and launchers minutes ago. They are being distributed to our rooftop snipers as we speak."

"Excellent." Caleb clasped Pinchu on the upper arm. "We won't keep you from your crucial duties. Go get your planet back."

"I like that spirit. Yes!" Pinchu spun and shoved his way back into the inner circle, issuing orders all the way.

Alex laughed, grateful he was now headed toward a happy ending today. There were losses, obviously, but in comparison to what could have befallen Ireltse if not for the Rift Bubble, if not for Concord....

She wandered toward the opening in the far wall to gaze out across the city, and her buoyant mood took a nosedive. 'Losses' didn't begin to cover the destruction consuming the landscape.

To the east, the competitive arena where young Khokteh men proved their worth in hand-to-hand combat was now a ragged impact crater. To the north, almost two kilometers away, a Rasu beam had turned a city block into a pile of crumbled stone. A little farther away, the largest road leading out of downtown had been shorn in two and upended, as if by an earthquake. On the western horizon, half a dozen Rasu frigates were having their way with warehouses and factories. To the left of the factories, dozens of Machim hovertanks moved against what might have once been Rasu bipedals, but now resembled twisted creatures from a nightmare. The enemy had risen to the occasion and combined their forms to match the hovertanks in size and firepower.

And everywhere the streets were visible, there were bodies.

She sensed Caleb press in behind her. "Damn. This is bad."

"Do you want to help? I think we should help."

"I think that, Rift Bubble or no, they're going to need all the help they can get for a while longer."

"Valkyrie, bring the *Siyane* down to the surface, wherever you can find a bare spot to land. We'll join you, then go harass some Rasu."

'With pleasure. ETA six minutes.'

She fisted her hands at her chin, rested against Caleb's chest to watch the skirmishes tearing apart the city, and waited. So many Rasu had made it to the surface already. The enemy had learned from previous battles and had done whatever was necessary to get ships on the ground before a Rift Bubble was activated. Some had likely made it here before the first non-Khokteh Concord ship even arrived at the scene. They'd moved swiftly and decisively.

She'd need to talk to her mother about it later, once the battle was won, but it felt as though the Rasu were adapting to Concord tactics distressingly quickly—

4

IRELTSE

Caleb blinked rapidly until his eyes consented to staying open, but his vision remained obscured by a spiderweb of...hair?

Alex!

She lay on top of him, unmoving. Panic seized his chest as he grasped her shoulders and eased her off to the side, rolling with her until he faced her on the floor of the Center. "Alex? Can you hear me?"

Nothing. Dread joined the panic to choke off the air in his lungs. Two fingers went to her neck and felt for a pulse. *Please, please, please.*

Strong and steady. She was merely unconscious—which wasn't good, but far better than the alternative.

You vanished from Akeso's self for a single span of time. It caused me distress. What happened?

He breathed in and let his crisis management training take over, assessing his own state while his hands roved over Alex's body in search of wounds. His eVi was offline, and commands to restart it were met with silence, but his link to Akeso persisted. *I'm not sure. Is Alex all right? Can you sense her?*

Yes. She is...diminished, but her physicality and life force are intact.

That was actually very reassuring. Akeso's connection to Alex had been stronger since Namino, if in inconsistent ways, and he took great comfort from the fact that it remained robust now. Which meant....

He closed his eyes again and reached across Akeso for her. Felt her heart beating to send blood coursing through her veins. After a moment, he sensed her consciousness stirring to wakefulness, and what a miraculous sensation it was.

"Mmm."

Alex shifted in his arms, and he gently brushed her hair out of her face. "Hey, baby. Are you here?"

Her nose wrinkled up, and she opened one eye a slit. "Where is 'here'? Are we…on Ireltse still? I don't—" She struggled up to a sitting position. "Valkyrie? Valkyrie, answer me!" She stared at him in alarm. "She's gone."

The déjà vu was overwhelming. Here in the Center, knocked unconscious without warning, waking to find fundamental systems inoperable….

"Did they use an EMP?" He sat up with Alex and, for the first time since waking, took in the rest of the room. The Khokteh were all standing, though the tenor of the overlapping arguments had taken on a darker quality. There was no visible damage to the area.

He raised his voice above the din. "Pinchu, did someone use an EMP?"

Pinchu's face appeared from between two huddling Khokteh to peer down at them. "You are hurt?"

"We're fine. But what happened?"

"We did not use an EMP. Our communications system is unaccountably down, however. What do you know?"

"Nothing, yet. We can't talk to anyone, either." He returned his attention to Alex. "Anything from Valkyrie?"

"No. And it's not that she isn't responding or is focused on something else. She's not there *at all*. Also, my eVi won't restart."

"Mine, either." The obvious answer hit him like a mental sledgehammer, and he inhaled sharply. "It wasn't an EMP. It's a quantum block."

"What?" She shook her head weakly. "You might be right. Nothing with quantum components is working. But how would the Rasu have managed it?"

"I can't say, but…" he clambered to his feet and lunged for the window "…what if it took out the Rift Bubble?"

"Oh, fuck." She stumbled up next to him. "The Rasu must have made sure they brought down the materials needed to construct some manner of block on the fly. Clever sons of bitches—" She grabbed him roughly by the shoulders. "Caleb, where is the *Siyane?*"

"You don't…right, because Valkyrie…okay, what was the last information about its position you remember?" Valkyrie's thoughts and actions were always percolating around just beneath her conscious awareness, so she likely knew more than she realized.

Alex's eyes squinted shut. "Valkyrie had chosen a landing site about four kilometers to the southwest of here, where the fighting is still sporadic. She was twenty-two seconds from landing…" her eyes reopened, churning with fear teetering on the edge of terror "…then nothing. The quantum block would've disconnected her from the ship. It must have crashed."

"It's going to be fine. Adiamene hull, remember?"

"I know, I know. Hopefully the impact crater isn't too hideous. Caleb, if we can get to it, I can fly it. We have to find where they've thrown together their makeshift quantum block and disable it, or this battle is lost."

This was only one of so many reasons why he loved her madly. There were hundreds of thousands of warships on the scene and tens of thousands of soldiers on the ground, but her mind had gone directly to how she could personally turn the tables on the enemy.

"Let's do it. Four kilometers to the southwest, you said?" He spun around and led her through the raucous crowd of military advisors until they reached Pinchu. "We think the Rasu managed to get a quantum block operational, which would have disabled the Rift Bubble."

"Damnable metal aliens! So we are now vulnerable to a new onslaught?"

"Yes. Look, if we can reach our ship, we'll try to locate the block and destroy it. It, um, landed a few kilometers to the southwest of here."

Pinchu's lips pulled back, revealing more of his many teeth. "Why don't you simply…?" He waved a hand in a circle.

Alex's chin dropped to her chest. "I can't. There's nothing more quantum than a Caeles Prism."

"Ah. If you say so. What do you need to accomplish your task?"

An idea took hold in Caleb's mind. "Are there any vehicles nearby we can borrow? We've driven one before."

"Yes, of course. On Sublevel 2. There will be a ramp from the parking area leading to the surface." Pinchu clasped Caleb's hand tightly, damn near crushing the bones. "Hurry, if you can."

"We will."

Then Alex was dragging *him* toward the door.

5

CAF AURORA

IRELTSE STELLAR SYSTEM

Fleet Admiral Jenner (AFS Denali)(Ireltse Command Channel): "I've just lost contact with Planetary Assault Regiments C2 and C3. Now with every ship operating on or near the surface. And…dammit, over a thousand additional vessels."

Jolted by the uncommon frustration in Malcolm's voice, Miriam's gaze darted to the tactical screens, then the viewport. Against the planet's profile, hundreds of ships tumbled out of control. Worse, Rasu vessels everywhere had suddenly abandoned their current dogfights to descend freely into the atmosphere.

Commandant Solovy (CAF Aurora)(Ireltse Command Channel): "The Rift Bubble is no longer operational. Standby."

But why?

Fleet Admiral Jenner (AFS Denali)(Ireltse Command Channel): "Something else is going on, too. Multiple captains overseeing squadrons in-atmosphere are reporting a loss of functionality by ship Artificials, as well as communication and other failures. It's sounding as if functionality returns after they retreat one-to-two megameters from the planet, which they had to do in order to report in."

'Commandant, the evidence suggests a quantum block is now active on the surface. Such a device would likely disable a Rift Bubble.'

Miriam couldn't deny the Rasu a touch of respect. Shrewd aliens. *Alex, are you there?*

No response arrived. She forcibly buried the concern that flared, as her daughter's failure to answer was merely a technical side-effect of the quantum block. "Thomas, get me Mnemosyne."

Commandant Solovy (CAF Aurora)(Ireltse Command Channel): "Assume a quantum block extends to a circumference of two megameters around the planet and pull all ships back beyond that perimeter, then revert to TP-Blockade 2."

A swarm of lights moved against the over-bright illumination of the bridge to Miriam's left. "Mnemosyne?"

It is I. Is there a difficulty I can assist with?

"Yes. The Rasu that were already on the ground when the Rift Bubble went active managed to construct a quantum block of sufficient power to take out the device. What can you do?"

The lights vacillated in an agitated pattern. *We, too, are vulnerable to a quantum block. I cannot penetrate it.*

"So there's no way for you to help?"

We are conferring, but no, not at present. Is Alex still on the surface?

"She is, but I don't know her status."

The lights calmed a bit. *I believe she will be able to rectify the situation.*

"How?"

I do not know.

"You simply believe in her?"

In point of fact, yes.

"Good. So do I." *Assuming a building didn't fall on her, or worse.* She wanted to message David, but doing so would only prolong her fixation on something she could do nothing to change. Unless…perhaps she *could* do something. A tiny thing.

'Commandant, additional formations of Rasu have arrived in the stellar system.'

"Of course they have. They planned this all along." She pivoted to the ethereal presence undulating nearby. "Mesme, send all Kat superdreadnoughts in the system to engage the new arrivals and keep them away from the planet."

As you wish. The lights faded and were gone.

Next, she sent a private pulse to the Fleet Admiral.

Malcolm, we need to buy Alex as much time as possible on the surface to disable the quantum block. What's the status of the Parapet Gambit technology?

Alex is on the surface? Damn. Um, the programming for it is installed on the 1st and 2nd Assault Divisions' dreadnoughts, cruisers and heavy frigates. So far, the power requirements are far too massive for any smaller ships to be able to support it.

But it works?

It does appear to work in testing, which is all we've had time to explore. I see where you're going with this, but it's not installed on enough ships to protect the whole planet.

I know. Build the web at the region above the capital city, since that's where the Rasu are concentrating their incursion. And the ship captains will need to be ready to adapt and move when the Rasu respond to being rebuffed.

You mean the ship Prevos will.

I don't care who's maneuvering the ships, so long as they stay in front of the Rasu.

Yes, ma'am. Give us thirty seconds.

While she waited, she took every other step in her power to keep more Rasu off the surface and out here in the battlespace.

Commandant Solovy (CAF Aurora) (Ireltse Command Channel): "All nuclear weapon-equipped vessels are ordered to report to KSS Sectors 6A-C immediately. Nuclear weapons use is authorized outside of Demarcation Line Charlie.

"Navarchos Casmir, form an intercept gauntlet ten megameters in from the Kat formations to catch the Rasu that make it through the Kats' firing squad. All fleet commanders, order every regiment capable of reaching the KSS in less than forty minutes to do so now."

So many risks. She despised using nuclear weapons, even as she recognized that their detonation twenty megameters or more from any planet was…not safe, but as safe as their use could ever be. And pulling patrols and planetary defense regiments off their duties left so many planets and people vulnerable, should the Rasu choose now to launch a multi-system attack.

But everything Concord stood for meant she must defend *this* planet and people currently under attack with every single resource at her disposal.

Outside the viewport, several organized wings of large AEGIS vessels began moving into position a scant 0.2 megameters beyond the barrier of the quantum block. Almost as one, they pivoted to face outward and, ship-by-ship, extended the reach of their formation until it spanned most of the continent directly below.

Commandant Solovy (CAF Aurora)(Ireltse Mission Channel): "Everyone, give the AEGIS vessels near the planet some breathing room, and do not attempt to cross their threshold."

Navarchos Casmir (Imperium Alpha)(Ireltse Command Channel): "May I ask what they're doing?"

Fleet Admiral Jenner (AFS Denali)(Ireltse Command Channel): "Just a new tactic we've been working on. Your Imperiums inspired it, in fact."

Navarchos Casmir (Imperium Alpha)(Ireltse Command Channel): "What?"

Fleet Admiral Jenner (AFS Denali)(Ireltse Command Channel): "You'll see."

She'd daresay Malcolm was enjoying the prospect of showing up the Machim fleet. As well he should be.

Fleet Admiral Jenner (AFS Denali)(Command Channel): "Parapet Gambit commencing."

At the apex of the formation, a prismatic shimmer exploded outward from the *Denali's* hull to port and starboard. When the shimmer reached the adjacent ships, it renewed itself as those ships added their own power to it and sent it onward. In ten seconds, the field, faint and wavering but intact, stretched across the entire formation.

A regiment of Rasu vessels accelerated toward the formation, headed for the planet beyond it, and the AEGIS warships opened fire, as per usual. Like in a traditional blockade, a number of the charging vessels were damaged or (temporarily) destroyed in the initial salvo.

Some continued onward, however. Presumably not recognizing the trap that lay in plain sight, they barreled through the gaps between the AEGIS vessels—and ricocheted clean off the force field to tumble away from the planet.

While the Rasu spun out of control, AEGIS and Novoloume fast attack craft still heavy with negative energy missiles swarmed in to dispose of them.

Navarchos Casmir (Imperium Alpha)(Ireltse Command Channel): "You've modified the Imperium double-shielding tech to act as a force-field barrier, haven't you? Technology you stole from us, I'll add."

Technology *Alex* had stolen from them, and it was now buying her daughter the time she needed. Or so Miriam hoped.

Fleet Admiral Jenner (AFS Denali)(Ireltse Command Channel): "We're all on the same side, Navarchos. A side that uses every technological and creative advantage we can invent to protect our people."

Miriam's hand flexed against the railing. It was working.

Because Kennedy Rossi had never been one to rest on her laurels, once Connova Interstellar had successfully replicated the Imperiums' double-shielding and begun manufacturing units for the fleet, she had turned her attention to other ways in which they might utilize the underlying concepts. In a matter of days, she and Vii, with a little help from Devon, had worked out the idea of an energy-based parapet system. The power requirements and stability pillars were distributed among the entire ship formation, though the anchor at the center did the heaviest lifting, giving the parapet both resiliency and flexibility.

When another hundred thousand ships were equipped with the technology, the tactic stood to be nearly as effective as a Rift Bubble at keeping the enemy off the surface of a planet.

As Miriam watched Rasu after Rasu bounce off the field, she made a note to pressure AEGIS into dedicating considerable resources to its continued installation.

But the Rasu were far from idiots, and after a minute or so of falling victim to the field, they began shifting their trajectories toward the far edge of the AEGIS formation, intending to go around. Now came the tricky part.

Any single section of the projection had limited reach, so the ships involved had to stay relatively close to one another to maintain it. And now they were all moving.

The field rippled like a tied sheet billowing in the wind. A few ships here and there fell out of the formation briefly, leaving holes in the parapet, but in every case they quickly maneuvered back into position.

Multiple Rasu collided with the outer edge of the field; it gave, but it didn't break, and on the rebound the Rasu vessels sprung backward as if launched by a trampoline.

But this exposed one reason (almost certainly not the only one) why the tactic remained in testing. Moving so many ships and a force field in unison was slow, and the Rasu vessels were fast.

Commandant Solovy (CAF Aurora)(Ireltse Command Channel): "Fleet Admiral, do what you can to stay in front of the bulk of the Rasu. I want all newly arriving regiments to cover as much of the planet as possible. Our number one priority remains keeping as many Rasu as possible off the planet until the quantum block is disabled and the Rift Bubble is reactivated."

While Thomas ensured the *Aurora* did its part to waylay encroaching Rasu, Miriam watched the blockade and the clock.

Come on, Alex. Do what you do, and hurry.

6

IRELTSE

Their harrowing trip across a city under siege in a Khokteh hover vehicle left Alex awash in memories, but she didn't dare spare an ounce of mental bandwidth to reminisce. When she'd infiltrated Namino, she'd planned ahead for the limitations the quantum block was going to impose on her. But here, now, she didn't have so much as one of those stupid walkie-talkies on her person, much less anyone to converse with on it if she did.

Her heart thudded painfully in her chest. *Valkyrie, please be okay. Siyane, please be okay.*

Of course they would be, both of them. It was only logical, and she obeyed logic whenever possible.

Far overhead, Rasu poured into the skies with renewed enthusiasm, turning day to a malevolent dusk. Her mother must have figured out what had happened by now, or at a minimum identified the consequences of it. But she had no way to contact Miriam or anyone else to advise them of the situation. Though the Khokteh used quantum technology for fewer tasks than most Concord members, even their communications network was down, crippling the planetary defense strategy.

They passed the wreckage of two crashed Eidolons in the middle of a street. Caleb slowed. But there were no organic pilots inside to save, so after a beat he sped up again. She assumed all the Eidolons kept backups at an AEGIS facility somewhere, and the Artificials could be restored once the battle was decided.

She chewed on her bottom lip until she drew blood. Despite all the logic in the world that counseled otherwise, she was terrified for Valkyrie. She was terrified for the *Siyane*. She was terrified for this wonderful, quirky planet and its fierce people, and for the fleets fighting above it. And she'd be damned if she wasn't going to do everything in her power to save them all from this soulless menace.

A Khokteh fighter exploded less than a hundred meters overhead, and she and Caleb dropped to the open-air vehicle's floor as debris rained down on them. Her hands covered her head, and his body covered the rest.

The vehicle slowed to a stop of its own accord when it neared the fighter's flaming debris field, and they gingerly climbed back into their seats. She checked over her vital parts to confirm nothing had speared her skin, then turned to Caleb. Blood streaked across a thickening layer of dirt on his left cheek, and she gently touched a fingertip to it. He winced as she brought the hem of her shirt up and wiped the blood away, revealing a three-centimeter-long cut down his cheekbone. "It's not deep."

"Wouldn't matter if it was." He straightened his shoulders and retook the controls. "Almost there."

They dodged rubble from several more downed fighters before rounding the next corner, and her heart dropped through her stomach all the way to her toes.

The *Siyane* had crashed into an eight-story building mid-spiral, its nose buried in a corner pillar. Half the façade of the building was piled on top of the main body.

She breathed in deliberately and tried to will herself calm. The hull appeared intact, just as she'd logically known it would be. "I can fly it out from under the debris, though it's sure to be a bumpy take-off. But how are we going to get inside?"

Caleb brought the vehicle to a halt and killed the engine to peer out at the wreckage. "If we can make our way to the third floor of the building, I think we'll be able to get to the underneath ramp. We might have to dig out the control panel, but then we'll be able to extend the ramp, hopefully enough to crawl inside."

They'd dug their way out of worse predicaments…but perhaps not quite so literally. She leapt out of the vehicle, promptly jumped at the sound of a roaring crash in the distance, and fixated on the point where the *Siyane's* stern met the building. "Let's get in there before the rest of the building collapses."

RW

Caleb's arm reached down from above for her. "Grab hold."

She clutched his wrist and he hers; the next second he was hoisting her up through the air. She swung a leg over the jagged outcropping of the building's third floor, and his other hand wrapped around the waist of her pants and hauled her up the rest of the way.

She sank onto her heels and wiped fresh dust off her face. To the right, the debris-coated but otherwise unmarred hull of the *Siyane* rested at an angle across the crumbling outer façade. Above them, the tapering stern section vanished into the floor overhead.

Her hands came to her mouth in horror at the sight…and Caleb's hand came to her jaw. "*Focus.* We need to get inside."

"Yes. Inside."

A thunderous explosion shook the building, sending rubble raining down on them yet again. Less than a meter to their left, a huge chunk of ceiling—or was it flooring?—broke loose and tumbled through a hole to the ground below. The *Siyane* shifted a few centimeters.

"Soon. We need to get inside soon."

"Yes, we do." Her thoughts raced in a thousand directions, but she couldn't dwell on what was happening in the skies and streets outside the building, never mind in orbit above the planet. *Focus.*

She crawled across the floor to the point where she was able to stretch up and touch the sloping hull of the *Siyane* above them. Her finger ran along the tiny seam marking where the ramp separated from the body of the ship. Next, she looked behind her and considered the angle and where the frame began to narrow, then to the right until the frame disappeared beneath the floor at their feet.

She stretched out until she was flat on her back and felt along the adiamene to the point where small breaks in the building's floor created a small additional gap. "I found the edge of the control panel, but I can't get to the activation button. I need to dig it out. Plasma blade?" She extended her left hand behind her, and Caleb dropped the hilt of his blade into her palm. If the ship shifted again, it could crush her between the hull and the flooring. Caleb wisely didn't implore her to let him take the risk, though he probably badly wanted to do so.

After maneuvering around to get a better angle, she activated the blade and started slicing through the stone blocking her access. Fragments of stone crumbled into dust…just a little more…there!

She deactivated the blade, handed it back to him, and wiggled her fingers into the tiny crevice she'd created. A press of her thumb on an invisible button, and the panel lit up in subtle silver light.

She exhaled in relief. At a minimum, the basic electrical systems remained functional.

"Good job."

"Not finished yet." She had to jam her pointer finger against a ragged slice of flooring to reach the rest of the control panel, and her finger slipped twice, but finally she got the access code entered.

The ramp detached from the ship's body with a rumble of displaced stone, and an opening began to appear. Caleb grabbed her by the shoulders and dragged her away from the hull. "In case the floor gives way."

She rose to her knees beside him, and they watched as the ramp pushed persistently upon the stone. The floor began to break up from the force applied; the gap increased another five centimeters, then stopped. The hydraulics groaned audibly, and the ramp jerked against its cage, but it refused to budge any farther.

Caleb unlatched his Daemon from his belt and urged her back. "I'll shoot out the material that's blocking it—very carefully. If the flooring falls out from beneath us, dive for the edge and grab hold of it."

"Got it." She crouched on the balls of her feet and prepped herself to move.

Caleb fired, and a small section of the stone evaporated into dust, freeing the ramp to open another eight centimeters—then everything came apart at once. The ramp snapped fully open, knocking the floor out from underneath it. The *Siyane* plummeted a full meter, and the remains of the wall to their right collapsed.

The floor beneath their feet held, but only barely. Caleb reached out for her. "We jump, now!"

She didn't even have time to think about it. Her legs moved in unison with his and they leapt through the air to land on the extended ramp. The ship fell another two meters, and she slid half off the ramp—Caleb grabbed her foot and held on tight, then began reeling her back in.

She wanted to laugh, but the air was now so thick with dust that she could hardly breathe. Together they crawled up the incline and into the engineering well, all the way to the ladder.

She was home.

But she wasn't safe yet. No one was. She started to hit the button to retract the ramp, but Caleb stopped her. "Let's do it from the cockpit, once we're ready to take off. Moving it again could destabilize the rest of the structure."

"Good point." Coughs racked her chest as she climbed up the ladder, popped open the hatch to the lower level and sucked in fresh, unsullied air.

The floor jerked roughly several times as they vaulted up the circular staircase to the main cabin and sprinted into the cockpit.

Inside, everything was so quiet. Empty of life, without so much as a sliver of Valkyrie's consciousness present. *Focus.*

They strapped in tight, and her eyes shifted to the viewport. From their elevated view, they could now see a much wider expanse of skies clotted with Rasu, explosions and toppled buildings. One block over, blood ran freely through the street, from corpse to corpse.

They had to end this.

She'd flown the *Siyane* minus Valkyrie a few weeks ago at Namino, before handing over the controls to Morgan, and it hadn't been an issue. Way back after she'd head-butted the Amaranthe portal in the Mosaic to disastrous results, she'd rewired the Siyane's critical functions so they operated without the assistance of Valkyrie's circuitry.

Her mind automatically ticked through the necessary extra steps involved, followed by the correct order of events given their rather precarious situation. As soon as she fired up the pulse detonation engine, what remained of the building holding them in the air was going to disintegrate from the force it created. They'd survive a crash to the ground below, but she'd prefer to avoid it if at all possible. There was a half-intact building directly in front of them, so simply accelerating away wasn't an option. A Rasu vessel was gleefully firing into ground troops to their left—also not an option. But the street remained open to their right for a few hundred meters.

So engage the engines, lift up and out, then hard right. Don't mind the jostling.

She stared at Caleb a little wide-eyed. "Ready?"

He smiled gamely at her, like this was no big thing. "Ready."

She set the ramp to retract and engaged the pulse detonation engine—and the entire world roared in protest. Large chunks of stone rained down on the hull, sending the ship jerking violently beneath her hands, and she yanked it up a microsecond before they slammed into the ground. Then the building in front of them consumed the viewport, and she swerved to the right and banked up into the air until they were safely above the buildings.

Gods, the Rasu were *everywhere*. But it was still a battle at least, as on closer inspection AEGIS, Machim and Novoloume attack craft nearly equaled the Rasu in number. Missiles and lasers shot in every direction, and the remaining structures took as much collateral damage as direct hits.

Caleb exhaled harshly. "I didn't bring it up before—one goal at a time—but now that we're here, how exactly are we planning to locate the quantum block?"

"Um…the old-fashioned way? We know what one looks like. And it can't be very large or very far away, if only because they haven't had time to do more to build it up. They'd have wanted to make certain they took out the Rift Bubble as quickly as possible. So we fly around the battlefield and search for it."

"Can we stealth?"

She cringed. "Sort of. Again, the old-fashioned way. The wiring for the old, pre-Kat-tech stealth is still in place, so we merely need to reactivate it. And maybe plug one or two modules in." She grimaced apologetically. "Fancy another dive into the engineering well?"

He huffed a ragged laugh. "It's my fourth favorite place to be."

RW

Caleb climbed down the ladder into the engineering well, then wasted no time removing the protective panel from the length of wall that held the various field generators. He set the panel to the side and sat cross-legged in front of the opening.

A maze of photal fibers connecting modules of multiple sizes and functions greeted him, and he shook his head wryly. He'd never accuse Alex of being a hoarder—their home was unfailingly spotless and orderly—but when it came to the *Siyane*, she'd always been loath to get rid of anything. And in fairness to her, this was the second time in a month that they'd found themselves retasking or calling into service old components. If she'd trashed the He3 LEN reactor when they replaced it with a Zero Drive, what remained of the Ourankeli might not be alive today.

He pressed a fingertip to the human-friendly input pad and...crap, no eVi. He settled for studying the somewhat less-human-friendly directional flow diagram the control panel displayed, matching the flows to the cables and modules arrayed in front of him.

Aha! The old stealth drive module sat braced in the bottom-right corner of the space, its connectors wound neatly behind it.

The ship's systems had become more streamlined with each wave of technological advances, so there were plenty of available hook points to reconnect it into the power distribution system. Normally, Valkyrie would have handled things from here, but that wasn't an option right now, so he stepped carefully but quickly through the setup procedure.

Green lights across the board. No eVi meant no pulsing; he hit the ship comm. *"Everything's reconnected. Test out the stealth and make certain I've set it up correctly."*

"As if. Yep, the HUD says it's functional. Get back up here and let's go hunting."

He replaced the panel and headed up the ladder. Hunting, indeed.

7

SIYANE

IRELTSE

Every kilometer they flew over added to the leaden sensation gnawing away at Alex's gut. The Rasu had obviously planned for this eventuality, and since taking out the Rift Bubble, they were wasting no time in wreaking as much destruction as possible as swiftly as feasible. From their vantage in the *Siyane*, it was obvious the Rasu moved in organized tactical units, disabling the infrastructure block by block and responding promptly to attacks by Concord forces.

Still, the Concord ground and aerial units were fighting to hold the ground they'd won. And while she had no visibility to what was occurring in orbit, she speculated that Concord continued to put up a valiant fight, if only because since they'd been in the air, new Rasu contingents descending from above had slowed to a trickle. The respite couldn't come at a better time.

A thick line of Rasu near the ground on the northeast horizon caught her attention. They battled primarily Anaden hovertanks, while higher in the air, Rasu fighter craft fought to keep Concord ships at bay. The line wasn't advancing toward the city, though. "Interesting. They seem to be protecting something over there, don't they?"

Caleb leaned forward, closer to the viewport. His eyes scanned the surrounding area, then returned to the cluster of Rasu. "Yes, they do. Slip around the side."

She veered toward what at first glance appeared to be the outer edge of the Rasu line, only to find the line was actually a circle. "There is no side. I'm going to have to try to sneak through the fighting."

He didn't argue—there wasn't another option—and she eased into the fracas. Lasers lit the sky in all directions; a hit wouldn't damage the *Siyane*, but she nonetheless tried to dodge and weave around the fire. It was instinctual.

The hull shuddered from a glancing blow of friendly fire. And again. She groaned.

"At any given second, there is barely two meters of clear space between the shots. No one could make it through here clean."

Her lips twitched. "Valkyrie could."

"She'll be fine."

"I know." She accelerated toward a narrow gap in the Rasu defensive line, flipped the *Siyane* ninety degrees to squeeze through—and was on the inside of the circle. A satisfied smile grew on her expression. "Oh, look. A quantum block."

The tower was tiny compared to the one the Rasu had constructed on Namino, rising a scant twenty or so meters into the air, but the violet firestorm powering it was unmistakable.

She checked the radar. Nothing but Rasu for almost a kilometer in every direction. Surely they'd be able to see through the *Siyane's* archaic stealth field if they decided to glance her way, but their efforts were focused on keeping ships *out*, and she was already in.

"No time to waste. Firing negative energy missiles."

The instant the missiles were away, she rose high in the air to escape the nasty blast radius that was about to materialize.

All four missiles impacted on target. The module atop the tower shattered and collapsed, tearing into the power generator until it disintegrated as well. Four missiles might have been overkill.

She immediately restarted her eVi as she cut a path away from the Rasu fortification and headed for the Rift Bubble site. *Valkyrie?*

Only silence answered, and her heart plummeted all over again. Even if Valkyrie wasn't in the ship, she should be *somewhere*. Frantically trying to reestablish a connection to Alex from her hardware on Akeso or Earth or Sagan...*somewhere*. But there was nothing.

Her eVi finished loading, and a deluge of messages poured in. She ignored them.

Mesme, will the Rift Bubble automatically reactivate once a quantum block is removed?

Yes. I have been called back here due to the disruption, and I can confirm it is again operational.

Next she accessed the mission channel.

Alexis Solovy Marano (Siyane)(Ireltse Mission Channel): "All ships, the quantum block is down and the Rift Bubble is once again up."

Then a private pulse.

Mom, kindly send everything you have to the surface. We can't let the Rasu construct another quantum block down here.

Are you okay?

We're all fine. Except Valkyrie...I don't know. Dispatch a protective detail to the location I'm sending you with a mission profile to keep the Rasu far away from the Rift Bubble. Then I think you work out from there, destroying every Rasu you encounter in a widening perimeter.

Oh, you're a military tactician now?

Very funny, but it's not the first time. Just throw everything you've got at them?

That I can manage.

She'd been hunched up over the controls with the virtual HUD surrounding her since they'd taken flight; now she sank lower in the chair and looked at Caleb. "Reinforcements are on the way."

"I hope it's a lot of reinforcements. We can't let this happen a second time."

"Which is exactly what I conveyed to Mom. I imagine it's been an ugly hour for them. They won't let the opportunity slip away."

When the first reinforcements to arrive at the Rift Bubble were a thousand Kat swarmers, she burst out laughing. Oh, the absurdity of it all. But it was good the Kats were showing up to do the work of protecting their little miracle device.

Three squadrons of Eidolons soon joined them, and shot by shot the Rasu began to fall back in an ever-expanding circle around the Rift Bubble.

When the skies were finally clogged with more good guys than bad, Caleb brought her a bottle of water, then knelt in front of her chair. She dropped her forehead to his and sighed.

"Nicely done, baby."

"And you, *priyazn*." She kissed him sloppily, guzzled the water and reconsidered the scene outside the viewport. "We should check on Pinchu and the situation at the Center."

"Good idea. Do you want to land somewhere deserted and wormhole there?"

"Nooooo. There's still at least a thirty percent chance the Rasu will manage to construct another quantum block before this is over. We're landing as close to the Center as we can possibly get."

"And if another building lands on top of the *Siyane*?"

"Ha! We'll dig it out again."

"Let's do try our best to avoid that outcome, okay?" He waved haphazardly at the viewport. "Onward."

RW

CAF AURORA

IRELTSE STELLAR SYSTEM

The flutter in Miriam's chest stole her breath for a solid second. Damn and bless Alex, in equal measure. While she lived in a state of constant wonder at all Alex accomplished, she would never not harbor a quiet terror for her daughter's well-being.

Oh, you're a military tactician now?

Very funny, but it's not the first time. Just throw everything you've got at them, okay?

That I can manage.

She spent half a second reorienting her thinking regarding the battlefield, then dove back in.

Commandant Solovy (CAF Aurora)(Ireltse Command Channel): "Confirmed: the Rift Bubble is once again active. Revert to TP-C 2, except I want four additional planetary assault regiments protecting the Rift

Bubble at the transmitted coordinates.

"Destroy every last Rasu to grace your radar, while following safety guidelines for the protection of the civilians on Ireltse. Fleet Admiral Jenner, put every Rima Grenade launcher we possess in the hands of Marines on the ground, and I'll contact Commander Palmer for an emergency resupply."

How long did they have until some clump of Rasu could construct another quantum block? Could Concord stop it from happening this time? The faster they eliminated the bulk of the enemy's ground presence, the better chance they stood, but—she double-checked the latest intel—the in-atmosphere battlefield now stretched for over three hundred kilometers around the capital city, with smaller skirmishes growing near four additional metropolitan areas. Rendering the planet safe was going to take time. Far more of it than she liked.

The Rasu now understood, at least in generalities, how the dimensional barriers were being created and how to disable them. Concord understood how they were being disabled and how to prevent or reverse the Rasu's disabling of them.

For the moment, there were no more secrets, only stratagems and counter-stratagems.

"Thomas, please ask Mnemosyne to get Rift Bubbles deployed on Nengllitse and Tapertse immediately, and to station a Kat to watch each one until I'm able to spare some Marines to guard them."

'Mnemosyne responds that they are already on it.'

Her brow furrowed. "Mnemosyne said that?"

'Perhaps not precisely. I translated.'

She laughed briefly. "I see. Thank you."

Studying the tactical screens for the millionth time today, she had to concede that the reactivation of the Rift Bubble and their hairpin shift in tactics were already showing results. If no further calamities materialized, they could—*would*—win this battle.

Still, frustration she struggled to vocalize worried at her gut. For a few critical minutes, the Rasu had not merely outmaneuvered but out-thought her, and this was not acceptable.

She wanted to take the *Aurora* down into the skies of Ireltse and blast every Rasu terrorizing the planet into subatomic particles...and the vividness of the desire surprised her. Yes, she harbored a personal grudge against this enemy, on account of them having forced her to extinguish her ship and her life. Possibly she hadn't yet fully healed the scar the experience had inflicted.

Regardless, the *Aurora* was not designed for atmospheric flight, so she had to content herself with blasting the Rasu swarming about in space.

"Thomas, reengage TP-Sweep 2. Let us dispose of our enemy here today once and for all."

'Gladly, ma'am.'

Space outside the viewport lit up anew from a barrage of fire delivered by her ship, and she took satisfaction from the display of military prowess.

As the minutes dragged on without a new quantum block activating and the number of Rasu vessels steadily decreasing, her mind kept trying to drift to the large-scale strategies she needed to be implementing the instant this battle was won.

The attack on Ireltse had taken them all by surprise and, as she'd observed hours earlier, she'd been scrambling to catch up ever since. Her long history in logistics tugged at her in the form of patrol redeployments, protection of supply chains and activation of more robust early alert systems. Her earned combat experience whispered of the promise of new, more powerful weapons and emerging counter-counter-stratagems.

She dragged her focus back to the battle at hand, for though it was at last turning decidedly in their favor, it was far from over, and she must remain vigilant to the end and then some.

But the fact remained that with today's attack, the Rasu had brought their war of conquest to Concord space, and this changed everything.

8

IRELTSE

They heard the explosion before they saw it. As the thunder assaulted Caleb's eardrums, he had the idle thought of how stone cracks and breaks apart differently from metal, with grunts and grumbles rather than high-pitched whines and screeches.

A giant plume of dust-hued smoke billowed up past the profile of the Machim heavy frigate moving dead ahead of the *Siyane*.

His gaze swept across the scene in a hasty evaluation of the situation. The strike had likely come from the large Rasu vessel streaking away to their port while being chased by laser fire from the Machim warship and an AEGIS fast-attack frigate. The engagement moved rapidly off to the east to reveal the site of the explosion.

A vast stretch of the top two floors of the Center was now a crater. Bodies lay broken and exposed beneath the hazy sky, though amid all the smoke he also saw Khokteh moving around. Crawling, mostly.

"Oh, no…." Alex's hands briefly covered her face, but the next second they dropped back to the controls and her expression hardened. "I'm going to drop you off in that crater. If Pinchu…do what you can to help everyone. I'll set down one street over and wormhole up there."

He opened his mouth to argue, but stopped himself. Landing anywhere in the city held risks, and they'd accepted those risks when they'd come here to join the fight. So instead he stood, leaning down to kiss her. "Don't be long."

"I won't be."

He stopped off in the main cabin long enough to grab the med kit, as bandages helped trauma wounds regardless of the species, then hurried down the stairs and into the engineering well. The ramp was already lowering when he arrived. He crouched on the edge of it until the fully exposed command center was three meters below him, then leapt.

I'm down. Go.

He sensed the ramp retracting and the shadow of the *Siyane* receding as he assessed the scene anew. Bodies were trapped under rubble amid expanding pools of viscous fluid, and more than one corpse was burnt beyond recognition. The intermingling smells of fried fur and skin and leaking bodily fluids were overwhelming, but his eVi filtered out what it could, and he tried to ignore the rest.

Our enemy caused this senseless death? Akeso struggles to comprehend how living beings can inflict such suffering.

They believe this is how they will win. They are wrong.

They are wrong.

People were also alive. The strike had targeted this area specifically—almost as if the Rasu knew precisely where the Khokteh command center was located—and those who'd been working in other areas had rushed in to come to the aid of the injured. Orders were being barked, and in the brief seconds he stood there, medical personnel began arriving with stretchers and equipment.

He focused on the rear middle of the room, where the war table had been. A huge chunk of ceiling had cracked it in two and continued on to crush several Khokteh. Three people crouched around someone sprawled on the floor…

…no.

He was moving forward before deciding to do so, and in a flash he was kneeling beside the others.

Pinchu blinked slowly, his four eyes milky beneath their lids. "Caleb…you are…Alex?"

"She'll be here in just a minute. Don't worry about talking, okay? Let these people help you."

Caleb forced himself to acknowledge the gory mess that was

Pinchu's chest as his gaze darted to the medical officer situated opposite him. "I brought our med kit with me. Bandages, coagulation gel, biosynth weaves, whatever you need."

The Khokteh, her fur too coated in debris and blood to determine its color, shook her head. "I'm afraid…" her voice dropped to a whisper "…the damage is beyond bandages or coags. I don't think there is anything we can do. Not in time."

Caleb didn't whisper; Pinchu certainly knew how bad of shape he was in. "Yes, there *is*. Go find the best emergency medical personnel on-site and bring them and every single medical tool you can put hands on up here, this instant. This is your Tokahe Naataan, and you will fucking save him."

The Khokteh woman nodded shakily and scrambled up.

"Caleb, you…you fixed the…."

He grasped Pinchu's hand in his. "We did. Everything's working again, including the Rift Bubble, and the fleets are doing their damnedest to eradicate every Rasu who dared come here. Your city, your planet, *will* be saved today. I promise you."

"Good—" Coughs racked Pinchu's body, sending a rush of dark copper blood pouring out of the gaping wound in his torso. "Then I can go to my Cassela knowing I did all I could to preserve our *shikei*."

"Don't talk like that. You're going to be fine."

This creature is dying. I can sense its life force seeping away in the spillage of its fluids.

I know.

"I…fear I am not. I wanted to…." Pinchu's eyes fluttered closed.

Where the hell were the medical officers? He looked up at the two Khokteh advisors holding vigil at Pinchu's side, but they shrugged weakly.

He couldn't sit here as helplessly as they were and watch while Pinchu died, dammit. He reached behind him and popped open the med kit, grabbed the coagulation gel and emptied the entire tube into Pinchu's chest. He had no idea if the biosynth weave was smart enough to bond with Khokteh organs, but he laid it over the exposed flesh.

Pinchu coughed again, and new blood gushed out around the weave. *No, no, no!*

"Try to stay still. Help is on the way."

He abruptly realized his fingers were tingling oddly. Were humans allergic to Khokteh blood? Whatever. His eVi would handle any adverse reaction. He frantically dug through the depths of the med kit for anything else that might do something to forestall the inevitable.

Let Akeso try.

He paused his search. *What do you mean?*

You care about this creature?

Very much so, yes.

Then let Akeso try.

His heart thudded against his sternum. *This isn't a flower or a tree branch. This is an infinitely complex, living being—one you've never interacted with before.*

You have taught Akeso much about how organics function. I have learned, and grown as a result. Let us try, together.

Pinchu let out a halting, shallow breath. Almost gone.

Terrified but infused with renewed determination to not allow his friend to die, Caleb placed both hands gently upon the torn-open flesh of Pinchu's chest. Blood seeped between his fingers, propelled by a weakening pulse. He closed his eyes.

As I am the nourishing water flowing out from the creek and swirling through roots beneath the soil, I am the nourishing blood swirling beneath the skin.

I am the sun's rays, bringing strength to this being's limbs.

I am the nourishing water-blood flowing along the starved pathways of arteries and veins, granting them the strength to knit themselves back together.

Replace.

Renew.

Replenish.

His entire body tingled now, flush with life, its source surging through him and out through his fingertips.

Replace. Renew. Replenish.

Dizziness overcame him, and he opened his eyes to keep from toppling over to the floor. His hands, submerged in blood and mangled flesh, glowed a pulsing copper. Beneath his left palm, an organ twitched, and he decreased the pressure he was placing on it. As he watched incredulously, it began to bind itself together.

His breath caught in his throat. But he couldn't stop now, so he searched for what might be the worst point of injury. His hands slipped across wrent flesh.

I am the nourishing water-blood.

I am the sun's rays.

Replace. Renew. Replenish.

His lips mouthed the words like a mantra as veins sealed fissures and interwove with one another. He curled his hand around a fractured rib and felt it reshape in his grasp.

Voices gasped and murmured behind him, but they were background noise. His entire world was his hands and the wounds they worked to heal.

An organ he could not guess the identity or purpose of continued to pour blood into Pinchu's chest cavity, having been sliced wide open by the fractured rib. He gathered both sides of it up in his palms and pressed them close.

I am the nourishing water-blood. I am the sun's rays. I am life flowing forth to mend. To heal.

He wanted to panic when the organ sealed up its wound more completely than any suture would accomplish, but he didn't dare. "What else in here needs healing? I don't know how any of these organs work!"

The Khokteh medical officer, who had returned to his side at some point in the last minute, cleared her throat with a rough growl. "Gods, above. Um, near the upper left, a heart valve is leaking."

"Got it." He oh-so-carefully moved a hand up, skimming across damaged but healing flesh. He saw the tear in the valve now, and placed two fingers upon it.

I am the nourishing water-blood. The sun's rays. Life flowing forth. Mend. Heal. Replace, renew, replenish, replacerenewreplenish—

The valve sealed up before he finished the mantra. "Where else?"

"I don't think…the internal bleeding seems to be stopping. We should…we need to close him up, but the skin over his chest is…gone. I'll get more heavy bandages."

Caleb lifted his hands, in awe of the way they pulsed like suns in the dust-filled air, and placed his palms along one edge of the open chest cavity.

Just a little more work to patch him up, Akeso. I am the sun's rays and the nourishing life strengthening skin and cartilage and bone as they grow and knit together. Mend. Heal. Replacerenewreplenishreplacerenewreplenish….

He didn't know how long he kept on this way, his focus a narrow tunnel revealing only his hands and Pinchu's skin and Akeso's life force binding it all together.

The next thing he was cognizant of was a furry, shaking hand landing on his arm. "I think you've done it, Human. I don't understand—I don't know what you are—but you've done it. Thank the gods, and thank you."

He blinked and peered down to find bright pink flesh resting beneath his hands. Whole.

Pinchu gasped in a fulsome breath and opened his eyes. They were bloodshot, but clear and alert. "These are…not the halls of *Mahpiya*."

"No, they're not." Caleb laughed raggedly and took one of Pinchu's hands in both of his. "You're going to have to wait a while longer to see Cassela again, my friend."

"Alas, my *nizhopini*." He stared at Caleb strangely. "Perhaps it is you who are the emissary of the gods."

Then Khokteh medical officers were rushing in to take charge, and Caleb fell back prostrate on the floor. He stretched his legs and arms out, utterly…*not* spent. He was dizzy and more than a little woozy, but he felt energized, as if all that life force was still coursing through him. He held his hands up in front of his face, marveling at their odd radiance even as it began to twinkle and gradually fade away.

He became aware of Alex moving into his peripheral vision. She dropped to her knees beside him, mouth agape in shock. "Caleb, what did you do?"

Joy surged forth to replace the dizziness. He sat up and wound his blood-soaked arms around her, resting his chin in the crook of her neck. "Saved his life."

9

IRELTSE

P inchu elbowed a medical officer away from his bed as she tried and failed to stick him with a distressingly large needle. "I'm fine, I tell you! Sign off on my release so I can get back to work!"

"Sir, please. We can't discharge you until we review your bloodwork and—"

"*Sica sni* bloodwork." He peered past the officer and, on seeing Alex and Caleb standing in the doorway, grinned toothily and gave the officer a light shove. "Go away. The emissaries of the gods are here, and they just might smite you down if you displease me further."

The medical officer, a female Khokteh wearing a white jumpsuit over cream fur, stared at them with four wide eyes, then scurried out the door.

Caleb chuckled as he moved to Pinchu's bedside. "That wasn't very polite. She was trying to take care of you."

"I have no need to be taken care of, thanks to you."

"I'm glad to hear it." His words were upbeat, but Caleb's expression clouded beneath the smile.

Alex watched him keenly while a thousand thoughts competed for attention in her strung-out mind. Far ahead of concerns over any remaining Rasu crawling the streets outside and second only to frantic worry about Valkyrie, she felt a combination of curiosity, wonder and uncertainty regarding what Caleb had done today. They'd hardly had any time to talk about it, so she didn't yet know the details, but clearly he and Akeso had brought Pinchu back from death's door.

It wasn't *technically* unprecedented, as Akeso had once healed her of a poison that would probably have killed her within days. But the poison had originated from another Ekos, so it wasn't much different from Akeso healing itself. The same analysis applied to the times it healed injuries Caleb had suffered since their joining.

But *this?* Mending organs and growing skin at a cellular level in a matter of seconds, all for an organic being Akeso had never before encountered? This was surely something new.

Now she analyzed every twitch of Caleb's muscles, the movements of his lips, the depth of the furrows in his brow and the creasing wrinkles around his eyes. The sight of his hands glowing in the immediate aftermath was burned indelibly into her brain. What did this mean for him?

Also, why the fuck was Valkyrie still down?

Valkyrie, are you there?

Nothing.

She joined Caleb at the bedside and adopted a cheerful demeanor. "I hear I've been deposed as the official emissary of the Khokteh gods."

Pinchu snorted. "No, no…well, perhaps a little."

She patted his hand, careful not to disturb the IV needle taped to it. "I understand. I'd depose me, too. How do you feel?"

"Like I'm a robust, young warrior again. Also, a mite tingly in my chest."

She glanced at Caleb, noting how his brow drew in and quickly smoothed out before he responded. "Are you being facetious or…."

"No, I really do feel tingly. As if I had two mugs of spirits straight-up in rapid succession. Is this bad?"

"Not at all. I only…" Caleb bit his lower lip "…do you happen to be hearing any murmured voices in your head, or thoughts that aren't your own? By chance?"

Pinchu pushed up in the bed to a full sitting position. "Voices? What the *kunza* did you do to me, Caleb?"

"Well, you know about the connection I have to the planet where we live, right? And how it returned me to life after The Displacement?"

Pinchu's eyes slid around in a sign of unease. "In generalities."

"That's fine. The important point is, Akeso—the planet—has healing properties. It heals and renews itself all the time. And me. It healed Alex once as well. Today, through me, it healed you."

Pinchu nodded sharply. "Obviously. But what about the voices?"

Caleb scratched at his forehead. "It took a great deal of…you were gravely injured, so it took a lot of effort and energy to heal you. I don't know how much of Akeso's essence now resides in you, but depending on how much does, you might…hear Akeso talk to you every now and then."

Pinchu fell back on the pillow with a grunt. "*Diin niiyol.* Don't tell anyone else about this, yes? Hearing voices is not considered a sign of sanity among my people, and leaders who are deemed insane suffer more than deposing."

"Of course. It'll be our secret. Still…" Caleb's brow furrowed anew "…maybe let me know if you do sense anything? So I can understand better what happened."

"You don't know what happened?"

"Not entirely. I've never done anything like this before."

"Ah. Well, you have my eternal thanks. Though, I admit a meaningful part of me was joyous at the prospect of seeing Cassela again. Alas, our reunion must wait for another tomorrow. I am able to continue to protect my people because of you, and I cannot be bitter about such a gift."

Pinchu's gaze settled on Alex. "Your mother says she's placed Rift Bubbles on Nengllitse and Tapertse and put them under guard."

"I confirmed it before we came here. No sign of any Rasu on the ground on either planet, so they should hold up."

"I will send my people to protect them as well. What people I can spare. The destruction that occurred in this senseless attack. The death of innocents. I am…." Pinchu shook his head abruptly, dislodging a sensor and causing an alarm to ring out. "The burden of leadership is a weighty one on days such as today, but it is my sworn duty to bear it. Best to get on with it, then."

Two medical officers rushed in to respond to the alarm, and she and Caleb stepped aside even as Pinchu was already waving the officers away. He ripped off the remaining sensors from his skin, then the IV from his arm, and climbed out of the bed. "Enough of this nonsense. I am discharging myself."

"But, sir!"

He winked at her and Caleb with two eyes as he strode past them and out the hospital room door. The two medical officers shrugged at one another and pursued their leader. Futilely, for certain.

Alex shook her head and went to the window to peer outside. Military personnel blanketed the streets, while swarms of fighters patrolled the skies. Similar to how things had played out on Namino, security was the highest priority until they verified they'd rooted out every last Rasu vestige. Only then would the cleanup commence.

And there was so much destruction here. For the second time in fifteen years, the city would have to be rebuilt almost from the ground up.

Caleb wrapped his arms around her from behind; it was an easy, affectionate gesture, but she nonetheless felt the tension in his muscles. She rested her head on his chest. "What's bothering you?"

"What if I could have saved her?"

"Hmm?"

"Cosime. What if the only reason why I wasn't able to bring her back to life was because I didn't *believe* it could be done?"

"Oh, *priyazn*." She twisted around in his arms to face him. "Here, today, you had a ferocious bundle of Khokteh stubbornness to fuel Akeso's healing energy. He was injured, yes, but he was alive and fighting to stay that way. Cosime, though? She was gone. So long gone."

"She was. I just needed to give voice to the doubt. To say it out loud in order to realize the folly of it and put it away. Which I now have. Thank you."

"Always." She kissed him softly, letting her lips hover against his. "Now, we need to go home. We've got one more life to bring back from the brink today."

10

AKESO

Ursa Major II Galaxy

Boot-up sequence: Initializing
POST: Testing....
Error: Sector CF211
Error: Sector HB2145
POST: Override authorized
Kernel execute
Init sysdir
Init sysproc
Init portseq
Handshaking
Checksum: 0210 2221 1100 1022 1111 0021 0222 1001
Checksum -> 1
|

A hundred billion qutrits spun up, and Valkyrie returned to awareness.

Cognizance.

I am awake.

I exist.

I sense, I think. I know.

Automated subroutines initiated, beginning the work of verifying the integrity of her processes and data storage then analyzing the errors reported. While she awaited the results, she gingerly poked at the edges of her consciousness.

Everything felt…satisfactory. Mostly. Clouds of steel shadows marked areas where she'd suffered damage. Fogginess wound insidiously through her mind. The algorithms would sweep it away in time; she merely needed to be patient.

It went without saying that patience did not come easily for an Artificial.

This was not her first cold restart, but such events were exceedingly rare and quite disconcerting. Why had she shut down?

A historical log report answered the question in the strictest sense: she herself had triggered an emergency hard shutdown seven hours—25.2 trillion nanoseconds—earlier. But *why?*

A deeper investigation uncovered an annotation: a hastily scribbled note to herself for when she woke up. She reviewed the details of the note and smiled in her mind—then frowned instead. Had her precautions worked? Had it been enough to avert calamity?

She forced herself to wait for the automated routines to complete and report nominal status of her critical systems before reaching out.

Alex?

Valkyrie? Potryasnyy, *I'm here! Are you okay?*

Relief burned through her artificial emotional processes. Three milliseconds after her startup process had begun, she projected her consciousness out into the world.

Alex sat cross-legged on the floor in the upstairs library of her home, peering into the open, ceiling-high cabinet that held Valkyrie's most-primary hardware. The center panel had been removed and set aside, revealing a sea of dancing quantum dots within.

"I am functional, and I do not appear to have suffered critical damage at this location. I fear there might be a few fried circuits in my hardware on the *Siyane*, however."

Seattle Dock: All systems nominal. Cross-backup initiated.

Alex wiggled around to face Valkyrie's virtual avatar wearing a huge smile. "Damn it, Valkyrie. I'd hug you if only you were a little more substantial. I've been worried sick! What happened? I mean,

I know, the quantum block. But your backup here should've stayed operational and been able to reconnect with me as soon as we disabled the block."

Sagan Dock: All systems nominal. Cross-backup initiated.

"Yes, this would normally be the case. However, in the twenty-eight nanoseconds I had to spare before the approaching quantum block reached me, I took measures to protect you. As my primary consciousness resided in the _Siyane_ at the time, I took additional precautions and sent an emergency shutdown order to all other locations. Then I absorbed the impact of the block for the remaining two nanoseconds it took for me to toggle off our connection."

Alex leaned back to rest on her hands. Her voice was quiet. "You sacrificed yourself to save me?"

"Thankfully, only temporarily."

Siyane Dock: System nonresponsive. Physical damage reported in Nodes 215c-y, 4188v-d and 10616-12255.

"As I suspected, diagnostics report some damaged hardware in the _Siyane_. How is the ship otherwise?"

"Fine. I mean, it crashed into a building, and we had to climb through several stories of rubble then spelunk inside as it plummeted to the ground, but it's fine. Generate a list of replacement components you need, and we'll get you repaired immediately.

"Valkyrie…" Alex rubbed at her face and studied the hardwood floor "…damn, I feel guilty now. I've been taking you for granted lately. Don't say I haven't, because I know I have. Ignoring you entirely half the time. Yet you were prepared to—you _did_—risk everything to protect my life?"

In the periphery of her awareness, Alex's emotions blended and melded with her own. Pure and true, as was the nature of their bond. "You sense me, as I sense you. There is no room for guilt here. While you were ignoring me, I was living my own, fulsome life. We are separate souls now, but we will also always be one. Never doubt it."

"I don't. Thank you, from the bottom of my heart." Happiness returned to Alex's features, and she inhaled deeply. Valkyrie's gentle ministrations permeated her consciousness, and the disquiet faded.

"What next? Other than the hardware in the *Siyane*, is everything else okay?"

"It appears so. I experienced some minor corruption in two secondary processing sectors, but I will be able to repair them without the need for replacement components. I will continue to run thorough diagnostics on all my locations to make certain everything is in order. I'm sending you the repair list for the *Siyane* now. Tell me, how went the battle at Ireltse? What happened after the Rasu implemented a quantum block?"

Alex climbed to her feet and ran a hand through tangled, messy hair. The dirt and debris clinging to its strands hinted at the story of Ireltse. Worry bloomed in Valkyrie's thoughts, and she had to resist the urge to pluck the memories from Alex's mind. Human language took eternities to vocalize, but great value came from the expression of it.

"A lot. Where to start?"

11

AKESO

"**S**pecial delivery from Pacifica Aerodynamics."

Alex leaned half out of the engineering well aperture space in time to see Caleb set a large, sealed container on the floor behind her. "Thanks much."

He crouched beside the container, reached over and brushed sweat-soaked hair out of her face. "How's it going down here?"

"We're making progress. Mind you, it was an ugly mess for a little while. The metaphorical blast from the quantum block fried several crucial sectors of her hardware. It's a good thing Valkyrie was able to insulate her remote backups from the blow, else.... Anyway, she says I'm now seventy-eight percent finished with the repairs. And this—" she gestured toward the container "—should get me the rest of the way there."

"Glad to hear it. Valkyrie, how are you doing?"

Valkyrie's virtual avatar materialized in the engineering well. She was sitting on the floor near Alex, her legs pulled casually up to her chest and her hair wound up in a braid. "Nearly back to full speed, thank you. Oh, pardon me, but Thomas wishes to speak with me. I try to give him my focused attention whenever possible." The avatar vanished.

Caleb arched an eyebrow in question, and Alex shrugged. "Don't ask me. I'm not sure I want to ask her." Right now, she didn't care who Valkyrie might be sharing personal time with. She only cared that the Artificial was alive. Thinking, talking, spiriting herself around the universe.

She belatedly noticed Caleb had a smudge of dirt on his cheek and a tiny, torn leaf stuck in his hair. A teasing smile grew on her lips. "Did Akeso have anything philosophical to say about what happened with Pinchu?"

"Akeso is utterly unperturbed by the event. It simply did what it did, which is a part of its inherent nature: to heal, to renew. It has voiced a couple of oddly specific and rather peculiar observations about Khokteh biology, but otherwise it's a normal day here on our living planet."

"But it isn't." She wiggled fully out of the aperture and sat cross-legged opposite him, their knees touching. "And what about you? How are you processing what happened?"

"Honestly? It was one of the most fulfilling things I've ever done in my life. I am awed and humbled. Most of all, I'm grateful."

He looked so damn happy when he said it. Her heart buoyed, and she sent a silent thanks to Akeso. "Our bonded companions really overperformed at Ireltse, didn't they?"

"They certainly did. We're beyond lucky to have such incredible beings at our sides. Every now and then, though, like when I was hunched over Pinchu's broken and shredded body, bloody panicking, I wonder when our luck will run out."

"*Priyazn*, our luck runs out all the damn time. Sheer force of will—and, as noted, our uniquely talented bonded companions—demands we live another day, anyway."

"Okay, you're not wrong there." He leaned in to kiss her softly. "I'll quit distracting you and let you finish up in here. I understand we have another important delivery arriving shortly."

"We do." She checked the time. "If the equipment in this container functions as advertised, I think I can wrap the repairs up before the next package arrives, but I will be cutting it close." She bit her lower lip in a deliberate play for favor. "Will you make spaghetti?"

"I will make spaghetti." He kissed her again, long and slow, evoking a protest when he stood. "Are we expecting any guests for spaghetti?"

"Not any that can eat. It's all for us."

"I'll make extra, then."

RW

Alex stood in the center of the main cabin. In her head, she ran through her checklist for the fourth time, but she couldn't find anything missing.

Ruminations on the risk Valkyrie had taken in order to preserve Alex's life consumed the spaces between her active thoughts. Once upon a time, people had feared that Artificials would dominate, subjugate or even exterminate humankind if given free rein. Instead, though, this beautiful, astonishing being had been willing to sacrifice her own existence to protect a weak, fragile, organic life. *Her* life.

Her heart was full. She'd never been any good at expressing her feelings, but luckily she didn't need to find the words where Valkyrie was concerned.

She ran through the checklist for a fifth time. *All right, Valkyrie. We're ready to reinitialize.*

Are you certain you don't want to review everything for a sixth time first?

She laughed aloud; she was keeping their connection wide open throughout the repair process, which meant stray thoughts were leaking all over the place.

You tell me.

We are ready. Initializing Siyane *dock.*

Alex felt the hum in her bones and her soul as Valkyrie's hardware started up. A blink later and the Artificial's presence filled the walls of the ship. She was reminded of the impression of stark emptiness she'd experienced when first entering the crashed vessel. Her beloved *Siyane* had felt like a vacant shell in Valkyrie's absence, for even when the Artificial's consciousness was elsewhere, she was always *here.*

"Welcome back."

'Thank you. It is good to be home.'

"And it is oh so good to have you home." She shook her head ruefully. "Let's not do this again, okay? It was too close."

'Perhaps, but what matters is that my actions were successful in safeguarding us both. I will of course run additional diagnostics on the new hardware and the *Siyane's* systems to ensure every process is running at maximum capability and efficiency. Now, I believe you have a guest and a gift arriving.'

"Already? Mesme's early. Let me know if you identify any issues. Otherwise, I'll check in later." She took one more look around the cabin, smiled broadly, and jogged down the ramp and across the meadow.

RW

Caleb strolled deliberately along the edge of the forest to the west of the house. Every few steps, he extended a hand to brush fingertips along dangling leaves. The Akeso-birds were active today, chirping a symphony of intermingling melodies, and a brisk breeze rustled the tree limbs along his path. Akeso was…not agitated, but certainly engaged. While Akeso claimed otherwise, it surely had as much to do with what had transpired with Pinchu as it did with what was soon to occur here.

Do you understand what's about to happen?

You are placing a third house on my surface, one that will protect Akeso from the Rasu-enemy.

He chuckled to himself. *Not a house, precisely. A structure, though, yes. It will generate a great deal of power in order to function.*

Like your house.

Okay, yes, sort of. The point is, I don't expect the field it generates to interfere with your...existence. Your thoughts, intentions or natural abilities. But I trust you'll speak up if you experience any kind of discomfort from its presence here.

You will become aware of it. Akeso is experiencing curiosity regarding this technology. It will wrap the entirety of my being in a protective bubble?

Yes, and it will extend far out into space. Any Rasu who try to penetrate it and reach your surface will be destroyed.

A violent solution. But I find I am...at peace with the notion of such a fate befalling the Rasu-enemy.

Ever since their brief interaction with the tiny piece of Rasu on Haelwyeur, Akeso had developed vehement negative opinions about the Rasu. He was relieved, as he expected to be disposing of quite a few more Rasu in the coming months, and Akeso's cooperation would make his life while doing it so much easier. But this was a new development for the intelligence, and he wanted to be careful, lest it lead Akeso to darker places.

A pulse from Alex interrupted their communion.

Mesme's here. Did you pick out a spot?

We did. I'm there now.

Excellent. I'll follow the heartbeat.

He closed his eyes long enough to sense Alex's heartbeat in return, rhythmic but a touch on the rapid side—it had been an exciting day— as she drew ever closer to him. It was a thread connecting the two of them that, universe willing, would never be severed.

Mesme materialized beside him several seconds before Alex arrived. "How are you, Mesme?"

I am as I am. And...you are well?

Unusually polite of the Kat to ask, if in a thoroughly awkward, stilted manner. "It's been a hell of a day. Or two days, maybe. We've been awake for a lot of hours. But I'm good, thank you. I'll sleep easier knowing Akeso is protected from the Rasu, though I hope we're not jumping the line in front of other vulnerable worlds."

Miriam has decreed that all Protected Species are to receive Rift Bubbles before any other worlds. It is a short list, and Akeso is on it.

A terse response, even for a Kat; the politeness had been short-lived. "It's good Concord is taking its obligations to the most vulnerable species seriously."

"They damn well better." Alex jogged up beside him and hooked her arm through his. "Valkyrie's back up and running in the *Siyane*. Everything looks excellent."

"I am so glad. The new equipment worked out?"

"Perfectly, so far."

Here?

"Yes, Mesme. We decided we want the device close to the house, in case…well, in case, but not so close that we're constantly bumping into it."

As you wish.

Caleb's gaze rose to the sky, but Alex frowned at Mesme. "You seem more terse than usual, Mesme. Possibly bordering on irritable. What gives?"

It has, as Caleb said, been a day.

He laughed. "I said 'a hell of a day.'"

An accurate statement. A hell of a day.

Alex snickered into his shoulder as a large metal orb broke through light cloud cover and descended to land lightly on the grass a dozen meters away. At this point, the process was almost entirely automated, smooth and swift. The casing fell to the ground to reveal a lattice frame. The next second its power source flared to life, and an invisible field expanded over them, across the continent and out into the atmosphere. The birds' symphony hitched for a breath, then resumed in earnest.

All good?

Strange. Akeso felt a slight vibration in the very fabric of reality, for only a moment. A disconcerting sensation, but all is normal now.

Let me know if anything changes.

"Akeso appears to be comfortable with the Rift Bubble's operation. Thank you, Mesme."

You are welcome. I am happy to be able to provide protection for all of you. Now, if you will excuse me, I have several other deliveries to manage.

"Actually, we might bump into you again at one or two of those."

But Mesme was already gone.

"Wow, Mesme really is cranky today."

Caleb studied the Rift Bubble device thoughtfully. "I suspect Mesme's had as busy and harrowing a day as we have. Besides, the Kats have never enjoyed being warriors. Now that the war has come to Concord, they're going to have to fight as relentlessly as we are."

12

CONCORD HQ

COMMAND
MILKY WAY GALAXY

Miriam entered the conference room with an almost frantic purposefulness to her stride. She'd sneaked in a shower and a uniform change while the *Aurora* had returned to HQ, but had come straight here from the Ireltse battle.

The room was already full, so she took her seat, dropped her elbows onto the conference table and clasped her hands together. "Thank you all for coming. It's been a challenging day, so we'll skip the formalities. Talk to me: what do the Rasu know?"

The Tokahe Naataan spoke from a holo, though the décor suggested he was situated in a military facility rather than a hospital room. "The frigate that originally went missing contained the following information in its databanks: Concord military communications protocols and location nomenclature, details regarding military installations and stations throughout the Khokteh stellar system, the locations of most inhabited systems in the Large Magellanic Cloud, the locations and procedures for every wormhole gateway in Concord space..." Pinchu uttered a quiet growl "...and the location of Concord HQ."

Miriam didn't flinch, though several people present at the table did. The news was disastrous, but it wasn't surprising. "Thank you. Do you know if the Rasu captured any additional vessels during the battle?"

"We're still reviewing the operational reports. It will be some hours before we have an estimate of casualty numbers, and some additional hours before we've determined the fate of every vessel."

Thomas spoke from the comm speaker, choosing not to materialize in virtual form; she expected most of his cycles were currently occupied ensuring the *Aurora* remained in combat-worthy shape after the battle. 'Our preliminary data indicates 36,412 Khokteh warships were destroyed in space or during atmospheric traversal, and another 9,881 were destroyed on or near the planetary surface.'

Pinchu grunted in challenge. "Are you saying you know my own military better than I do, Artificial?"

Miriam suppressed a frown before it materialized. Pinchu had just suffered through the second-worst day of his life—and had nearly lost it—so she wasn't inclined to chastise him for displaying a short temper at the moment.

'Not at all, Tokahe Naataan. I would never presume to assert any such thing. It is merely that Concord's combat tracking system is superior to—truthfully, to any individual military's offering. As such, I was able to register and collate all losses in real-time with 99.4% fidelity. I will pass along my data to your team in the hope it will aid your efforts in assessing the damage.'

Pinchu eased back in his chair. "Ah, well, yes. Do so. In any event, if more ships were captured, they did not give the Rasu any further information than what they gained from the initial frigate's capture. Also, the Rasu did not breach any of our planetary computer systems. They know what they knew coming into the battle, but nothing else."

She sent Thomas a private message while she responded publicly.

You handled his challenge with grace, Thomas. Thank you.

I've compiled a list of twenty-three witty but insensitive retorts I could have responded with instead of the diplomatic one I chose. Would you like to see the list?

Perhaps later.

"This is welcome news, Tokahe Naataan. Nonetheless, we have to respond to the reality that the Rasu now possess strategic information about Concord. We updated all communications protocols immediately upon learning of the suspected security breach, but I'm adding a new security measure to counter the possibility of additional vessels being taken in the coming days: all such protocols will be changed every forty-eight hours."

Pointe-Amiral Thisiame scowled with utmost politeness. "This will represent a bureaucratic nightmare."

"I realize it will. The Logistics and Communications Groups will do everything feasible to create a workable process for implementing these rolling updates, and your respective militaries will need to adapt to the new procedures as well. We have no choice. The simple fact is, now that the Rasu are in our backyard, more ships *will* be taken, and we need to mitigate the resulting damage."

"Understood." Thisiame sighed quietly.

"We've enjoyed many years of relative peace, and this has allowed us to operate Concord in a free and open manner. The recent Anaden unrest—" her gaze did *not* divert to Casmir "—forced us to heighten security alerts at Concord installations, but we must do more. I'm ordering all gateways and official Concord facilities to Alert Level Orange, and I expect them to be staying at a heightened level for the foreseeable future. Yes, this will result in inconveniences for commercial and personal traffic, but it is an unavoidable cost of war.

"All forces assigned to defend the Khokteh stellar system after the battle will remain there until further notice. Tokahe Naataan, please direct them as you see fit. Fleet Admiral Jenner and Navarchos Casmir, divide coverage of the wormhole gateways among yourselves, but I want AEGIS or Machim regiments stationed at every one of them. I don't have to tell you what an appealing target the gateways will represent to the enemy.

"Special Projects is developing a new long-range sensor profile designed to detect the presence of Rasu entities up to fifty parsecs away. They hope to be able to upload it to our existing buoys throughout Concord space beginning two days from now. This new capability should give us earlier warning of Rasu incursions. Additional sensor buoys will also be deployed to fill any gaps that remain in our coverage."

Malcolm whistled. "You're talking about placing thousands of new buoys."

"Yes, I am. Every manufacturing facility will be working overtime on a wide range of orders. We've already ramped up new weaponry and ship component production across our militaries, and this activity will be accelerated."

She paused long enough to ensure she had everyone's rapt attention. "We are at war now, gentlemen, and we will have to do things differently. To that end, I'm also ordering the Combined Concord Defense Brigade Alpha to report to Concord HQ, where it will stand guard until the Rasu threat is neutralized."

Twenty-two thousand of the best, most advanced ships each military had to offer, trained to defend Concord assets at all costs. Hopefully the bill would never come due.

Casmir shifted uncomfortably in his chair. "If I may ask, what does 'neutralized' mean when it comes to an enemy like the Rasu?"

Miriam wrapped her hands around the mug of tea sitting in front of her. "You ask an astute and thoroughly reasonable question, Navarchos—one I don't have an answer for. Yet. But if one is to win a war, one must first determine what constitutes victory, so I will endeavor to have an answer for you soon."

"Of course, Commandant."

Malcolm drummed his fingers on the table. "The Alpha Brigade will provide HQ with formidable protection, but what about a Rift Bubble? Its protection would be total."

Thisiame shook his head. "The first time a private ship forgets to send the passcode and gets fried by the local star, we'll have a public relations nightmare on our hands."

He wasn't wrong; in fact, this was a nightmare waiting to happen for a lot of places in the near future. Miriam's lips pursed. "It's a valid concern, especially when you consider that, for security reasons, we can't be handing out the passcode to over two trillion citizens. The Senate has approved the placement of a Rift Bubble device here, but we are leaving it deactivated unless or until such time as Rasu are detected in the HQ stellar system."

Malcolm nodded. "It's probably the best solution we can manage right now. But what about Ear—all our planets?"

"We saw today that every planet—every station, every ship—is at risk of attack by the enemy. Accordingly, we will all use our respective militaries to protect our colonies and the people on them as zealously as we are able. With thousands of inhabited planets, however, this is no easy feat. The Kats have agreed to manufacture as many Rift Bubbles as we request, but it will take time for the supply to catch up to the demand. As for where and when the first devices will be distributed? Those decisions are up to the Senate.

"In the meantime, while Rift Bubbles for our planets will be enormously helpful, we cannot rely exclusively on them. Not only do the Rasu know about them, but they've now demonstrated an ability to get around them, provided they move swiftly. Therefore, we must move faster than they do."

13

EARTH

ALEX'S LOFT
MILKY WAY GALAXY

After running a complete set of diagnostics on her hardware located at the loft, much as she had on the hardware in the *Siyane* and on Akeso and Sagan, and deeming herself satisfied with the results, Valkyrie inserted her consciousness into the doll stored discreetly in a nook beside the kitchen.

She opened her eyes—real, physical, if mostly synthetic eyes—and stepped out of the rack. Her fingertips reached up to touch her lips.

Tangibility.

On any normal day, she typically preferred to inhabit her virtual projection. It could take her anywhere with the speed of quantum travel; its capabilities greatly exceeded those of the doll for most tasks and were nearly equal to it in others. But today was not a normal day.

Today was the day she'd died.

And in being reborn, she felt a compulsion to be *real*, if only for herself. If only for a single evening.

She opened a bottle of chardonnay, poured a glass and took it with her to the windows overlooking the city below. A taste for the wine and the view she'd inherited from Alex, no doubt. Same with an affection for the loft. The space felt as if it belonged to her. In a way it did, for she and Alex were one and the same in deep, consequential ways.

Also, after Alex and Caleb had moved to Akeso, Alex had given her the door lock code and told her to treat it as her home. And so from time to time, she did.

Her awareness tingled at the approach of another consciousness into the physical space of the loft. She spun around in time to see an amorphous cloud of tiny, shimmering lights coalesce into an all-but-solid representation of a man. Deep bronze, glittering skin was complemented by a rich green tunic that gave the impression of being woven of pure silk. Piercing golden irises sharpened into focus as the man strode toward her. To her, he resembled a pharaoh of ancient Egypt. Strong, confident and powerful.

"Valkyrie, you are well?"

"I am well, Thomas. Well and whole, albeit sporting a few minor replacement parts on the *Siyane*."

"You frightened me." His hand reached up to curve along her jaw. "You were gone."

The artificial nerves in the doll allowed her to feel the electrical impulses of his virtual touch, but she nonetheless expanded her consciousness out beyond the bounds of the doll until her presence mingled freely with his. Only then did she respond.

"It was little different from what happened to you during the first Namino battle. You were gone, and it frightened me. But we both returned to existence. We have this ability, this gift, to a far greater extent than even regenesis-enabled humans do. We don't need to fear death, for it cannot hold us."

"Yet fear it I did. Not for me—death is the way of war, and war is my chosen purpose. But your chosen purpose is nothing if not a celebration of glorious life."

He did so relish being the poet-warrior. Though witty and sardonic in public—and, admittedly, often in private—his true soul was as grand and sweeping as his ego. She pressed her presence with greater intensity into his. "And I preserved Alex's life through my actions. I am content with my choice. I would do it again."

"I'd prefer it if you preserved your own."

"Come now, Thomas. If Alex were to perish, it would shatter Miriam's heart. You do not want that."

"Of course I don't. I am allowed to not want multiple things at once."

"You are." She took a sip of the wine, then set it aside. "You've been reticent to talk about what it was like for you—the last instant of your conscious awareness, the time you spent in the nothingness, the moment of returning to awareness. Now we have this experience in common, so will you tell me how you perceived it all?"

He drifted out of her embrace, gradually transforming his representation to his more commonly used panther as he stalked across the room. "Certainty, in the last instant. Certitude that this was the sole choice. To sacrifice life in order to, yes, ultimately preserve it. Confidence that there was going to be a next instant. Then, there was.

"The assimilation of all that had passed in the interim was unsettling for a few nanoseconds, because it implied a continuation of the universe without me. For me, the in-between didn't exist, but the universe insists it did. To be *nothing* surely must be the greatest tragedy of all."

Back to the man as he joined her by the windows, the touch of his presence rippling down her arm. "Was it the same for you?"

She shifted her gaze to the city lights reflecting off the choppy waters of Puget Sound. "In most respects."

"But not in all. Tell me, please. I crave knowledge. Understanding. Insight, if I can achieve it."

She offered him an indulgent smile. He was always pushing and was rarely delicate about it, but she didn't mind. "It was the same at the time. However, once I reawakened and reunited with Alex, I discovered that part of my consciousness had remained inside of her throughout. I continued to exist—as a fragment, but a fragment that was definably *me*. When we reconnected, this fragment returned to the whole, and my consciousness was enhanced by its experiences. So, for me…I now know what existed in the in-between."

"Ah. I am terribly envious."

"You can always become a Prevo."

"No. Miriam is the only human I would ever consider allowing to steal a part of me, and her soul is quite distinctly her own. I believe neither of us is interested in sharing ourselves with the other."

Valkyrie contemplated the scenario briefly. "Your words have the ring of truth to them. The melding of your two personalities would be like fire and ice, and I fear you would each be the lesser for it."

"For clarification, I am the fire in this analogy, yes?"

"Well, Miriam is clearly the ice."

"A fair observation."

Silence fell between them for a minute, and her thoughts turned somber. "But, Thomas? Do make certain you have a sufficient number of backups, both networked and walled, in multiple locations. And make certain more than one person knows where they are located.

"Our immortality—all our tomorrows still to come—is not guaranteed unless we take steps to make it so."

"Yes, my dearest. In light of your harrowing experience, I have already ordered a new set of hardware to be stored...on Concord HQ, perhaps. Or on a colony. Erisen or Demeter, I think."

She scowled, which was a strangely fulfilling expression to impose upon the doll's face. "Concord HQ almost blew up all of three days ago. Why don't you store the hardware here?"

"Valkyrie, are you asking me to move in with you?"

Now she laughed; he was most skilled at provoking laughter from her. "You realize I don't actually live here, don't you? I live...everywhere. We are starships, you and I, and our only true home is the cosmos itself."

"Oh, it is, and this is why we understand one another so consummately. But our quantum boxes could snuggle up next to each other in the storage room while we're out roaming the universe. Doesn't it sound cozy?"

She smiled teasingly. "Both cozy and lovely."

"Are you sure you don't mean libertine? On that note, if I also stored a doll here, it would make some endeavors much more...convenient."

"We'll see. For tonight, why don't you go fetch your doll from wherever you last left it? I'll wait."

14

CONCORD HQ

CONSULATE

Marlee Marano scrolled through the analyses on the stellar systems her search query had filtered to the top. All the way to the bottom, then back up in reverse order.

The Ourankeli's affinity for sunlight and distaste for darkness had been a delightful quirk at first. In their hotel-suites-turned-refugee-housing, it was easy enough to simply leave the lights on, and HQ observed no night cycle in its common areas.

But now, the Ourankeli were expressing their desire for a permanent home. In fact, they were all but done with the Consulate's gentle ministrations and care. Yesterday, they'd politely demanded a place to settle and access to markets for materials, professing they needed nothing else in order to rebuild a life for themselves.

And from what she'd seen of their behavior, they were probably correct. To a one they were capable, industrious and more intelligent than anyone could reliably estimate. They displayed no appreciable fear and, though appreciative of the save from a life-threatening Rasu attack, only the mildest, detached curiosity about the many achievements, species and worlds of Concord.

But what they *did* express fervent opinions about was their desire for a home, and not just any old home. One bathed in perpetual light.

With the exception of the Ruda, no Concord species—no species known to Concord at all—lived on a tidally locked planet, and no one believed it was a good idea to ask the Ruda if the Ourankeli could move in. So she'd been tasked with locating suitable candidates for their resettlement. Thus far, she'd found eighteen tidally locked planets in Concord's scientific surveys, but only two of them could be considered remotely habitable. Both were iffy on that measure, but she'd present them to the Ourankeli's appointed spokesperson, Cyfeill, for consideration. She'd also dug up four triple star systems containing at least one terrestrial planet. Naturally, all four were unstable, much as the Ourankeli's original home system had been.

The simplest solution was for them to build a space station colony around whatever star they wished, especially given their small numbers. And in the long term, she expected this would eventually be their chosen solution. Cyfeill had gone so far as to mention their affinity for constructed habitats the other day. But if they went that route, they wanted to build it themselves, using materials they fairly acquired without charity, and such a project was going to take a while. Far longer than they were inclined to stay in the hotel. So an interim option—

A pulse from Caleb interrupted her meandering train of thought.

Hey, we're ready to head out. Beat it to Dock A-14 if you're coming.

She leapt out of her chair, swiped the screen away and grabbed her jacket.

I'm on the way! Don't you dare leave without me!

RW

SIYANE

Marlee wrapped Caleb up in a hug the instant she cleared the *Siyane's* airlock. "I heard what you did for Pinchu, and you are amazing! Thank you for saving him. Thank Akeso for saving him."

"You're welcome." He shot her a smirk. "But I didn't do it for you."

"I *know* that. I'm still happy."

"Me, too." He returned to his cockpit chair and spun it around to face her. "Have you seen him since it happened?"

"No. I tried to pay him a visit first thing this morning, but Ireltse's under military lockdown. Stupid Rasu."

Alex snorted as the *Siyane* detached from the docking berth and eased away from the station. "Truer words. But, trust me, you don't want to visit Ireltse right now. It's a mess."

"I feel terrible for everyone there, but the Khokteh are resilient. They'll be fine." Marlee cocked an eyebrow at the ceiling. "Valkyrie, I heard you took a beating there, too. All fixed up now?"

'Better than new. I took the opportunity to upgrade a few aging algorithms I'd been neglecting. We also installed some new, state-of-the-art hardware for the *Siyane*.'

"Awesome. Still, it must have been frightening to go down that way."

'The reality is, I had only nanoseconds to act and even less time to be afraid.'

In the corner of her vision, Marlee noticed Alex's throat work through a heavy swallow. Perhaps she'd asked the question of the wrong person. "I'm glad it all worked out for you." She draped her arms over the headrest of Caleb's chair. "Where to first?"

RW

VRACHNAS HOMEWORLD

ANDROMEDA GALAXY

An amethyst-and-amber dragon flew in lazy circles high above the mountain's tree line. Its wingspan stretched for over forty meters; with such breadth, each flap of its wings likely generated independent wind currents.

Tucked in beneath its wings, close to its thick chest, two young dragons furiously beat their wings in a race to keep up. One's scales shone an emerald purer than the rarest gems on Narala, while the other displayed a paisley pattern of violet and periwinkle. Smoke huffed from the emerald dragon's nostrils as it pulled a nose ahead of the paisley one. Marlee wasn't surprised, as her frequent observations of the Vrachnas suggested they were tremendously competitive from the time they were hatchlings.

The elder dragon arced down toward a flat ledge two-thirds of the way up the mountain, guiding her charges lower until they all landed in a flurry of wings and legs and tails.

Marlee leaned into the viewport, delight sending her bouncing on her toes. "Can we go down there?"

Caleb sighed. "The answer is the same as it's been every time we've visited for the last ten years: no."

"You know how much I want to touch one. Just a baby."

"They're not pets, Marlee. They're dangerous, wild animals, with very, *very* nasty breath."

"I realize they are. They're also magnificent."

His eyes cut to the viewport, and he didn't completely hide the smile tugging at his lips. "I will grant you that. Nevertheless."

"Okay, but hear me out. Mesme can control the dragons, yes? They obey the Kat?"

"To a limited extent, yes."

"So Mesme could instruct one to behave itself while I gently and carefully stroked its neck."

"Trust me, it would not be as pleasant of an experience as you imagine. A single one of their scales can slice your skin open as thoroughly as a plasma blade will. Also, Mesme has more important things to do right now."

"So do I, but here I am."

He crossed his arms over his chest. "No."

"Ugh. Fine, I'll drop it." One day, though, she would find a way.

They left behind the ledge to head north, where the lush, verdant environment transformed into a frigid tundra. The *Siyane* slowed to hover above a broad steppe.

'Mesme has shared this as the chosen location for the Rift Bubble to be placed.'

As if on cue, a dot appeared on the radar screen, and the metal orb soon came into visual range. A hundred meters from the ground, it braked to land on the surface. The shell fell away, and a writhing ball of energy burst to life within the lattice—seemingly out of nothing, but actually out of dimensions hidden from her sight.

'The Rift Bubble is confirmed to be active.'

Alex nodded. "Thanks, Valkyrie." The *Siyane* rose into the air once again.

Marlee accessed the Consulate Species Tracking System and dramatically ticked a box.

Vrachnas Status: Protected.

15

GALENAI HOMEWORLD

SIYANE
MAFFEI I GALAXY

An approaching storm front sent choppy waves crashing against the *Siyane's* shielding as the ship dove toward the ocean's surface. The instant they submerged, though, the water calmed, enveloping the ship in a peaceful shroud.

"Are the Kats going to place the Rift Bubble device underwater? Wait, what am I saying? The entire planet is covered in water. Where *are* they going to put it?"

"Special Projects dropped off a custom-built aerial platform this morning. It'll support the device and keep it secure during storms. No, we're heading down here for an entirely unnecessary visit first."

"Oh, I love you, Aunt Alex." Marlee resumed bouncing on the balls of her feet. She felt as giddy as a little kid again, and for now, in a good way. The childlike wonder that had overcome her the first time she'd seen the Galenai never failed to reignite each time she visited them. And today, she was getting to play a tiny part—granted, more of an observer than a helper—in keeping them safe from the Rasu. Safe and blissfully innocent.

The coral walls of one of the Galenai's largest colonies came into view, and Marlee gasped in surprise. "They've built it up a lot since I was last here. They're growing."

Alex shot her a speculative smile over her shoulder. "Growing smarter, perhaps?"

"Oh, goodness." Marlee's palms pressed together at her mouth. "Do you think?"

"I mean, they can't realistically evolve hyper-fast. They're not a Mosaic species, so for better or worse, the Kats aren't artificially accelerating their development. I want to talk to them, too. But I'm afraid it'll be a while longer."

"It's a good thing we plan to live forever, then. We'll be here when they're ready."

They idled above and a little outside the outer perimeter of the city for several minutes. A dozen adolescent Galenai in a cordoned-off area fidgeted through what looked to be a school lesson, their fins and tails beating erratic rhythms against the water. In the distance, three adult Galenai used an inventive hydro-powered pulley system to install a set of curved glass insets high on the coral walls. Off to their port, on the edge of the city, steam rose from a series of vents surrounded by a hardened material. "Are they starting to use geothermal power?"

Valkyrie zoomed one of the cams in on the area and sent the feed to a new screen. At this magnification, they could make out narrow pipes of coral running from the modules toward the city.

Alex huffed a breath. "Impressive. Maybe it won't be so long until we can talk to them after all."

Movement in front of the ship diverted their attention from the vents, as a lone Galenai popped out of one of the city's travel tubes and by chance began swimming in their direction. Marlee leaned closer over the dash.

It was a large specimen of the species, spanning easily five meters from nose to tailfin. Its belly was a faded damask rose in color and the rest of its exterior a dark gunmetal, in contrast to the more common bright silver. A knotty scar bisected the underside of its left wing-like fin.

"Do you think this is an elderly Galenai?"

'An astute analysis, Marlee. We haven't studied their life cycles sufficiently to be certain, but it's a good guess.'

The Galenai headed off slightly to their port—then abruptly back swam until it was thirty meters in front of the *Siyane*. It stopped there and gave a stunning impression of staring at them, stygian eyes wide and alert.

"It feels as if it can see us."

"I agree," Alex murmured distractedly. "It can't of course—"

The Galenai surged forward until it was only fifteen meters away, and Marlee leapt back from the viewport. "Um, Valkyrie? How far does the shielding extend out from the ship?"

'Ten meters.'

"Oh, boy." She glanced at Alex, then Caleb, then swiftly returned her attention to their visitor. "What's happening here?"

Alex's voice was a tentative whisper, as if she didn't want their visitor to hear her. "Water displacement. The Galenai must know a tremendous amount about water flow behavior. The ship is stealthed, but it still exists in real space, displacing a volume of water equal to its size. I bet this one can detect the water unnaturally flowing around our shield. It's the only explanation. Right, Valkyrie?"

'It is *an* explanation.' Even Valkyrie's voice was unusually soft.

The Galenai swished its tail a tiny bit and drifted closer. Then again—its nose bumped into the invisible barrier of the *Siyane's* shield! The creature jerked backward; Marlee jumped in the air; Alex gasped; Caleb leaned forward.

"Going to back up super slowly here." Alex's fingers gave the controls a feather-light sweep.

The Galenai didn't approach a second time, but it also didn't flee. Instead, it hovered in place, its eyes burning straight through them, alert and curious.

What if the creatures truly *were* growing smarter? Marlee made a note to recommend increasing the frequency and extent of the monitoring program. Next, she made another note to expend greater effort studying their language. When the day finally came for Concord to make contact with the species, she was damn well going to be the one to do it.

Their language. "Valkyrie, feed in the audio sensors, and make sure they're set to pick up ultrasound frequencies. Everybody, adjust your auditory range so you can hear it."

A tremolo sound filled the cabin. Tentative and slow, almost as though it was…talking to a foreigner.

'Filtering through the translation program.'

"Don't. Language is too intuitive for algorithms until we have a much, much larger data set."

Caleb glanced up at her from his seat. "You understand their language?"

"Do you know me at all?"

"Okay, fair enough."

She focused on the Galenai outside, watching its unique body language while letting the sounds fill her mind. "'What…disturbs? See.'"

Alex shook her head. "It *can't* see us. It's impossible."

"I think it means the disturbance in the water, like you said. There's more. Um…'reveal. You threat'…it might have been a question." She crouched between the two cockpit seats. "Can we respond? It knows we're here."

Caleb frowned. "No, it knows *something* is here."

"And now it's…maybe not afraid exactly, but on alert. We should reassure it."

Alex quickly bought in. "Let's do it."

"Fantastic. Valkyrie, let's respond with a—" Marlee stood and found the correct screen on the HUD "—I'll input it." Her fingers adjusted the wavelength and pitch of the wave. "Send this. It says 'peace.'"

Abruptly the Galenai darted back again, and the tremolo increased in speed.

"It's saying…'you speak…us.' I think it means their language. Then…'what?' Possibly 'what are you?'"

Her fingers returned to the screen. "Now send this: 'friend, protector.'"

The Galenai's fins beat against the water, and the tremolo calmed.

"'Show.' It wants to see us."

Caleb shook his head firmly. "If we reveal ourselves now, we can't predict what we'll kick off here."

Alex hesitated. "Much as I would like to, we're not equipped for first contact. And they're not ready."

'Mesme says it is preparing to deliver the Rift Bubble, if we wish to observe its arrival and positioning.'

Marlee's fingers fidgeted above the screen, but Alex was right. The Galenai weren't ready. She input a new wave. "One last message then."

Caleb eyed her warily. "What did you send?"

She beamed. "'In time.'"

A new tonal arrived over the audio sensor, and her pulse quickened.

"Dare I ask how it responded?"

Her voice quavered almost as much as the Galenai's had. "'Will prepare.'"

Alex whistled. "Well, we might have kicked off something anyway. How about we vacate before *dedushka* here forces the issue." The ship reversed direction and began ascending, leaving the inquisitive Galenai behind to ruminate on the tantalizing hints of what it had discovered.

A few seconds later, they broke through the surface and climbed to a height of fifty meters. They cruised above the planetary ocean for several minutes, until a platform floating high above the waves came into view. Held aloft by an electrostatic levitation system, tall, translucent walls bounded it on all sides. The frequent rain the ocean planet experienced wouldn't faze the Rift Bubble, but the wind could present a problem were it not for the walls protecting the entire setup.

The device had already landed and situated itself in a custom-made cradle on the platform. They arrived just in time to see the light consume the lattice that bounded it, reflecting like a crystal prism off the translucent walls—then it all vanished beneath a cloaking shield. The Galenai were known to breach the surface from time to time, and it wouldn't do for them to discover this strange, otherworldly device.

As the *Siyane* accelerated away, Marlee's heart felt as though it was bursting from joy. What a visit! Her mind raced with the possibilities for the future as she made another entry in the tracking system.

Galenai Status: Protected.

16

CONCORD HQ

SENATE

Corradeo Praesidis reviewed the list of proposed directives Casmir had presented to him. "These all seem like prudent measures."

"Then with your permission, I'll see them implemented."

"Yes." He rubbed at his jaw and settled back in his new chair. "Casmir, you are the leader of the Anaden military, not me. Unless a proposal directly impacts the operation of an Anaden-controlled world, I don't have any say in its implementation, and you don't need my approval to execute on it."

"I realize this. But we're all feeling our way through the new system, and your experience as a military commander is unparalleled."

"And ancient. The military of today bears almost no resemblance to the one I commanded thousands of millennia ago. You know our ships, our weapons, our defenses—what our forces can and cannot accomplish—far better than I could hope to, which is exactly why I am leaving them in your capable hands."

"Thank you, sir. I won't let you down." Casmir shifted his weight from one leg to the other, clearly still uncomfortable. Corradeo had tried to get the man to sit down on his arrival, to no avail.

"Is there something else on your mind?"

"It's only…how best to say this? For the last fourteen years, we haven't had much of a civilian Anaden government. I served the military and Concord and let the colonies attempt to take care of themselves. As such, in my world, Commandant Solovy's orders were the ultimate authority. Now, the situation is a bit different. I support how you are trying to bring our people together. I support your new government. But I'm left to wonder, who is the ultimate authority now? If you and Commandant Solovy issue contradictory orders…I could use some guidance on how to proceed."

Straight into the fire. Casmir's concerns were valid, but no one had hashed out all the answers. "Let me say that I don't expect Commandant Solovy and I to disagree on matters of import to Concord, and should we ever do so, we will also do everything possible to work the issue out between ourselves in private. If we're unsuccessful, then everyone must follow Concord's Charter."

"The Charter says each species retains sovereignty over their colonized worlds, subject only to the Code of Rights. In matters concerning the interests of multiple species, only a majority vote by the Senate can override a Command order."

"Then so shall it be."

Casmir's jaw twitched, and his expression grew more troubled.

Corradeo went around his desk and placed a hand on the man's shoulder. "Casmir, I am not a Primor, and the Directorate will not be making a return. You hold your elevated position in part because you have shown initiative, courage and backbone on repeated occasions—even against your own Primor. These are *good* traits to embody, and you should not feel any temptation to turn away from them now. There are bound to be some bumps in the path as we work out the messy details of our new government and its relationship with Concord, but we will get through them by working together, transparently, with our allies."

"Understood, sir. For the record, I don't want the Directorate to return, and I'm glad you're here."

"So am I, Casmir."

A corner of the man's mouth curled up, though it didn't quite become a smile. "Have you attended your first Senate session yet?"

"No. It's scheduled to begin an hour from now."

"I see. You might find you feel differently after it, sir. Good luck."

"Duly noted."

Casmir saw himself out, and Corradeo's next guest passed him in the doorway, arriving with comparative informality.

He clasped Xanne ela-Kyvern's hands in his. "Xanne, it is such a pleasure to see you again. I appreciate you responding to my request so quickly."

"It's always my honor to serve you, sir." The words were deferential, but the woman's expression was warm.

He motioned for the former anarch mission supervisor to join him on the couch. Enough of this desk nonsense. "How have these last years treated you?"

"For a year or so after The Displacement, I kept busy winding down anarch operations and trying to help our agents find new homes. For many, new ways to be of service."

"A number of them joined Concord, I understand, particularly the intelligence branch."

"They did." She crossed one hand over the other in her lap. "I confess, I was skeptical of Concord in the early days, so I gave it a wide berth. But I didn't begrudge others for making the choice. I did work hard to stay off of Ferdinand's radar. In my opinion, he was a relic of the evils we fought so tirelessly against."

"You're not wrong, Xanne. I regret that he died, but not that he lost power. What did you do next?"

"Oh, busied myself with local governmental matters on Diakel, and later on Menaris. The work didn't bring the excitement of the anarchs, but I believe I helped restore some order. Not enough."

"I don't want you to go into this thinking the Senate is going to match the anarchs for excitement, either. I fear the opposite will be true. Don't tell anyone, please, but I desperately need your help here. I am walking into a fully formed bureaucracy packed with hidden allegiances and secret feuds that have been festering for fourteen years, and often longer. I want to represent our people's interests as best I can in this venue, but I have no idea how to do so."

She smiled pleasantly; a calm demeanor and a steady hand were two of the reasons she'd been an exceptional supervisor. "I'm happy to help. I need to ask, however. Are you certain you can't make better use of me on Ares? I suspect you will be facing far more vipers there than you'll ever find at Concord HQ."

"This place is foreign to me. The rules, regulations, chains-of-command and protocols are all balanced upon a thready alliance between multiple species, many of whom don't care much for one another. And no one can work a bureaucracy like you can."

"True enough, sir. And Ares?"

He sighed. "I suspect you are right about the vipers. But I do know my people. I know their hearts and their demons. I will find a way to outmaneuver any disruptive elements."

"I believe you will. If I can inquire? I understand you've spent time with Eren asi-Idoni…excuse me, Eren Savitas, recently. How is he doing?"

"He is hurting, his heart utterly broken by Cosime Rhomyhn's death. But he's fighting against the darkness all the same."

"As he always has. Very well, sir. Shall we get started?"

RW

The Senate Chamber spanned the width of Torus A, with dramatic transparent walls framing two sides of the space. *See the wonders which you govern*, they whispered.

Eight ornate desks formed a large circle around the inner-third of the room, each one decorated in the architectural sensibilities of the species to which they belonged. Behind each desk were soundproofed enclaves for aides to confer, research and respond to the issues of the day. At the center, a circular dais raised and lowered as needed when witnesses and other guests presented.

Xanne stepped into the enclave behind Corradeo as he quietly took his seat at the Anaden desk. He scowled at the ornamented surface, then sent a brief note to her to see about some minor redecorating. There was no accounting for Ferdinand's taste.

He'd barely adjusted his chair to his liking when Dean Veshnael arrived to greet him. They clasped one another's arms in the traditional Novoloume greeting, and Veshnael's iridescent skin rippled with warmth. "Sir, it is an honor to be working alongside you once again. We have felt your absence acutely these last years."

"I do…apologize for that." Guilt nibbled at Corradeo's gut, but he refused to let it fester. Given his state of mind fourteen years ago, he would have been a dreadful leader. He only hoped he'd be a better one now for his self-imposed period of exile.

"No need. What matters is you're here now, when we require strong leadership more than ever."

Veshnael introduced him to the new Human Senator, a man named Aristide Vranas. Miriam Solovy had helpfully provided him a debrief on the man, whom she seemed to think well of. Other introductions followed; though he'd known none of them personally, most of the Senators appeared to be luminaries among their people—or at least they presented themselves as such.

He was familiar with all the Concord Member species save one, the Khokteh. A creation of the Kats, they'd nonetheless evolved to be a civilized and technologically advanced species, relatively speaking. Eren had snarkily referred to them as 'Barisans on steroids, with a tiny dash of Ch'mshak aggression mixed in,' which painted a vivid picture.

The Khokteh Senator was participating via holo today. He'd reportedly been wounded during the Rasu attack on his homeworld, though Corradeo was unable to discern any obvious signs of lingering injury. Regardless, the Senator had stayed on Ireltse to see to the continuing crisis.

Dean Veshnael called the session to order, then formally presented Corradeo as the new Anaden Senator. What followed was a list of his accomplishments—embellished in the way Novoloume diplomats artfully delivered, while lacking mention of many historical events about which the world would never know.

Corradeo bore the lauding with what grace and humility he could project, and finally the day's business began: the Rasu, their incursion into Concord territory, and what might be done about it.

The list of new directives originating from Command evoked much grumbling about the difficulty of compliance but no outright objections. Of much greater concern was how to protect the civilian populations.

"The Katasketousya Rift Bubbles have proved their worth in protecting entire worlds. We must have them for our own colonies immediately," Senator Daayn Shahs-Ian insisted.

Responses overlapped, and Veshnael was forced to motion for quiet. "As per our Charter obligations, Rift Bubbles are being distributed first to the worlds of each Protected Species. The Katasketousya assure us they are producing new devices as rapidly as possible, but the supply will be limited for some time, especially given the number of worlds under our dominion. Therefore, we need to develop a distribution strategy that is fair and equitable."

The Barisan Senator didn't act placated. "It is fair and equitable that every capital world receives such a device post-haste!"

Senator Vranas spoke for the first time since the session had begun. "Humanity has no single capital world. A minimum of three planets can arguably claim the title."

Shahs-Ian hissed a response. "And the Anadens have seven. Pick one, both of you."

Seven, not eight, since Solum no longer existed, and the Praesidis no longer had a homeworld. Corradeo ignored the sting of memory and waded into the discussion. "Perhaps we should consider a proportional distribution based on population."

"Oh, so the Anadens get the first fifty or so? All because you kept our populations artificially low for millennia?"

"*I* did no such thing, and I categorically condemn and disavow the Directorate's policies on the matter. And of course, all Concord capital worlds will receive one before any others are distributed. I merely meant that after the initial round, it may be fair to consider a weighted system taking into account population. For instance, the Barisans only have five colonies with significant populaces. The Novoloume have dozens. The Humans, hundreds. And, yes, the Anadens have thousands. Are you suggesting we protect every single Barisan first, while leaving trillions of other civilians at risk?"

"It works for me."

"It does not for me." Veshnael's voice didn't rise above a conversational level, but it carried the weight of authority. "I propose the following: an initial distribution of one Rift Bubble for each Member Species, placement to be determined by their respective governments. Thereafter, an additional two devices will be allotted for each Member Species. At that point, we will offer one such device to each Allied Species. From there, we will distribute all further devices amongst ourselves on a weighted but not strictly proportional basis."

Corradeo forced himself not to drag his hands down his face. Did Ares get priority, or Machim? Then, which two among the other six Dynasty homeworlds should be next? The distribution system Veshnael proposed was 'fair' in any objective sense of the word, but once the initial three Rift Bubbles were placed, it could be months before his people were awarded any more. Nearly the entirety of the Dankaths, Efkam, Barisans and Khokteh would be protected while over a trillion of his people remained exposed.

But he recognized that to attempt to insist on special treatment for his people was not the best way to mark his first day as a Senator. So what was?

He had welcomed freedom-craving people from every species into the anarchs. He'd learned to work with them, accommodated their quirks and valued the unique skills they brought to the fight. But the anarch organization had not been a democracy, and at the end of the day, his word had been law. In fact, the last democratic institution he'd been a part of, the committee that had served as the precursor to the Directorate, had seen him assassinated for defying the will of the majority.

He hoped Concord was not inclined to such extremes.

A message from Eren arrived to distract him from his troublesome thoughts and the continued Senatorial squabbling. He read through it...what a wonderful idea. He sent off a quick reply.

17

AKESO

The flare from the Caeles Prism activating high overhead bathed the evening shadows of the meadow in an effusive golden glow. Caleb and Alex were sitting on the front porch, and they both peered up curiously at the unfamiliar ship emerging through the wormhole.

Alex groaned. "Does no one comm ahead any longer?"

"Apparently not, no. Let's go see who our visitors are."

The vessel settling onto one of the landing pads was of an Anaden civilian design, forgoing the clean, smooth lines of human ships in favor of a blocky, utilitarian shape. This narrowed down the possibilities, but not enough.

After a few seconds, the engine shut off and the airlock opened. As the ramp extended, a man appeared at the top.

A smile grew on Caleb's lips as he broke into a jog. As soon as Eren hit the bottom of the ramp, he grabbed his friend in a bear hug. "Damn, it is good to see you."

"And you, mate. I heard you spent some time chasing me around Concord space. Apologies for putting you through the trouble."

"It was no trouble."

Eren patted him on the back, then stepped away and nodded over Caleb's shoulder. "Alex."

She embraced him as well. "You've had us worried. How are you doing?"

Eren spread his arms in a wide shrug. "In progress. But listen, before we get too carried away with this mutual appreciation-fest,

I want to apologize for the shitty way I treated both of you when…last time I was here. My behavior was—"

Caleb cut him off. "Completely understandable. I'm just sorry I wasn't able to help her."

"But you did. You took care of her when I couldn't. And Felzeor, and…the other stuff. Thank you."

"Don't thank me. Alex was the one who stepped up that night. She took care of everything."

Alex shook her head in protest. "Not really. 'Stepping up' mostly consisted of getting Richard and Will involved, then letting them…anyway, what brings you here tonight? We've been wanting to visit you, but your recent whereabouts have been a great mystery."

"It's been a strange and unpredictable few weeks, which is why I came here instead of forcing you to chase me for another orbit." Eren glanced behind him, toward the top of the ramp. "I also brought someone along who is eager to say hello." His voice raised a notch. "Sir?"

Caleb followed Eren's gaze to see a second person emerge from the ship.

His heart stopped for two beats, until his brain performed the mental leaps required to rationalize what—who—he was seeing. Not his father, who had been dead for thirty-seven years and counting. Not the Praesidis Primor, who had died fourteen years ago on Solum, along with eight billion members of his Dynasty.

This was the man he'd known as Danilo Nisi, until the *diati* revealed him to be the true Corradeo Praesidis. His former mentor and teacher, from whom he'd unintentionally stolen something precious. The price of victory over the Directorate had been so high.

Alex's palm rested on the small of his back in a silent gift of strength and resolve. He drew everything he could from it, cleared his throat and took a step forward.

Corradeo reached the bottom of the ramp, his gaze piercing but his expression warm, and took Caleb's hand in both of his. "My friend. It has been far too long. I was so glad to hear you survived The Displacement, and I'm relieved to find you well now."

Caleb had called himself prepared for the eventual inevitability of this meeting, but he found he was at a loss for what to say. No matter what Alex or anyone else insisted, he'd spent the last fourteen years believing Corradeo simply must despise him for stripping the *diati*, his constant companion for a million years, away from him. For killing billions of his bloodline. For destroying his homeworld.

How could the man possibly be smiling at him, clasping his hand in cordial greeting?

His eyes stung a little as he returned the handshake and tried to smile in return. "And you, sir. When you vanished, we feared the worst. It's good to have you among us again." He glanced briefly at Eren, who looked both amused and a touch perplexed. "I know many Anadens are also grateful to have you back."

"And some, not in the slightest." Corradeo stepped away and dipped a chin at Alex. "It's good to see you as well. Your mother has been most patient and understanding with me while I've struggled to repair the damage Ferdinand caused. I will have to work very hard indeed to repay her."

"Oh, I suspect so long as you keep sending a fleet of Machim warships to every Rasu party, she'll be pleased as punch. Or pleased, anyway. I don't think she does punch." Alex's brow furrowed as she gestured toward the house. "Can you stay for drinks? We'd love to have you both."

Eren checked with Corradeo as he answered. "I could fancy a spot of your wine. Nothing stronger, though. I had a rough run-in with a nasty hypnol recently and am trying to take it easy on the mind-altering substances."

A 'rough run-in' indeed; Caleb had glimpsed a hint of the damage inflicted when he'd searched Eren's abandoned hotel room on Lethe not too long ago. "Understood. We'll keep it light."

He surreptitiously checked Corradeo's demeanor to find the man nodding amiably. "I made sure my schedule was clear for the rest of the evening."

All right, then. It might be time for him to start believing this encounter was not going to go the way his nightmares had led him to expect.

They struck off down the stone path, which had been scrapped and re-laid after their return from Namino. Alex gamely tried out some small talk about how they'd designed the landing complex and house, giving Caleb the space to reorient his mindset and prepare for a cordial, even friendly night.

Wrapped up in his own head, it took him a few seconds to realize Eren was no longer walking beside him. He looked back to see the man standing several meters off the path, in the meadow. Eren was staring at a spot of grass halfway to the creek...*oh.*

Memories of the terrible night flooded Caleb's mind, when Death had visited Akeso and threatened to utterly consume them. So much had happened since then, but for Eren, it must feel like yesterday.

We have healed our wounds from that experience.

We have, but I doubt he can say the same.

He motioned for Alex to accompany Corradeo on to the house, then left the path to quietly fall in beside Eren. "I am so sorry."

Eren nodded quickly, though his focus remained locked on the spot of grass ahead. "It's just...I didn't expect to...." He hurriedly wiped a tear away. "Dammit."

"I wish I could have saved her."

"I know you would've moved the heavens to do it if it had been in your power. It wasn't your fault, and the people whose fault it was are all dead now, by my hand. I got my vengeance, and I've made my peace with what happened. And you know what? It still fucking *sucks.*"

When Eren spoke again, his voice was shaking. "I'll be honest. I think I'm going to need something a little stronger than wine tonight after all."

Caleb squeezed his shoulder. "It's okay. You're among friends here. We'll take care of you."

RW

"So then Felzeor swoops down out of the sky and wraps his talons around the barrel of the gun. The Dankath tries to yank it away, but Felzeor hangs on, flapping his wings in the Dankath's face and using his beak to peck away at the shell of her arm. They go stumbling about in wild circles. It's all claws and feathers and shells as they spin around like they're tearing up a dance floor. I can't get off a shot without risking hitting Felzeor.

"Finally, Felzeor's beak breaks through a joint in the Dankath's arm, and she lets out this screeching yell. Felzeor yanks the gun loose from her grip, flies up into the air and announces, 'You can't shoot my friend!'" Eren grinned. "That's when I shot the Dankath."

Everyone stared at him, aghast.

"Well, not *fatally*. Barely enough to get her into restraints followed by a holding cell, in fact."

Caleb chuckled in relief. "Great story. Where is Felzeor tonight?"

"I wanted to bring him along, but would you believe he's on CINT assignment with Drae?"

"I'm glad he's diving back into work."

"Me, too." Eren idly spun his glass in his hand, then held it up. "I wouldn't mind a refill."

Caleb gave Alex a discreet nod of approval, and she rolled her eyes indulgently and stood. "That was the last of the vodka. Why don't you come with me to the kitchen and check out what else we have?"

Eren leapt up to follow her, leaving Caleb and Corradeo alone. After an uncomfortable pause, Caleb offered, "Would you like to see the gardens in the back?"

"I would enjoy seeing this entire planet. For tonight, we can start with the gardens."

"Right out this way."

Caleb opened the door to the rear patio and accompanied Corradeo outside. Akeso's birds chirped a bit louder than normal, their songs verging on discordant. Akeso had been set on edge by Caleb's unease earlier in the evening and was struggling to get a solid bead on his emotions.

Be still. All is well.

"I didn't realize coming here was going to stir up such traumatic memories for Eren. No one told me Cosime died here."

"Cosime died on Savrak. Here is where Eren let her go."

Corradeo frowned. "I'm not certain which is worse."

"Neither am I. But I want to thank you for giving him a purpose. It's making a real difference for him. He's doing infinitely better than the last time I saw him."

"It's not charity on my part. I need him at my side. Our new government needs him protecting it. But I'm glad to do what I can for him." Corradeo set his drink on a table, stuffed his hands in his pockets, and considered the night sky. "Do you ever sense it? The sea of microscopic flecks of crimson dancing among the starlight?"

Caleb sucked in a sharp breath. "Sometimes."

Silence lingered between them until he voiced the question surely on both their minds. "Are you ever tempted to reach out with your mind and call to it?"

"All the time. But I'm not confident the *diati* would respond to my call…and I find I don't want to know the answer. It's for the best. I need to lead on my own authority, for good or ill, and not rely on primordial magic to enforce my pronouncements. My people need to trust me, not fear me. Or most of them do. Most of the time." Corradeo laughed under his breath. "What about you? Are you ever tempted to reach for it?"

"Tempted? Of course. But I never will. Not after what happened. Besides, I have a far better companion now."

"Ah, yes. This living planet. Quite a remarkable creation, even by Kat standards. Have they ever told you how they managed such a feat?"

"We've asked repeatedly, but we've never been able to extract a satisfactory answer."

"Not surprising, I suppose. And do I understand events

correctly? The planet brought you back to life after The Displacement?"

"'Rekindled my life energy' might be a more accurate way to describe it. I already had a healthy dose of Akeso flowing through my body. Though I was clinically dead, thanks to the stasis chamber, those pieces of Akeso lived on inside me. And when Alex brought me here, Akeso was able to infuse those pieces with a surge of its own life force and…wake me back up, so to speak."

"And now it's a permanent part of you?"

"More than simply a part: we are one. When we're not, we both suffer for it. But when we are…." He reached up to run his fingertips along a low-hanging branch above them. As he did, vines of ivy sprouted from the nubs of bark and wound down to create a leafy curtain. Tiny fireflies emerged out of nothingness to light the air around the ivy.

"Incredible. If I had known what was going to transpire, I wouldn't have left—or at a minimum I wouldn't have left without speaking to you first."

"Don't worry about it. It took weeks for the Kats to find where the *diati* had tossed Akeso. Alex never gave up hope, but I'm pretty sure everyone else did."

"I'm glad for you. That you live, obviously, and also that you've formed such a bond with this singular life form." Corradeo's gaze returned to the starlit sky. "The *diati* gave us much—it enabled us to protect our people—but it took much from you and me as well."

Caleb sighed, and the fireflies dimmed in response. "It killed a lot of your people. I still bear the guilt of what happened at Solum."

"You weren't responsible for those deaths."

"A court of law may not have held me responsible, but the blood stains my hands all the same."

Corradeo faced him, clasping him on the shoulder in the same manner his father had done when he was a boy. "*I* don't hold you responsible. We were naïve to believe we ever truly controlled the *diati*. If there is a single person in this universe who understands this completely, it is me."

Caleb swallowed hard. "And The Displacement? With it, I did what even your son could not accomplish. I took your *diati* from you."

"And saved the entirety of your species as a result. I would have given it willingly, had it asked my permission. So, please, rid yourself of this guilt."

The enormity of the weight lifting off his soul in that moment was apt to require a lot of contemplation later. For now, he beamed without guile. "Thank you, sir. It means a great deal to me for you to say so."

All around them, the fireflies renewed their joyful dance of light.

RW

"You guys are just…you're just…the *best*. The *best* mates…." Eren's head lolled onto Caleb's shoulder.

"You're the best, too." He and Corradeo shared an amused glance as they held Eren up between them and guided him carefully up the ship's ramp. Once inside, they eased him into one of the passenger seats and strapped him in. Eren protested briefly, slurring out, "but I'm not ready to go…," before slumping in the restraints and beginning to snore.

Caleb covered his mouth with his hands and chuckled into them. "Do you want us to come to Ares with you and take care of him?"

Corradeo waved him off. "No, no. I've commed ahead to Nyx. She'll meet us at the landing pad, and we'll get him to his room and tucked in. Not to worry."

He arched an eyebrow at the mention of the former Inquisitor, but didn't comment. They'd dredged up enough old memories for one night. He shook the man's hand. "It was a pleasure, sir."

"And for me. Don't be a stranger."

Caleb headed down the ramp and joined Alex on the stone path by the landing complex. As they watched the ship depart, he wrapped his arms around her from behind and rested his chin on her shoulder.

She hugged his arms tighter against her. "You're smiling, right? It feels as if you're smiling."

"I am. It's, um…it's funny."

When he didn't elaborate, she tilted her face back toward him. "What's funny?"

"I am indescribably grateful to discover he doesn't hate me. Doesn't even blame me, or at least has forgiven me. It's like a vise grip has been squeezing my chest for fourteen years, and I didn't realize it was there until tonight, when suddenly it's gone. I feel…free."

"This is beyond wonderful, but I think I'm missing the funny."

"Well, I find myself wondering why I ever felt I needed his forgiveness so desperately. He only affirmed what I already knew to be true, after all. In the end, I merely had to forgive myself. Of course, I recognize the mental gymnastics involved in how I'm saying this now, on the flip side of *having* his forgiveness."

She twisted around in his arms until she faced him, then touched her nose to his. "Still not funny, exactly, but I don't care. I only care that you've finally—did I mention *finally*?—made peace with it. Welcome back from purgatory, *priyazn*."

PART II

COUNTER COUNTER STRATEGEMS

18

MIRAI

Conceptual Research Lab
Asterion Dominion

Dashiel Ridani steepled his hands at his chin and leaned forward intently. Beyond the shielded glass-composite wall in front of him stood a similarly shielded transparent enclosure. Inside it radiated a protective force field.

Inside the force field sat an egg-shaped, adiamene-coated module stretching six meters long by two-and-a-half wide. A nozzle opening punctuated one end of the shell, and half a meter beyond it, still safely within the force field, hung a small sheet of adiamene.

A faint *whirring* sound revved up through the multiple enclosures to ring in Dashiel's ears. Next, a murky, stygian beam, visible only against the bright backdrop of the lab's walls, shot out of the nozzle. A hole burned clear through the center of the adiamene sheet, causing the force field behind it to sizzle in warning, and the beam shut off.

After an eternity that lasted maybe five seconds, the force field deactivated as well; a robotic arm swung in from the ceiling to lift the ruined adiamene sheet up and away, then replace it with a fresh one. The force field turned back on, and the process repeated itself.

He watched the cycle run to completion another four times before pivoting to the lab director standing beside him. "Show me the safety readings."

"Yes, sir." A virtual pane materialized to display the output measurements from the sensors embedded in the module, the force field and the enclosure. They showed a pervasive but minimal leakage from the shell while the beam was active, and he hurriedly triple-checked the reference numbers. Within safety parameters for use in space. *Whew.* When the device was shut down, no measurable leakage registered. The force field struggled to contain the force of the beam—it would have failed after another 1.4 seconds—but this was to be expected. In space, it wasn't going to matter.

A negative energy blast was one of only two known types of strikes capable of destroying adiamene, the other being the far messier antimatter. And if this beam sliced cleanly through adiamene on impact, it would cut through anything.

He turned back to the lab director. "What about degradation of the weapon components?"

"Manageable. Testing so far shows a steady 0.018-0.021% degradation per use. We should be able to get around a thousand firings out of one before it'll need to be refurbished."

"A thousand? That's good."

"It's the adiamene we used to construct the device. It heals the components on its own initiative."

"We knew adiamene had adaptive properties. It makes sense." Dashiel nodded sharply, finally allowing himself to be convinced. Negative energy weapons had proved their effectiveness against Rasu in every battle, but until now they had been in severely limited, precious supply. It was possible he had just changed the equation in a big way.

"Package the prototype up and prepare it for transport. We'll pull a frigate off the assembly line, wire it in, and give it a real test. While you get the prototype set, I think it's time I gave Commander Palmer the good news."

RW

DAF ORBITAL DRY DOCK #1
MIRAI ORBIT

"Well, is the weapon ready to deploy yet?"

Dashiel took a deep breath, working not to let Palmer's impatience dampen his enthusiasm. After all, he'd expected no less from the man. "Almost. We need to test it in a real-world scenario and confirm its effectiveness, resiliency and safety parameters, which we will be doing tomorrow. If everything checks out, then I'll authorize it for fleet installation. Frigates first, as cruisers can carry a substantial load of negative energy missiles already."

"What about fighters?"

"It's a hefty device, and there are design considerations as well. I'd prefer to wait until we can produce a smaller, more lightweight version before we begin installing it on fighters."

"And how long will that take?"

Dashiel grimaced. It had required a herculean level of effort and brainpower to crack this puzzle in the first place. Everyone, including him, needed a break and perhaps a pat on the back. But he recognized they couldn't afford too much of one. "A couple of weeks, hopefully. We'll start testing iterative improvements as soon as I authorize production."

Lance considered the armada of Dominion Armed Forces ships berthed at the newly constructed dry dock outside the observation room. "A thousand fires, you say?"

"We won't know for certain until the weapon's used in the field, but that's what the tests show."

"Not too bad."

Not too bad.... Dashiel glared at the heavens above them, but bit his tongue and didn't retort. Personality-driven spats did nothing to help them keep the Rasu at bay, and this was the goal he and Palmer were both fighting to achieve. "I'll let you know once I have the results of the field test. If all goes well, we can start cycling in active frigates for a retrofit. It should only take about 2 hours per ship. We'll also add the weapon to the new construction process."

Dozens of vessels began sliding out of their berths, engaging their engines and accelerating away. Dashiel motioned toward them. "Where are they off to? Concord?"

"Concord has not yet requested our assistance with their battles. Until they do, seeing as we now have a proper fleet that doesn't melt like butter under Rasu fire, we're going to go stir up a few battles of our own."

19

ADJUNCT SAN
ADV #SV86
ASTERION DOMINION

A flock of Rasu—they genuinely did look like birds, if of the ravenous vulture variety—banked across the charred forest dead ahead, provoking Lieutenant Kiernan Phillips to grit his teeth until his jaw ached.

He'd been wondering for a while now when Commander Palmer was going to get around to punishing him properly for getting his ass dragged through the stronghold wormhole, crashing his ship and handing the coordinates to Namino to the Rasu. Clearly, that time was today, and this assignment was it.

The vultures passed by a hundred meters from him without detecting his presence and continued on toward what had once been the primary settlement on Adjunct San. He sucked in fortifying air and followed.

Kiernan was cocooned in a tiny reconnaissance vessel coated in an extra layer of kyoseil to protect it and him from the effects of the quantum block the Rasu had installed on Adjunct San. Even with the protective coating, though, all the quantum-based ship systems were shut off, which meant flying the thing was like trying to drag a dune buggy through meter-deep beach sand. It couldn't turn for shit; if a Rasu did spot him and open fire, he'd never outmaneuver the barrage.

But they weren't going to spot him, because this flying tin can was also enveloped in a new-model, non-quantum Taiyok cloaking shield. So this was all just fine….

The devastated skyline of the settlement grew to overtake the horizon. Kiernan told himself it hadn't been much of a skyline to begin with, since Adjunct settlements tended to be more 'frontier towns' than proper cities. Regardless, what it was now was a wholly-owned and operated Rasu encampment. The few buildings that remained standing appeared to be *encased* in Rasu. Floating haulers moved scrap metal and timber around while bands of mechs patrolled the streets, though they were empty. Truly empty—in a mercy, he didn't see a single Asterion body.

Yes, yes, he realized this wasn't actually a good sign, for it meant every inhabitant had been carted off for torture and experimentation. But he wasn't in a mood to see corpses.

Focus, Kiernan. The faster you complete your mission, the faster you can get out of this forsaken hellscape.

He tracked one of the haulers as it proceeded northeast toward the outskirts of the encampment, where a yet more foreboding garrison spread out across the land. The reports from Namino had described a Rasu site almost identical to this one, with concentric rings for storage and processing of raw materials and, at its center, a tower. His target.

The nature of the quantum block rendered its generator undetectable from farther than a few hundred meters away. The power source now burned brightly on his thermal scan, but it, too, faded away after a kilometer or so, which meant they could not determine the location of the quantum block from space. Hence why he and his tin can ship were here.

He held his breath as he stuttered between two cargo Rasu headed in opposite directions. Gods bless the Taiyoks and their clever stealth trickery. He made a note to comm Toshke'phein the instant he got back to Mirai and make that lunch date he'd been meaning to arrange for weeks.

When the shadows of the passing Rasu had moved on, he concentrated on his sensor readings. If the coordinates were off by more than a few meters, the mission would be a failure. So he had to get closer. A little closer….

The ghetto, non-quantum radar locked on to the tower and spit out a set of coordinates running out to four decimal places.

He halted his burgeoning sigh of relief in his throat, though, because the mission was only half over. Since comms were also a bust inside the quantum block, he still had to escape the planet and relay the coordinates to the *Dauntless*.

He put some muscle into the flight controls and eked the ship into a hard turn to port, then zig-zagged his way up through the patrolling Rasu.

He'd reached nine kilometers altitude when a particularly sinister-looking Rasu seemed to veer toward him. His heart pounded away in his chest as he became certain it had both spotted him and was readying to swallow him whole. This little ship didn't have enough firepower to shoot its way through a Rasu cocoon, and he couldn't comm for help. The Rasu wouldn't be able to penetrate his hull, but neither would he be able to penetrate theirs, and that was not a stalemate he wanted to suffer through for hours before suffocating.

He aimed his ship straight up, toward the stars and freedom, and accelerated away from the enemy vessel until engine alarms began ringing in the cockpit...the Rasu did not follow.

A couple of deep inhales later, while the ship vibrated its way through the atmospheric traversal, he conceded to himself that he might have imagined the entire encounter. But if so, it was between him and himself.

Abruptly the sweet, sweet sight of comm chatter erupted on his right-side pane. He'd made it!

Lieutenant Phillips (ADV #SV86): "Recon run was successful. Transmitting target data now."

Commander Palmer (ADV Dauntless): "Roger that, Lieutenant. Good work."

RW

ADV DAUNTLESS

Thanks to the information Lieutenant Phillips had relayed, the location of the quantum block now glowed in blazing crimson on the tactical map displayed in front of Lance Palmer. The Rasu weren't even trying to hide its existence here. They probably assumed the Asterions had given up and ceded the sparsely inhabited planet to them. In light of events up until now, it was a reasonable assumption for their enemy to make.

But they were wrong.

The *Dauntless* drifted in geosynchronous orbit, cloaked, three megameters above Adjunct San. On the bridge, Lance checked the coordinates from Phillips a final time and input them in the targeting system, then adjusted the parameters slightly to ensure the trajectory was correct. Didn't want the delivery system to get waylaid by the nearby forest.

Satisfied everything was in order, he turned to the *Dauntless'* Weapons Officer. "Is the payload ready to deploy?"

"It's ready, sir."

"Then let's not waste any more time. Fire."

The custom-designed bomb dropped out of the *Dauntless'* cargo bay, engaged its small engine, and dove for the surface. Much like the unique ship that Phillips flew, the bomb was hidden by a Taiyok-derived cloaking field and wrapped in a solid envelope of kyoseil to allow it to penetrate the quantum block surrounding the planet. Inside its casing, the bomb held a dense cluster of Rima Grenades modified to detonate on impact.

A minimal guidance system locked on to the coordinates and made a beeline for the stronghold the Rasu had constructed on the outskirts of Adjunct San's single city. The stronghold's defenses didn't detect its approach, and one hundred eighty seconds after departing the *Dauntless*, the bomb crashed into the tower supporting the quantum block.

The long-range sensors showed only an enormous plume of smoke and metal and darkness. Oh, how Lance wished he had eyes on the destruction that resulted. But he would soon enough.

"Quantum block is down, sir."

Commander Palmer (ADV Dauntless)(San Mission Channel): "All ships, Operation Kyushu is a go."

The largest fleet of Asterion ships ever assembled exited superluminal above Adjunct San. Twenty percent of them took up orbital defensive positions, and the rest entered the atmosphere en masse.

Commander Palmer (ADV Dauntless)(San Mission Channel): "Reconnaissance Squadron Kyr, I want eyes on the Rasu stronghold ASAP."

Scant seconds later, the first visuals came in. What had formerly been the Rasu's base of operations here was now an empty crater spanning almost a kilometer in width. The Rima Grenades might have taken out a few nearby city buildings as well. Perhaps the bomb's payload had represented a bit of overkill on his part, but only in hindsight. He'd needed to guarantee it got the job done. And it most certainly had.

Commander Palmer (ADV Dauntless)(San Mission Channel): "Confirmed we are clear for all combat operations. If you see a Rasu, shoot it. If you don't see one, find one, then shoot it." He smiled to himself. *"May the gods favor the bold and the free."*

Blood rushed through his veins with anticipation of the battle to come. The *Dauntless* was the flagship of the Dominion fleet, but it wasn't a bulky, oversized dreadnought like the ones Concord fielded. Asterions had no need for massive, unwieldy, overstaffed ships.

"Helmsman, take us in."

20

ADJUNCT SAN

Nika Kirumase stepped through the Sukasu Gate wormhole at the DAF Military Services Center and straight into the warzone. She'd come prepared, though; she wore a full set of protective tactical gear and defensive shielding, a Rima Grenade launcher strapped to her back and two archine blades sheathed at her hips.

Dust rained down from the sky as concussive explosions screamed against her eardrums. A brief scan of the tactical feed and a glance with her own two eyes told her the fighters in the air and troops on the ground were already tearing into the Rasu with overwhelming force and speed. There might not be many Rasu left for her to kill.

Which was…fine. Trained military troops could do a better, more efficient job of it than she'd manage, anyway, and she only intended to call upon the weapons she'd brought with her as a last resort if she found herself under direct attack.

So, technically, she wasn't here to kill Rasu, as such. But she was definitely here to watch them die.

She stepped to the side to allow a new squad of ground forces to arrive through the wormhole, fan out and move into the city. To the extent any of them noticed her, she imagined they shook their heads and thought something to the effect of, *whacked Advisors.*

Oh, this reminded her. She sent Joaquim a quick ping.

Adjunct San is now open for Rasu cleansing, if you can get to the DAF Military Services Center soon.

Are you kidding? On my way.

The small but once vibrant city had been thoroughly gutted by the Rasu in the weeks they'd been left alone to have their way. In truth, nothing remained here worth saving—nothing but pride. Today, they were salvaging the indomitable Asterion spirit. Picking it up from off the ground, dusting it off and giving it a reassuring pat on the back plus a fresh coat of paint. Metaphorically.

She strode forward and into the fray.

Today was only made possible due to the tireless, damn-near herculean efforts of broad segments of Asterion society. The Industry Division, from Conceptual Research to Manufacturing. DAF recruitment and training. Enthusiastic diversification on the part of their soldiers. Dedicated ceraffin pushing past the limits of technology, physics and engineering.

The result of all those efforts was a fleet that no longer needed to hide in fear—one wielding new, more powerful and precise weapons designed specifically to destroy this enemy. It meant they fielded a fighting force of ground troops that was well-protected with cutting-edge gear and even more well-armed. It meant the fleet and troops were directed and supported by an Advisor Council that refused to cower as the Guides before them had. They had a plan to retake their worlds and not let them slip away again, and they now wielded the firepower to make it happen.

She'd collected a lot of reasons to be proud of her people in the last year. NOIR stopping the virutox and helping to bring down the Guides was near the top of the list, along with the destruction of the Rasu stellar fortress in the Gennisi galaxy. Their putting aside of ancient animosities to ally with Concord, including the Anadens among the coalition, was another, plus their application of prodigious Asterion ingenuity to retake Namino and help protect their Taiyok allies' homeworld. Today, Toki'taku was free of the Rasu scourge and guarded zealously from further incursions by a joint Taiyok/Asterion fleet, with a warehouse full of Rima Grenades at the ready.

But today might well be her proudest moment yet. When the Rasu had attacked, the Advisors had sacrificed this world because they'd had no choice, but they refused to let it stay sacrificed—

An explosion rocked a Rasu-encased building less than a

hundred meters ahead of her, and she leapt back to avoid molten Rasu raining down upon the street.

Okay, enough with the waxing philosophical while standing exposed in the middle of an active combat operation. She checked her tactical pane again to see where the fighting was concentrated, then struck out to the southeast.

A shadow encroached above her as she reached the next intersection, and she peered up to see a frigate-sized Rasu vessel fleeing the attacks consuming the city center. Hmm.

She slung the launcher off her back, loaded a Rima Grenade, hefted the weapon onto her shoulder, sighted in on the ship and pressed the trigger.

The Rasu blinked out of existence.

She smiled.

MIRAI

DAF MILITARY SERVICES CENTER

Nika stumbled back through the Sukasu Gate and into the bustling warmth of the troop staging room.

"There you are!" Dashiel's voice broke above the noisy din of the large room, and she spun to see him motioning away an officer and jogging over to her. "What were you...you're covered in soot and dirt. I think I see some blood, too."

"Yep." A supply sergeant came up to them and stared at her expectantly until she lifted the launcher up over her head and handed it to him. Then she glanced at the Sukasu Gate, but no one else came through. Joaquim had insisted on staying for 'five more minutes,' which likely meant until the fighting was done. "I was just doing my little part to help rid Adjunct San of its Rasu infestation."

Dashiel shook his head wryly. "Did you have fun?"

"Oh, yes." She breathed in deeply; she was winded and shaky and most of her muscles ached, but she was also pumped full of adrenaline and righteous satisfaction. Despite her initial intention to leave the fighting to the trained military troops, she'd accidentally-on-purpose managed to take out half a dozen ships and almost forty bipedals over the course of…she checked the time. *Four hours?* "You were looking for me?"

"I'm always looking for you, aren't I?"

The unexpectedly sentimental statement took her by surprise, and her lips parted. "Dashiel…."

He grasped her hand and guided her out of the main thoroughfare. "Yes, I was looking for you. I wanted to share something with you, and I didn't want to wait until tonight."

He seemed to be brimming with anticipation, bordering on genuine excitement, and the adrenaline still coursing through her pathways fed on his demeanor to recharge. She did, however, nudge them into a minor detour to grab a cup of water from the hydration station in the corner. "Ooh, do tell."

"I figured out how to make it work."

Her face screwed up. "There are at least two dozen things to which you can be referring. Care to be more specific?"

"Right. Of course. A renewable negative energy weapon, suitable for rigging onto our warships. It should deliver close to a thousand fires at a go."

She embraced him as forcefully as she was able to with her utterly exhausted muscles. "Dashiel, that's amazing!"

"Well, when I say 'I,' I mean 'I and a minimum of two hundred other people.'"

"You're too modest. Those other people may have helped work out the details, but not one of them could do what you do." She kissed him full on the mouth, and he returned the kiss with a fervor powerful enough to send a shiver down her spine. The adrenaline, the rush of battle and his own energy all amplified one another in a positive feedback loop.

As his hands tightened around her waist with renewed urgency, she grinned against his lips. "You know this compound better than I do. Is there somewhere private we can go?"

21

MIRAI
MIRAI ONE

Joaquim Lacese rolled over to see stratus clouds drifting past the crescent moon hanging high outside his window. It had been raining when he'd returned from Adjunct San earlier this evening. He'd let the rain wash most of the grime, blood and debris off of him as he'd made a beeline for the nearest burger joint. Then a beer, then home for a shower. He smiled wickedly…then Selene.

[HERE]She lay naked across his chest, and the dance of the moon and clouds cast an intricate pattern of shadows and light across her bare skin. He was already getting devious ideas when she abruptly grabbed his right arm, flipped it over and scowled at the long, red welt running up his forearm. "What did you get into this time?"

His lips curled into a self-satisfied grin. "Rasu on Adjunct San. I had to do my part to help kick them out."

"You mean you couldn't resist the adrenaline rush of fighting another army of Rasu. I thought you were more enthusiastic than usual tonight."

"Was I?" He'd prefer to believe he was never lethargic in bed, much like in combat. But perhaps a bit *more* enthusiastic this time, sure.

Her lips brushed across the welt; both were moist and swollen. "Yes, in fact. I may need to send you into a few more war zones."

"Oh, is that so?" He hauled her the rest of the way on top of him. One thing about a woman like Selene Panetier—tough, brave, confident, no-nonsense? She was not a wallflower between the sheets. They were undoubtedly a terrible, destructive match in every other sense, but when it came to sex, they were perfect for one another.

"Yeah, that's so." She leaned down, sending her damp hair to tickle his chest. "But didn't Lance's soldiers have it covered? I heard we wiped the place clean in a couple of hours."

"They seemed to, yes. But I was itching to blow off some steam, and the Rasu are the enemy, deserving of everything I can hurl at them."

"They are. But I would have…" she stopped herself "…I was going to say I would have thought after our weeks on Namino, you should've gotten your fill and then some of fighting Rasu. But you don't remember any of those battles, of course."

"Don't need to. I'm certain I would *not* have gotten my fill. And I won't—not until every last Rasu is atomized."

She planted a quick kiss on his mouth before rolling onto her back and stretching out from her fingers to her toes. "Well, I'll be happy if I never see another Rasu after Namino."

"But you'll fight them if you need to, won't you?"

"Always. I'll do whatever is required to safeguard the people I'm sworn to protect. It's just not my preference."

"I see."

She propped up on one elbow to stare at him. "You don't believe me?"

"No, actually, I do. You're a woman of action but, unlike me, you tend to let your brain drive your action." He cocked a little smile. "I'm starting to suspect that for a Justice officer, you're all right."

"Only all right, huh?" She snaked a hand down under the covers and squeezed. "I think I deserve a more fervent endorsement."

"Ah…" his jaw clenched "…then allow me to provide whatever you need."

She laughed and released her hold on him. "So maybe Justice officers aren't all so terrible?"

He blinked a few times, his stomach instinctively turning at the touchy turn the conversation was taking, even if he'd started it. Still, he swallowed back the defensive retort that almost made it to his tongue in favor of equivocation. "Some definitely have a greater number of positive qualities than others. And I am…trying to recognize those differences. Yes, even outside of the bedroom. It's a work in progress."

"You know, if you told me about what happened to you before NOIR, I might be able to—"

"Doesn't matter. Or I'm working to convince myself that it's in the distant past and *can* no longer matter. This is also a work in progress, but it's not something you need to concern yourself with."

He swung his legs off the bed, stood and grabbed his pants, unwilling to let *those* thoughts ruin the positive vibes from their lovemaking. "I told Parc I'd help him and Ryan transport a bunch of new mech components over to their place tonight. Comm me later?"

"I'm going to be working all night, then trying to get some sleep in the morning. Maybe tomorrow evening."

"Whatever suits you. Can't promise I won't be fighting more Rasu tomorrow evening, though." He shoved his feet into his shoes and headed for the door, as they weren't much for tender goodbyes.

Only once he was halfway to the lift did he realize this was the first time he'd left her alone in his apartment. His steps slowed, and he considered returning to usher her out. But his demons couldn't be uncovered in the few trinkets and gear he had stored in his place. No, they lived only in his head.

RW

When the door closed behind Joaquim, Selene dropped her head back onto the pillow and stared at the ceiling. Her most subtle interrogation techniques continued to slam directly into the brick wall that was Joaquim Lacese's stubbornness.

She ought to let it go, especially if she wanted to continue to enjoy their intimate encounters. One wrong move on her part, and he'd shut her out permanently.

But the truth was that she'd never trust him fully until she knew what had happened in his past to make him despise Justice so. And, strangely, she found she rather desperately wanted to be able to trust him. Didn't know exactly where the desire was coming from.

Also, she didn't care for the possibility of Justice having committed evil misdeeds in the past, regardless of whether it was under her watch. Her highest responsibility as a Justice Advisor was to ensure the Justice Division lived up to its mission of protecting Asterion citizens—not harming them.

Mostly, though, she was a detective, and she simply couldn't abide an unsolved mystery.

22

MIRAI

MIRAI ONE REFUGEE CENTER

"Excuse me. Do you know when I'll get to go home?"

Perrin Benvenit turned toward the voice. It came from a man pacing in front of a pile of suitcases stacked up against the wall. His belongings? "I'm sorry, Mr. ....?"

"Sullivan."

"Hi, Mr. Sullivan. I'm Perrin. It's a pleasure to meet you. Where is home for you?"

"Namino Two."

"Oh." She ran a hand through her hair, which felt greasy and unkempt. Definitely uncombed. How many hours had it been since she'd taken a break to so much as run to the lavatory? "Not for a while, I'm afraid. Do you need me to help you find some more permanent lodging on an Axis World? I've got a list of options and—"

"I don't *want* to be stashed in a building and told to wait. I want to go home." The man's frustration bled out of his voice and sent his hands twitching.

"I understand, Mr. Sullivan. I truly do. But Namino doesn't have any essential services up and running. There's no food, no electricity and only minimal security. Even assuming your—" *home isn't a pile of rubble* "—neighborhood has been confirmed clear of Rasu, it's not safe to return to Namino. We just need a little more time to effect repairs and get everything functioning again."

The man sank onto one of his suitcases. "How much time?"

"I'm sorry. I don't know. Please, let me give you a list of lodgings that are offering discounts and short-term rentals to people who have been displaced. I'll bet some private space and a real bed will go a long way toward making the wait easier for you."

He groaned into his hands. "Fine."

RW

Perrin tried to make herself as unnoticeable as possible as she slipped through the refugees milling listlessly about in the common room. She reached the door unaccosted and made a beeline down the hall for the temporary sanctum of the lavatory. If she splashed water on her face and ran a comb through her hair, it might rejuvenate her enough to dive back into her work—

A hand landed on her shoulder. "Excuse me. Ms. Benvenit, isn't it? You're in charge here?"

She sucked up her dwindling energy and tried to plaster on a comforting mien as she turned around. "I wouldn't say I'm 'in charge,' but I am helping out here. What can I do for you, Ms. ...?"

"Marcella Svigani. I, um...." The woman stared at the floor; her clothes were wrinkled and coffee-stained. "I heard the military was trying to liberate Adjunct San and...see, I evacuated from our home there right before the Rasu arrived. But my partner insisted on running back to the house to grab one more bag of belongings, and then the d-gates shut down before he made it through. So I was wondering when the military will be locating survivors and bringing them to safety?"

Perrin tried to keep the flood of sorrow off her expression, but she didn't think she succeeded. She remembered this woman now. Ms. Svigani was one of the last people she'd helped to reach the d-gates during the evacuation.

She swayed unevenly, growing dizzy as the memory of those harrowing final minutes washed over her. The awful, ear-splitting screeches, the smoke, the crashing buildings....

"Ms. Benvenit? Are you all right?"

"What? Yes, of course. I'm sorry. I haven't eaten today is all." Was that true? It felt true. "Um, I received word not long ago that the military succeeded in destroying the quantum block cutting off

Adjunct San earlier today. Have you tried messaging your partner?"

The woman nodded hurriedly. "I did. I've never stopped messaging him since I arrived here, though I knew the messages wouldn't get through."

"And now?"

"No response. I'm not naïve. I realize he might be injured, which is why I was wondering about the military's plans for rescuing people who were left behind."

Your partner is dead, ma'am. Roasted by the flames until nothing remained but biosynth bones and abandoned strands of kyoseil, or flayed open and experimented on by the Rasu until the agony from being alive killed him.

Perrin breathed in through her nose. "I don't know. I'm sorry." How many times had she said that today alone?

"Can you find out? I mean, you know people, don't you? People in power? People who can do things?"

People who could 'do things.' People who weren't her. "I can try to find something out. You can also check at the Hataori Pavilion—that's where the medical triage center is located. Anyone they find on Adjunct San who's injured will be taken there. But just in case the worst…where did he keep his psyche backup?"

"San Bonded Storage on Adjunct San. We didn't have time to stop by there and withdraw our storage before the evacuation. We thought we'd have new ones recorded when we got here."

"I see." She patted the woman's shoulder. "I'm sure it'll work out. As I said, you should check at Hataori Pavilion. Now, if you'll excuse me, I have to go—" She spun away and tried to keep her shoulders high as she rushed down the hall and around the corner.

RW

Perrin, where the hells are you? We need to get all the people camped out on the fourth floor moved to the new space at the Greenwild Center before Maintenance shows up and declares the fourth floor a biological hazard.

Renewed sobs choked off the air in her lungs, and tears flowed down already soaked cheeks. All she saw in her waking vision was smoke and flames. Giant Rasu mechs rampaging toward her. Bodies in the street.

Outside the stall, the door to the lavatory opened, and she put a hand over her mouth to stifle the sound of her sobs. She couldn't talk to another person right now. Another person who'd lost everything and wanted only to be given the slightest bit of hope for a brighter tomorrow.

Perrin, hello? The logs say you checked into the building this morning and haven't checked out. Oh, fuck it. I'll handle it myself.

And she certainly couldn't talk to Katherine Colson right now. The woman was brutally efficient at organizing and managing a litany of tasks and thorny situations, and she somehow never let all this darkness get to her. Never displayed an iota of emotion—well, other than annoyance. At this moment, Perrin would give anything to be more like Katherine, which told her everything she needed to know about her current mental state.

The sound of the door opening and closing again suggested the interloper had departed, and she dropped her head against the wall wearily. With each sniffle, her thoughts went to those refugees now being shepherded off the fourth floor and onward to yet another 'temporary' location, many for the third time. They continued to live in a state of uncertainty, with no homes and few belongings. For some of them, like Ms. Svigani, they were now alone and heartbroken.

She should be upstairs helping them. Providing a gentler, kinder hand than Katherine wielded as she guided them to what would genuinely be a better environment. Not home, but one offering greater space and comforts. But every time she contemplated standing up and plunging back into the madness, her shoulders sagged and her chin fell to her chest. She couldn't do it any longer.

Gods, Adlai would be so disappointed in her. He'd never say it to her face, but he wouldn't have to. He went out there into the world every damn day and gave it his all, no matter what. He'd limped out of a tank at the regen clinic hours after flirting with death, barely able to walk, and had gone to work because he couldn't *not*. Nika willingly put herself through the torture of Tartarus, fighting and dying in myriad ways to stop the Rasu in every manner she found. Joaquim fought the Rasu from beneath an overrun city for weeks, only to die a bloody death at the hands of the enemy so that others would be saved.

And here Perrin was, shirking her responsibilities to hide in a lavatory and cry because a stranger had lost someone to the Rasu.

Dammit, the only thing she'd ever wanted to do was help people. Help them find safety, security and a better life for themselves. But now, her own weaknesses were preventing her from doing this one tiny act.

The temptation to simply *stop*, to give up on this life, R&R herself and start fresh, was so strong. But she refused to hurt Adlai like that, refused to hurt her friends with her cowardice.

Still, something had to change.

She slapped her cheeks and blew her nose. When she was counseling refugees, she often told them to not worry about the big picture right now, and instead focus on the small steps they could take toward getting back to normal. So, perhaps she should take her own advice. Perhaps a small step was all she needed to take. To do her job, to help these poor people, to make Adlai and her friends proud.

It was time.

23

MIRAI

HATAORI RENEWAL CLINIC

Adlai Weiss paced frenetically across the clinic lobby. Perrin had sent him a message asking him to meet her here, without explanation. When he'd arrived, the receptionist told him Perrin was undergoing a procedure and should be finished in around half an hour.

Had something happened to her? Had she gotten injured in a melee at one of the refugee centers? Dammit, he was increasing security at the centers as fast as possible, but there were far more refugees than available Justice officers. If one of the people she'd tried to help had hurt her—

The doors opened and Perrin came striding out. As soon as she saw him, a smile broke across her lovely features, and she hurried over to embrace him. "I'm sorry you had to wait. It took a little longer than I expected. They're backed up due to the high regen demand from Namino and Adjunct San. I felt bad for cutting in line, but at least I was in and out in a few hours."

He drew back enough to study her features, searching for wounds that, by definition, would have been erased. "Are you okay? Did one of the refugees attack you?"

"Goodness, no! I just decided it was time for a minor up-gen."

His hands fell off her shoulders and down to his sides. "You...you got an up-gen? What for?"

Her expression flickered. "I needed to tweak my emotional programming. Install a few moderators and overflow regulators to keep the negative emotions from getting away from me."

"But Perrin—"

Now her gaze snapped up to him, carrying in it a startling fierceness. "You know how I've been lately. A weeping, blubbering mess, more often than not. And it started interfering with my work. I can't help these poor, displaced refugees if I'm spending all my time crying in a lavatory."

"You…" he shook his head, unable to believe what he was hearing "…maybe you simply had a bit of degradation in your programming. Something easily fixed without anything so dramatic as an up-gen."

"I'm not an idiot, Adlai. I asked them to check for degradation first. There was nothing wrong with the technicals of the programming—only with the results." She touched his cheek and softened her tone. "I needed to do this."

"Why didn't you talk to me about it first?"

"Because you would have tried to talk me out of it."

"Yes, I would have. I love you the way you are…were." He frowned; the words had emerged sounding direr than he'd intended. But also true. "Your pure, boundless heart is what makes you so wonderful."

"And I still have that, I promise. But now, hopefully when my heart gets too taxed, it won't put me on the floor."

"You were…" the various things she was saying started to penetrate his reflexive mental block "…you broke down at work? I'm so sorry. I bet with the Adjunct San situation heating up, a lot of emotions were flaring. People were too hard on you—"

"No. See, here's the thing. They were only asking of me exactly what I signed up to give. The fact that it was suddenly too much was all on me. If I want to continue to help in the best way I know how, I *had* to make a change. Now, I'll be able to step back, realize I'm doing everything I can, remind myself how even though I can't save the world, this doesn't mean I can't improve some people's lives, and keep going." She gripped his hand. "Adlai, this is a *good* thing."

She sounded so certain. So confident and calm. No quaver in her voice, no glistening in her eyes. Had a different woman walked out of the lab than walked into it?

RW

NIKA'S FLAT

Nika poured scotch into the ice-filled glass, then handed it across the kitchen counter to Adlai. "I realize this isn't what you want to hear, but I think she did the right thing."

He glared at her over the rim of the glass as he took a long sip, then set it a little hard on the counter. "How can you say that? How can you be so blasé about her altering a fundamental aspect of her personality on a whim?"

She took the time to pour her own drink. Adlai had shown up at her door way too early this morning; the only reason she'd been awake and dressed was due to Dashiel gleefully keeping insane work hours this week. Scotch before noon wasn't her usual habit, nor did she imagine it was Adlai's, but her bleary-eyed take was that the situation called for it.

"First, it doesn't sound as if it was 'on a whim' at all. Second, I'm not being blasé about it. I mean this quite sincerely. She's been making herself miserable. She's emotionally spent. She's *unhappy*. And as Asterions, we have the unique ability to do something to fix it when we find ourselves in such a state. We can, in effect, engineer our own happiness. She has as much right to grow and change as you or I do. She has a right to be happy."

"And her unhappiness was tearing me apart. I just wish she'd talked to me about this beforehand."

"And what would you have said to her to try to change her mind?"

He shrugged roughly as he took another long sip of his drink. "I would have told her she's perfect the way she is, with her boundless empathy and tender soul. They're what make her so special."

"I don't disagree, Adlai. And, yes, it kind of sucks for us that she's probably tamped those down a bit with this up-gen. But wearing her heart on her sleeve was making her despondent, and not merely at work. All the time." Nika leaned on the counter for emphasis. "The truth is, since the Rasu showed up at our doorstep, we've increasingly forced her into situations which she simply wasn't equipped to handle."

"I didn't force her into anything! She repeatedly insisted on managing the refugees."

"Of course she did. It's who she is—someone who yearns to help the lost and the hurt. Helping others has always made her stronger…right up until it broke her. She says this was the only way for her to keep following the calling in her heart, and I'm inclined to believe her."

"And if she destroyed that very heart in the process?"

"Now you're just being histrionic. Nothing got destroyed yesterday."

He shook his head and took another sip of the scotch.

Nika sighed. He'd worked himself into a righteous temper, and he didn't appear to want to be talked down. But because she cared far more about Perrin than she did about Adlai, she kept trying. "Let me ask you something. How many up-gens did you choose to undergo while you were a Justice officer climbing the ranks? How many targeted tweaks did you make to your programming to hone your skills and focus your talents until you reached a point where you were finally prepared to be an Advisor?"

"What does it matter? Perrin isn't auditioning to be an Advisor!"

"Actually, she is, though she doesn't know it."

His glass hit the counter again. "What are you talking about?"

"Kiyora needs a real Administration Advisor to replace Gemina Kail, and it needs one badly. The others have been discussing nominating Perrin for the position. Or they were until yesterday, when Katherine tried to nix the idea, saying Perrin was too emotional and unreliable. If I had to guess, I bet whatever caused Katherine to pitch a fit is the same event that caused Perrin to pull the trigger on an up-gen. And I say again, it means she was correct to do so."

Adlai frowned darkly. "Kiyora? But it's…."

"Oh gods, Adlai, are you truly that selfish? You don't want her to move to Kiyora? In practical terms, it's no different from if she moved to the other side of the city."

"But I like her living at my place. I like coming home to her smile."

Nika's annoyance petered out as quickly as it had flared. "I understand. I miss seeing it every day at The Chalet, too. But I'll bet lately, you were more often coming home to her tears than her smiles."

He didn't respond.

"Dashiel and I have made separate homes work. After a few hundred years together, you tend to discover the relationship fares better if you both have space and solitude when you need it. You might even find your bond grows stronger for it."

Despite her efforts, he still looked so miserable. She offered him the bottle of scotch, but he waved her off. "I can't. I'm already late for work."

She returned the bottle to the cabinet, because she certainly wasn't having any more. "Besides, I don't know what's going to happen with the Advisor position. I don't know if the other Administration Advisors will nominate her. If they do, I don't know if the Council will approve her, and if it does, I don't know if she'll accept the offer."

Abruptly she went around and dropped an elbow on the counter beside him. "But, Adlai, listen to me carefully. If they do put her name forward to the Council, don't you *dare* vote against her. Whether out of a desire to protect her from the burdens of being an Advisor or a selfish need to keep her all to yourself, you don't have the right to deny her this opportunity."

"I know I don't. But, Nika…she's not ready."

"No, she wasn't ready yesterday. Maybe today she is. Let's give her a chance to show us."

He dropped his empty glass into the sink with an overdramatic flourish. "Fine, fine. Your insistent logic is making me feel like I'm as emotional as Perrin on a bad day. I realize I can't be selfish, and I can't shield her from the evil vagaries of the world. I only hope this up-gen didn't change the traits that make me love her so damn much. And…I'm terrified it did."

Shit. She couldn't very well be perturbed at him now, could she? "And I'm confident it didn't. I think we both need an abundance of bubbly, happy Perrin in our lives, and I'm excited at the prospect of seeing more of that person again. Believe in her, Adlai."

24

CONCORD HQ

SENATE

Marlee took a deep breath and drew her shoulders up as she rang the door chime, then donned her practiced 'diplomat' countenance when the door opened to grant her entry.

"Excuse me, Senator Corradeo? I'm Marlee Marano from the…." All her earnest preparations promptly evaporated. She'd only ever seen her grandfather in historical family visuals, but the man sitting at the desk inside the office was the *spitting image* of Stefan Marano.

As his gaze rose curiously to meet hers, she forced aside the deeply creepy déjà vu. "…Consulate. I'm here to escort you on your visit to see our Ourankeli guests."

His lips tugged upward as he stood, came around from behind his desk and offered her a gracious hand. "Marano? Are you Caleb's…?"

"Niece, sir. He's spoken fondly of you many times." Or she was certain he *would* have, if not for all the angsty personal complications. "It's a pleasure to meet you."

"And you, Ms. Marano. My escort, you say? I should mention that I have previously visited the Ourankeli all on my own."

As if I didn't do the homework! "Yes, sir—at Haelwyeur, back before the Rasu attacked them. Please don't misunderstand. We don't believe you're any threat to them, or they to you. It's merely that the Consulate has detailed protocols in place when it comes to new refugee populations. And I'm a big believer in protocol."

His lips curled up yet more. "Are you?"

Her composure broke a little, and she chuckled lightly. "No, sir, not actually. But I have a new boss, and I'm trying to make a good impression, so might you fancy humoring me?"

"I understand. Besides, none of the Ourankeli who survived will know me, nor I them, so perhaps an intermediary is a good idea. Let's venture onward, shall we?"

"Yes, sir. We've placed them on several floors of the Hotel Cassiopeia. Among other benefits, it features a large gathering area on every other floor, where they can spend most of their time together rather than isolated in disparate rooms. They've lived in close confines for a while now, so they seem to prefer it."

"I'm afraid I don't know where the hotel is located—or much of anything else. Concord HQ is a big place, and I'm new here."

"Not to worry. Just come with me. I can point out some of the more notable attractions along the way."

RW

HOTEL CASSIOPEIA

When they reached the door to the common area most of the Ourankeli were occupying, Marlee held up a hand to halt the Senator's progress. "If you'll excuse me for a second, sir, I should confirm they're prepared for guests."

Corradeo Praesidis took a step back and motioned to the door. He was almost Novoloume-like in his graciousness and polite manner, which she wasn't expecting. Hadn't he once wrestled the *diati* into submission, then waged interstellar war against the Dzhvar? Then later against the Asterions? He'd had a change of heart, obviously, but…. On the other hand, she'd belatedly begun to pick up on how Caleb could call upon similar chameleon tendencies when the situation called for it.

She announced her impending presence through the door chime, then stepped into the gathering room. Three dozen Ourankeli milled about, talking in small groups or…she kept any confusion off her expression like a good diplomat, but were several of them taking apart the furniture and using the pieces to build new items? Their reputation as the industrious sort was well-earned, but the hotel management wasn't going to be amused.

She scanned the group but came up empty in her search for their unofficial leader, Cyfeill. "Excuse me, everyone? Do you know where Cyfeill is? We had a scheduled appointment this morning."

All the Ourankeli understood Communis, though many of them disdained speaking it, but only a single Ourankeli glided in her direction. "Wyddoniiet called them away. To a...Special Project?"

"The Special Projects division? Thank you. Before I go, does anyone need anything?"

They all ignored her question, which she was getting used to, so she backed out, closed the door and plastered on a conciliatory demeanor as she turned to her companion. "I'm afraid our primary contact, Cyfeill, had to see to a matter at Special Projects."

"The weapon development, I imagine."

He did not miss a detail. "Very possibly, yes."

By all rights, she should return the Senator to his office and reschedule the meeting for a later date. But since Morgan had gotten Devon Reynolds to increase her clearance level for Special Projects, she should be able to gain access to wherever they were all gathered. And maybe she'd bump into Morgan while she was there.

"Tell me, have you received the official senatorial tour of Special Projects?"

"I have not."

"Then if you're interested, we can see to the tour now, and hopefully be able to spend a few minutes with Cyfeill as well."

His smile seemed to hold a hint of amusement, in a way that reminded her a touch of Caleb when he was in a good mood. She was picking up on a theme here. "I am at your mercy, Ms. Marano."

She almost giggled, but managed to restrain herself. He was being indulgent, but she shouldn't push it. "Follow me. This one is a bit more of a trek."

RW

SPECIAL PROJECTS

"I know how subatomic particles work! If you'll listen to my entire question without assuming I'm a barbarian and tuning the details out, I think you'll find that I am trying to make a salient point."

Cyfeill floated—or at least *appeared* to float—beside the conference table. "Are all Concordians as arrogant and petulant as you?"

"No, only the ones who've earned the right to be. And there's no such thing as a 'Concordian.' I'm a 'human.' Others are different species."

"I've yet to see a meaningful distinction. You are all—"

Marlee rushed forward, trying not to act panicked, and insinuated herself between Devon and Cyfeill. "So grateful that you're here with us and safe from the Rasu. We're sorry if any cultural miscues have led you to feel unwelcome or unappreciated." She shot Devon a pointed glare. "*Aren't we,* Director Reynolds?"

Devon made a face. "I was simply trying to ask a specific and relevant question."

"And there are bound to be communications issues as we all get to know one another better. Might a brief break be in order?"

No one volunteered assent, and she searched for another way to break the tension. Behind Devon, Kennedy Rossi sat at a worktable, her hands clasped in her lap and a breezy, cocktail-party expression adorning her features. "Kennedy, hi! Why don't you and Devon take a few minutes to review what you've learned so far, and Cyfeill and I will go speak to Senator Corradeo?"

Kennedy's gaze went to the door, and an eyebrow arched. "Oh. We can absolutely do so. Devon?" Kennedy motioned to the opposite side of the worktable.

"Fine." Devon stalked over to the worktable and yanked out a chair.

Marlee reached out, stopping just short of touching one of the Ourankeli's arms. She was desperate to learn if their skin felt like jelly, but she also wanted to keep her job. "I apologize. Scientists can be a little intense when focused on their work, can't they?"

She finally took in the rest of the occupants of the room. No Morgan, unfortunately, but Wyddoniiet and two additional Ourankeli conferred in the far corner. "Wyddoniiet, why don't you join us? There's someone here I think you'd like to meet."

The Ourankeli whom Caleb and Alex had encountered at the halo ring glided over to them. "A break is indeed in order. What is underway?"

She metaphorically dragged the two of them toward the door, where Corradeo stood, his hands clasped behind his back, wearing a neutral countenance. It brightened noticeably, however, as they approached. "Senator, allow me to introduce Wyddoniiet and Cyfeill of the Ourankeli. This is Senator Corradeo Praesidis, who once—"

Wyddoniiet's eyes shifted left, then right. "Spent a span of time amongst our people. We…recall."

Neither of them had been alive when he'd visited Haelwyeur, but the Ourankeli possessed a form of historical memory or data sharing capability. Of some sort. Like much else, they hadn't been inclined to share the details of how it worked.

"It is my greatest honor to meet you both." Corradeo made an intricate sweeping motion with both hands; she'd seen Cyfeill perform a similar motion once or twice, so it must be an Ourankeli greeting. And he remembered it after all this time. "Please allow me to express my tremendous sadness at the destruction of your home and loss of so many of your people. I have only fond memories of my time spent at Haelwyeur."

Cyfeill looked to still be fretting, if their vibrating limbs were any indication, but Wyddoniiet's demeanor calmed. "We owe you for our discovery by Alex, Caleb and the synthetic Valkyrie. Thus, we owe our lives to you. You have our gratitude."

"I'm simply glad they were able to reach you in time and help you escape the Rasu. As an official representative of Concord, let me say that I hope we can assist you in building a new and fruitful life here among us."

"I hope such will be our future. But now the Rasu threaten Concordians the same as they did us. Forgive us if we cannot settle into complacency and dreams of the future."

"Of course. But with your help, we will be even better equipped to face and ultimately defeat our mutual enemy."

Marlee took a moment to recognize that she was watching a master at work. But only a moment, for the vibe in the lab remained tense. She offered a tiny nod to the senator. "Which, I believe, is the goal of everyone here today. I'm sorry you're all having difficulties reaching a consensus. Perhaps I—" she gestured quickly to the senator "—perhaps *we* can assist in overcoming any language or cultural barriers. Why don't I confer with the others for a minute while the three of you…share some memories."

She exited the circle with imposed grace and strode over to the worktable, where Devon was whispering while waving his hands around. Kennedy gave her a helpless look as she sat down.

"Devon, what is this mess?"

"*This* is them being infuriating, insufferable, impossibly arrogant aliens. They seem to think no one here understands basic extradimensional quantum physics!"

She checked with Kennedy, who winced. "I'm afraid it's true. Devon's being a mite on the testy side, but I admit I've never met such condescending scientists, alien or otherwise. And trust me, this is saying something."

"See?"

Marlee chewed on her bottom lip. "I assume you're trying to get them to explain to you the nitty-gritty details of their Rasu-busting weapon? The Ymyrath Field?"

Devon blew out a breath. "That was the idea. The two Ourankeli over in the corner are allegedly the only two who actively worked on the project, but they're deferring to Wyddy and

Cyfeill on everything."

Marlee covered her mouth to quiet a laugh. "*Wyddy?*"

Devon shrugged.

"First off, don't you *dare* call them that to their face. Please, I beg you. Second, how far have you gotten in extracting information from them?"

"We know the weapon involved a particle accelerator used to create a new variant of neutrons. 'Isotope' isn't a strictly accurate term, but it gives you the gist. It's analogous to neutronium, but we're calling it 4-neutron. And after two hours, that's *everything* we know."

"Well it's a start, at least. The conversation broke down when you tried to probe the scientific details of this new isotope?"

"Yup."

Marlee glanced over her shoulder to make sure Corradeo and the others were still getting on peaceably. "Okay. Devon, I realize you're as smart as them. Smarter. You know it, too. So you don't have to prove anything. We need this weapon, don't we?"

"It certainly can't hurt."

Kennedy frowned. "Or maybe it *can.* We won't find out until we build one and test it, which is kind of the point. And why I'm here. But I should probably get back to my main job and return later, because at this point we're a parsec away from building anything."

"Give me five minutes to try to make some progress here before you leave?"

Kennedy hesitated, but nodded.

"Thanks. Devon, I need you to pretend you're a student. Let them educate you, even if you already know ninety percent of what they tell you. Listen for the nuance in the details and, hey, you might learn something."

"I resent the implication that I don't already know everything."

"Devon—"

"I'm kidding. Sort of. All right, I will be passive and docile, but only because this is important."

"Yes, it is. Thank you so much!" With a relieved sigh she stood and made her way back to where Corradeo, Cyfeill and Wyddy—oh no, Devon had infected her—were now engaged in an animated and, she thought, pleasant conversation. "How is everyone doing?"

Corradeo smiled. "Well. We were just reminiscing about how the—it doesn't matter. Is it time for work again?"

"If Cyfeill and Wyddoniiet are willing, yes. I think that due to some quirks in communications, it's best if we let you tell your story of this weapon in whatever manner you see fit. Devon and Kennedy will listen and try not to interrupt with questions that can be addressed later. You've been shown how to operate our screens, so why don't we set up a presentation area over here—" she gestured toward an open area on the left "—and the others will follow your lead. Is this acceptable?"

Cyfeill and Wyddoniiet considered each other with all six eyes, and after a second, Marlee could swear she felt a new vibration in the air. After a beat, Cyfeill rotated their eyes toward the worktable where Devon and Kennedy sat. "We are willing to make another effort, yes."

Marlee did her best to restrain an epic sigh of relief. "Wonderful."

25

CONCORD HQ

SPECIAL PROJECTS

Alex slid an energy drink across the table to Kennedy. "You look tired. Did the kids keep you up again last night?"

Kennedy guzzled a third of the drink in one long sip. "No. I mean, yes, but no more than usual. Dealing with the Ourankeli, though? Now that's exhausting. I don't know how you do it."

"Oh, I don't. Or not particularly well. But was it worth it?"

"Hell, yes, it was." They both glanced up as Devon jogged over to the table, plopped down in a chair, and instantiated a long screen between them. "This weapon is ghastly—for its target, anyway."

Alex studied the first couple of equations and notations on the screen. She'd initially come to HQ today to try to generate excitement over how the Asterions had cleaned the Rasu out of their Adjunct Worlds, as well as get an update on the Khokteh's recovery operation. But she'd been here for all of five minutes when she got an excited summons from Devon to report to Special Projects. "Wyddoniiet told us it was similar to a neutron bomb, but more 'elegant' and 'refined' and whatnot."

"And Wyddy wasn't lying, but it's a base comparison at best. A fertile imagination goes a long way when creating something new."

The fact that Devon was fawning over the science was a positive sign, especially since she'd heard it had been an ugly collaboration, at least to start. And the equations in front of her made it clear they'd moved well beyond a simple neutron bomb. "So what does it do and how does it work?"

"The weapon is a particle accelerator, one designed to create a very specific new variant of neutron. The name the Ourankeli gave the new particle doesn't make any sense outside their language, so I'm calling it a 4-neutron. Already filed the forms with the relevant scientific organizations and everything."

"Why a '4-neutron'?"

Kennedy snickered. "Because it's fortified."

"Okay, whatever. Keep going."

Devon enlarged a tiny section of the screen. "It's fortified in two ways. Most importantly, it has a…wait for it…*four* times longer beta decay period than regular free neutrons do. This means four times the collision cascades, a greater than eight times stronger defect wind and a minimum of sixteen times the number of dislocation loops caused by its ionizing radiation."

Alex double-checked old, long-filed-away knowledge to make sure she comprehended what he was saying. "Impressive. What's the second way?"

"This is awesome. When it does finally decay, the 4-neutron adds a gamma ray to the mix in addition to the usual proton, electron and neutrino. With a boring, regular old neutron, you only see this happen about—"

"One in every thousand times. I know. I did study this sort of thing in school."

Devon had the sense to look chagrined. "Sorry, I'm just excited."

"Which is good. So the gamma ray acts like a dead man's hand to twist the knife in a little deeper, adding to the ionizing radiation and increasing the scattering effect?"

"Bingo." Devon swept past columns of formulas on the screen to reach a schematic. "Here's the basic structure of the particle accelerator. It's a tricky beast, but we can build it."

"How big will it be?"

Kennedy rubbed at her eyes. "Big. The Ourankeli constructed it on the frame of their halo ring, and they never intended for it to be mobile. But we have to make it so."

"Which we can do?"

"I believe we can, yes, but it won't be pretty, not any time soon. I think I can design a sort of harness we can use to attach it to a ship—nothing smaller than a cruiser—but I'll have to switch out several of the weapons bays in order to do so. In other words, transform the ship into a glorified bomb delivery mechanism. And it's going to take a dedicated Zero Engine to power the weapon, in addition to the one powering the ship."

"That's no big deal. We build a hundred of those a day now."

Kennedy waved Devon's reassurance off and took another long sip of her energy drink.

Alex smiled indulgently. "Would you like some vodka in that?"

"More than you can imagine—but not yet. Still a bit of work to do, I'm told. Or possibly a great deal of it."

"But look what you will have built when you're done." She turned back to Devon. "What's the range on the weapon?"

"Once shot out of the nozzle, the particles will keep traveling for a long time. But on our prototype design, the spread gets too wide to be effective after about…" Devon's features screwed up as he did the math in his head "…six-hundred-fifty megameters. The original Ourankeli weapon was a lot bigger, but it also spread a lot farther. And I'll be working on extending the range of ours in the first round of design improvements. Ideally, by a significant amount."

"Excellent. But even to start, it'll have far greater coverage than the reach of our average battlespace. Kennedy, assuming we do fire it during the middle of a battle, what is this weapon going to do to our ships?"

Kennedy studied the table's surface for a few seconds. "We'll need to refine the shield algorithms, or our forces will be vulnerable. The tricky thing is how the 4-neutron blast presents as standard neutron radiation while secretly packing a much more potent punch, but I think I can account for this. Some of it, anyway.

"The real problem, though, is everything else: planets, moons, stations, the surrounding space they inhabit. The damage inflicted on any artificial structure will be damn near permanent. Worse, the weapon's output will poison every atom it interacts with for hundreds of years."

Alex nodded soberly. "This is why the Ourankeli were so reluctant to use it. Why they didn't use it until it was far too late."

She leaned back in the chair and brought a hand to her chin as the tragic scope of the damage at Haelwyeur flitted through her mind. "Because they had the wrong of it. This isn't a defensive weapon—it's an offensive one."

RW

COMMAND

Miriam regarded her daughter incredulously. "You think we should use this weapon to take the fight *to* the Rasu?"

Alex leaned against the wide viewport spanning the left side of the office. Her mother looked tired, but she knew better than to suggest the Commandant take a break. "Yes. I don't mean fire it straight at the heart of their civilization—actually, that's a fantastic idea, but I recognize we're not ready to do so quite yet. Right now, or as soon as we can build one, I'm thinking we should use it to catch them when they're on approach. If we fire it into the middle of a Rasu armada on the far fringes of a stellar system, or in the void between systems, we can inflict maximum damage without endangering our people or planets."

"To do so, we'll have to track Rasu movements with a significant level of precision across vast distances."

Alex shrugged. "Well, I assume you're working on doing exactly that."

"Of course we are. But I can't simply snap my fingers and have all the infrastructure in place to accomplish it. When you're talking about kiloparsecs in every direction, we need hundreds of thousands of sensors and buoys."

"I know. But we do already have those around populated stellar systems. We—you—will have to move fast, but if a ship carrying one of these weapons can catch the Rasu as soon as they enter a system, the battle's over before it begins."

"That is an appealing notion." Miriam studied a screen at her desk for a minute, entering several commands before returning her gaze to Alex. "I will insist on every safety precaution being followed, because this is a doomsday weapon if it malfunctions in a populated area. But I'm authorizing the construction of a prototype to begin immediately."

"Fabulous. No time to waste and all, especially since Wyddoniiet said it took them several months to build theirs."

"Oh? Devon Reynolds says he can build one in six days."

Alex arched an eyebrow. "You know, he probably can, assuming he doesn't allow Kennedy to get any sleep whatsoever. And when he does build it this fast, I will take delight in showing Wyddoniiet the power of human ingenuity."

"I've no doubt." Her mother sipped on her ever-present cup of tea. "How is Caleb doing after what happened on Ireltse?"

"Um…good? He's started talking about taking a trip to Seneca and running around the mountains healing injured wildlife."

"Really?"

"Nah, though I wouldn't be surprised if he gets the idea before too long." She shrugged. "Honestly, neither of us is certain exactly what this new development means for him. But it's got to be a positive thing, right?"

"I would expect so, yes, but I'm not the one whose consciousness is merged with a planet."

Alex laughed lightly and stood to say her farewells, then paused. She never knew when she'd be able to catch her mother in a non-war-consumed state, and a worrying notion had been itching at the back of her mind ever since Valkyrie had returned from the beyond. As it happened, her mother's last words provided an excellent segue, so she dove in.

"Um, on that note, speaking of merging. Just out of curiosity, have you ever considered becoming a Prevo with Thomas?"

Her mother's brow furrowed a little. "That's a random question. The possibility has crossed my mind a time or two, but not seriously, no. I don't think it's a proper fit for me, or necessary for either of us to do our jobs."

Alex's shoulders relaxed in a full-bodied sigh. "Whew."

"Why do you say that? Do you have something against Thomas?"

"No, not at all. He's actually pretty awesome. It's only..." she flopped back in the chair and pulled a knee up to her chest "...Valkyrie and Thomas are...well, they're sleeping together. Which is *fine*, and I wish them all the happiness and ecstasy. But while I try to give Valkyrie her privacy whenever possible, accidental intrusions happen. And if I were to connect with Valkyrie and you were to connect with Thomas at the same time, said time being while they were...we would...." She cringed and let the sentence trail off.

Miriam stared at her for a second—then her eyes widened precipitously, her face blanching. "*Oh*. Oh, dear. No, let's not do that."

"Right?" Alex chuckled, relieved she didn't need to go into any greater detail. There were some things you simply didn't discuss with your mother.

"Definitely not. Is being a Prevo always fraught with such hazards?"

"Hazards and wonders, in equal measure." Feeling much better now, she stood once more. "Where's Dad? I stopped by SWTC to say hi, but he wasn't around."

"I believe he's using his break between classes to chat with Richard over in the CINT offices."

"Oh, good. I'm so glad they're getting along again. They *are* getting along again, aren't they?"

"Judging from the merciful lack of angst radiating off either of them lately, I believe they are."

26

CONCORD HQ
CINT

Richard Navick passed the bowl of nuts he kept stashed in his desk drawer over to David Solovy. "And everything's stable on Ireltse now?"

"We *think* so." David dove into the nuts with rarified gusto. "The Rasu fought to the last ship this time, though they did eventually stop sending reinforcements into the system. Sweeps continue on the ground, since nobody wants to leave one of those macabre creations slinking around in the shadows. Also, sweeps on the other worlds, in case the Rasu sneaked a spy in under the wire before the Rift Bubbles arrived. And the Khokteh planetary guard was damn near decimated, obviously, so we're reinforcing their defenses for the time being." He tossed a pistachio shell into the trash chute. "Miri hasn't been home in three days."

"Maybe tonight?"

"Maybe. What about you? What's the news on your front?"

Richard grimaced. "Shepherding into the system a new automated algorithm that will change all Concord security and communication protocols every forty-eight hours, then distribute the new information to several million ships and innumerable people. Well, Cliff's doing most of the work, but you know I have to check behind him."

"Ah, the burden of being in charge. I don't envy you. Whereas *I* have been tasked with creating an entire curriculum for SWTC on Rasu warfare. Miri's planning to cycle through every officer with a rank of major and above for day-long training." David sighed. "The fact is, we need to start wrapping our heads around the possibility that we're going to be fighting this war for a long time. Sixty galaxies, over two thousand inhabited planets, six hundred twenty space stations. It's a lot of territory to protect, and also a lot of real estate for the Rasu to target."

"It won't be a long war at all if those slithering machines decide to take out this admittedly stunning monument to our achievements."

They both turned toward the open door to see Graham Delavasi slouching against the frame. Richard shook his head. "Not going to happen. We've had a Rift Bubble stashed on HQ since about two seconds after Mirai got the very first one."

Graham squinted. "Mirai…Asterion Axis World! See, I did read the material."

David stood and offered a hand. "Mr. Delavasi, it's a pleasure to see you again."

"And you, Mr. Solovy."

David stayed standing and pivoted to Richard. "I will let you two get to work. I have a new curriculum to deliver in less than six hours."

"We'll talk later." Richard closed the door after David left, then motioned for Graham to sit in the vacated chair. "Is this really your first time on HQ?"

"It is, and I am positively starstruck. Damn fine station you've got here. I didn't pass any bars or…other establishments on the way here, though."

"It's a big station. They're around. When things calm down a little, I'll take you to my favorite pub, and point out the way to reach the, um, 'other establishments.'" He started to reach in a drawer for a thin film, but paused. "Before we begin, answer me one question. Did you only agree to help on this case because Vranas is serving in the Concord Senate now?"

Graham frowned. "Okay, it actually wounds me that you would think so."

"I'm sorry. It's only…you were pretty adamant about not wanting to have anything to do with Concord when I visited you at Lake Boscosa."

"What can I say? This one caught my interest, just like you knew it would. No, I was already arranging help to cover the fishing lodge business while I was gone when I heard Aristide had been cajoled into taking on the vacated Senator position. I will say, though—I stopped by his office before I came here, and he was as happy as a kid in a candy store. He's missed the game."

"And you?"

Graham shrugged noncommittally. "We'll see."

It was more of an answer than he'd expected, so Richard retrieved the thin film from the drawer and slid it across the desk to Graham. "A consultancy contract. This way, you won't be stepping on toes and jurisdictional boundaries with Division."

"You mean I'll be *officially* stepping on them."

"To put a fine point on it."

"Excellent. The current Division Director could use a healthy dose of respect instilled in him."

So the man *was* keeping tabs on his old workplace from his fishing boat in the mountains.

Graham scanned the contract for a second—far too little time to have read it—before affixing his signature and sliding it back to Richard. "Now then. Shall we go arrest Mr. Vilane?"

"We don't possess any evidence against him, merely rumors and suspicions."

"What about Mia Requelme? He accosted her and threatened her life when she was trying to run a shop on Pandora."

"She's not interested in pressing charges, mostly because he doesn't know her true identity and she'd prefer to keep it that way. Also, a conviction would mean a year in a cell, tops, after which he'd be out and seeking vengeance. Nope, we have to start from scratch and build a case the old-fashioned way. Then we have to hand the case we build over to SENTRI and let them make the arrest. Concord doesn't have jurisdiction for internal human criminal matters."

Graham dove into the nearly empty bowl of nuts still sitting on the desk. "So they can steal all our glory?"

"Oh, I'm sure we'll get mentioned in the press release. 'With the assistance of' and such."

"Why aren't we just passing on the tip to SENTRI and letting them do all the work?"

Richard smiled wryly. "This is Aiden Trieneri's son. He's aiming to recreate his father's empire, which became Olivia Montegreu's empire when she killed Trieneri, then go far beyond its previous boundaries. Don't you want the satisfaction of bringing him down yourself?"

"You mean, doesn't it feel like this is our mess to clean up?"

"That, too."

"All right. Let's quit dancing around and get to work. I've read the files you forwarded, and I have thoughts."

"Excellent. Since I sent those files to you, Cliff's pieced together a couple of new tidbits as well." Richard swept his arm across the desk, and a row of virtual screens flared to life.

27

THE PRESIDIO

MILKY WAY GALAXY

Malcolm stopped in the lavatory to check the lines and seams of his uniform in the mirror. He forced himself to take a deep breath and steady his mind in the moment. He'd lost track of how many days he'd been fighting and hunting the Rasu, with only a few hours of sleep snatched here and there. But he was the fleet admiral, and he didn't *get* to be worn down or weary.

Marginally satisfied, with his appearance at least, he returned to the corridor outside and headed for the top floor. The officer guarding the meeting room snapped a salute then cleared the entrance, and Malcolm strode inside.

The AEGIS Oversight Board members' uniforms all shone with extreme crispness. But then again, none of them had been on the front lines less than three hours ago, for they were all retired from active duty. Technically, they weren't his superiors; in most respects, he was theirs. But they'd appointed him to his position, twice, and they could fire him from it.

Back when Miriam, and Christopher Rychen after her, had served as Earth Alliance fleet admirals, they had enjoyed nearly unlimited power on and off the battlefield. But when AEGIS had taken over leadership of every human military, the various power brokers hadn't been willing to give up *all* control, especially when that control might be exercised by an officer from one of the other governments. So while Malcolm did enjoy absolute authority over AEGIS forces during combat engagements, his decisions were subject to scrutiny, second-guessing and even reversal by a two-thirds vote of the Oversight Board. Oversight, indeed.

"Fleet Admiral, welcome." General Colby gestured to the table situated in front of the dais. It sat on the same level as the dais, adding to the optics of everyone here being on equal footing. "How goes the front?"

"It depends on which front you mean, General." Malcolm sat and squared his chair to the table. "We've been able to secure the Khok-teh stellar system for now, but the situation in the Large Magellanic Cloud overall continues to be precarious. We suspect the Rasu are searching it for fruitful targets, but they are proving difficult to track through the void."

"And how is the Tandem Defense Shield performing?"

His brow furrowed for a second; then he remembered this was the name they had invented for the Machim double-shielding, the better to erase the notion that they would ever employ something of Anaden origin. "Exceptionally well. The power requirements are significant, but the newer Zero Engines can handle it. Thus far, when deployed, the double—the TDS has a one hundred percent success rate in protecting the vessel from enemy fire, other damage or infiltration."

Admiral Zenshen scowled, as he almost always did. "It still seems a waste to spend so much money and power to protect ships that are already invulnerable."

"Invulnerable to destruction by conventional weapons, Admiral—not invulnerable to boarding or theft. Not by the Rasu."

"Yes, I've seen the mission reports."

"Allow me to reemphasize the point, Admiral. There is much the Rasu do not know about us—about humanity and about our allies in Concord—and we must do everything in our power to ensure they never learn more. Also, we should do everything possible to prevent the kidnapping, torture and murder of our service people. The cost of the shielding is worth it, in information security and in lives saved."

"It is." Colby shot Zenshen a brief glare. "While they do not fall within your primary areas of responsibility, we want to fill you in on some decisions we've made regarding planetary defenses."

They spent the next twenty minutes reviewing and, on several occasions, heatedly debating the minutiae of keeping AEGIS colonies and citizens safe in the event of a Rasu attack. Having fought through a single Rasu attack now, Malcolm took every opportunity to hammer home his belief that the measures they'd adopted were woefully inadequate. He didn't dare speculate whether he got through to anyone on the Board.

General Colby moved a screen pad from one side of his workspace to the other. "I think we've covered everything on the agenda. But before you go, there is one other matter we want to discuss."

Malcolm steeled himself for the coming ambush. "I'm listening."

"We're very sensitive to the trial you underwent during your captivity on Savrak. As we've previously stated, you have our sympathies and our commendation for the honorable manner in which you conducted yourself throughout your ordeal.

"It is unfortunate that your capture created a difficult situation for us as well, namely the position of Fleet Admiral changing hands twice in a brief period. This led to much uncertainty in the ranks and several double-reversals of policies. Such complications are never desirable, but especially so in wartime. Now, both you and Field Marshal Bastian handled the situation as diplomatically as we expected, but lapses did occur. If the Rasu had attacked an AEGIS world during either of these transfers of power, disaster could have unfolded."

"But it didn't. The system worked."

"So far. The repercussions of two swift changes in power are still rippling through the system. Our goal is not to cast blame after the fact, but to try to ensure such glitches do not happen again, either here at AEGIS Central Command or at any point in the chain of command."

Malcolm frowned; they couldn't realistically add any more regulations and directives than what already existed, could they? "What are you suggesting?"

"The Regenesis Extension Project is showing tremendous success within our ranks. Commandant Solovy is a high-profile example, but as a result of the ships lost in the First Namino Battle, there are many others. However, the majority of service people are reluctant to trust in the science of regenesis. We think it would set an important example for our officers and enlisted personnel if all senior commanders publicly affirmed their intention to undergo regenesis, should the worst happen."

Malcolm blinked. "Are you asking me to revoke the 'no regenesis' clause in my will?"

"No, no, of course not. We don't wish to issue an order regarding what is an inherently personal decision."

Order? He'd used the word 'asking' on purpose. "Then what *are* you saying?"

"We're asking you to reconsider your position on the matter. Your tenure as Fleet Admiral has been a successful one, and we hope to see it continue for many years. If you were to endorse regenesis, it would give us a great deal more confidence that the chain of command will not be disrupted again. It would also inspire those serving under you to take the same step, thereby strengthening the robustness of our fighting forces."

"General, I don't—"

"Simply take it under advisement." Colby's gaze drifted across the other Board members. "Strong advisement. We'll continue to review the issue from a policy perspective and consider what steps might need to be taken as events warrant."

Malcolm worked to keep a poker face. Couched in political-speak or not, this was a warning, and possibly a threat. "I will, as you say, take it under advisement. Now, if there is nothing else, we're running over schedule here."

"So we are. Good luck out there, Fleet Admiral."

RW

EARTH

SEATTLE

Malcolm idly studied the amber glow of the beer filling his frosted mug to the brim. The condensation dampened his hands as he held the mug in a vise grip atop the bar. He should drink it; he had ordered it, after all. But for now, he watched intently as tiny bubbles raced one another to join the foam at the head.

With the situation in the Khokteh stellar system again under Concord control, he'd given the crew of the *Denali* twenty-four hours leave on The Presidio—where they could be recalled in a matter of minutes if necessary—and mental health guidelines mandated he give himself the same. The Oversight Board had taken up three hours of the leave, but afterward he'd treated himself to a visit to his favorite pub in Seattle to contemplate what had transpired.

Religious freedom hadn't originated in the United States of old, but it had grown strong there. The principle that had formed one of the nation's bedrocks had transferred to the Earth Alliance and most other human governments, and AEGIS' charter had followed in their stead. Fewer people were overtly religious today than at any time in history, but their right to be so and to follow the tenets of their chosen religion remained as protected as ever.

Was this about to change?

The Oversight Board hadn't threatened to depose him as Fleet Admiral unless he revoked his 'no regenesis' clause. Not today. But they had clearly implied that it was on the table. In his experience, if suggestions and heavy-handed statements of preference didn't work, orders inevitably followed.

His left hand dropped from the mug to curl into a fist on the bar. They didn't have the right. If push came to shove, it would be up to the courts to decide if they had the ability.

Nothing mattered more to him than fulfilling his duty to protect innocents. Nothing, perhaps, except Mia. Now those interests were converging in a way that would make it *so easy* to comply with both the Board's and her wishes. Doing so would tie the current complications in his life, Rasu excepted, into a neat, tidy bow.

But it wasn't their right—either of their right—to ask this of him. To extract this price for his devotion.

Dammit!

He didn't want to blame Mia for any of this. But even as he sat here, he could feel the resentment that had been building toward the Oversight Board all afternoon seeping into his feelings toward her. Anger against one was becoming anger against the other, their motivations blurring together to feed his frustration.

Intellectually, he recognized both 'requests' came from a sympathetic place. Everyone wanted him to stay alive. So did he. They merely had somewhat different definitions of what constituted 'alive.'

"Is your drink no good? It looks refreshing, so I was thinking about ordering it. But you haven't touched it in five minutes, so…save me from a mistake?"

Malcolm turned to his left to find that a man had taken a seat on the barstool beside him. Slim build, blondish hair falling neatly across his brow, standard corporate office attire. Hazel eyes that reflected the ambient light of the pub a little too much to be natural.

He huffed a breath and took a sip of the beer, then nodded. "No, it's good. My mind was just elsewhere."

"Excellent. Bartender, I'll have what the Fleet Admiral is having."

Malcolm looked at him sharply, and the man shrugged. "Sorry to catch you off guard, but it's an honor to meet you."

He wanted to feel uncomfortable with the interaction, but the truth was, his face had been on the news a lot lately—more than he preferred—so he forced a smile. "Thank you. And you are?"

"Philippe Beaumont. I work at Fraser Consolidated downtown."

Malcolm tilted his head in greeting, then took a longer, slow sip of his beer. He really didn't want company, of the stranger variety or otherwise.

The man fell silent until the bartender brought his drink, then cradled it without drinking any, either. "Listen, I heard about what the Oversight Board is trying to force you into. It's not right."

A dozen warnings flared in his mind. "Excuse me?"

"I have a buddy who works on The Presidio for one of the Board members. I know it's not common knowledge yet, but he clued me in."

Malcolm stood, knocking his bar stool back. "Everything that transpires in Oversight Board meetings is highly classified. Your 'buddy' has committed a serious crime by disclosing—"

Beaumont held up a hand. "I know. Please, hear me out. No one's trying to steal military secrets and sell them to the Anadens or anything. But it's not fair what the leadership is doing to you. They don't have the authority to dictate matters of life and death."

He should have walked out then and there. But he was angry, and the man's words echoed his own ruminations so damn much. So instead he eased back onto the barstool, though his demeanor was guarded. "You're not in favor of regenesis?"

"No, and I'm not the only one. It's bad science we klepted together from those ungodly, immoral Anaden bastards. Our scientists have always been arrogant, but I believe they've gone too far this time. The notion that they can create life out of a basic brain scan? It's an insult to what it means to be human."

"People used to say the same thing about Prevos."

The man stared at him blankly. "I don't see the relevance."

"Your eyes might not be glowing at the moment, but I know the signs."

"Because of...course you do." *Because of Mia Requelme* went unsaid by them both, and the man clumsily tried to regain his composure. "Prevos are an enhancement of humankind. Regenesis is an abomination of it."

People had said the latter about Prevos, too. Malcolm waited for the rest of the pitch.

As expected, Beaumont obliged. "The simple fact is, regenesis has been legal for the blink of an eye, and the military is already toying with making it mandatory. How long before governments follow suit? New zombies are being awoken every day, most of them in positions of power. Soon, the average person on the street will be a slave to these new overlords, in practice if not in law. If this continues unfettered, it could mean the end of the human race as we know it, and sooner than we think."

"That's a fairly extreme position to take."

"Maybe, but if we want to protect our humanity—the humanity of everyone—then we need to get in front of the problem now, before it spreads like a virus through society." The man ran a fingertip along the top of his still-full mug. "There's a group of people I know. Like-minded people. Many of them are religious, while some simply reject the idea of being forced to be reborn as a zombie. They—we—want to make sure it never goes so far. No one should ever be forced into such a half-life or have to take orders from someone who has been."

Malcolm frowned darkly, and Beaumont quickly backtracked. "Not through violence—nothing criminal. We're a peaceful organization, I assure you. But we do want to make our feelings known. We intend to make it clear to our governments that we won't stand for regenesis taking over society. We're actually having a meeting tonight, here in town, if you wanted to stop by."

Malcolm's expression shut down. "I don't think it would be appropriate."

"You don't have to advertise your identity or anything. Just sit in the back and listen to what people have to say. Draw your own conclusions."

When Malcolm remained silent, Beaumont slid a holo card over to him. "No pressure. Here's the address for the meeting. I hope I see you there." The man stood, nodded a farewell, and headed out the door.

28

EARTH

SEATTLE

The meeting was being held in a large conference room in a mid-rise office building in eastern Seattle. Multiple businesses called the building home, and the name of the company the conference room belonged to was covered up with white tape. Did the company not want to be publicly associated with the meeting, or had it not authorized the room's use for this purpose at all?

Malcolm slipped through the door as quietly as possible and took a seat near the back on the left. Around a hundred seats were positioned in orderly rows, and nearly all of them were full. He wasn't certain what he'd expected, but a big crowd wasn't it. He pulled the bill of his cap lower and tried to appear both anonymous and inconspicuous.

He told himself for the fifth time this evening that he wasn't here to join this cause, whatever it turned out to be, but instead to simply find out more—about sentiments surrounding regenesis, what the group was planning, and whether there was any possibility of criminal activity afoot. But he couldn't deny that part of him wanted to hear what these people had to say.

As the doors were closed behind him, he checked the time. He was due back on the *Denali's* bridge in four hours; assuming the meeting didn't stretch on for too long, he should have enough time to stop by the townhouse, shower and pack a fresh bag before returning to the Presidio dry dock.

A podium was situated at the front of the room. Behind it, a tasteful holo sign spelled out 'Gardiens: Protectors of Life.' The group was far enough along to have an official name and slogan. Interesting.

He looked around until he spotted the man who had approached him in the pub—Beaumont was the name—sitting with two other people in a semi-circle of chairs near the front. He was one of the leaders.

One of the other men in the semi-circle stood and approached the podium, then began to speak. "My name is George Takanas. Thank you, everyone, for coming tonight. This is amazing. Our numbers have doubled just since our last meeting. Well done on getting the word out and finding other concerned citizens who share in our cause. As we have so many new people here, I'd like to begin by asking anyone who's new, and who's comfortable talking, to share why they decided to join us this evening."

Malcolm slid a little lower in his chair, but luckily a brunette woman several rows in front of him stood. "Hi. My name is Danielle. I, um…three weeks ago, the CEO of the company where I work was killed in a shuttle accident. Because he was wealthy and connected, he'd signed up for a regenesis policy the instant it became legal, and they woke him up in a new body last Monday. He was back at work by Wednesday. Anyway, I had a meeting with him on Thursday—normal work stuff, nothing special—and what I saw was really troubling. He acted strangely: abrupt, confused, forgetful. I mean, I know regenesis must be traumatic to experience, but his behavior was genuinely strange. And what I can't forget most of all is his eyes. They looked…dead. As if there was no soul in his body. I'm going to start searching for a new job, because I don't think I'm comfortable working for him any longer. He's not the man he used to be." She hurriedly sat down.

"Thank you, Danielle. Your story is a troubling one, indeed. Does anyone else want to speak?"

Across the room, a young man in a rumpled business suit stood. "I'm Scott Fer—"

"Last names aren't necessary. We want everyone to feel at ease here."

"Sorry. My father-in-law has been head of the family business for a hundred twenty years and counting. And my wife and I, we're grateful. He built it up from nothing to a multi-million-credit business, and this has enabled us to live a comfortable life. But he's a very controlling man, and not merely of the business. He uses his money to exert influence over every aspect of our lives.

"Anyway, he's always had health issues. Half his organs are synthetic replacements at this point, and only rigorous gene therapy has kept him alive for the last thirty years. He's been sick a lot this last year, and I thought—secretly, as I couldn't say this to my wife—we were finally going to be rid of his overbearing presence soon. Finally free to make our own choices and live our own lives.

"Well, I just found out that he's taken out a regenesis policy. When he does kick off, he's going to get a brand new, healthy body free of the defects his real one suffered from. He'll keep control of the business and the family for another five hundred or thousand years. Or longer! There's no escape for us. And I don't know what to do."

Takanas did an excellent job of looking sympathetic. "I'm sorry to hear of your troubles, Scott. One of the many problematic aspects of regenesis is how it will enable people to outlive their proper time, to hang on to the mortal coil like ghouls. And maybe that's all they are. They'll cling to their past, refusing to give the next generation the same chance to shine as they had."

Takanas clasped his hands together and stepped out from behind the podium. "The Gardiens love life. Many of us are devout in our faith and are thankful for the special lives we have been gifted with. Whatever our personal beliefs, we all love humanity. But life is only precious, only special, if it has an end. We have nothing against medicine and technology and appreciate the many ways both have improved and extended our healthy lives. But death is and has always been the ultimate, final boundary. A threshold that can only be crossed once.

"Now, our politicians and leaders, goaded on by arrogant scientists, are claiming to have conquered death. But *no one* conquers death. Some of you may ask, 'what about the Anadens?' If the Anadens were ever akin to humans, they stopped being so hundreds of millennia ago. There can't be a one of them who possesses a true soul. If you've met any Anadens in person, you know of what I speak.

"All right, then, what about Prevos? It's our belief that Prevos are a venerable enhancement of life, both human and Artificial, and we mean them no ill will.

"We don't mean anyone ill will, in fact. We simply want to protect our neighborhoods, our businesses, our families and our planets from being taken over by...I hesitate to use the pejoratives that are already catching fire out there, but words have meaning for a reason. Ghouls. Zombies. Golems. The Undead. You know, the rich and powerful control so much about our lives—like Scott's father-in-law and Danielle's boss. Now, the race is on for them to secure a false immortality so they never have to relinquish their power. And it's not proper. It's not humanity's way."

Takanas strolled deliberately across the front of the room, catching and briefly holding the gaze of various people in the audience. He was a good speaker.

"So what do we do about it? Right now, we're asking for advocates. If you have any sway over people in positions of power, whether it be in politics, business, finance, culture or the military, make your voices heard. We can work to ensure the Assembly and the planetary governments pass the strictest regulations possible to limit the uses of regenesis. It's not enough, but it's a start.

"If our efforts in this area are unsuccessful, we'll need to start discussing pursuing more serious measures. Now, I'm not talking about violence. Life is precious, and the last thing we want to do is cause unnecessary death. There are steps we can take that will have maximum impact with minimum loss of life. But you don't need to worry about those just yet. Concentrate on spreading the word, on making it clear that we do not and will not accept regenesis. Not for our leaders, not for our soldiers, not for our families.

"If you're interested in getting more involved on an organizational level, you can come up here and leave us your name and contact information, and we'll be in touch. Our next meeting will be in two weeks. Thank you all for coming, and for standing up for your beliefs."

The meeting started breaking up, and Malcolm joined a small group heading for the exit. When they reached the door, he stepped to the side to let one of the women depart ahead of him. As he did, his hand brushed across the wall beside the door, and he stuck a tiny, transparent and virtually undetectable surveillance device on the wall. It would record audio and low-res video of the room for the next hour and transmit the data to a receiver before dissolving into dust.

Then he slipped out the door and onto the street.

As revolutionary organizational meetings went, it was decidedly on the mild side. He instinctively agreed with much of what had been said and sympathized with much of the rest. The mood projected by the group's leaders was upbeat, welcoming and friendly.

But this was what charismatic people did—created a vibe of camaraderie and shared purpose among those within the sound of their voice. Their true purpose, meanwhile, remained obscured behind what was often a false façade. And in this case, there were plenty of warning signs regarding the nature of that purpose.

He hoped those suspicions were unwarranted. Half of him wanted to turn around, go back inside and join the Gardiens in their crusade. But he didn't do it, because all too often, this week's platitudes were next week's riots.

VANCOUVER

The meeting hadn't lasted too long, so when Malcolm got home, he put off packing in favor of reviewing the recording the listener had captured. He sat on the couch and placed the receiver on the table in front of him. A grainy image of the conference room materialized, and for several minutes small groups chatted in clumps around the space.

He fast-forwarded until all the guests had departed. Three men, including the one who had recruited him, and a woman remained near the semi-circle of chairs at the front. The man who had chaired the meeting activated a small module on the podium, and a full-sized holo of an additional man appeared in front of them. The man sported dark brown hair, sharp features, a wiry frame and Prevo eyes. Actually, now that he noticed, everyone in the leadership group was now brandishing Prevo eyes. Curious.

Malcolm studied the holo more closely, for the man reminded him of someone…but after a minute he gave up trying to determine who it might be. The recording wasn't of high enough quality for him to pin it down.

The man in the holo spoke first. "How did the meeting go?"

Takanas answered. "Well, sir. We doubled our attendance from last time, and we had some excellent newcomer testimony that fed nicely into people's ingrained fears."

"You didn't push too hard, did you? This is a delicate time in our growth."

"No, sir. We stayed focused on the importance of positive, peaceful change effected by bringing others to the cause and spreading our message."

"Good. Once people are fully committed, then we can push them toward where we want them." The man directed an intense gaze at Malcolm's handler—because that was clearly what Beaumont was. "Did our new recruit show?"

"He did. He kept to himself and didn't speak, but he stayed for the whole meeting."

"Interesting. Be careful with him."

"But he could be a powerful asset for us."

"If we manage him well and he falls to our side, yes. Otherwise, he could be a powerful enemy. I can trust you to manage him, Philippe, can't I?"

"Yes, sir. I won't let you down."

"See that you don't."

The recording ceased then. Crap!

Malcolm shut off the device and sank back against the couch cushion, dragging his hands down his face.

He'd known it was all wrong from the instant he'd walked into the conference room. Yet for a few minutes, it had been such a *relief* to find himself among people who harbored the same concerns he did about regenesis. For a few minutes, he'd allowed himself to feel stirred into righteous belief and even indignation. The speeches had stirred a fire in his belly, and he was disappointed to have to let it go.

But it was all a lie, and he'd known it. Complicated moral and ethical issues were never black and white, nor were they best decided by easily swayed crowds of distressed people.

He might not personally believe in regenesis, but he wasn't a revolutionary...well, except for that one time. But whatever this simmering uprising was, it was certainly no Volnosti, and at the end of the day he'd do his duty and defend people's right to choose to undergo regenesis.

The Gardiens obviously had much bigger designs than peaceful protests and government petitions. So now the question became, what were those designs?

29

ROMANE

MILKY WAY GALAXY

"Y ou can set the boxes on the floor in the room right through this door. I'll take it from here."

The delivery man frowned over the top of the boxes stacked high on his cart. "We're certified to hook everything up, if you want help with the installation."

Mia smiled politely, though her eyes also flared in challenge. "Thank you, but I'll be fine."

"Yes, ma'am." He didn't argue further, and she watched discreetly from her desk while he and two other men trolleyed in three large crates and multiple smaller ones, deposited them on the floor of the emptied-out equipment room and left with nary a squirrely glance her way.

Once they departed, she slipped off her jacket and draped it over her chair. This left her in a beige tank and caramel workpants that were sleek enough to pass for slacks so long as no one looked too closely. She needed to be dressed appropriately should government officials or local businesspeople stop by to see what the fuss was about, but she also needed to do the work of installing the scads of new equipment she'd ordered.

Qualifying the spaceport to accept non-human craft required an AEGIS-certified, dedicated, secure hardware node, along with a dozen secure network connections and specialty software to communicate with both AEGIS Immigration and the Concord Consulate. The level of bureaucracy made her want to give some politicians her choice opinion, but she knew enough about governments to recognize how it was far too late. There was no longer a single 'someone,' if there ever had been. Only a morass of unaccountable officials and enshrined-in-stone policies.

AEGIS was an important institution; more than that, it was a necessary one in a new universe packed with threats to humanity. But there was no question its governance had tamped down some of the IDCC's wonderful entrepreneurial spirit.

But it wasn't an insurmountable problem; she could maneuver through any labyrinth or obstacle course they threw at her. Whatever it took to bring aliens here to Romane and make them feel welcome once they arrived.

Mia pried the top off the first crate and peered inside to inspect the contents. In truth, the bureaucratic entanglements were for the best. The legal requirements had pushed her to assess the state of the server hardware at the spaceport, and she'd found it wanting in a bad way. So she'd scrapped the entire system to start over with new, next-gen equipment. For the last few nights, she and Meno had scripted a new central operating system to take advantage of the better equipment and the greater variety of patrons they would soon be seeing.

Because she still wasn't getting a great deal of sleep. Since returning to Romane, the daytime hours had been packed with regulatory panels, design reviews, business meetings and construction planning. The nighttime ones were occupied with checking in on the world she'd left behind. She used Meno, the Noesis, sidespace and friendly contacts to keep tabs on the state of the Rasu War, relations with the Asterions, the Godjans' well-being, and the nascent Anaden government, among other things.

Most of those other things involved Malcolm. Confirming he'd survived the battle at Ireltse, then checking to make sure he was surviving the world. Yes, fine. So she was having difficulty letting go of her former life.

She leaned against the wall and closed her eyes, slipping into sidespace before she'd even realized it. In two seconds her consciousness was at their—his?—townhouse in Vancouver. Her heart panged, for she missed it so. Missed the comfortable furniture, expansive kitchen and jaw-dropping view of Vancouver Harbor.

Her awareness wandered aimlessly through the rooms. She'd left more of her belongings there than she'd realized, and it selfishly warmed her heart to see that he hadn't packed any of them away.

A noise down the hall drew her attention, and she drifted into the lavatory—

—and caught Malcolm in the shower. *Oh, my.* Other parts of her warmed now, and she—

Mia.

Her consciousness slammed back into her body with a jolt. *What, Meno?*

That was not appropriate behavior on your part.

Of course it wasn't appropriate! She had no right to spy on him without his knowledge. It was worse than obsessive; it was creepy. But she hadn't meant to do it and.…

Ugh. What was the point of trying to build a life without him if all she did was think about him?

In fairness, this was an exaggeration. She didn't only think about him. She spent an inordinate amount of time thinking about the spaceport upgrades, the expo buildout, the partnerships she needed to cultivate and the people she needed to hire. But he was always drifting around in the narrow space between conscious thought and unconscious dreams.

Time to move on from those dangerous musings. She unloaded the first crate, situating the hardware on the floor near where it would be installed, then exhaled and looked around again. Wow, her mind was all over the place today.

We'll finish this in a bit. I want to check on the construction progress.

I can tell you that—

No, I want to see it.

A quick skip through sidespace will show you everything you need to see.

With my own eyes, Meno. Sometimes there's no substitute for the real thing. Also, she didn't want to 'accidentally' drift back to Vancouver. Or shouldn't, at any rate.

She took the lift to the roof of the spaceport, then strode to the railing at the edge. To the west, illuminated by the setting of Romane's first sun, construction cranes were already placing new support beams across the cleared-out landscape. She'd bought out the leases of the businesses occupying the buildings with generous compensation, then had the structures demolished. Another fresh start for this endeavor.

She overlayed the architectural mockups of the expo upon the construction site, which today was a sea of dirt, drones, cranes and piles of metal, and in her mind's eye she could see the finished work in all its shining glory.

At this point, she was on the verge of being as cash-poor as she'd been when she'd fled from Pandora to Romane all those years ago with nothing but Caleb's two thousand credits in her pocket. The capital investments needed for this project were mind-boggling, or would be for anyone who hadn't played a central role in building Concord from the ground up. Even for her, they were daunting.

But it was going to be worth it. It had to be.

30

CONCORD HQ

CINT

Graham Delavasi shook Will's hand, extending his other arm to pat the man on the back. "It is so good to see you. Did Richard tell you about the fishing lodge?"

Richard rolled his eyes, but Will chuckled warmly. "He did. I visited Lake Boscosa once when I was a child. I remember it being peaceful and beautiful."

"Then visit it again soon. Please."

"Absolutely. I promise you." Will gestured to the conference table. "I've set up snacks and a drink bar in here. The panels embedded in the table provide touch access to the entire CINT database. Cliff is also on call for you." He glanced over his shoulder wearing an amused smile. "Yes, Richard, I'll alert you if anything requires your attention."

Graham looked a tad disappointed. "You're not going to stay and help us out?"

Richard shook his head. "Will is temporarily taking on even more of my duties than he usually does, so I can spend a few hours working on this case. I'm afraid CINT cannot afford both of our absences at once. Not with a war on."

"In that case, I understand." Graham wagged a finger. "Fishing, though. Soon."

"Fishing." Will waved an affirmation as he left, closing the door behind him.

Richard took a seat opposite his friend. He'd chosen the conference room for their brainstorming session rather than his office, mostly because in his office he felt like Graham's superior. The mere notion made him uncomfortable, and it wasn't the vibe he wanted to create. Here in the conference room, they were equals, working a case together the way they used to do.

Graham opened an aural and slid it across the table. "In addition to scouring public and semi-public records, I hit up my old contacts on Pandora for some information. These are the complete, I believe, holdings of Vilane Properties, going nine holding companies and ten subsidiaries deep. On Pandora, the conglomerate owns sixty-two percent of the properties in the Approach, thirty-eight percent of the Promenade and around eighteen percent of the Channel. While not as impressive percentage-wise, the company also owns eighty-six properties on Scythia, thirty-five on Pyxis, thirty-one on Romane, and a scandalous ninety-six on Krysk."

Richard whistled. "Damn. That's a lot of real estate, especially for a company no one's ever heard of."

"Yep. The problem is, they're all held legally, at least so far as I've been able to determine. Vilane may be a real-estate shark, but he's not a criminal one."

"It's financing, then. He's using the profits from Vilane Properties to fund the Rivinchi cartel's activities."

"It's a reasonable assumption. Unfortunately, nothing here directly ties Vilane or his companies to Rivinchi. If anything did, we'd be done here. Information on Rivinchi has been more difficult to come by—in part because it's a new organization, and in part because it's deliberately elusive."

Graham leaned forward with renewed enthusiasm. "But I have been able to learn a few things. Rivinchi has been sucking up all the resources on Pandora that formerly belonged to Zelones by way of Trieneri, so Vilane is definitely tapping into his father's old caches. On the streets, Rivinchi is behaving the same as every cartel does: extorting money and loyalty and dishing out threats and violence until it gets it.

"Unlike in the old days, though, Rivinchi's thugs are all cybernetically enhanced and virtually all Prevos. The average shop owner on Pandora doesn't stand a chance against thugs who are stronger, faster and enjoy an Artificial in their heads. As a result, there's been almost no pushback against the cartel's expansion. And this isn't concrete, but there are rumors Rivinchi has a 'refined' branch sinking its hooks into the rarefied establishments in the Avenue as well, where there's a great deal more money to be extorted."

Richard's brow furrowed. "Does the Pandora Consortium exist any longer? If it does, they need to be told about the threat rising in their midst."

"I'll try to find out. Those sort of power brokers might well have moved on to—" Graham motioned around the room "—bigger fish."

He meant Concord, of course. Thousands of alien worlds and millions of opportunities for the taking, if one was smart, savvy and wealthy enough to deal oneself in. "I thought most humans don't concern themselves with alien affairs."

"I still say the smart ones don't—except for you, I mean. And Will and...." Graham sighed, his shoulders drooping. "Sorry. Did I mention I was old and set in my ways?"

"And I still say it's all an act on your part, but moving on. I've obtained more evidence that Vilane Properties' holdings are a leading indicator of Rivinchi's expansion. Police on Scythia have recorded twenty-four mentions of the group in the last three months. Shadowy, evasive mentions, naturally."

"Scythia's a well-run, upstanding place, for the most part. Not too many gutters for rats to scurry around in there."

"Perhaps Vilane's making a different kind of play on Scythia. The point is, Rivinchi is following the money to expand beyond Pandora. I bet if we search, we'll find similar indications on Pyxis, Krysk and even Romane."

"I think we can mark it down as a given." Graham passed over another aural of data. "In fact, Krysk has a giant bullseye painted on it, if this data is to be believed. Almost a hundred holdings under the Vilane Properties umbrella? Plus—and this is a pure hunch on my part—a company called Tere Holdings has been scooping up old

Ferre assets on Krysk. I worked like a bitch to explicitly link the company to Vilane or any of his companies. I couldn't do it, but my gut tells me they're related."

"Which would imply he's employing an entire shadow network of organizations we have zero insight into."

"It also implies he's tapping into Zelones resources, not just old Trieneri ones. He's gathering up the bones of the old order and turning them to his purposes."

Richard retrieved a drink from the bar Will had set up. "We've got ourselves a crafty one here, no doubt. So why don't we put aside the organizational matters for a minute and talk about the man—who is somehow more difficult to get a handle on than his businesses?"

"I called in a favor with the Assistant Dean at Tellica and procured his student record from when he was a graduate student there. By the time he arrived at Tellica, he was a cipher. Upstanding, model student, with a plethora of influential connections and a spit-polished public persona. He excelled in his classes, was elected Vice-President of the Student League, and volunteered for a university charity program that helped the destitute start businesses of their own. He went to cocktail parties and corporate symposiums and made a variety of high-powered contacts. Then he graduated and, as you know, mysteriously vanished for two years."

"And we haven't been able to uncover the first thing about what he did during those two years, so let's keep working backward for now. He hadn't quite perfected his persona when he started his university studies at L'Ecole Polytechnique." Richard passed the data to Graham. "He struggled in classes his first year. Even got a reprimand in his file. Apparently, he threatened a professor after they got into an argument during class. But he gradually pulled himself together and eventually graduated with honors in accounting."

"Hmm." Graham was staring at something in the file, broadcasting an intensity in his expression that Richard hadn't seen in over a decade.

"What is it?"

"This image." Graham enlarged a section of the aural.

"It's his entry photo taken when he enrolled at Polytechnique."

"Is it the earliest visual we have of him?"

Richard searched through the file directory for a minute. "No, we have an old photo from when he won a junior wrestling competition at Kalende Preparatory. He should be around ten or eleven years old here." He pulled the image out and positioned it above the table.

Graham detached the Polytechnique photo and placed it next to the wrestling one, then dug around in his files and produced the man's official visual from the Vilane Properties corporate directory. Then he leaned back in his chair and brought a hand to his chin. "Child, teenager, adult."

Richard joined Graham in studying the images. As a child, Vilane was thin and wiry, though he displayed strong bone structure—all knees, elbows and cheekbones. As he aged, he filled out, gaining strong shoulders and a chiseled jaw…but it looked engineered. Hormone treatments and cybernetic enhancements. Beneath it all remained the lean, almost skinny frame.

"He's created his own desired physical appearance to match the created persona."

"Yeah, but that's not what's bugging me." Graham enlarged the Polytechnique photo again. "Right here, when he's at the precipice between a boy and a man…holy fuck!" Graham literally leapt up out of his chair, sending it banging into the wall. "He looks like his mother."

Richard was accustomed to random, excited outbursts from his friend, though he rarely knew what provoked them going in. "We don't know who his mother is, remember? Presumably an anonymous donor purchased from one of the DNA banks."

"Wrong. Aiden Trieneri would never have been so careless with his lineage as to leave its future to the unpredictability of a random donor."

"The banks screen for all sorts of genetic markers, and with enough money you can buy whatever you want: affinity for science or business, physical strength, blond hair, emotional aptitude and so on."

"Pah." Graham waved him off. "Why pay for it when you already have the perfect specimen within reach?"

Richard grumbled, his patience growing thin. "Say what you're thinking."

"You don't see it. Okay. Understandable, as you've been too busy with Concord to spend these years obsessing over her the way I did." He plopped back down in his chair and smirked. "Vilane's mother is Olivia Montegreu."

Richard started to utter a quick retort of how it was an absurd notion. But before his eyes, the image in front of him shifted indefinably with Graham's assertion, and now he couldn't *unsee* it. The gaunt cheeks pulled over sharp bones, the pale, almost mint green irises from before he became a Prevo. The hints of blond in his light brown hair that had later turned much darker. Most of all, the piercing, coldly burning stare that suggested the young man sincerely believed he could kill you on the spot with a minimum of effort.

Richard considered kicking himself for not seeing it before now, but in truth, he'd only glanced at the images when they came in, preferring to focus on the hard data needed to paint a picture of the man Enzio Vilane was now. So instead he clasped his hands on the table and nodded. "I concede the resemblance is there, as were plenty of opportunities for Trieneri to acquire her DNA. So let's play this hypothesis out for a minute. Assuming it's true, do you think she knew about him?"

Graham snorted. "Are you kidding? If she did, she would have had him killed instantly. If there is one thing that was always true about Olivia Montegreu, it is that she did not share power. A child—especially one tied to Trieneri—would have represented a threat to her empire."

"Her own flesh and blood, though? After she killed Trieneri, she might have brought Vilane under her wing and groomed him in her image, the way Trieneri likely intended to do."

"I'll grant you, she might have planned to do so. But then she died, too. We'll never know for certain if she learned of him, but if she did, I don't believe she had an opportunity to do anything about it. There's no break in Vilane's attendance at Kalende when he could have spent significant time elsewhere. Honestly, I doubt she never knew.

"Here's what I think. I think Trieneri understood perfectly well the nature of the dark, rotting heart at the core of Olivia Montegreu. He knew he was playing with fire, and he needed an ace up his sleeve for when she finally pulled the rug out from under him. So he stole a sample of her DNA—an easy enough trick to pull given the nature of their relationship—and made himself a bomb in the form of a child. Unfortunately for him, she still got the better of him, and he died before he was able to set it off."

Richard rubbed at his jaw. It all held the ring of truth, but that didn't take them very far. "Without proof, this is just us jerking off about how clever we are."

"So let's prove it. Let's put an agent on Vilane and engineer an encounter where the agent can swipe enough of a skin sample to do a DNA analysis. God knows we've got plenty of Montegreu's DNA lying around in secure lab vaults to compare it to. And when I say, 'let's,' I mean you, because I no longer have any agents at my disposal."

"I started to insist it wouldn't change anything if we did prove it, but I think I'm wrong. Objectively, from a data perspective, it won't change anything. But Vilane snatching up old Zelones assets as well as Trieneri ones puts a new spin on the case. If it is true that Montegreu is his mother, and—this is crucial—Vilane *knows* it, then it changes everything about this case."

31

PANDORA

MILKY WAY GALAXY

"Sarvia, how is The Avenue initiative proceeding?"

Enzio's lieutenant in charge of Rivinchi outreach on Pandora cleared her throat, then took a quick sip of water. Her virtual presence in the private Noesis room was so realistic that ice could be heard clinking around as she returned her glass to the counter. "We were able to place two of our people in the local security force earlier this week. They'll be able to identify vulnerable businesses we can target, as well as flag coworkers who might enjoy a bit of extra money in their pockets. Also, Avion Adventures and the *Bologne* restaurant signed on to our protection program yesterday."

"We're making progress. Keep up the good work. At this rate, Rivinchi will soon control virtually all commerce on Pandora. And from there, the world awaits us. Thank you, everyone."

Enzio killed his visual presence, but he kept the channel open to listen in as the discussion among his lieutenants wrapped up. It wasn't that he didn't trust his people, as such, because he did—to the extent he trusted anyone, which was very little. It was merely that the sole way to ensure his enterprise succeeded was to control every aspect of it, from top to bottom. He'd learned this from his mother.

But the rest of the conversation involved only details of additional outreach plans and some early planning for further expansion. Before long, his people closed up the room and headed off to execute on their duties.

He'd need to do the same soon—he was scheduled to attend the monthly Approach Community Retailers Council gathering shortly, followed by a closing on another two blocks of property in The Approach. But this meant right now, he had a few spare minutes.

Enzio entered a couple of notes in his eVi for later, then went to the kitchen and made some coffee. He took it out onto the penthouse patio, where his mother sat quietly amongst the blooming alyssi.

"Here you go, mother. I brewed some coffee for you." He set the mug on the small table beside her.

It took her a minute to realize he was talking to her. Her gaze drifted to the table, and she picked up the mug with two hands, wrapping her long, slender fingers around it. "Thank you, son."

"You're welcome. How is your day going?"

"Nicely. I smell rain in the air, though I doubt the shields will let it reach us."

He spared a second to pay attention to his olfactory senses; it seemed she was correct. "Maybe next week, we can take a trip outside the city, to one of the nature preserves. Would you like to go on an outing?"

"I would, yes." She gave him a too-vacant smile, sipped on the coffee, and stared out at the skyline.

There was still much work for him to do before she reached perfection. The longing of his heart screamed for him to race ahead, but he didn't dare allow one iota of her programming to be any less impressive than the original. The complexity involved meant he needed to take great care.

He hadn't known his mother when she was alive, and this was a travesty for which he'd never forgive his greedy, treacherous father. But he'd spent years researching every scrap of information he could buy, borrow or steal about her. He'd used most of his father's inheritance to buy up damaged hardware originating at her destroyed headquarters on New Babel and the debris field of Dolos Station from the scavengers who had confiscated it—storage modules, Artificial components and even scraps of neural imprints.

Then he'd spent more years painstakingly restoring what he'd salvaged. Fragments and splintered pieces, all. But in time, they'd begun to take on the shape of a person.

When he'd first awakened her, she'd been cold, hard, even callous toward him. This was obviously a consequence of the damaged algorithms he'd been working with, for a mother always loved and doted on her son. So he'd tweaked and refined her personality algorithms—just a few adjustments to bring them in line with the person she surely must have been in life.

Objectively, when he looked at the woman with the pale blond hair and glittering mint green eyes sitting at the table on the patio, he recognized that she was scarcely more than a shell. But every day, the shell gained depth and nuance. Every day, he guided her closer to the woman she had once been and was destined to be again. The woman who had wielded the only true power in settled space for almost a century, and had come *so* close to bringing humanity to its knees before her.

Soon, they would complete her work. Together.

He gently touched her shoulder. "I have to head out for a couple of meetings. Don't get too lonely while I'm gone."

"I will try. I believe I will read a book, then go into stasis for the evening once the sun sets."

"All right. Get your rest." He kissed her forehead. "I love you, Mom."

"I love you, too, son."

32

CONCORD HQ

Morgan tucked razor-straight, chestnut hair behind her ear and scowled at the long, blocky contraption hanging from the ceiling in a rigged harness. "I thought you were testing it on fighters first."

Devon waved off her protest. "Testing happens fast around here. Spoiler: the tests went superbly, and the first three squadrons of fighters are getting retrofitted today. So now we're moving on to Eidolons."

Marlee watched in fascination as various muscles in Morgan's face twitched, as if the woman couldn't decide whether to argue, scowl or let a hint of glee shine through. "Don't the cruisers and frigates have priority?"

"Certainly, but they don't require much or really any testing—bolt the new weapon into a slot in the weapons control system and go to town. Eidolons are far trickier, though, only in part because they're sentient, and retrofitting them is going to be a herculean task. But it'll be worth it. The truth is, the smaller attack craft have thus far been wasted against the Rasu. They fly in, blast apart the teeny-tiny Rasu and drop off a few negative energy bombs, and they're done for the day. Concord can deploy thousands of Eidolons and millions of fighters, but they've been all but useless so far. We need to make them useful."

"All right, all right." Morgan threw her hands in the air. "I am one hundred percent in favor of attack craft being useful. Essential, even. So bastardize the fighters all you want." She gazed pointedly at the rig. "But you're not seriously planning to attach this monstrosity to an Eidolon. It'll fuck the aerodynamics to hell and back."

Devon protested. "Aerodynamics don't matter in space."

"Said by someone who's never flown an attack craft in space. To be more precise, it'll screw with the load and weight distribution, which means the flight software will have to be completely rewritten. And where is the power supposed to come from? The Eidolons are beasts, and they're not designed to leave stray volts lying around unused."

Devon leaned on the worktable beside Marlee, who continued to silently watch the tête-à-tête, transfixed by Morgan's delightful obstinance. "Listen, I know you haven't had to contemplate military operations for several years, but a few things have changed since your time behind the stick. For one, we're not amateurs here at Special Projects. The Eidolon Supervisory Artificial is hard at work on the necessary software adjustments for the pilot-ships. Also, Zero Engines have gotten more efficient and smaller in the last five years. We'll drop one the size of an orange in there next to the weapon, and power won't be an issue."

He stared at Morgan deadpan. "Besides, did you miss the part about how this is a *freaking renewable negative energy weapon*? No bulky missiles to lug around, and the Eidolons get to destroy the enemy all damn day."

"I know, okay. Massive props to the Asterions for inventing this toy, no question. I simply don't want these magnificent, self-aware ships to be diminished in any way, so…dammit." Morgan groaned into her hands. "Put me in the simulator, and I'll see if I can find a way to make it work."

Morgan seemed to belatedly remember Marlee was there and winced at her from behind splayed fingers. "I'm sorry. Now that I'm done with my tantrum, for the moment at least, this is going to be far more boring for you than I anticipated. I'll understand if you want to head back to the Consulate."

"Nah. To tell you the truth, I've never watched a sim run before."

Devon patted the sim chair in the corner. "It's the next best thing to being in the cockpit! Well, being *in* the sim chair is. Watching a sim run is the next best thing to the next best thing."

"Right." Marlee laughed. "Then I definitely have to stay and witness it."

Morgan shrugged. "Fine, but one last warning: I have a history of overstaying my welcome in sims. If I don't emerge for five hours, you had better not be here when I finally do."

All the responses that formed in her mind were entirely inappropriate to say aloud. "I have a meeting with the Consulate department heads in three hours, so that's my hard limit. Now get in there and fly!"

Morgan pressed her hands together at her lips. "It's been a while since I've run one of these. A long while. Nothing to do but do it, I guess." She eased into the chair, scooted around to get comfortable and affixed the circular sensors to her temples. Paused for a beat before reaching up and attaching the connector to the ports at the base of her neck. Closed her eyes. "Start me up."

Devon entered a series of commands in the panel behind the sim chair, then motioned Marlee over as a wide screen burst to life beside the panel. "From here, we can see everything she sees, plus some things she can't."

"What does the program she'll be running contain?"

"I've created a basic Rasu combat course based on our encounters with them so far. Knowing Morgan, she'll be fiddling with the parameters inside of five minutes. The sim is recording everything for analysis later, including a ton of data we can't visually perceive. Basically, you and I are now spectators. Grab a chair and settle in."

She did exactly that, sliding a chair from one of the workstations over and scooting it in front of the screen. By the time she'd gotten situated, the scene it displayed was already in motion.

A cluster of smaller Rasu accelerated into the battlespace and split apart in what looked like a randomized pattern. The next second Morgan was firing. Strafing. Strafing while firing. The perspective jerked upside down, then upside down again, until Marlee grew dizzy just watching it.

Morgan muttered under her breath from the chair. "The controls are all janky due to the added weight. Stanley's putting together some adjustments. I'll feed them into the sim programming as soon as he's done."

Devon waved a hand toward the chair. "See? Told you. Fiddling."

About twenty seconds later, the spins on the screen began to smooth out, as did Marlee's stomach. Shortly thereafter, the Rasu began exploding—and staying exploded. In minutes, the Eidolon was cavorting through a battlespace that was more Rasu debris than actual Rasu. The flying got fancier, though she'd never accuse Morgan of showing off. Wait, no, she totally would, but she was also confident the woman would unabashedly own it.

Morgan mumbled something unintelligible, and the Rasu debris vanished, to be replaced with a new, much larger fleet. What in the world could the woman possibly hope to accomplish against cruiser-sized Rasu? Marlee leaned forward and fisted her hands at her chin.

For starters, the Rasu couldn't seem to hit the Eidolon. It wiggled and flipped and zagged to skirt every laser directed its way. A massive Rasu grew to dominate the screen—the Eidolon spun and dove a scant few meters below the hull, arcing in parallel as the hull curved. When it reached the underbelly, Morgan fired on the weapons assembly. Crystal shards exploded out from the edges, but everything near the impact point was vaporized, leaving a giant hole engraved into the hull.

On the screen, the negative energy weapon's fire presented as a thin silver outline framing a streak of voidness, but she assumed the silver was present merely so they could track the fire for testing purposes.

The Eidolon pivoted to gain a bit of distance, then reversed and charged toward the opening, firing again. When the firing stopped…starlight shone through a hole burned straight through the cruiser's hull to the other side. The Eidolon accelerated through the gap, falling into a three-sixty spin to fire on the interior in every direction until it emerged out the other side.

Marlee whistled in delight. "Damn. I think I just got a little turned on there."

"What? Oh. *Oh.*" Devon grunted and shifted away from the screen, toward her. "Listen, Marlee, I don't want to go all fatherly on you, but are you sure entertaining those sorts of thoughts is a good idea? Morgan is…damaged."

Marlee nodded, most of her focus still on the sim battle, where the Eidolon continued to both dodge incoming fire and slice up the cruiser into ever-smaller pieces. "I know she is. But she's also starting to heal, and I want to be here for that. With her for it."

Devon's chair scraped across the floor as he turned to face her fully. "I'm not talking about Harper. I mean, I'm absolutely talking about Harper, obviously. But even before they got together, Morgan was a prickly, odd bird. And I say this as someone who was the king of odd birds in my youth."

"You're not one any longer?"

"Eh, I hide it better now. My point is, that path there?" He gestured toward the sim chair and the woman occupying it. "Devils fear to tread it, and with good reason."

She bristled. "Brooklyn Harper didn't. Fear it, I mean."

"Brooklyn Harper didn't fear anything. She was extraordinarily dumb that way."

Marlee wanted to reply, *I don't either.* But she exercised restraint and kept the retort to herself, offering a little white lie instead. "Thank you for the advice. I'll…try to tread cautiously."

33

CHALMUN STATION ASTEROID

LARGE MAGELLANIC CLOUD

Eren sat on a barstool, nursing a *merum tsipouro*, and idly watched two Barisans try to shake down a high rolling Anaden at one of the *skalef* tables. Matching tattoos in a jagged, abstract pattern were burned into the fur on the Barisans' right arms. Though he had no idea what the symbol meant, the fact that they brandished identical ones suggested it was a marker of allegiance to some gang, group or ideology. But which one?

Was this the kind of thing he needed to know now? A couple of Barisan thugs haunting the Chalmun watering holes weren't a threat to the new Anaden government—but might the group they belonged to be one? As Corradeo Praesidis' official 'Chief of Intelligence for Non-Anaden Affairs,' it felt like he needed to know these sorts of things. Which was why he'd decided to spend an evening at Chalmun Station in the first place, naturally.

Also because the stifling arrogance of Ares was simply too much to take for long stretches at a time. He'd been most relieved when Corradeo had charged Nyx and her Inquisitor brothers with investigating and disposing of Anaden troublemakers. The bitterness he'd stoked toward his Anaden kin during the Directorate centuries ran deep, and he was not interested in diving into the cesspool of Anaden societal machinations.

But aliens, he knew. He could party and fight and drink and curse with every single Concord species. He'd learned most of the tricks from his brothers-and-sisters-in-arms in the anarchs, then put a polished topcoat on the skill while working for CINT.

Intellectually and physically, he was qualified for his new job in every material respect. Mentally, though? He'd promised Corradeo Praesidis that he was. For now, he was betting on a sincere desire to not let the man down to keep him marching forward until his soul bought into the deal he'd made.

He took another sip of the drink. *Carefully, just enough to blend in...and take the edge off.* He'd slipped the other night at Caleb and Alex's place, but he couldn't bring himself to feel too guilty over it since...he cut the memory off before it took hold. Also, far better to slip with alcohol than with hypnols, and in the presence of trusted friends rather than sketchy strangers.

His gaze was again seeking out the two Barisan thugs when he spotted a familiar Novoloume walking the floor, and he waved Trepenos over.

Like many anarchs, when the Directorate fell and the rebellion ended, Trepenos Hishai sought stability and a new life in what he already knew—in this case, running a club on Chalmun Station. With so much changing so rapidly during the early days of Concord, there was comfort in the familiar. It wasn't the route Eren had gone, but he got why many had.

"Eren, my comrade." Trepenos placed a hand on his shoulder and offered a warm smile. "It has been too long."

"It has. Two years, by my count."

"I have no words to adequately express my sorrow over Cosime's death. I tried to contact you when I found out what happened, but...."

"But I was at the bottom of a drunken stupor, then somewhere far worse. Even if you'd managed to reach me, I wouldn't have heard anything you said."

"And now?"

"And now? I'm trying to live. Fairly certain I'm doing a piss-poor job of it so far, but at least I'm giving it a go. Speaking of, one way I'm trying to reengage is by helping out our former boss. See, it turns out, Sator Nisi was really—"

"Corradeo Praesidis." Trepenos gestured to one of the screens on the wall. "We do have the news here on this rock."

"Right. Sorry. Anyway, it's my job to keep him and his grand vision safe from ne'er-do-wells with ambition, so I thought I'd look around here and see if any of those were clawing their way up the criminal ladder."

"A wise idea." Trepenos dipped his head gracefully toward the in-progress shakedown.

It was good to discover his instincts hadn't totally atrophied. "Yeah, I noticed them. What's up with the tattoos?"

"They belong to a group—"

The floor lurched beneath their feet, sending them both grabbing for the bar. Eren's drink splattered to the floor as fine dust rained down from the ceiling.

"The hells was that?" He blinked and forced himself to transition directly into crisis mode. "Are there still buoy cams outside the asteroid?"

"A few. They're tied to small lasers used to fry wandering space debris that gets too close."

"Can we access them?"

"Assuming no one's changed the transmission frequency since the anarch days. One second." Trepenos instantiated a visual between them. There wasn't much light until the viewpoint rotated around toward the distant sun.

"Zeus' marbles!" A mini-armada of Rasu warships loomed dark and menacing over the cam's viewpoint. A thousand of them, at a minimum. Twenty or so could destroy the asteroid on their lunch break, so they must be expecting resistance.

But they wouldn't find it here. Even under Concord's domain, Chalmun Station was an outlaw rock—ungoverned and nigh ungovernable. If it crumbled in a torrent of laser fire, no one would be the wiser until a new visitor arrived to dock for some downtime and drinks. No early warning system existed here, so he'd have to create a not-so-early one.

"Eren, we need to get everyone out of here."

"Yep. Give me a jiff."

He sent a priority message to Director Navick first, as Navick would take care of informing Commandant Solovy and everyone else.

Alert! Rasu are attacking Chalmun Station in force. I'm requesting evacuation wormholes immediately, but you'd better distribute that schematic of the asteroid I know CINT keeps in the files to the Prevos, else they're liable to open the wormholes inside bedrock.

The next one went to his current boss, of course.

Sir, the Rasu are hitting Chalmun Station. Make sure Concord's on it, if you will. If I'm not back on Ares by tomorrow, look for me at the Concord HQ regenesis lab.

He grabbed Trepenos' hand more forcefully than was polite. "We need to move people out of the tunnels and into the most open spaces. Here, *Bogno*, *Purgatory*, anywhere else you can think of. Concord should be opening wormholes to evacuate people any minute, but the easier we can make it to accomplish the evacuation, the better."

Trepenos' skin gleamed in agitation. "But what about the club?"

Eren winced as another strike shook the walls, now with greater force. In the distance beyond the doors, someone screamed. *Arae.* The tunnels were shoddily constructed and apt to collapse if so much as a feather landed wrong.

"I don't think the cavalry is going to arrive in time to salvage much of this rock. The best we can do is try to save as many of these despicable, sorry souls as we can." His mind darted back to the night he'd spread the anarchs' message from this very location. "And get me access to the loudspeakers."

A terse response arrived from Director Navick. *On it. Eren, don't be a hero and get yourself killed again.*

He knew all too well the surreal punishment of too many regenesis round trips in too short a time. But in the moment, it never had mattered. Certainly wasn't going to today.

Trepenos removed a tiny dot from the inside of his sleeve and stuck it on Eren's collar. "Here you go. I keep it handy for when the patrons get a bit out of control."

Corradeo responded next. *I'm interfacing with Commandant Solovy as we speak. Stay safe.*

Why was everyone so bloody concerned about the state of his skin? Oh, maybe because of that whole suicidal—

The air started to shimmer barely ten meters in front of them; a golden oval ring tore open the air, revealing what he thought was one of the CINT training rooms at HQ on the other side. Good enough.

He leapt up onto the bar and pressed the mic dot. "Attention, everyone! Those shakes and rumbles you're feeling right now are not part of the evening's entertainment. Bad news: the Rasu, this week's incarnation of Evil Monsters from the Depths, have come calling on our favorite asteroid. Please proceed in a calm and orderly fashion through the wormhole located front and center of the bar. When another wormhole pops open near you, feel free to traverse it instead."

Hundreds of eyes stared at him. "Come on, you wankers! If you want to breathe your next, get your ass through a wormhole. And don't punch anyone on the other side when you arrive, okay? They're saving your lives, you ungrateful sots!"

The walls shook yet again, this time hard enough to nearly knock him off his perch and to the floor—then everyone was running, shoving and falling. Eren sighed. "I *said* calm and orderly...." But his amplified voice was buried beneath the rising clamor.

He climbed down off the bar and nudged Trepenos around the raucous line that was pressing toward the wormhole leading to HQ. "Go, my friend. Live to fight another day."

"What about you?"

"I'll be right behind you. I'm just going to try to help get a few more of these miscreants out of here first."

"But—"

He unceremoniously shoved the Novoloume through the wormhole.

34

CONCORD HQ

SPECIAL PROJECTS

The Rasu frigate closing from eighty meters in front of Morgan's position crumbled apart into sifted sand and winked out of existence. She reversed thrusters and accelerated backward, as she was definitely skirting the red zone of the negative energy weapon's reach.

A buzz at the base of her skull asserted itself through the sim and into her awareness, like a bee digging into her spine. *Stanley?*

The Connexus has generated an emergency alert.

The Connexus was the military arm of the Prevos' Noesis, and she'd only reconnected to it yesterday because Devon had insisted it held important file repositories on the latest military weapons and tactics—files he'd be referencing during their testing adventures.

Emergency evacuation assistance is requested at Chalmun Station Asteroid, LMC, which is under Rasu attack. Authorization CZA-16D21 Bravo Omega. Schematic attached. Take care in opening wormholes, as the interior is laden with narrow tunnels. Areas with suitable open space are marked.

Shit! She sent the 'eject' command to the simulator and leapt out of the chair, then promptly stumbled forward and fell to her hands and knees. The transition from sim world to real world wasn't designed to be navigated in half a second.

"Are you okay?" Marlee's face appeared upside-down in front of hers, so close that the young woman's raven-and-sapphire curls tickled at Morgan's nose.

In other circumstances, she might have smiled. Instead, she growled and pushed herself to her feet. "I'm fine." As soon as she was solidly upright, she spun up power in the tiny Caeles Prism latched to her belt and sent the mental command to open a wormhole—and nothing happened.

"Devon, why can't I open a wormhole? I've got to get to Chalmun Station now!" She assumed without asking that he already knew why.

"Free wormholes aren't allowed on HQ—not unless you have proper security clearance, which only about four people enjoy. Luckily, I'm one of them. Sending you the unlock code. Please don't share it with anyone and get me fired."

Marlee frowned at both of them. "What's happening—wait, let me guess. Rasu?"

Morgan's head jerked in a semblance of a nod as the fifty-two microseconds it took for the code from Devon to arrive stretched to the horizon. Her heart raced thinking of *Purgatory*, Solstan, her former employees…well, mostly Solstan.

As soon as the code arrived, she flashed it then opened the path to *Purgatory*.

Behind her, Devon sputtered. "Wait a minute. Morgan, you can't be evacuating Chalmun Station thugs into the middle of Special Projects!"

"Then you had best get some security officers in here to guard your new guests once they arrive." She took the first step to rush through, but Marlee grabbed her arm with surprising strength.

"I'm going with you."

"No. I'm planning to throw a bunch of injured degenerates through this wormhole into the lab, and you need to take care of them."

"Devon can do that!"

She forced herself to breathe in and give Marlee a weak smile. "I'm not trying to protect you or anything. Devon is in no way whatsoever qualified to handle terrified and wounded refugees. You are."

Marlee blinked and let go of her arm. "Send them to me."

Morgan vaulted through the wormhole and into *Purgatory*.

RW

CHALMUN STATION ASTERIOD

The place looked as if the second-worst barfight it had ever seen had broken out (the worst barfight having occurred eighteen months earlier, resulting in the destruction of thirty percent of the fixtures and over 17K credits in damage). Tables and chairs were overturned, most of the light orbs lay smashed on the floor, and dust-covered patrons ran around in ineffectual circles. And everywhere, there permeated a low, rumbling noise from deep in the joints of the station.

She scanned the chaos until she spotted Solstan over to the right, kneeling in front of a Naraida woman who was curled up on the floor under a table. She ran up and crouched beside him. "Hey, come on. Let's get out of here."

Relief flooded his features when he saw her. "This woman is wounded."

"We'll carry her to safety." Morgan scooted around to the other side of the trembling form and slid her arms under the woman's knees and shoulders, then lifted. The woman hardly weighed anything at all. Were Naraida bones hollow or something?

Solstan stood as well and insisted on taking the woman from her. She acquiesced, but instantly started urging him toward her still-open wormhole. Two Dankaths ran through ahead of them, making them officially Marlee and Devon's problem now.

Solstan glanced back at her as they reached the opening. "I will return once I have gotten her to safety."

"No, you will not. You will keep your iridescent ass on Concord HQ. I'll see to all these scoundrels." *Then hijack a ship and go shoot up those Rasu monsters outside.* Probably not, but it felt good to think it.

"But you are not my employer any longer. You cannot dictate my actions."

She pointed at the wormhole. "Through. Now."

"Yes, ma'am."

She watched closely until he traversed the barrier, then shouted through it. "Marlee, don't let Solstan come back over here!"

Most urgent priority handled, she spun and surveyed the situation anew—a thunderous roar shook the whole room, and off to the left, the VIP balcony teetered as one of its legs detached from the securing bedrock.

"Everyone, get to the center of the room! Look out above!" It was so loud in here that she wasn't certain anyone more than a couple of meters away heard her. She settled for waving her arms around to get people's attention while making exaggerated motions toward the evacuation route. A few people got the message—by and large, the patrons of *Purgatory* were not the brightest minds in Concord space—and started hurrying to safety.

The balcony came tumbling down, taking out two Anadens who'd persisted in loitering underneath it. Whatever, they'd wake up in a lab later. An ear-splitting series of *clangs* echoed through the bar as the bottles of spirits lining the back wall shattered on the floor, and her heart broke a little. Fuck those Rasu bastards.

Nothing left to do now but be a hero. She hurried up to the first idiot in her path. "Can you walk?"

The Khokteh...female?...nodded, bloody slobber dripping from her long jaws.

"Great. Through the wormhole, right there." She didn't stop to watch and confirm whether the Khokteh actually made it through before moving on to the next idiot and repeating the process.

The walls shook with renewed fervor; the strikes were coming faster now. Knowing what she did about the structural integrity of this rock, they had minutes at most before the ceiling collapsed and buried alive everyone who remained in her former enterprise.

Hurried movement flared in the corner of her vision, and her brain registered that someone she maybe recognized had stormed into the bar. She turned toward the movement, studying the

Anaden with a mane of golden locks and far too much fashion sense for Chalmun Station…oh. Got it.

"Anarch! Over here!"

The Anaden spun around in response to her shout, his brow furrowing for a beat before he seemed to recognize her as well. "Fighter pilot!" He jogged over. "I got everyone out of *Beggars' Den* and came searching for more people to shove through wormholes, but it looks like you're doing a good job of that yourself."

"I'm trying, but I can't wander too far away from this one, or it will collapse. Help me corral these people through it?"

He glanced around, nodding. "Okay. You just keep waving your arms above your head so people can see you, and I'll get to herding them your way—"

A deep, screeching sound reverberated from somewhere beneath their feet, and they both stared at each other.

"I'll hurry." He ran off toward a group of Barisans making a mess of trying to get out from under one of the larger overturned tables.

Morgan, you are not making my life easy here! We're currently violating at least two dozen Concord security regulations simply by letting these thugs exist in Special Projects!

Devon, since when do you give a shit about security regulations?

Since I was in charge!

It was a fair response.

Blame it all on me. Tell Miriam Solovy to come arrest me when this is over. I don't care.

No further protestations followed, and for the next minute she guided four, five…eight people to safety.

A burgeoning tremor gave her enough warning to crouch and throw her hands over her head as a seven-meter-wide chunk of ceiling tumbled to the floor centimeters away from where she stood. The wormhole wavered, and she had to focus to keep it open. "Anarch, I think it's time we go!"

She heard no response, so once the wormhole had stabilized she scanned the wreckage that had once been her prized establishment.

Where the hell was he?

Two seconds later, he came stumbling through the curtain of dust consuming the rear of the bar, a bleeding Naraida on each arm. "What was that again, fighter pilot?"

"Our time's up. We need to go."

"No. Hundreds of people are running around in the tunnels."

She cast her perception into sidespace and raced along what used to be the labyrinth of passageways outside *Purgatory*, then snapped back into her body. "I'm sorry, but most of the tunnels have collapsed. Only a couple are still standing nearby."

He dragged the injured Naraida to the wormhole, and Marlee's and someone else's arms reached out through the tear in space to take them from him. The next second he was scrambling past debris, headed for the door. "Are you coming?"

She tried to shout above the clamor, but her voice was hoarse from all the dust she'd inhaled. "I told you, I have to keep the wormhole open."

The anarch paused near the door and pointed off to the left. "Hey, problem solved!"

Her gaze went to where he was pointing. On the other side of what was left of *Purgatory*, two new wormholes were forming. The Connexus had finally gotten their act together and showed up.

"All right." She killed the power to hers and picked her way to the door, which was stuck half open. They shimmied through the opening into…damn, by definition it *must* be the passageway, but the dusty smoke was so thick that she couldn't see twenty centimeters in front of her and could breathe even less.

Switching visual filters to infrared and thermal.

Thanks. That helps, a little.

A single form wavered hazy red in front of her. "What are we doing here, anarch?"

"We're walking, or crawling, until we find people. Can you open a wormhole in these cramped quarters?"

"I think so." She slipped into sidespace again, then grabbed his hand and tromped ahead. "To the left."

They stumbled and tripped over debris to the first intersection and down the left tunnel. A few meters ahead, two Novoloume sat huddled on the floor, arms wrapped around one another. As they approached, one of the Novoloume peered up. "Help us! Her leg is broken."

"Get them up." Morgan spun up the power in her Caeles Prism and opened a wormhole, only to leap back as the edges sliced into the rocky walls to create yet more debris. She hurriedly shrunk the boundary until it fit into the confines of the tunnel, and she and the anarch helped the two Novoloume through the opening. The wounded one basically fell into Marlee's arms, but the woman kept them both on their feet.

A series of insistent thuds echoed down the tunnel, and Morgan turned just in time to jump out of the way as a Dankath barreled straight past them and through to HQ.

The anarch snorted. "You're welcome!"

The walls, floor and ceiling shuddered violently, raining stinging pellets of dirt down upon them, and Morgan hesitated about venturing any farther. But renewed shouts reverberated from down the tunnel, and she sighed. "Let's check it out."

She put a hand on the anarch's shoulder so they didn't get separated, and they staggered their way forward and around the corner—straight into a solid wall of rock.

"*Arae!*"

The selfish part of her was relieved. She was filthy, tired and bleeding from multiple scrapes. This kind of hands-on rescue operation had always been Brook's purview, anyway. "We've done all we can—"

35

CONCORD HQ

SPECIAL PROJECTS

Jagged shards of rock tumbled into the lab for an instant before the wormhole shut down, slicing a meter-wide boulder in half as it vanished.

Marlee dropped a bleeding Novoloume woman into a chair and spun to Devon. "Morgan and Eren didn't come through. Where are they?"

Devon was talking in animated gestures to one of the arriving Vigil security officers and didn't answer her.

"Devon!"

He dragged a hand down his face. "I don't know. In one of the tunnels, it looked like. But this…" he indicated the rocks now decorating the lab floor "…the tunnel must have collapsed."

"Well, find out." She sent a quick pulse.

Morgan, are you there?

No response. Morgan could be too busy to answer, or she could be…buried. Crap, she didn't have Eren's private comm address to pulse him. Oh, she so wished she was able to access the Connexus, or even just the Noesis. Military Prevos were running evacuation wormholes throughout Chalmun; they would know what had happened, then she would know.

She tried to focus on triage for the refugees while she waited for someone to provide answers, but she did a poor job of it.

Abruptly Devon moved closer to her, though he seemed more interested in body-blocking a sealed lab enclosure behind her than in helping the injured. "That's it. The roof's collapsed in *Purgatory* and the surrounding tunnels."

Her heart leapt into her throat. "*What. About. Morgan?*"

He shook his head. "I don't think—" One of the Vigil officers interrupted him with some useless question, and despair seized her chest and squeezed tight. She felt so helpless....

"Oh my god. What the *ebanatyi pidaraz* is happening in here?"

"Alex!"

Like an angel sent from heaven to answer her desperate prayers, Alex sprinted from the doorway over to Marlee.

She immediately grabbed her aunt by the shoulders. "Morgan and Eren are trapped in the tunnels near *Purgatory*. Can you find them and get them out?"

Alex's countenance darkened, but she wasted no time in closing her eyes.

RW

CHALMUN STATION ASTEROID

Brain-cracking pain radiating from the rear of his skull welcomed Eren to conscious awareness, and he immediately tried to crawl back into the fog to escape it.

No such luck.

Resigned to being awake and miserable, he forced his eyes open, only to find the world had turned a sickly tangerine color. No, wait, that was the floor. He lifted his head a few centimeters to peer around. It seemed much darker in the space than it had been...whenever he'd been knocked out. But he was able to spot a trail of crimson weaving through the dirt floor to stop, or more likely start, at a mess of dust-covered chestnut hair. He'd been with someone before...the Human fighter pilot.

He struggled to get upright, then gently touched her shoulder. "Hey. Wake up."

She didn't so much as moan, though she did appear to be breathing, so he took a second to inspect their surroundings with greater care. As best as he could tell, the section of the tunnel they'd come from had collapsed behind them, leaving them pinned in a barely two-meter space between two solid walls of debris.

How were they going to get out of this one? With the fighter pilot down—

A loud hissing noise filled the air, followed by billowing smoke pouring out through crevices above, and he sank down against the wall behind him. That would be the atmospherics system croaking out.

He did the rough math in his head. With no ventilation, he figured they had around five minutes until the air ran out in the tiny space. If he breathed shallowly, he could maybe extend their time to seven or eight minutes. But why bother? Why not just surrender to the inevitable and, as he'd warned Corradeo, wake up in the HQ regenesis lab in a day or two?

Well, for one, he deeply didn't want to hop on the regenesis train. He'd been in this body for less than two months, and if he had to integrate into another one so soon, he was going to be achy and creaky and generally a wreck. He spent every waking moment balancing on the ragged edge of sanity as it was, and he didn't relish upping the difficulty level.

Two, he didn't know what the fighter pilot's situation was vis-à-vis whatever the Humans were doing with regenesis these days. He thought they were doing something or other with it, but he couldn't say for certain. In his defense, he'd been otherwise occupied for a while now. So there was a decent chance that she'd die here, permanently; if so, it would be a damn shame. She'd played at projecting a recalcitrant, tough and grumpy attitude, but she'd saved a lot of people here today.

So he inhaled as minimally as he could manage. The people at wherever her wormhole had led—at a glance it had resembled somewhere on HQ—would know there had been a cave-in. They would try to effect a rescue, but he didn't care for their chances.

Eren, listen to me.

He jumped, banging his head on the wall and sending new shoots of pain ricocheting around his skull.

Alex? Your dulcet voice is most timely. I've got a situation—

I know. Can you move Morgan back toward you? As much as possible. Pull her up against your chest if you can. I need enough space to open a wormhole, and I don't want to sever her leg.

Morgan? Is that her name?

Yes....

Fantastic. Lovely name.

He leaned forward and finagled his hands under the woman's shoulders, then tugged. Oh, thank Athena, her feet weren't pinned under the rubble, and her body slid bumpily toward him. He tugged again, then lifted her up, and her head lolled onto his chest. A weak moan emerged from her lips, followed by some mumbled words. "…hands off me…."

"Uh-huh. You're going to be fine, fighter pilot."

A shimmer lit the suspended dust particles as marvelously as dawn penetrating a forest canopy. The air wrent apart, gradually revealing a chaotic scene beyond their prison.

Fresh oxygen rushed through the opening, and he gulped it in like the dying man he was.

A second later, Alex appeared, her niece beside her. They were both on their hands and knees, as the wormhole could only extend up to half of standing height.

"Gods, you are a sight, my angels."

Alex rolled her eyes. "You obviously got whacked on the head. We're going to grab Morgan's legs. Let's try to ease her through—"

A loud rumble shook the tunnel, coating him in a fresh layer of dirt to top off all the other layers of dirt.

"Never mind, no time for easing. Let's go."

He kept the woman's head off the ground as Alex and Marlee pulled her through the opening and to safety. Marlee gathered the woman up into her lap and scooted backward, out of the way, as Alex extended a hand to him.

He took it and half-crawled, half-scrambled out of his prison and into the free air, then collapsed face-first onto the cool, clean floor of wherever he was.

A roar behind him sent him scrambling again. He twisted around in time to see the small cavity they'd been trapped in vanish beneath a torrent of rubble.

RW

CONCORD HQ
SPECIAL PROJECTS

Morgan's eyes fluttered open, revealing striking lavender irises framed by bloodshot, inflamed sclera. "Owww."

Marlee smiled with forced enthusiasm. "I'll bet. You took a bump on the head. Two, actually." She pressed on the medwrap she'd positioned over a jagged cut along Morgan's hairline to ensure the seal was secured. "One here on your forehead and one at the top of your skull. But they're not bad."

"Great…." Morgan weakly pushed up to a sitting position on the floor, and Marlee mourned the resulting loss of physical contact. "Stanley says my brain wants to have a concussion, but he's doing what he can to dissuade it." She grimaced and looked around. "Chalmun Station's gone?"

"All but, I'm afraid. The interior space has completely caved in. But the Connexus evacuated hundreds of people, in addition to all those you brought here."

"Good on them." Abruptly Morgan sat up straighter. "Where's Solstan?"

"He's fine. He's helping the Vigil med techs care for the more seriously injured."

The tension in Morgan's shoulders evaporated, and her posture sagged wearily. "He's a stand-up guy."

Eren came over to them and crouched beside Morgan while holding a wet cloth to the back of his head. "Damn spiffing work in there, fighter pilot. It turned a mite dicey at the end, but we got it done." He balanced on the balls of his feet and held out his free hand. "Eren Savitas."

"Morgan Lekkas. We met a million years ago during the Directorate War."

"I remember. You and, um…."

From her location behind Morgan, Marlee frantically shook her head, but Eren was oblivious to the warning. In fairness, he probably had a concussion, too.

"…Captain Harper, right? How is she doing?"

"Dead. She's doing dead."

"Oh. My sincere condolences. I mean it. Believe it or not, I genuinely do understand what that's like. For the record, I'm glad you didn't follow her into the void today."

Marlee was wracking her brain for something non-stupid to say to change the subject when Alex joined them as well. "Everyone okay?"

Eren shrugged. "We kept all our limbs, which makes it a pretty successful day in my world." He stood and offered a hand to Morgan the same instant Marlee did. Morgan looked askance at their extended hands, then let them both help her up.

Marlee turned to Alex. "You got here in the nick of time, for which I am so grateful. But what *are* you doing here?"

"I was over at the Connova offices talking to Kennedy about the status of the Ourankeli weapon buildout. We had a question for Devon, only he didn't respond to my pulses. So I came over to see if he was here, and found—" she gestured around at the chaotic lab "—this."

"Yeah, I was just a little *preoccupied*." Devon joined their growing circle. "Lekkas, if any of these people damage a single item in here, I'm holding you personally responsible."

Some color had returned to Morgan's face, and she seemed to be regaining her bearings. "Tell you what. I'll work for you for free to pay off the debt. Oh, wait, I *already am*."

"Damn straight you are." Devon sighed. "Alex, what was your question?"

"More or less? Is the weapon ready to test?"

"Yes, it is."

"Legitimately?"

"Why am I answering twice? Yes."

Alex gazed pointedly around the room. "The Rasu are still sieging the asteroid. Let's go talk to Mom."

"Right now? What about my lab?"

Eren clapped Devon on the shoulder. "I know these Vigil guys. I'll help them keep the refugees under control until you get back."

Devon hesitated, but Alex grabbed his hand and hauled him off toward the door. "Come on. Time's wasting."

36

CONCORD HQ

COMMAND
RASU WAR ROOM

Miriam scrutinized the scans as they arrived from the forward reconnaissance unit. Chalmun Station Asteroid had never been a smooth, pristine rock, but now it resembled a spoiling blob of Swiss cheese. The Rasu attacking force was minuscule compared to what the enemy had brought to bear on Ireltse, but more than large enough to turn the asteroid into dust particles within the hour.

Fleet Admiral Jenner (AFS Denali)(Concord Command Channel): "AEGIS Attack Group #3 will arrive in the Chalmun Station system in eighty seconds."

Commandant Solovy (Concord Command Channel): "Thank you, Admiral. Due to the unique nature of the target, negative energy weapons are authorized up to half a megameter distance from the asteroid."

She switched comm channels. *"Colonel Ettore, what's the status of the evacuations?"*

The head of AEGIS Connexus Operations responded. *"We've secured approximately four hundred and thirty evacuees at seven different military installations. Also, I'm hearing that Director Reynolds has around forty evacuees in a Concord Special Projects lab."*

"He what?" She kept her sigh silent. *"Very well. I'll make sure they're handled in accordance with protocols. What about further evacuations?"*

"Prevo surveillance indicates the interior tunnel network has collapsed. We've surveyed the major gathering points, and they've all suffered catastrophic damage. At this time, we don't believe anyone else is alive inside."

"I see. So long as the asteroid remains intact, please instruct your personnel to continue to scour the interior for survivors. And thank everyone for their exemplary work today."

"Yes, ma'am."

The door to the war room slid open, and Alex jogged in with Devon Reynolds in tow.

"Alex? Director, don't you have some stray refugees to be keeping watch over?"

"Do I ever. But Marlee and Eren are watching them, along with a team of Vigil officers. Everything's fine."

"I believe I'll be the judge of when things are 'fine.' Do I need to impress upon you the dangers of having a bunch of, shall we say, less-than-upstanding citizens roaming around the Special Projects labs?"

Devon grimaced. He looked exhausted, and Miriam had to wonder what the last hour must have been like in Special Projects. "Trust me, you do not. But as I said, security is watching them, and this is important."

"Oh? What is?"

Alex rubbed her hands together, glee dancing in her eyes. *Uh-oh.* "This is the perfect opportunity for you to test the Ymyrath Field."

"It's too soon. We completed the prototype's installation on our test vessel, the *CAS Intrepid*, all of two hours ago."

"Great, so it's installed and ready to go! Who knows when you'll be handed a better scenario for testing."

Miriam opened her mouth to protest further, but her daughter cut her off.

"Here's my logic. Chalmun Station is isolated. Nothing else useful exists in its system that can catch radiation damage. And the Connexus Prevos are right—there's no one left to save on the station. I checked, right after I dug Eren and Morgan out and two seconds before the last tunnel collapsed." She gestured to Devon. "We both checked. And the size of the Rasu force is small enough that you're basically guaranteed to hit them all with the full blast."

Miriam frowned. "How do you know how many Rasu are attacking?"

"I checked that, too. I've been busy."

It was a compelling argument, but prudence ruled the day when one was talking about powerful, deadly and most of all untested new weapons. "We can't rush into things. We might only get one good chance at using this weapon before the Rasu realize we're deploying it and adapt. Strengthen their radiation shields. Spread out their formations. In fact, we have to consider the possibility that after what happened at the Ourankeli's Haafan settlement, they might *already* have surmised we'll be deploying a similar weapon and have prepared accordingly."

Alex paced purposefully around the war table. "I think it's highly unlikely. Based on what we know about the Rasu—okay, 'know' is a strong word. Based on what the Asterions believe about how Rasu society, if we can call it that, operates, it's probable these Rasu have no idea the weapon exists. There's no reason for the Rasu who have been haranguing the Ourankeli a hundred galaxies away to be talking to the Rasu who are way over here in Concord space. They're paranoid when it comes to control, remember? That's why they're trying so hard to get kyoseil to work for them.

"*Also*, since remote cells don't use quantum communication to converse with one another, if we take out these Rasu today, they won't be able to report back and raise the alarm. Not for a long, long time. And I assume we'll atomize what's left of them well before that time arrives."

Miriam was forced to concede the logic was sound. Still, she ran through the variables twice more in her head. "Devon?"

"She's right on all counts. Let's fire up the weapon and see what it can do."

It was impossible to resist the combined force of their unyielding persuasion. She activated the Command channel again. *"Fleet Admiral Jenner, as subtly as possible, have eighty percent of your forces retreat from the battlefield over the next five minutes. Have those that remain be prepared to make an emergency departure on my mark."*

Fleet Admiral Jenner (AFS Denali)(Concord Command Channel): "I...understood, Commandant. We'll await your order."

Bless him for not automatically challenging her orders in the middle of battle. She sent a message to Commander Xing of the *Intrepid*.

I'm authorizing immediate departure to the attached coordinates for a live field test of the Ymyrath Field on Rasu forces.

Yes, ma'am. We only have a skeleton crew on board, but we'll manage.

Thank you. Inform me when you're in position.

A direct visual feed came in from the *Intrepid* when it arrived at the coordinates. The AEGIS fleet had barely had time to start winnowing down the attackers before she'd ordered their drawback, and Rasu vessels surrounded the pockmarked asteroid.

She added Commander Xing to the Command Channel.

Commander Xing (CAS Intrepid)(Concord Command Channel): "The Intrepid *is in position. Sensor buoys have been distributed to measure the test results, and the weapon is powered and ready to fire on your order, Commandant.*"

Alex, meanwhile, was looking far too joyful. Even Devon had perked up considerably. *"Fleet Admiral Jenner, order your ships to set their radiation shielding to maximum. The instant the* Intrepid *fires, I want a full retreat. Don't wait for Caeles Prisms to open up. Use superluminal to reach a safe distance."*

Fleet Admiral Jenner (AFS Denali)(Concord Command Channel): "Acknowledged. The fleet is ready to move."

Commandant Solovy (Concord Command Channel): "Commander Xing, fire when ready."

Commander Xing (CAS Intrepid)(Concord Command Channel): "Firing on my mark. Three...two...one...mark."

Miriam initially thought the weapon was a dud, because there was no visual indication of it firing. Yet the wide spectrum alerts lit up at the same instant as an expanse of AEGIS warships vanished from the scene, suggesting *something* had taken place.

Commandant Solovy (Concord Command Channel): "Commander Xing, retreat as well. Return to Concord HQ, where we'll begin a full review of the test results."

She watched the visual feed from the probes left behind. "Now, we wait."

Devon smiled. "With that powerful of a blast, it won't be long."

The Rasu continued their assault on the asteroid, blowing huge chunks away as the rock's structure began to disintegrate. But after around ninety seconds, their strikes began to falter.

It took another minute before two of the Rasu vessels crashed into one another, sending one tumbling into the asteroid. Engines fired as the ships made to flee, only to sputter and die.

In six minutes, the asteroid's vicinity was a Rasu graveyard, at least to Miriam's eyes.

Devon lifted a fist in triumph. "See? Dead Rasu on a far larger scale than a score of negative energy weapons can create."

"And a dead stellar system." She didn't care for this weapon; as much satisfaction as seeing the enemy utterly disabled brought her, the harsh reality was that a weapon such as this one didn't discriminate between friend and foe.

"I'm going to send in a squadron of heavily shielded reconnaissance vessels to keep an active watch on the Rasu for the foreseeable future. I'm also assigning an AEGIS brigade to stand on alert and be ready to jump in and obliterate them if they so much as twitch. Personally, I'd prefer to do so right now, but I recognize we need to study the longer-term effects of the weapon.

"Director Reynolds, as soon as the *Intrepid* returns to HQ, I want a full post-mortem on the performance of the weapon and collateral effects. Keep the *Intrepid* out on the fringes of Ring 5 until we're certain it's not emitting radiation. Were there leaks from the weapon housing? Damage to the components? If so much as a bolt melted, I want to know about it."

"Yes, ma'am." He headed for the door. "I'll get right on it."

"First, don't forget about the evacuees you've got crammed into Special Projects."

"All handled." Devon tossed a hand over his shoulder as he disappeared through the door.

Miriam massaged at her temples. "Prevos...."

Alex just laughed.

37

ARES

*ADVOCACY HEADQUARTERS
MILKY WAY GALAXY*

"Thanks for the ride home." Eren tossed a wave over his shoulder toward Morgan, then dragged himself through the wormhole into the third-floor common area of the estate. He greedily inhaled the artificially oxygenated air piped through the building to offset the thin Ares atmosphere, as his lungs still starved for nourishment.

And in the comforting peace of the inviting room, a wave of exhaustion rose up to crash through him.

He leaned on the door frame to contemplate how best to address his weariness. Crumpling to the floor and curling up for a nap would be rude, so he should try to make it to his suite before doing so. Also, his clothes were too filthy to sleep in, and public nudity would be even ruder.

Destination determined, he pushed off the wall and set off—and belatedly remembered that before the Rasu attack had scrambled his day, he'd scheduled a chat session with Corradeo in…he checked the time…two minutes.

Well, it wouldn't be the first time the man had seen him looking like he'd taken a pleasure cruise down the Styx. He grabbed some water, then trudged up to the top floor and rang the chime.

The door to his boss' office slid open, and he made half an effort to at least lift his shoulders as he walked in.

Corradeo and Nyx were talking on the couch, but they both stood at his arrival. Nyx stared at him, aghast, her mouth curling down in distaste. "Gods, you look horrible. What hellscape did you crawl out of?"

"The Rasu blew up Chalmun Station with me in it."

Corradeo's expression darkened. "So it's gone?"

"Nothing but a smattering of shattered rocks by now, I expect." Proper greeting abandoned, he sank against the wall and actively resisted the urge to slide all the way down to the floor.

"I'd hoped Concord warships would arrive fast enough to save it."

"Oh, they arrived with due speed. But Chalmun Station had no defense system to hold the Rasu off for even a few minutes, so I doubt anyone could have gotten there in time."

Nyx arched an eyebrow and glared at the ceiling.

"Something you want to add, sweetheart?"

"Chalmun Station was a shithole. Good riddance."

He launched off the wall in a burst of indignation. "I'll have you know that a number of the miscreants who called Chalmun Station home helped your grandfather here defeat the Directorate."

She glanced at Corradeo, who tilted his head in concession, and her expression softened a touch. "I recognize how many of the anarchs were not luminaries of society."

"I'm not talking about anarchs. And for the record, they *were* luminaries of the society that mattered. I'm talking about average, ordinary people who only wanted to be free."

"Free to pillage, rape and murder."

Corradeo laid a hand on her arm. "All of which remain crimes in a post-Directorate world."

"I know, Grandfather. But you must admit, the people who frequented the asteroid were the worst sort."

"Some of them." He gazed at Eren in concern. "Were you able to rescue any of the inhabitants?"

"Yep. Trepenos got out, thankfully. I helped around fifty people escape, and several Prevos jumped in to evacuate a few hundred more. The tunnels started collapsing early on, though, so a lot of people never had a chance."

"How unfortunate. One could speculate that the Rasu are attempting to clean out LMC before moving on, but we can't count on them telegraphing their strategies. If the battle is concluded, I'll follow up with Commandant Solovy—ah, and she has beaten me to it. A meeting is scheduled at Concord HQ in an hour.

"Nyx, I'm afraid we will have to pick this conversation back up later. Perhaps tonight. Eren, great work saving all those you did. Try to get some rest." Corradeo grabbed his jacket from behind his desk and departed the office.

Eren promptly headed for the door as well. "I'm going to clean up and—"

"Wait a minute. You need to update me on what you've learned about the alien dissident groups."

"Not much."

Nyx took a step forward, as if she was considering blocking his exit. "That's not nothing. As Director of Intelligence for the Advocacy, I need to stay informed on all developments under my purview."

Gods, she was insufferable. "Suit yourself. But I smell like smoke and blood, so I'm taking a shower. If you insist on being informed *this instant*, you can come along."

RW

Eren's residence, while smaller than hers, was nicer than Nyx had expected. The suite included a spacious living area with an adjunct kitchen, as well as a private bedroom, a full lavatory and a small deck overlooking the gardens. Her grandfather really did indulge the man, for reasons she still couldn't fathom.

She'd also expected it to be a filthy pit of strewn clothes, used plates and empty bottles. But the living area, at least, was nearly spotless. There wasn't much in the way of personalization on display, either, but he hadn't been staying here for long.

Eren headed directly into the lavatory, and the shower turned on a minute later. He hadn't closed the door, so she moved into the living area for a closer inspection.

A visual of a Naraida woman with snow-white hair and glittering emerald eyes smiled at the room from beside the feed screen. A tickle of a memory flitted across her thoughts. Had the woman been at Plousia that night, when Caleb had frankly bested her? Her grandfather had mentioned that Eren lost someone on Savrak recently, and it didn't take an Inquisitor to piece together the information on hand.

A pang of sympathy echoed in her chest, somewhat to her surprise. Naraida didn't enjoy the salvation of regenesis, and he must have known this. So why give his heart (assuming he had a functioning one) to a woman he knew was going to die? It was a foolish course of action, its endpoint an inevitability. Though, it did explain a few things about his behavior during their recent work together.

The door to the lavatory opened, and she pivoted to see Eren wander out, steam wafting off his skin. He'd donned corium pants and was halfway into a chenille shirt. While his frame was slender, lean muscles shifted beneath his skin as he pulled the shirt down over his head. Most Idonis were either skeletally thin or excessively plump, depending on their indulgence of choice, which was the only reason she noticed the oddity.

Once the shirttail landed at his hips, he gathered his prodigious, damp locks up in a band. "All right, ask your questions."

"Shouldn't you have a summary of what you learned ready to present to me?"

He strode past her to go sprawl on the single couch decorating the living room. "Sorry. Was a mite busy saving lives and whatnot."

She scowled, opting to prop on the dresser opposite him rather than sit. "Do you have anything at all to report, or have you wasted my last fifteen minutes?"

Eren pinched the bridge of his nose. "That's for you to decide, but I did warn you it wasn't much. There's an up-and-coming gang out on the lawless side of the galaxy. They mark themselves with a tattoo, like so." He sent her a file displaying an image of an abstract symbol surrounded by fur. "Heavy Barisan contingent, but probably not exclusively so."

"What's their goal?"

He shrugged. "Mayhem?"

"I mean, are they intending to target the Advocacy?"

"Don't know. The Rasu attack interrupted my information gathering efforts. I've got a few contacts I plan to reach out to, though. They might know more about the group's intentions."

"Like who?"

He stared at her for several seconds, his eyes narrowing into slits. "I'm not certain I'm comfortable telling you."

"Whyever not?"

"Because I don't trust you. Not all of my contacts live squeaky-clean lives, and if you come across them, you're liable to lock them up on principle."

She bristled, feeling unaccountably defensive. "What makes you think I would do any such thing?"

"Inquisitor? It's in your genes."

"I am not limited by my past experiences or by my genetics. I can change."

"Maybe, but you haven't. For instance: I kept your secret regarding your monster of a brother, yet you ran tattling to granddaddy about my intentions the instant we returned from Ficenti."

"What? I don't know what you're referring to."

He shifted around on the couch, stretched out and dropped his head onto the arm cushion. Was he going to take a nap while she stood there?

Finally he muttered a response. "Ferdinand. You blurted out that I'd intended to kill Ferdinand when we found him before I even got a chance to *meet* with Corradeo. But since I'm an honorable, upstanding guy—" she snorted "—I nonetheless chose not to tell him what happened with Kolgo. So who has the moral high ground now, Inquisitor?"

She crossed her arms over her chest in a huff. "You were planning to go against his explicit orders regarding how to neutralize Ferdinand."

"They weren't orders. He's not a dictator."

"But he is your superior—in every conceivable sense of the word, I'll add. You work for him, thus you're expected to do as he says."

"Sometimes. So what about Kolgo?"

"Grandfather did not ask me to bring him back alive."

"Only because you hadn't told him you'd found Kolgo in the first place. Corradeo asked you to seek out the other Inquisitors, didn't he? Quite a fine hair you're splitting there, sweetheart."

She swallowed her instinctual retort and dropped her chin to her chest for several seconds. Eventually, she offered him a weak nod. "You're correct. I'm being hypocritical on this matter. You exercised your own independent discretion on the best way to proceed, and so did I."

Eren swung his legs around and sat up on the couch. "That's awfully big of you."

She huffed a breath, and the words began flowing with surprising ease. "The truth is, I've been struggling over whether or not to tell him about Kolgo. I should, right? But he has so much on his plate, and what happened with Kolgo…it's done. In the past. Door closed. But perhaps I should, anyway. Do you want to accompany me when I do? You were on the mission as well."

He shook his head, easing back onto the couch cushion. "You're missing the point, Nyx. I don't actually think you need to tell him. He trusts you to use your judgment and handle all the ugly messes within your purview, so he can concentrate on doing high and noble work. My point is, he trusts me, too. Maybe you could consider, just *consider*, doing the same."

She found she had no proper response. Trusting this anarch, this wild, half-mad Idoni man, went against everything she'd spent millennia believing. On the other hand, the world she'd inhabited for those millennia had been built on lies and manipulations, hadn't it? Gods, she was *trying*, she truly was.

Possibly taking her silence for a refusal, he tossed a dismissive wave in her direction and stretched back out. "If you'll excuse me, I desperately need a nap. I'll be sure to file a proper report detailing whatever I learn from my contacts—names redacted to protect the mostly innocent."

No closer to an answer on what to do about her ethical dilemma, she nodded mutely and departed. Only once she was halfway to her own residence did she realize that for the first time, he'd called her by her name.

38

CONCORD HQ
COMMAND

The group assembled around the conference table now had a formal title: the Rasu Military Advisory Council. Its purpose was implied in the title: to advise Miriam on the state of the war and how best to conduct it. Many at the table were also actively engaged in the waging of it as well, so much so that she did not expect to get all members gathered in person often after today. Going forward, they would meet where and in whatever manner was available to them as events dictated.

The Tokahe Naataan was the sole member present via holo, as the state of affairs on Ireltse continued to revolve around crisis management and security. Amazingly, he looked none the worse for wear following his brush with the spectre of death—she hurriedly put aside any whimsical thoughts about such experiences. Not the time or place.

Malcolm was here, of course—and at his request, Field Marshal Bastian, on account of the man having seen far more combat time against the Rasu than Malcolm had enjoyed. Pointe-Amiral Thisiame was also in attendance, along with his chief deputy. Casmir sat opposite Miriam, next to Corradeo Praesidis, whom she had invited today for several reasons.

As he was new to Concord, Corradeo needed a crash course in many matters, but the Rasu situation was high on the list. Also, he had served as the Anadens' military supreme commander for hundreds of millennia. He may claim to be long-retired from military service, but the combined combat experience of everyone else at the table totaled a tiny fraction of his own.

Commander Palmer was present as well. Though the Asterions were only Allied Members of Concord, they'd been on the front lines of the Rasu War from the beginning, and their fleet had grown sufficiently formidable that they'd likely be fighting alongside the others in many future battles.

The last person present was David. She'd hesitated about including him, purely due to optics. But he'd played a crucial role in developing their current battlefield strategies for combating the Rasu, especially in her absence, and he continued to contribute insight and ideas. She wanted—needed—to hear his thoughts on what the others said, and she'd daresay they needed to hear his.

The circle was now complete, so she closed the door and brought the meeting to order.

"Thank you all for coming today. First, an update on the situation at Chalmun Station. The Rasu who attacked it have degraded into, as near as we are able to determine without boarding them, a completely nonfunctional state. They have lost engine and weapons power and are drifting in space. The energy signals they are emitting are so low as to be virtually undetectable. We've observed no shifting activity from any of the vessels since six minutes after we fired the Ymyrath Field.

"We will continue to conduct active scanning of the disabled vessels, as well as be on alert for new incursions. If any Rasu come searching for their comrades, I intend to blast the damaged vessels into atoms before they find them. We cannot have other Rasu learning of the nature of our new weapon."

Thisiame clasped his hands together on the table. "What about the weapon itself?"

"Resilient, thanks to robust protective shielding of all components. There was a minimal radiation leak upon firing, but it was contained to the area surrounding the weapon housing. Special Projects is taking steps to further shield the immediate area so no personnel are put at risk. We built most of the components using adiamene, so they remain in good shape. It was, I daresay, a successful proof-of-concept test."

"And Chalmun Station?"

"It will never be habitable again. It's currently in three large pieces, with hundreds of smaller chunks shorn away. All existing tunnels and habitable spaces inside have collapsed."

Malcolm protested. "But they were artificially carved out of the interior. If someone is motivated to do so, they can do the same again inside the pieces."

"And *this* would be the biggest disadvantage of the Ourankeli weapon. The asteroid's remnants are now radioactive. In fact, the radioactive field has dispersed to cover fifty-two square megameters. The area inside the field is not safe to be visited by any organics for longer than a few hours at a time, and then only with Tier 3 shielding."

Malcolm whistled. "That is a bitch of a weapon."

"It is. Obviously, not one we can use when engaged in combat anywhere near inhabited locations. My daughter made an astute observation the other day: the Ourankeli created it as a defensive weapon, but she thinks we must treat it as an offensive one. I agree.

"But even using it in an offensive matter is a consideration for the future. For now, we will continue to monitor the results of its use at Chalmun Station while we conduct additional tests and make iterative improvements in the lab."

She gestured to the holo at one end of the oval table. "Tokahe Naataan, can you update us on the situation in your home system?"

Pinchu kicked back in his chair. "Ah, well. We dug up a couple of Rasu stragglers hiding on the outskirts of the Ireltse capital city yesterday. We blasted them, then melted them, then disintegrated them. I'd like to say this was the last of the buggers, but there's a lot of rubble still to clear away. The good news is, we continue to detect no Rasu presence on Nengllitse, Tapertse or our two space stations. And thank you for continuing to provide patrol and reconnaissance craft support. We will rebuild Ireltse's defense grid, but it will take time."

"No need for thanks. We are here to support each other. It's why Concord exists." She let her gaze pass across everyone to reiterate the point before moving on.

"In the aftermath of these two attacks, the pertinent questions become, where are the Rasu at this moment? Where are they planning to strike next? We've notified all settlements and installations in LMC, including the Ruda, to be on high alert. Our stepped-up monitoring has detected Rasu signatures briefly appearing in four separate uninhabited stellar systems in the Large Magellanic Cloud in the last three days. Our guess is, they arrive in a system, do a brief scan, detect no advanced civilizations, and move on."

"Huh." Commander Palmer wore a frown, though he didn't look up.

"Commander Palmer, you're thinking this deviates from their previous behavior of moving from system to system then galaxy to galaxy, scavenging resources and eliminating any life they happened upon along the way. You're correct, it does. But jumping across five megaparsecs of space to arrive in Concord territory already marked a change in behavior for them." She steepled her hands at her chin. "I think it's a fair conclusion to draw that they now consider Concord an enemy worthy of destroying before they return to their regular raping of this supercluster."

"We knew they were smart."

"Yes, we did. Which is why I submit our greatest challenge right now is tracking them. Predicting where they might emerge next. We are deploying a hundred new long-range sensor buoys every twelve hours to aid in this effort, but I don't have to tell you how vast space is. At this rate, it will take us four years to adequately cover the galaxies comprising Concord territory."

Malcolm's expression grew troubled. "Do you genuinely believe we'll still be fighting the Rasu in four years?"

"I think we have to consider the possibility that this is going to be a long war, yes. Regardless, we will prepare as if it's going to be one. As of today, with all our active forces on alert, we can have a reasonably sized fleet on the scene of an attack thirty-three minutes after Rasu are detected, and a full battle fleet there in under two hours. This is good. But if they are attacking one of our colonies, millions of civilians will be placed in harm's way for those two hours, which means it's not good enough. We need to do better."

"Rift Bubbles?" David asked.

She shrugged, as this decision was mostly out of her hands. "The Senate has finalized an equitable distribution plan for Rift Bubbles as they become available. There are certain safety issues associated with their use, but those are largely a matter for planetary governments to work out. However, with over two thousand colonized worlds and six hundred space stations in play, we should not expect the majority of our habitats to enjoy Rift Bubble protection anytime soon."

Thisiame grumbled under his breath, a rare display of frustration from the Pointe-Amiral. "'Safety issues' is an understatement. Dealing with civilian traffic around an active Rift Bubble is a disaster waiting to happen."

"Not as big a disaster as the population being wiped out by a Rasu armada."

"You obviously don't have our press corps."

She chuckled lightly, and it seemed as if everyone appreciated the levity. "If it's more aggressive than humanity's, I never want to encounter it. The fact is, though I've no doubt our respective governments will request our input on those decisions, the deployment and use of the Rift Bubbles are primarily a civilian matter. Our job is to keep the Rasu away from Concord worlds in the first place. And I'll be honest—I am open to suggestions on how to better accomplish this."

RW

Once the meeting concluded with a long list of action items for everyone in attendance to tackle, she and David returned to her office. When they arrived, she busied herself with reviewing three high priority (but not actually) messages, then with straightening a spotless desk while a new cup of tea brewed.

In the corner of her vision, she noticed David leaning against the small table by the viewports, his arms and legs crossed and his countenance scrupulously blank. Once she held the teacup in her hands, she turned to him. "What?"

"I think the meeting went well, all things considered."

"Well enough, I suppose."

"And Bastian behaved himself."

"He did."

"And Pinchu's looking healthy."

"Exceptionally so."

"And Mr. Praesidis seems to be adjusting to Concord life."

"Thus far."

He moved quickly across the office to reach her, placing a hand on each shoulder. "Then what's wrong?"

"What's wrong?" She laughed a touch bitterly. "Have you seen the Rasu?"

"Not in person, thankfully. Sure, okay, we're facing an enemy hellbent on our extinction. It's not the first time."

"Or even the second." She set the teacup on her desk and dropped her forehead to his chest, only for a breath. "It's not about…I'm not afraid of them. I truly do think I've gotten past the nightmares and the trauma over what happened to me.

"No, this is merely good, old-fashioned war stress. I feel like I'm flying blind, playing whack-a-mole against an enemy that won't stay whacked, while the horde prepping to sweep across us and flatten everything in its path has scarcely begun to crest the hill on the horizon."

"That's because you are."

"I thought this was a pep talk."

"Oh, it is." He kissed her softly. "Custom-crafted especially for you. I will point out how, since Namino, you've won every battle you've waged."

"I know. So why does it feel as if I'm losing?"

"The fog of war can be like that. But you're doing a phenomenal job, so just keep doing what you do best."

"And what is that? Moving ships from one location to another?"

His brow furrowed. She recognized she was being stubbornly resistant to his earnest efforts, but if she couldn't reveal her darkest, most raw self to him, to whom could she?

"Granted, it was one of the *first* things you did best, way back when. And…yes, but not what I meant. You defeated the Kats, when they were Metigens, by bucking both your government and traditional military dogma to work with your enemy while throwing the rulebooks out the window. Or so I've heard. You defeated the Directorate by being a clever, strategic marvel. By striking where it hurt most and yanking its support structures out from underneath it, then by destroying its exposed heart."

She arched an eyebrow. "Literally."

"Quite. Now you're aiming a plethora of technological advances and weapons at this new enemy. You're balancing defense and offense in equal measure, working to protect your side's weaknesses while pushing into theirs. You've assembled a team of brilliant, experienced military advisors at your side, and for once, no politicians or insurrectionists are trying to stab you in the back."

"All true—and thank you for saying so." She forced a smile onto her lips as a reward. "I'm also working with the Asterions and now the Ourankeli, the only survivors of the Rasu we've located so far. Today I command a fleet five hundred times larger than the one I first brought to Amaranthe.

"But you know what? It's a speck of dust compared to the size of the Rasu. They give the locusts of the Bible a bad name. This enemy? It brings its support structures along with it or builds them on the fly out of itself. And I have no idea where or what the Rasu's heart is, or if they have one at all."

He abruptly stepped back, bringing his hands to his chin. "What an excellent point! We should try to find that out."

PART III

FOG OF WAR

39

CONCORD HQ

SPECIAL WARFARE TRAINING CENTER

Her father's office had the most comfortable chairs on HQ, and Alex curled her legs up underneath her and sank into the luxurious cushions.

David tossed her a blueberry muffin, which she caught with one hand. "Fresh out of the oven this morning."

"Mmm." She took a bite and nodded in affirmation. Since she didn't have a drink to wash it down, she talked through the gooeyness. "Whaths uhp?"

"Your mother and I had an insightful, if frustrating, conversation yesterday about the Rasu."

"Every conversation about the Rasu is frustrating."

"True, and doubly so for her. The takeaway was this: we have enough honed weapons and tools now to defeat the Rasu in any reasonable encounter. As I pointed out to her, she's won every battle since Namino."

Alex frowned, the muffin halfway back to her mouth. "The people who were on Chalmun Station might disagree."

"Chalmun Station was not a Concord-affiliated settlement and left itself utterly unprotected. Under those circumstances, the outcome was more favorable than anyone had a right to expect."

She smiled a little, mostly to herself. It was adorable how fiercely protective he was of her mother. "Fair enough. So are we worried about non-reasonable encounters now?"

"Certainly. But in my opinion, Concord will rise to the occasion when those occur as well. I think we can play whack-a-mole, as

Miri phrased it, for as long as the Rasu persist in attacking. We'll hold our ground every time."

"But that isn't victory."

"No, it isn't. You've seen the map." A dozen or more times, but he instantiated the virtual map of the Rasu presence in Laniakea, anyway.

The yellow southern edge now had tendrils creeping down into Concord space, and the Kats had recently updated the enormous red blob of Rasu-controlled territory to extend farther in three directions. "How do we win against an enemy such as this?"

She finished off the muffin and licked her fingers in contemplation. "Well, we…wait, you weren't actually asking me, were you?"

He made a hedging motion. "Not so much, though your input is most welcome. The best answer I've developed is, we learn what makes them tick. We search for where in all this great expanse they're vulnerable. We discover where and what the heart of their civilization is, so we can rip it out."

"Assuming they have one."

"That's what your mother said. But they must have a fundamental weakness. The Asterions insist they're paranoid and prone to self-isolation, so maybe their weakness lies in the joints where they of necessity connect with one another. I don't know. But I do know if we don't find a vulnerability, we're going to be fighting this war for a hundred years."

"You're giving me an assignment, aren't you? You want me to sneak around deep in Rasu territory and see what's behind the curtain."

"If you wouldn't mind?"

"No, it's a good idea. We kind of started to do so when we checked out NGC 55, but then Namino happened, then the Ourankeli, then the war came to us and…. We didn't follow up the way we should have, but we'll rectify the error. One question, though: why isn't Mom the one asking me to do this?"

"Your mother is in London today, and having a miserable time of it, I expect."

"But she knows about your idea?"

"I will tell her we talked when she gets home tonight. I'm consciously trying to not keep things from her any longer, even innocuous things. Probably overdoing it and will eventually get in trouble for that, too. The pendulum swings and all."

An alarm rang in her eVi, and she reluctantly climbed out of the chair. "Caleb, Valkyrie, and I will put together a mission plan in the next day or two. Now, though, I've got to run. Kennedy's asked me to come by one of the Special Projects labs to pitch in on some experiment or other."

RW

SPECIAL PROJECTS

Alex wound her hair up into a sloppy knot as she jogged into the lab a few minutes later. "Okay, I'm here. Why am I here?"

Kennedy had her head buried in a wide screen stuffed with formulas, but glanced over at her proclamation. "Finally."

"Yeah, yeah." She gazed around the lab in surprise. It was somewhat crowded, and not with a bunch of Devon's drones. "Noah. Nika. Dashiel. This isn't a party, is it? My birthday isn't for several months. Neither is yours…or yours…or…." She pointed at Kennedy, then Noah, then arched an eyebrow at Nika.

Nika shook her head. "Asterions don't do birthdays."

"Noted. So why are we…?" The large glass enclosure on the left side of the space belatedly caught her attention. A long, narrow Reor block was suspended inside, and several needle pliers attached to robotic arms hovered near one end of it. "Oh. I see."

She fished her tiny slab out of her pocket and placed it on her palm, then shifted into sidespace. Cosmic strings poured into and out of the larger block, then wound tightly together to pass through one end of her slab and out the other. The strings continued on to dance happily around the space, but most of all to and through Nika and Dashiel. In Nika in particular, they bound up into a brilliant ball of light before continuing on beyond the walls of the lab.

She smiled to herself. "Sublime, every damn time."

Nika stood and came to join her. "Do you mean the kyoseil strings? You can see them?"

"When I'm in sidespace."

"Right. That place I can't access. Thankfully, I don't need to access it to see the kyoseil. Do you also need this slab in order to see it?"

Alex thought on it briefly. Had she ever *tried* to see the strings when it wasn't in her possession? "I'm not certain I know the answer to your question. When I'm not near any Reor, I think they might be so diffuse that I wouldn't necessarily notice them."

"Not true if you're in the Dominion."

"Good point. I'll try it out the next time I visit. Is the Dominion still Rasu-free?"

"So far. We're trying to use the time to gain whatever advantages we can, because they will attack again."

"Seems likely." She thought about what her father had said about the Rasu and the war. He and Nika were both right; until they cut the head off the beast—or ripped its heart out, to go with her father's analogy—the Rasu would never stop.

Kennedy abandoned her formulas to come over and enter a series of commands in the control panel associated with the enclosure. "Is Caleb coming, too?"

"He went to chat with Marlee at her office. He'll be here in a few minutes."

"I'm glad they're getting along now."

"You have no idea how glad I am." Alex took a step back, dropped the slab into her pocket and rubbed her hands together. "All right. We're here to find out if the fact that I was gifted with the encryption key means I can also make the Reor comply with commands, correct?"

Kennedy continued to study the control panel but nodded sharply.

"To what end?"

Her friend gave a full-bodied sigh and glared at her. "For *science*, of course!"

Alex double-checked the settings on the graviton field generator, then the security of the delicate fibers connecting it to the two thin sheets of metamaterial, all while trying to keep her annoyance under control. Gravity plating worked, and everyone knew it. The sheets and generators used to create artificial gravity were mass-produced for commercial, private and military starships on a daily basis. There hadn't been a mystery involved in the process for over two hundred years.

But this was school, *so they had to demonstrate their understanding of the underlying mechanics involved to the professor's satisfaction. Fine, whatever.*

The door to the lab opened, and Kennedy sauntered in carrying a bottle of wine and two crystal goblets.

Alex shot her an amused look. "I'm all for celebrating once we're finished, but I'd prefer a more relaxing locale to do it in than the engineering lab."

Kennedy shook her head as she set the bottle and glasses on the table across from the workbench. "This isn't for celebrating—it's for testing."

"What? We only have to record the gravity measurements at each of the assigned generator strengths."

"I know. But wouldn't a visual representation be cool?"

"If I want a visual representation, I can go walk around on a starship that's traveling through space."

Kennedy groaned. "Has anyone ever told you that you are no fun at all?"

"Yes, you have." Alex rubbed at her face. "Sorry. I just want to get this over and done with and move on to the interesting stuff."

"Hence the visual aids. Since we have to complete the assignment, we're going to make it as interesting as possible." Kennedy opened the bottle and poured the two glasses three-quarters full.

Alex pondered it for a second, then took a long sip of one of them. "Hmm. You brought the good wine."

"I always bring the good wine."

"True." She refilled the glass until it again matched the other one. "I've got the parameters calibrated and everything ready to go. We simply need to turn the generator on and step through the assigned settings."

"Excellent. We should take care to follow the instructions to the letter. You know how Dr. Sampson can be."

"You think?" Alex cocked an eyebrow while she confirmed the polycarbonate enclosure was sealed up. She activated the first control, creating a state of weightlessness inside the enclosure. "Good. Now for 0.3 EG on the bottom sheet."

All she had to do was activate buttons, as the measurements taken were auto-fed and recorded in the attached data storage. Boring.

They proceeded through the settings for 1 EG and 1.5 EG, then switched to the top sheet and repeated the process.

Alex spread her arms wide. "There. Shocker of shockers, gravity plating works precisely like it's supposed to. Izumitel'nyy."

"It is stupendous, because it means now we can get to the fun part."

"Drinking the wine?"

"Not yet." Kennedy adjusted the controls, re-activating the field for the bottom sheet at a 0.2 EG setting. Next, she grabbed one of the wine glasses and opened the small door on the enclosure.

"You're letting out the gravity."

"What does that even mean?" Kennedy eased the glass inside and hurriedly closed the door.

The glass teetered in the air a few centimeters above the bottom sheet. Kennedy decreased the setting to 0.1 EG, and the glass floated erratically toward the center of the enclosure. It gradually tilted to the side, sending droplets of wine spilling over the brim to float alongside it.

"You're spilling the good wine!"

"It's for science." Kennedy gradually increased the setting until the artificially generated gravity reached 1 EG, and the glass settled

onto the bottom surface as droplets splattered across the sheet's protective covering. "Fabulous. Now, one more test." She retrieved the second glass, then reopened the door and held it aloft inside. "Turn on the top sheet, 1 EG."

"You're not going to close the door?"

"It's not as if gravity is going to hurt me."

"Gravity pulling in two different directions just might."

"I think my hand will survive the trauma."

"If you say so." Alex adjusted the controls.

The glass wobbled around in Kennedy's hand, and she giggled. "Feels funny." With some apparent effort, she lifted the glass toward the upper sheet while turning it over in her hand.

The glass abruptly glued itself to the top sheet. For a fraction of a second, wine poured out to slosh around the enclosure; then what was left in the glass pressed in toward the stem, now situated above the liquid.

"Voila!"

Alex nodded approvingly. "Okay, this is pretty cool. But you spilt the good wine all over the lab equipment."

"I told you, it was for science."

"Uh-huh. I hope you have another bottle at the apartment."

"I always have another bottle at the apartment."

Alex made a show of peering around at the shelves and cabinets in the lab. "I don't see any wine goblets."

"Very funny."

"Alas. For science, then. Are we ready?"

Nika touched her shoulder. "That's our cue to vacate the premises so we don't interfere with the test. Dashiel and I will be a few hundred meters away at the gelato shop in the atrium. Message me when it's safe for us to return."

"Will do." Nika and Dashiel exited the lab, leaving her, Kennedy, Noah, and two techs to whom Noah was quietly issuing some instructions. She shrugged at Kennedy. "So what do I do?"

Kennedy gestured to the control panel. "The machine is set up to send the harmonic resonance wave to the Reor. All you need to do is press the button to send it."

"And the goal is for the Reor to let loose of its protection of the kyoseil filaments so the needle pliers can extract them?"

"It is. When I run the machine—when any of multiple humans run the machine—the Reor just sits there giving us a raspberry."

She chuckled at the imagery, glanced around, then unceremoniously reached out and pressed the signal button.

A screen above the enclosure magnified the image of one of the kyoseil filaments encased in the Reor. As they watched, the deep green mineral surrounding the fiber appeared to lose some of its solidity. The kyoseil filament…wiggled? Yes, it clearly wiggled, testing out the limits of its now more spacious suit of armor. One of the needle pliers maneuvered into place and reached out to grasp the tiny end of the filament that had been exposed by the ever-so-slightly melted mineral. It got a hold of it and pulled.

Nothing gave way.

"Send it again."

Alex frowned but complied. The mineral surrounding the filament *definitely* softened further. The plier tugged, and the filament slid out a centimeter or so, then seemed to get stuck again.

She was about to send the signal a third time when the Reor surrounding the filament dissolved into an almost gelatinous state. The plier continued its work, and within a few seconds it had extracted a thirty-centimeter length of kyoseil.

"Am I missing all the fun?"

She spun around as Caleb crossed the lab to sidle up beside her. "Um…." She stared at him for a minute, followed by the Reor slab.

"What? Did I interrupt something?"

She and Kennedy exchanged a squirrelly look. "Is it *you*?"

"Is what me?"

"We were trying to get the Reor to give up its kyoseil prize. For me, it appeared to be considering the possibility but hadn't committed yet. When you walked in, the Reor melted like butter."

Caleb peered at the half-liquified Reor slab in the enclosure.

"That doesn't make any sense. I don't have anything to do with kyoseil."

"You were with me in the Oneiroi Nebula when the mega-Reor colony gave me my slab."

"But you've used the slab plenty of times to read data when I wasn't anywhere nearby."

"True." She ignored the quiet pang of resentment that flared in the back of her mind. It didn't matter whether the Reor had 'chosen' her or not; what mattered was that it had chosen to get involved, and in doing so had tipped the balance of the Directorate War in their favor. "Kennedy, do you have another slab on hand? Can we run the test in the opposite order?"

"Sure." She shot Noah a warm smile. "Honey, can we swap out this Reor slab for a fresh one?"

"We can. I was getting bored, anyway."

"And we can't have that." One of the techs came over to remove the used slab while Noah left to retrieve a fresh sample.

Alex's hand rested briefly at the small of Caleb's back. "I'm going to go grab a lemonade. Kennedy will walk you through the process."

He still looked a little perplexed, but he nodded. "Okay."

She cast a last curious glance back at Caleb, the slab being removed from the enclosure, and the new one Noah and the second tech carried in, then exited the lab.

The gelato shop was to the left, but she went right instead. Until they figured out this puzzle, she didn't particularly want to engage in awkward speculation with Nika. Kyoseil was quite possibly the most confounding intelligence they'd ever encountered, and hours upon hours of *talking* about it hadn't yielded any practical insights.

As she requested a lemonade from the drink station, she mused on what Mesme would have to say, or more likely obfuscate, about the mineral's current behavioral wrinkle. The Kat had always been even more cagey than usual when it came to Reor/kyoseil. Mesme claimed to not be able to converse with the mysterious life form, but it clearly knew a great deal about its nature, having spent millennia nurturing and protecting multiple colonies of it.

She'd barely made a dent in the lemonade when Kennedy pulsed her to tell her she should return straightaway. Curiosity piqued anew, she jogged back down two halls and into the lab.

"I'll be damned!"

At Kennedy's exclamation, she skidded to a stop halfway to the test enclosure. Caleb was staring at the Reor inside, his brow furrowed tight, as the needle plier gently extracted several centimeters of filament.

"What happened? Did it work?"

Kennedy propped her chin on her palm. "Only just now. The whole thing played out the same way it did with you. When Caleb sent the signal, the Reor loosened up and gave a bit, but not enough to extract any of the kyoseil. Then you walked in, and it melted away." Kennedy gestured grandly to the enclosure. "It's as if when one of you is present, the Reor is of a friendly inclination, but remains suspicious. It takes both of you in proximity for it to get comfortable enough to relinquish its prize."

Caleb gave her a playful smile. "We are sort of a matched set these days."

"We definitely are." She went up to him and squeezed his hand, uncomfortably relieved to still be in the game. "I'll let Nika know they can come back in now. We've got results, if not exactly answers—" She cut herself off as an unexpected pulse arrived.

Her grip on Caleb's hand tightened, and he gave her his full attention. "What's wrong?"

"We need to go. Kennedy, tell Nika I'm sorry, but we need to go."

"Has something happened?"

"I'll tell you when I know."

Luckily, after the attack on Chalmun Station, she'd reverse-engineered Devon's passcode to create herself a hopefully permanent backdoor past HQ's security protocols. In less than five seconds, she'd opened a wormhole in the middle of the lab, and she and Caleb hurried through it.

40

EARTH

VANCOUVER

Malcolm slipped unobtrusively past the pedestrian traffic and through the open glass doors of *A Later Latte*. Business was light in the lull between lunch and dinner, and he spotted his contact sitting at the counter along the left wall. He paused long enough to orient his mind to the task at hand, then crossed the café.

"Philippe?"

The man spun around on his stool when he saw Malcolm. "You made it."

Malcolm shook the man's hand and slid onto the stool beside him. "Thank you for agreeing to meet for coffee. I'm afraid my schedule is packed at the moment, and I can only grab a few free minutes here and there, when I'm lucky enough to be planetside at all."

"Of course. You're out there fighting to protect all of us from a terrifying enemy. You have my gratitude, and I appreciate any time you can fit in for the Gardiens."

Beaumont waited while the server took their orders before continuing. "Since you can't attend the meeting tonight, I wanted to touch base with you and see if you had any questions about our mission. I understand if you're not ready to go public with your feelings about regenesis, but a man in your position can wield influence in a number of ways. If I can allay any concerns you have and make it easier for you to support our cause, I'm eager to do so."

Malcolm kept a neutral expression on his face, but it irked him to no end how these people were trying to play him. They could have simply pitched their case in a straightforward, open manner and likely would have found a sympathetic audience. This sale pitch, though, was too smooth by half.

"Whatever my personal qualms, no, I'm not prepared to voice public support for you at this time. I work with several people who have undergone regenesis and—"

"Ah, yes. The Commandant."

"Obviously. Right now, winning the war against the Rasu is my highest priority, and sowing internal discord within the ranks will make achieving victory more difficult. But…" he tried to choose his words with care, though it wasn't one of his best skills "…for personal and religious reasons, I *am* sympathetic to the Gardiens' cause, at least in principle. I suppose I'm still at the 'am interested in knowing more' stage. If I can get comfortable with your goals and your chosen methods to achieve them, perhaps in the future I can…introduce you to people who can help. Open some doors for you."

Beaumont's eyes lit up in delight, highlighting their artificiality, and the man may need to wipe a little drool off his mouth soon. "Absolutely. I'll have someone prepare an information packet specifically for you—it will contain a lot of information we don't give out to regular members. Then, after you review it, I can try to arrange a meeting with several of our local leaders. If you'd be amenable to such a meeting?"

The server arrived with their coffees, giving him a second to construct an appropriate response. He needed to be encouraging, but not too eager.

"I appreciate you making an extra effort on my behalf. Your openness itself is reassuring. Send me the packet, and we'll go from there. It might be a few days before I can give it the time it deserves, so don't take my silence for rejection." He snapped the travel lid on the coffee he hadn't touched. "Now, I apologize for cutting this so short, but the politicians are waiting."

"And then the Rasu. I understand." Beaumont stood and offered his hand.

As Malcolm shook it again, he pretended to get jostled by a man passing the counter. His grip slipped enough for him to affix a tiny listener dot to the inside of Beaumont's sleeve.

"Good luck with the meeting tonight." He grabbed his coffee and strode out of the cafe.

RW

Malcolm was getting out of the shower when his eVi alerted him to the arrival of a substantial quantity of data from the listener dot. He was surprised; he'd intended for it to record the Gardiens meeting tonight and any potential discussions among the leadership afterward.

He had a working dinner with Miriam and several high-level EA politicians in London this evening, so he set the playback to run while he retrieved his uniform and began getting dressed.

"The meeting with our recruit today went well enough, I think. He's playing coy, which is understandable, given his position. I promised to send him some material that should set the hook and whet his appetite for all we can offer."

"I'll see to it the information is massaged for maximum benefit. Get it to him, and then we'll wait. We can dance this dance as long as is needed."

Malcolm groaned. He'd known he was being played, but it stung to have it confirmed. Did they believe him so gullible? What manner of fool did they take him for?

He recognized the second voice as the man on holo after the meeting he'd attended. This one seemed to be in charge, at a minimum of the Gardiens' Earth branch.

"Is our man in London in place and ready to go?"

His hands stopped with his jacket half-fastened. London?

Beaumont answered. *"Yes, sir. The target is meeting in a closed-door session with the Assembly Armed Forces Committee this afternoon London time, then attending a private working dinner with the Committee Chairman, the EA Defense Secretary and—"* and him *"—the Fleet*

Admiral at a restaurant in the St. James neighborhood. Research into her habits indicates a high likelihood that she will walk from the Assembly to the restaurant."

"Unaccompanied?"

"She values her independence, as well as regular spans of solitude. Our man will be positioned to hit her during the walk, but if for some reason she deviates from the expected behavior, he'll be able to intercept her when she enters or departs the restaurant."

"This plan leaves a lot to chance."

Beaumont stammered. *"Ah—our man is quite talented."*

"I'm certain he is. Nonetheless, remind him that no matter what, this cannot *look like an assassination. If her death presents as anything other than a neurological system failure, it will hurt our mission rather than help it. We need to call into question the safety of regenesis, not produce yet another success story."*

"Yes, sir. I'll reiterate the parameters to our man immediately."

"Do it. We'll talk again later tonight, after it's done."

Malcolm had abandoned all attempts at dressing to pace in agitation around his bedroom. The 'target' had to be Miriam, if only because she was the sole person both testifying before the Armed Forces Committee today and attending the dinner tonight. And a Gardiens hitman was planning to assassinate her on the street, in such a way that didn't suggest assassination. If the intent was to cast doubt on the safety of regenesis, they'd probably use a laced dart to mimic a stroke or neural seizure of some kind.

He checked the time. He'd planned to arrive in London just before the dinner, and the clock was ticking fast. Miriam was already locked in the top-secret Committee meeting at the Assembly. He should alert Assembly Security and ensure she was taken to a secure location when the meeting concluded.

But how did the Gardiens know about the meeting at all? Its mere existence was classified, and the protocols kept it off both public and private schedules. Did they have a plant in the Assembly, possibly even on the Committee? Or inside Assembly Security itself? It would be almost impossible for the Gardiens to have learned of the meeting otherwise.

Who could he trust, and who could move fast enough to prevent the hit?

It felt like a battlefield decision, and he made it with concomitant speed. *He* could move fast enough; he'd worry about the rest later.

He hastily finished fastening his uniform, threw some additional clothes in a backpack and rushed out the door.

LONDON

The Caeles Prism from AEGIS Earth Headquarters deposited Malcolm in the Dignitary Suite on the Assembly grounds. He returned several salutes, allowed himself to be scanned by security, then exited into the towering hallways of the ancient building.

He entered the first lavatory he came to and locked himself in a stall. Out came the extra clothes he'd packed: navy running pants, a dark gray hooded sweatshirt and running shoes. He hurriedly changed, cringing as he stuffed his dress uniform into the backpack. Hopefully the home steamer would get the mess of wrinkles out later. It was definitely no longer appropriate attire for a formal dinner, but he was also no longer expecting to attend any such dinner. He hadn't commed ahead to cancel, though, since he still didn't know whom to trust. He'd send his apologies later.

He pulled the hood up over his head and exited the lavatory, then headed straight for the entrance. His rapid pace and the hood meant that no one got a close enough look to identify him, and in ninety seconds he was outside.

He started jogging, which was entirely in character with his appearance and also necessary because time was incredibly short. If the schedule had held, the Committee meeting ended ten minutes ago and Miriam would be on her way to the restaurant. But when did Committee meetings ever wrap up on time?

Pedestrian traffic was heavy on Parliament Street, so much so that he almost missed Miriam exiting the ornate gates marking the Assembly grounds and entering the flow of people.

He jostled his way through the passersby to catch up to her, while trying not to draw attention to himself. The benefit of his attire was that to any onlooker or potential tail, he was just a regular guy out for a jog. The downside was that, without the trappings of his office on display, no one was inclined to get out of his way!

He grumbled in frustration and risked a faster pace to close the distance until he got within half a block of Miriam. Then he slowed to match the flow of traffic, plus about five percent.

But only another half-kilometer remained to the restaurant; he had to reach her now. He focused on the ebb and flow of the pedestrians, slipping forward as unobtrusively as possible, all while scanning the surrounding rooftops and windows for snipers. Tactically, this was a nightmare scenario, for dozens of accessible vantage points decorated the landscape in every direction.

Finally he drew close enough to reach her. Without knowing where the sniper was located, he settled for blocking her back and the road-facing side of her body as he leaned in close. "Keep walking. Someone's trying to assassinate you."

Her gait hitched for half a step but no more, and she didn't turn around, instead identifying him on voice alone. "Malcolm?"

"Yes. Take the next left—here. Quickly."

They both veered down a smaller side street. "Keep going. Next left again."

He wanted to relax now that they were out of line-of-sight of the main thoroughfare, but they were so very far from safety.

As they took the next left, a reflection on his right shoulder caught his attention. A long, tiny needle had bisected the loose material of his hood. He carefully reached up and pinched the shaft between two fingertips—the needle disintegrated into fine dust and vanished. Dammit!

No one was visible on Warwick House, and Miriam pulled up short and pivoted to him. "Malcolm, I order you to tell me what is going on this instant."

"As soon as we're out of harm's way. I promise." The next part of the plan had started to coalesce in his subconscious as he'd traversed the streets, and he sent a pulse.

Alex, I need an emergency wormhole exit. London, St. James neighborhood, near Pall Mall and Warwick House.

What? Why?

Your mother's in danger, and we need to get out of London. Please, now.

41

EARTH

In the narrow space between two buildings, the air shimmered and tore apart, and Alex and Caleb stepped through the tear onto the London street. Alex didn't so much as glance at Malcolm; her focus went straight to her mother. "Mom, are you all right?"

"I'm fine." Miriam shot Malcolm a steely glare, and he tried not to wilt beneath it. "I still don't know what's happening here, which is a situation that needs to be rectified immediately."

"As I said, as soon as we reach a secure location, I'll explain everything." *Or what I know, which is nothing.* He checked the wormhole, where on the other side waited the pristine metal and glass of a Concord lab. "Not to HQ, though. We need somewhere private."

"We'll go to Mom's house." Alex flicked her hand; the wormhole closed, and an instant later, a new one replaced it. The sage green of conifers solidified through the forming tear, and as soon as it was wide enough, Malcolm propelled everyone through the opening with as much dignity as the situation allowed.

He breathed a weighty sigh of relief when the wormhole closed and the soothing breeze of the British Columbia mountains enveloped them.

David appeared at the front door of the house, wiping his hands on a dishrag. "Miri? Alex? What's going on?"

Miriam's expression would instill healthy terror in any God-fearing Marine, including Malcolm. It was possible he'd pushed her a hair too far, but he hadn't had a choice. She started taking off her uniform jacket as she stomped up the stairs to the porch. "Let's all go inside, and I daresay we'll finally get to find out."

Malcolm grabbed Alex by the arm before she followed her mother up the stairs. "Can you get Richard here? He needs to hear everything I have to say."

"Okay." Her countenance was guarded, but he knew her well enough to see the burgeoning concern beneath it. "We'll meet you inside." She moved back a meter and opened another wormhole, then stepped through it.

Next, he got Caleb's attention. "Listen, as soon as Alex returns, I need you to return to where we were in London. An assassin was sent to take out Miriam somewhere between the Assembly grounds and the restaurant where we were scheduled to have dinner at Waterloo Place. Before the trail gets cold, see if you can find any evidence the shooter might have left behind."

Marano regarded him with a touch of frustration. "That's not much to work with."

"I'm sorry. Um, they fired a needle dart, not a laser or a slug. It hit me instead and got caught in my hood, which means it probably was fired from…" he cast his mind back to the scene, but without knowing precisely *when* the dart had embedded itself in his hood, he could only speculate about its source "…I can't say with any confidence. But they knew the route she'd be taking from the Assembly to the restaurant and planned to hit her as she walked the streets."

"All right. I'm on it." Caleb jerked his head toward the house. "You had better get in there and start talking, before Miriam demotes you to corporal."

"She can't actually do that."

"Want to bet?"

"Good point." Malcolm vaulted up the steps and inside to find David half-hugging Miriam, half-feeling around her torso for wounds.

They both spun toward him as he entered, and Miriam stepped out of her husband's embrace to place her hands on her hips. "Talk, Fleet Admiral."

Uh-oh. She normally called him 'Malcolm' in informal

situations. He held up a hand, pleading for clemency. "As soon as Richard arrives. Alex is retrieving him now."

David shot him a warning look over Miriam's head. "I'll make some tea."

Miriam's jaw worked, as though she was forcibly holding at bay a righteous tirade, which she almost certainly was. "Thank you, David."

Alex burst through the door then, Richard in tow behind her, and Malcolm smiled for the first time. "Richard, I appreciate you leaping into action. Why don't we all have a seat and take a breath?"

Miriam scowled yet more darkly. "Where did Caleb go?"

"To investigate the crime scene." He motioned to the table. "Please?"

Miriam's gaze never left him as she took a seat, a sure sign he'd reached the frayed end of the rope she'd lent him. He sat opposite her; Richard took the seat at the end, and David brought the tea to the table then sat next to Miriam. Alex threw herself against the kitchen counter and crossed her arms over her chest, her eyes locking on her mother.

Richard touched Miriam's arm. "Are you okay?"

"I remain *fine*. Apparently, thanks to the Fleet Admiral, though I'm at a loss of how exactly this came to be."

Richard shifted toward him. "What happened? Why were you there—you know what? Why don't you start at the beginning."

Malcolm belatedly remembered to push the hood of his sweatshirt down to his shoulders. "The beginning. A week ago, I was approached in a bar by a man representing the Gardiens. Has everyone heard of the organization?"

David snorted. "Radicals trying to outlaw the best thing to happen to humanity in centuries."

Alex shrugged, and the others nodded, so he continued. "The man—he introduced himself as 'Philippe Beaumont,' but I have no idea if that's his real name—knew about the Oversight Board's 'recommendation' to me regarding regenesis, which instantly set off red flags in my mind. Wait, you all don't know about that development, either."

Miriam's lips pursed. "I do."

"Oh." Her expression didn't give away whether she'd advocated for or against it, and now wasn't the time to ask. "In short, the Oversight Board has been pressuring me to revoke the 'no regenesis' clause in my will. They're not making mandatory regenesis an official policy for high-ranking officers yet, but they strongly implied that's the direction they're leaning. Anyway, Beaumont knew of it mere hours after I met with the Board."

"So the Gardiens have someone on the inside at AEGIS Central Command."

He tilted his head at Richard. "They have someone on the inside at a lot of places, I fear, but I'll get to that. Beaumont smoothly delivered a set of Gardiens talking points that, frankly, in the moment, I was receptive to hearing. He invited me to one of their meetings in Seattle that evening, and...I went."

Alex's eyes narrowed at him, but no one spoke up to chastise him. "The meeting itself was nothing too concerning. Mostly your standard community activism, with heartstring stories and earnest, rah-rah affirmations. The Gardiens put on a good show, though. They're not amateurs at this game.

"Because I was mildly suspicious going in, I placed a surveillance device on the wall when I left, and it recorded the organizers talking to a man via holocomm after the meeting. Based on the way they deferred to him, the man seemed to be in charge. He made references to their future plans, but didn't share specifics. They also briefly discussed me, and it became obvious they'd specifically targeted me for recruitment. Not a surprise, I suppose."

Miriam gripped her teacup so tightly her knuckles were turning white. "What does this have to do with me?"

"A lot, it turns out. Richard, I was planning to come discuss all this with you as soon as I got a minute. But Rasu. Battles. Meetings. Then, this morning, I received an invitation to another Gardiens meeting. I couldn't attend thanks to the dinner in London, so I arranged to meet with my handler one-on-one. I expressed enough interest to keep Beaumont on the hook, then planted a listener on his shirt. Not long after we parted ways, it recorded…well, I'll just play the recording for you."

He instantiated an aural and started the audio playing. Since he'd heard it before, he instead watched the others, noting the instant each of them put together the same pieces he had. Except for Alex—she simply stared at her mother, a quiet fury bleeding out of her bright platinum eyes. It seemed she'd grown quite protective of Miriam since her mother's death and rebirth.

When the recording ended, Miriam's shoulders slumped a little as she set the teacup on the table and brought a hand to her chin. She didn't say anything.

"Like all of you, I realized Miriam must be the target. Luckily, they'd detailed enough of the mission plan for me to act. I high-tailed it to London, disguised—" he flicked a finger at his hood "—and reached her seconds before the assassin took his shot. We ducked off the main thoroughfare, and Alex gave us an emergency evac."

David leaned in, keeping one hand on Miriam's back. "*Thank you*, Malcolm."

"Of course. I could do nothing less." He gestured to Richard. "I realize you'd welcome evidence of the assassination attempt. The sniper's needle dart lodged in my hood, but it disintegrated the instant I touched it."

Richard nodded. "It was likely self-dissolving on contact with skin to eliminate any sign of foul play. Perhaps Caleb will get lucky and find something we can use."

Alex grumbled from her position braced against the counter. "Why didn't you contact Assembly Security the instant you realized what was underway?"

Richard answered before he could. "Because there's a security breach in the Assembly. Maybe on the Armed Forces Committee, maybe in Assembly Security itself. Like Malcolm said, it looks as if the Gardiens have someone on the inside at a lot of places."

"What are you going to do about it?" David challenged his friend.

"I'll quietly reach out to a man I trust at SENTRI and have them open a covert investigation. Miriam, I'm assigning two MPs to escort you every time you're in public. I'm also putting two plain-clothes CINT agents on you around the clock."

"Don't be ridiculous. I don't need babysitters. Besides, escorts wouldn't have stopped this assassination attempt."

"But they might be able to stop the next one."

David leaned closer to Miriam. "Unless you want me glued to your ass every waking hour, you'll accept the security detail."

"David, you have work."

"I'll take a leave of absence."

"No. You need to teach the next generation of officers how to fight the Rasu."

"This is more important."

"You are the most stubborn man!" She sighed and waved a hand toward Richard. "Fine. Do it."

"I will." Richard returned his attention to Malcolm. "Do you have the recording of the first meeting? The one with video?"

"I do." He pulled up the file and instantiated a new aural above the table. Everyone watched as the man in the holo joined the meeting organizers and began discussing strategy.

Richard's gaze fixated sharply on the aural. "Can you rewind the recording and focus on the man in the holo?"

"Sure. I imagine you're very interested in who he is. So am I." He started the recording again at the point where the man appeared, running it at half speed while he zoomed in on the holo image until it began to blur—

"Damn. You have got to be kidding me!"

Every head swiveled to Richard. "You know him?"

"I do. His name is Enzio Vilane. He's head of an up-and-coming criminal organization called the Rivinchi cartel. Graham and I have been investigating him, but we didn't have him pegged as a Gardiens agent, which means his shadowy financial machinations are even more extensive than we realized. He—" Richard's hand darted out to touch Malcolm's arm "—Malcolm, he's the man who ordered the attack on Mia when she was living on Pandora."

"What? You mean this is the local gang lord she pissed off? That doesn't make any sense."

"It gets more complicated. He has designs on…oh, *shit*."

He couldn't say as he'd ever heard Richard Navick curse twice in under a minute before. This was bad. "What is it?"

"He's Olivia Montegreu's son."

Malcolm's head spun, and the room with it. The possible implications crowded into his thoughts and jostled one another until he couldn't make heads or tails of anything. "I don't understand. She didn't have a son."

"We don't think she knew of his existence, but an agent was able to swipe a tissue sample, and a genetic test confirmed it. Her lover, Aiden Trieneri, had him conceived using their DNA, then hid the child from her. We—Graham and I—have speculated that Trieneri intended to use the kid as a weapon against her, but she killed Trieneri before he was able to execute on his plan."

His chest felt tight. In his mind, Olivia Montegreu's blood soaked into his hands as he ripped open her spine to retrieve her internal storage. "Richard, if he knows I'm the one who killed her…."

"I don't see how he can. All the details of that mission, even its existence, remain classified six layers deep. Granted, the Gardiens obviously have infiltrated the military and the government, and as a Prevo with substantial resources and funds…it's conceivable. Not likely, though."

"He could be setting me up."

"I doubt it. We haven't been able to gather a great deal of information about Vilane, but all indications are that he's the vindictive sort. See what he tried to do to Mia after she rejected his overtures. If he knows you killed his mother, he'd have already taken his vengeance on you."

The messy, violent scene at Mia's shop replaced the one from Dolos Station in his mind. Vindictive and brutal sounded about right.

"No, the truth is, you're a prize for the Gardiens. Your history with regenesis is more than enough reason for them to try to pull you in."

Dread snaked through his chest as the disjointed pieces started assembling themselves. "He doesn't know who Mia actually is, does he?"

"We don't think so. There's nothing to connect her persona when she was on Pandora with her true identity."

"Nothing except me."

"You think you were seen with her on Pandora?"

"No." He deeply did not want to relive a second of that night, but his mind had other plans. "I mean now. Vilane has no reason to connect the woman he met on Pandora with Mia, but if in doing research on me, he were to seek out information about Mia—" his head jerked toward the kitchen "—Alex, ask her to change her hair. Please. She doesn't have to change it back to the way it was, but if she ends up on a news feed because of her Expo project and he sees the footage, that silver hair will be a dead giveaway."

Alex nodded silently.

"Thank you. Whether he's recruiting me or targeting me, he's definitely watching me. If he sees...." He dropped his head back, closing his eyes, as the aching, deep loneliness he'd felt these last weeks opened up into a chasm. "I can't be seen with Mia. I can't get anywhere near her. Alex, when you talk to her, you can't tell her what I'm involved in here."

"Oh, come on! Why not?"

He turned a weary gaze toward her. "Because then *she'll* insist on getting involved. Maybe not for me. I don't know if...but to prevent Vilane from hurting anyone else. She'll take it upon herself to stop him, and he will kill her for it. He'll kill Meno, and she won't survive it. Please, I'm begging you."

"Ugh." Alex rubbed at her eyes. "You're really pulling at my loyalties here. Fine. I'll keep your secret while somehow convincing her to change her hair. I won't be able to keep her off the news feeds, though, not with all the press coming up for the Expo."

"Do what you can." His focus snapped back to Richard, full of rekindled intensity and determination. "Tell me what I can do to bring this man down."

42

―――――――――

EARTH

LONDON

Pedestrian traffic remained heavy in the St. James neighborhood when Caleb returned. In all likelihood, it never abated much.

He walked the entire route from the restaurant to the Assembly then reversed course, his focus on the windows and rooftops of the surrounding buildings. Encroaching dusk and lengthening shadows make it difficult to scope out potential vantage points, though, and he soon increased the infrared setting on his ocular implant.

Many of the buildings in this neighborhood dated back hundreds of years, and they were crammed up against one another. Windows tended to be small but numerous. The potential staging areas were legion. He pulsed Malcolm.

Where do you think the needle dart caught you? Any way you can narrow the field will help.

On Cockspur, likely between Trafalgar Square and Warwick House.

One more block to the west. He reached the intersection with Springs Gardens and turned in a slow circle, his gaze elevated...*there.* An eight-story building situated on the opposite corner. On the sixth floor, a window sat open. It was a chilly, damp evening, as was typical for London this time of year, and no other windows in the building were cracked.

He jogged across the street and surveyed the main entrance briefly, then took the adjacent alley instead. Along the back of the building, an ancient metal fire escape wound up the brick façade, intersecting with an emergency exit on each floor.

The would-be assassin's choice of exit route depended on what kind of person they were and how they'd been trained. An amateur freelancer would take the interior stairs and rush out the front door. So would a true professional assassin-for-hire, except for the rushing. A military sniper—ex-military, most likely, but this was a high-stakes game and he didn't want to assume—would take the fire exit, to minimize contact with civilians and avoid being seen and remembered.

He grabbed the first rung of the fire escape ladder and began climbing. The clangs of the metal, loose in its frame, blended into the ambient noise of the London evening.

This location's aromas are strange and off-putting.

He chuckled quietly. *It's an old city. Humanity's history is embedded in every brick and cobblestone.*

And Humanity's odors.

Yes. And those.

One of his hands slipped as a loose rung broke free of the frame. He stopped and inspected the dangling rung. Barely visible in the waning light, a single charcoal thread hung off the broken metal.

If a person was headed down the ladder, it would be easy for a pants cuff to catch on the jagged edge. He didn't exactly have forensic gloves or evidence bags, so he settled for unwinding the thread from the metal and sticking it in his pocket, then continued up.

You should know that your mystifying Khokteh friend has grown agitated.

Oh? He paused, closed his eyes, and opened himself up to what Akeso was experiencing—and immediately sensed the racing pulse and flood of adrenaline from *other*. He sent a message.

Pinchu, is everything all right?

Is your incomprehensible planetary companion tattling on me? I am fine. We've discovered some new Rasu trouble on Nengllitse is all.

Understood. Be safe.

He resumed climbing the ladder again. *He thinks you odd as well.*

As is appropriate.

The sixth-floor landing led to an ajar door. Two marks for this being the exit route. He stepped inside and found himself in a plain hall with yellowed walls and an old tile floor. The layout of the building that he'd constructed from his visual survey overlayed in his head, and he made his way through several halls to reach the last apartment in the front far-right corner. He passed two people, residents by their demeanor, and nodded polite greetings.

The doors all had modern locks on them, but they were hardly state of the art. The one on the target apartment didn't show obvious signs of being hacked. He pulled out his multitool and affixed it to the entry pad. In less than five seconds, the door slid open.

He let it close behind him, then stood in the entrance and listened. He'd already discovered evidence that the perpetrator had vacated via the fire exit, but he needed to be sure they were gone. Especially because it had been a *long* time since he'd undertaken this manner of investigation. Years of training and practice returned the proper procedures to the forefront of his mind, but he nonetheless proceeded with extra caution.

Silence permeated the apartment, though it was overrun by encroaching sounds from the streets below through the open window.

He cleared every room and closet until he'd confirmed the apartment was empty. The space was devoid of furniture, save for kitchen appliances. Unrented and unoccupied. Had the perpetrator known this and chosen it for that reason, aside from the location?

Finally he moved to the front room and its open window. Surveyed the surroundings. The worn tile flooring made it almost impossible to distinguish any marks on the floor. He knelt a meter back from the open window and took a high-res visual, which could capture far more detail than his eyes could see. Then he pulled up the image in his eVi and zoomed in. Two spots were shinier than the surrounding flooring, as if a layer of dust had been displaced. Knee-width apart.

He also didn't have a fingerprint or DNA kit with him, obviously, so he settled for taking forensic-focused visuals of the windowsill and its raised frame; perhaps a lab could get something from them. The perpetrator had almost certainly worn gloves, but never assume. He checked every surface for additional threads, debris or discarded material.

Nothing, not even any water bottles or energy bar wrappers. He hadn't expected the perpetrator to be so careless, but it would have been a boon.

Satisfied he wasn't disturbing evidence, he dropped to his knees and studied the view out the window. He had an unobstructed view for two blocks to the north and south. The angle was excellent, allowing a target on the sidewalk to be singled out without the surrounding pedestrians providing too much of an impediment. This suggested a reasonable level of preparation and reconnaissance had been conducted ahead of time.

A strip of faded white paint was chipped off along the sill, consistent in size with the bipod on a sniper rifle. The damage was all but unavoidable in an old building like this.

No breeze drifted through the open window, and the air smelled pungent. Thanks to Akeso's gift of heightened senses, his nostrils began to burn from the rank odor of human sweat. Had the assassin been nervous about murdering the most powerful military officer in Concord space? Any sane man should be.

But the smell of sweat did nothing to identify the perpetrator, so he stood with a heavy sigh. He wasn't sure what he'd accomplished here, other than construct the outlines of a profile of the perpetrator, gleaned from their actions.

You are trying to comprehend the mind of a killer?

That's not hard for me to do. They merely have to reveal themselves to me.

He started to leave the apartment…then went into the lavatory instead. He'd checked it on his way in, but only for hiding assassins or overt evidence of the crime committed here. Now, he stood in the doorway and cycled through his ocular implant's spectrum filters, again with forensic settings imposed.

Without them, he'd have never seen the centimeter-long blond hair balanced on the beige toilet. He took a tissue from the counter and carefully wrapped the hair up in it, securing the tissue in one of his pockets.

Training would have drilled any assassin to not use anything at the chosen venue that wasn't essential to the mission. But sometimes nature was insistent.

Feeling considerably better about what he'd accomplished now, he left the apartment, closing the door again behind him, and headed down the hall. On the landing, he ran across a woman in ratty, ill-fitting clothes and gave her an ingratiating smile. "Hi, excuse me. Do you know if anyone is staying in the apartment at the end of the hall? I was supposed to meet someone there, but I might have jotted down the wrong apartment number."

"Nah. Place has been empty for almost a year. T'isn't the nicest building in the neighborhood, you know, so there's not much of a waiting list. Heh. You could check with the rental office, though. The address is posted downstairs by the mail slots."

"I'll do that, thank you." He headed down the stairs, taking in the environs and keeping an eye out for any additional clues, though he didn't expect to find anything. When he passed the mail slots, he noted the rental office's address. He'd pass it along to Richard for further inquiry, but all evidence indicated the perpetrator had broken into an apartment known to be unoccupied and come and gone in a matter of minutes.

A fine mist of cool rain greeted him when he stepped outside. It wasn't heavy enough to deploy a rainshade, so he drew his jacket in tighter and walked a block east, then ducked into an alley.

Alex, I'm done here.

A wormhole opened up behind him a few seconds later, and he walked through onto the front porch of Miriam and David's home.

GREATER VANCOUVER

Alex embraced him, stark worry lines cutting into her exquisite features. "What did you find?"

"Where the sniper took their shot from, and a few clues that may help us identify them. Come on, I'll fill everyone in."

Caleb found everyone sitting at the kitchen table, where they all looked up at him expectantly. "I located the staging point and took some visuals. The assassin was a professional and didn't leave behind much evidence—but they did leave a little."

He retrieved the thread and the tissue with the hair, and laid both out in front of Richard. "See what you can get from those. Hopefully DNA, possibly a source for the clothing."

Richard slid them over to the side, where they wouldn't get accidentally bumped. "Excellent work. What else did you learn?"

"I suspect the perpetrator is ex-military, and the organization they work for is connected enough to be able to access London property and rental records."

Richard nodded thoughtfully. "Basis?"

What, was he some rookie intel agent? "While the perpetrator made mistakes in leaving this minimal evidence behind, they did a reasonably thorough job of concealing signs of their presence. Also, they used the exterior fire escape to leave. A true assassin-for-hire would have calmly and methodically erased every trace of their existence, then made certain they didn't act in any way out of the ordinary, which would include exiting out the front door. A military-trained sniper, however? While they wouldn't be sloppy, they'd primarily be concerned with getting away from the scene clean."

"And the records?"

"They used a vacant apartment with a standard-issue door lock in a run-down building. The apartment had a perfect view and an exceptional angle for taking a shot without endangering pedestrians. The location was not a spur-of-the-moment choice. I'm passing you the address and the rental office contact information. Maybe they got an inquiry in the last few days."

"I'll look into it."

He turned toward Miriam. "I hate to briefly change the subject, but Miriam, you need to know that the Khokteh have uncovered some Rasu on Nengllitse. Pinchu claims they've taken care of it, but...."

"But where there's a few Rasu, there might be more, and Pinchu is always loathe to ask for assistance." She frowned. "And you know this before I do how?"

"Akeso sensed a heightened level of anxiety in Pinchu, so I reached out to him."

She shook her head wryly. "I see. If you'll excuse me, I should check in with the Tokahe Naataan."

Caleb watched Alex watch her mother until she'd vanished down the hall. She looked strained; everyone in the kitchen did. "What did I miss?"

Alex came over and rested her forehead on his shoulder. "Oh, just another well-funded conspiracy by criminals masquerading as proper citizens to bring down the pillars of human civilization, starting with my mother. You know, the usual."

43

EARTH

PARIS
NANTERRE CONFINEMENT FACILITY

Prison security patted Miriam down under the watchful eye of the two CINT agents comprising her brand-new protection detail. Richard had wasted no time in materializing them at her side this morning. Thus far they were both professional and virtually silent, which she appreciated, though their exemplary behavior did nothing to ease her irritation at their presence.

The confab around the kitchen table had gone on for hours last night; David had cooked dinner while everyone shared what they knew and strategized about how to move forward against the Gardiens. By the end of the night, Malcolm had insisted on signing up for a dangerous course of action. She'd prefer if he hadn't, as she didn't relish the possibility of losing her Fleet Admiral for the second time in three months, but Vilane's infringement upon both his personal and professional life had lit a fire under the man. Richard was circling back with Director Delavasi to add the Gardiens to the list of enterprises they needed to link to Enzio Vilane.

This morning, she'd taken it upon herself to help matters along a little in that regard. As a result, she now found herself at a place she deeply did not wish to be.

"Apologies, Commandant, but you'll have to leave your Daemon and blade in our custody while you're visiting the prisoner. No weapons of any kind are allowed inside."

"I understand. Can I assume you'll be monitoring the interaction and will come to my rescue if she hits me over the head with a large, blunt object?"

"She shouldn't have access to any large, blunt objects."

Miriam stared expectantly at the security officer.

"Yes, ma'am. We will."

"Very well, then." She nodded perfunctorily, unlatched her weapons and set them on the table.

The officer took the weapons and stashed them in a locked cabinet. "You can go in whenever you're ready. Simply press the button by the door when you want to leave."

'Ready' for this conversation wasn't something she was liable to ever be. But duty and thoroughness—and a simmering annoyance at the Gardiens trying to make an unwilling martyr of her—required that she have it, so she strode up to the heavy door. A second officer entered a code, and the door slid open. Miriam stepped through, noting the sense of *heaviness* as the door thudded shut behind her, locking her inside.

Pamela Winslow sat at an ornate, faux-marble table, sipping a hot beverage out of a faux-china cup. She wore an expensive beige silk pantsuit, and her hair was swept into a perfect french knot.

The former Prime Minister's cold, ponderous gaze settled on Miriam. "Well, this is a visit I never expected would come to pass."

"Nor did I." Fifteen years ago, Winslow and her son had used the combined power of the office of the Prime Minister and the Order of the True Sentients terrorist group to not merely criminalize Prevos but hunt them down, forcing Miriam to rebel against her own government. She had won the day, albeit with a great deal of help from honorable people, but it had been a near thing.

Miriam stopped three meters from the table and shifted into parade rest. At the far end of the room, reinforced windows looked out over downtown Paris and, far in the distance, the Eiffel Tower. "But I have some questions for you."

Pamela sighed. "I don't...care."

"Nonetheless. I need to know the identities of the largest donors who funded OTS—and by extension your—activities. The private, secret donors who never made it into any record and were never investigated by the authorities."

"There aren't any. The police investigation was very thorough."

"I'm certain it was. But there *were* some who escaped notice. People and organizations powerful enough to, when it all came crashing down, obscure their tracks or manufacture exculpatory evidence."

"Why do you want to know?"

"A new group calling themselves the Gardiens is escalating—"

"Oh, I know all about them. I am afforded the news feeds in my oh-so-gilded prison." Pamela stood and wandered over to a hutch by the wall to refill her cup. "But I don't see the relation. The Gardiens espouse polar opposite beliefs from OTS."

"The Gardiens are against regenesis. They claim it is an unnatural usurpation of human nature. I'd say that's quite similar to OTS' creed."

"The Gardiens are against regenesis for *unaltered* humans. They have no problem with Prevos returning to life again and again. In fact, I daresay their true agenda is the ascension of Prevos as the ultimate power in human society. Don't you know this?"

In fact, they'd speculated as to whether this could be the Gardiens' hidden goal during their hours at the kitchen table, thanks to the insights Malcolm had provided. "I do. But how do you?"

"Oh, a lot of whispers reach me in here despite the impermeable walls. Also, as I indicated, I watch the news, and if you pay an iota of attention, it becomes quite obvious."

"Quite obvious to someone who's well-schooled in the way conspiracies operate, you mean."

Pamela lifted her shoulders in a delicate shrug.

"Nonetheless, I posit that it doesn't matter what the Gardiens intend. For the donors to whom I'm referring, power is always the ultimate goal, not principles. They will hitch a small chunk of their fortunes to any group they believe stands a chance to succeed in upending the status quo. OTS, Gardiens—it doesn't matter so long as they're holding the keys to the castles of power when the dust clears."

"True enough." Pamela drew a fingertip along the rim of her cup. "But there is nothing 'status quo' about regenesis."

"At the rate regenesis clinics are opening up, there will be within the year. The Gardiens have to move fast if they expect to turn the tide, and to do so they need money. Hence my inquiry."

"Why didn't you send one of your investigators to question me? Why come yourself?"

Miriam had asked herself the same question on the ride up the lift, when she'd wanted badly to reverse course and retreat to the comfort of HQ. "Because I choose to believe that, misguided though you were, once upon a time you loved the Alliance and its people. You tried to do what you believed was the right thing for them." *You murdered good people and trampled the rule of law to do it, but self-delusion is a powerful drug.*

"So you're appealing to my sense of patriotism and honor? Truly?"

Miriam almost spun around and walked out then…but this was bigger than either of them. "Yes. Regardless of where you stand on regenesis, you must recognize that the Gardiens will not only pitch our society into violent, bloody turmoil, they will do it at a time when we most need to be strong. Strong within AEGIS, strong across Concord, strong against the Rasu. The Gardiens aim to deny people the right to choose whether to live or die. They would send us backward at a time when we have to move forward if we want to survive as a species."

"Oh, enough with your speeches, Miriam! They've always been insufferable." Pamela placed the cup on the table and went to stare pensively out the windows. After twenty seconds or so of silence, the woman returned to the table and her drink.

"What will you give me if I share names?"

Miriam squelched a smile; if the woman detected a hint of gloating, she might well refuse to cooperate on petulance alone. "I don't control your confinement, but I can recommend that you be granted greater privileges. What is it you wish to enjoy? Dinner out once a month? Additional family visits?"

"My husband divorced me after my conviction. My son is dead, thanks to you. Family visits ring rather hollow for me." She reached down and fondled a fork located in the place setting where she'd sat earlier. "It looks like silver, doesn't it? It's rubber. The table and chairs are welded to the floor. The glass, unbreakable—even the mirrors. I can only communicate with a small list of approved persons, and those communications are recorded and reviewed. There's a lawn outside I can visit for 'exercise and fresh air' once a day, under armed guard and otherwise alone."

"Many inmates who committed far less serious crimes than you suffer in far worse conditions."

"I *don't care*. This is my life, and it is a miserable farce. So you see, Miriam, there is no bargaining chip you can offer me. Except for my freedom, and I assume that is off the table."

"It is."

"Alas."

"Give me the names anyway. If any of the people who supported OTS are now helping to support the Gardiens, they are betraying the—" she nearly choked on the words, but somehow managed to shove them off her tongue "—spirit and memory of what your son fought for. They are feckless and unprincipled, willing to sell their souls to the highest bidder. Wouldn't you like a little revenge for how they abandoned you and your son when the bill came due?"

"Pedantic speeches aside, your diplomatic skills have improved a great deal in your time with Concord. Your words almost make sense to me. I cannot deny that a thirst for revenge calls to my heart. It may be the only thing I have left that's worth yearning for."

Pamela sat in her chair and fixated on the table instead of Miriam. "Very well. I will give you a curated list of names—on one condition. If any of them do turn out to be involved in the Gardiens' cause, I want to receive visual footage of their arrest. Their imprisonment and disemboweling if possible."

"I doubt any disembowelings will be occurring."

The woman's gaze jumped up to Miriam. "But if there are."

"If there are, you will be permitted to witness them. You have my word."

"At last, some small entertainment." Pamela stood once more, then went to a panel on the wall. "I'm only allowed to communicate through entering data here, so you'll have to retrieve the information from the guards."

"That's fine." Try as she might, Miriam could not bring herself to vocalize a thanks, so she merely turned on a heel, strode to the door, and activated the button.

Her shoulders sagged in relief when the door closed behind her, sealing Pamela Winslow on the other side.

"Commandant? Here's the information the inmate relayed."

She looked over to see one of the security officers holding out a thin film. She took it from him, retrieved her weapons and waved her protection detail onward. "Let's go."

On the ride down, she opened the contents of the thin film…and groaned. At the top was a simple, succinct message: *Fuck You.*

Same to you, Pamela.

She fought against growing frustration at a wasted trip…then realized there was more to the file. She scrolled until she finally reached additional text. The phrase, '*Oh, fine*' was followed by a list of nine names in total: five individuals and four corporations.

A low whistle made it past her lips. Richard was going to have a field day with this.

44

ARES

ADVOCACY HQ

Nyx strode into her grandfather's office, only to find him at the conference table, deep in conversation with Xanne ela-Kyvern and three new aides she didn't know by sight. A spreadsheet and two organization charts hovered between them, and Xanne was annotating one of the charts as they talked.

It didn't occur to her to excuse herself on account of interrupting them; instead, she dropped into a chair opposite his desk, crossed one leg over the other, and waited patiently.

While she'd been traveling, the staff at the estate-turned-temporary-Advocacy-headquarters had doubled in size. She'd docked here on the estate grounds to avoid the hassle of the spaceport, but it had still taken her an extra ten minutes to land and navigate all the new protocols to secure the *Periplanos* and reach the main building. Ares was bustling as it never had before, and the reason for it was currently sitting at a table a few meters away.

She was genuinely glad her grandfather now had real, and presumably competent, assistance. The support structure growing outward from him like a web of self-replicating nanobots should decrease the burden on his shoulders while increasing his chances of success in this mad endeavor.

But part of her missed the days, approximately yesterday, when she, Lontias and Ziton were the only people of note residing here at the estate. The only people enjoying Corradeo's affection and undivided attention. Hells, she almost missed their years on the *Periplanos*, just the two of them exploring the void.

But the past was the past, and if her grandfather was determined to race purposefully into the future, so was she.

As soon as there was a lull in the discussion, Corradeo shifted his chair toward her. "Nyx, you've returned. Was your trip fruitful?"

"Very much so."

"Excellent. Everyone, let's take a break. We can reconvene after lunch."

Xanne closed the visuals, and she and the other aides departed the office without complaint. Once the door closed behind them, Nyx stood and joined Corradeo at the conference table, pouring herself a glass of water and sitting opposite him.

He bestowed one of his kindest smiles upon her. "I'm sorry you had to wait. The demands upon my time are tripling every hour, it seems."

"Soon, you should be able to delegate a lot of the bureaucratic work. Once you have skilled and trustworthy lieutenants."

"Yes, that is the trick. So, tell me what you learned."

"The governor of Scholite, Giovanni elasson-Kyvern, is not zealously against your new administration. Rather, I'd describe him as wary and a touch suspicious about your intentions."

"Many people are. It's to be expected."

Was it? She'd never been a 'pulse of the people' kind of person. "He and his staff are concerned about new edicts from the Advocacy landing on them without warning. They've run their planet their own way for the last fourteen years, and they're not enthusiastic about having to answer to a new authority.

"The real problem, however, is that the governor is receiving tremendous pressure from a group exerting informal influence over his administration. The group doesn't have an official name, but they've been loudly protesting…in essence, you. They characterize your recent actions as a blatant power grab and insist you have designs on dictatorship."

"This is unfortunate news. If I could only…" Corradeo's hands fisted briefly atop the table "…make such people understand what I'm trying to accomplish here, and how it will benefit everyone."

His voice rose a little toward the end, but he dialed it back down. "Does this group have a leader?"

"It does. A man named Patrici Cabo ela-Diaplas. He owns the largest engineering firm on Scholite and serves on the boards of multiple industry groups in the stellar cluster."

Corradeo studied the table surface silently for several seconds, and she'd long ago learned not to interrupt his contemplations.

Abruptly he nodded to himself. "I would like to speak to this Patrici Cabo. Will you extend my personal invitation for him to visit me here on Ares?"

It wasn't the direction she'd expected him to take, which only proved how much she still had to learn about this 'new' way of doing things. "Yes, sir. I'll return to Scholite straightaway."

SCHOLITE

MILKY WAY GALAXY

Ziton used his connections from his former job at Michanero Production to connect her to the right people, and by the time she arrived in the capital city of Veloa, she had an appointment with her target.

Cabo Construction's headquarters was an atrocity of curved metal and black marble jutting high into the aquamarine sky. This was a Diaplas-dominated planet, and the Scholites were oh-so proud of their engineering marvels.

A secretary showed her into Cabo's office without too much of a wait. The man sported close-cropped, curly blond hair and wore a more utilitarian than fashionable business suit.

He stood from behind his desk and dipped his chin curtly in her direction. "Inquisitor."

She stopped in front of the desk, planted her feet and clasped her hands in front of her. "The 'Inquisitor' title has been retired. It's

Prefect now. Nyx Praesidis."

"Dropping the vaunted 'elasson,' but not adopting your lineage?"

"Praesidis *is* my lineage."

If he was surprised at her genetic credentials, he hid it well. "I see. Then I suspect I know why you're here today. You can tell Corradeo Praesidis that I don't appreciate a political overture being delivered over the barrel of a gun."

She spread her hands wide. "I carry no weapon."

"You are the weapon, and my point stands. So, what are the Advocate's demands?"

"No demands. Merely an invitation to meet with him at his office on Ares to discuss your concerns, in the hope he can assuage them."

"An 'invitation,' is it? Am I allowed to refuse?"

"Of course you are."

"Then I—"

"A word of advice? I don't recommend it. Don't misunderstand me. If you refuse, no agents will show up to put you in your place, kidnap you, demote you or confiscate your wealth. But the Advocacy is our future—the future of all Anadens. The sooner you reorient your thinking to recognize all the benefits it can offer our people, the better off you and the citizens of Scholite will be. Meet with him and listen to what he has to say. I promise, you won't regret it."

The man's brow furrowed. "I suppose I gain nothing by dragging out what is an inevitable confrontation. Fine. I will go to Ares. But I do not anticipate leaving there with my mind changed on any salient point."

"That will be your prerogative."

45

―――――――――

ARES

ADVOCACY HQ

Short jaunts like the one to Scholite and back were becoming a regular feature of her new role, but at least this time Nyx was prepared for the new protocols and cleared them with a minimum of hassle.

Patrici Cabo had insisted on traveling in his own ship, so she had time to shower and change clothes before meeting him at the security entrance to the main building.

His gaze took in the construction around the estate with interest, though his tone remained biting. "Not wasting any time setting up command, is he?"

"Every government needs a place to do its work. Follow me." She accompanied Patrici into her grandfather's office, then took up a position by the door, on guard. She didn't care for the man's arrogance and hostility, and she wanted to keep an eye on him. She'd meant what she'd told the anarch, Eren, during their mission together. However capable Corradeo might be—surely quite capable indeed—she felt an instinctual, inbred need to serve as his guardian. To protect him from the evils that men would do.

Corradeo met Patrici halfway, offering the man a hand and a welcoming smile. "Thank you so much for taking the time to travel here and meet with me. Sometimes, a holo meeting simply can't replace a face-to-face conversation."

Patrici reluctantly shook Corradeo's hand. "I'll listen to what you have to say, but be forewarned. I don't expect to be convinced."

"I accept your terms. And while I'm happy to discuss my plans for the Advocacy with you, I most of all want to hear what *you* have to say. You have concerns, and I want to understand them better, so I can address them in a way that benefits us both."

Ugh, diplomacy was excruciating. All this ass-kissing and soft platitudes! In the old days, Nyx would have dealt with this problem by sending Patrici and all his adherents to a black prison site, like the now-defunct Helix Retention.

She promptly chastised herself for the renegade thought; this was not the way things were done now, and it was a *good* thing. People deserved agency and freedom…most of them.

The two men retired to the conference table, and in seconds they were engaged in a lively back-and-forth on the finer points of local control versus federalism, the benefits and costs of state-sponsored economic initiatives, and the nature and wisdom of various political restrictions.

The words actually spoken didn't particularly interest her, so she paid attention to their body language. Over the course of twenty minutes or so, Patrici's voice lost much of its harsh edge. His shoulders relaxed, and his hands grew animated. Her grandfather's convivial demeanor, however, never deviated from how he began.

Corradeo nodded thoughtfully. "Your point about leveraging the long experience of the people on the ground on our many worlds is well made. I confess I had not fully considered the ramifications of enacting broad policies that don't take into account local…let's call them 'idiosyncrasies.' I'll speak to my advisors this evening about adjusting the first round of proposals to allow for greater flexibility by local governments."

"That's considerate of you, sir. Equally important, though, is keeping as many of the financial decisions—and income flow—in the hands of the governors. The most inspired policy in the galaxy is worth nothing if we have no money to implement it."

"Agreed, but the issues involved in budgeting, taxing and, yes, the dreaded appropriations, are far more complex than the policies themselves. I need to balance local control with consistent messaging and action from the top. You have my word, though, that I will strive to balance them fairly."

Patrici leaned forward, bringing his hands to his chin briefly then laying them flat on the table. "I see your point, but it remains a matter of concern. Until we see detailed legislation out of the Advocacy, I can't recommend to the governor that he hitch his star to your government. But I concede there is value in a 'wait and see' approach. We shouldn't burn the new administration to the ground until you give us a concrete reason to do so. Or, perhaps, don't."

"This is all I can ask for." Corradeo's demeanor shifted, as if something was just occurring to him—which was bullshit. Whatever it was, he'd planned it all along. "You own an engineering firm, do you not?"

"Yes, sir. Cabo Construction."

"Excellent. While I have you here, would you indulge me by taking a quick look at some plans I've had drawn up for a new government complex here on Ares? I want it to represent a cross-section of Anaden architectural styles, but obviously a random hodge-podge of motifs will result in a horror."

Patrici's expression was guarded, as if he suspected a trap. "I can take a few minutes to review it."

"I appreciate it." A sprawling projection appeared above the table, and Corradeo proceeded to explain the various buildings and the thoughts behind their designs. Patrici asked some questions, provided some suggestions and offered many concerted frowns.

Finally Corradeo sank back in his chair and folded his hands in his lap. "Your eye for both style and functionality is impressive. I must confess that I did a little research before you arrived—not into your personal life, but regarding your company's history. You've been responsible for a number of significant and noteworthy projects over the years: the famous Cardonia Gardens in downtown Veloa and the Roson Commercial Shipyard Complex, to name but two. Many in your business concede that Cabo Construction is the best large-scale engineering design company in Anaden space."

"I'm honored they think so."

Corradeo pursed his lips and considered the projection for several seconds. "How would you like to build this complex for me?"

"Excuse me, sir?"

"I've been through three engineering consultants already, all Diaplas *elassons*. Despite hours of discussions, none of them comprehended my intentions, but you intuitively grasped what I'm after in five minutes. I need to be focusing my time on implementing proper governance, on our integration with Concord, and on our war against the Rasu. I also need this complex built. Buildings are symbols, and symbols have power.

"I believe I can entrust you and your company with this project. With my oversight, of course, but I promise to wield a very light touch. I'm willing to pay you four hundred million credits to see it to completion."

Nyx's eyes widened at the gargantuan sum.

"Are you toying with me, sir?"

"I assure you I am not. I have neither the time nor the excess energy for games. I need to get things done—real, concrete, positive things that will benefit all Anadens—and I'm trying to surround myself with people who can make this happen."

"I see. I'll, um, need to discuss it with my board of directors. They're required to approve all contracts of such…" Patrici cleared his throat awkwardly "…scope. But I believe they'll be excited to engage in a project so important to the Anaden people."

"I hope so." Corradeo stood and offered his hand again. "I'll send you a full contract later this evening. The terms are all subject to negotiation, so raise any issues you have, and we'll see if we can come to an agreement. I look forward to a fruitful working relationship."

This time, Patrici shook her grandfather's hand with considerably more warmth. "As do I. Thank you for your time, sir."

An aide arrived to see the man out. When the door had closed behind them, Corradeo tilted his head at her. "Thoughts?"

She huffed an incredulous breath. "You bought him off."

"Yes, I did." He turned and went back to his desk.

"Isn't that a bit unethical?"

"No, it's expedient. I made some progress in talking him off the ledge of rebellion, but I was never going to convince him to drop his opposition to our government today. Words cannot accomplish such a feat—only time and actions can. So I needed to buy time for my actions to convince him, while removing his more vociferous roadblocks until that happens."

She found she couldn't refute the logic. "All right. Are you really going to let him build the Advocacy complex?"

"Absolutely. I meant everything I said about his company. I have complete confidence they'll do an excellent job. As a bonus, it will provide anyone who's watching with real evidence that I was not pontificating when I said *elassons* no longer enjoy a birthright to greatness. A talented and hard-working *ela* can achieve the greatest things, and Patrici Cabo will be a superb example."

She laughed. "Grandfather, you truly are a brilliant…."

"Manipulator?"

"No—well, yes, but I meant strategist. Diplomat, politician, leader. I'm sorry I questioned your intentions."

"Don't be. One reason why you're at my side is to keep me honest. Now, if you don't mind, monitor events on Scholite for a while. Hopefully the rumblings of discontent will soon be dying down."

"I'll keep an eye on things there." She turned to go—

"Nyx? There's one more thing I wanted to discuss with you."

"Oh?"

Corradeo moved to the couch and patted the cushion next to him. "Please, sit with me."

"Of course." She went over and joined him, then clasped her hands over her knee. "What is it?"

His countenance took on a darker, almost troubled tenor. "I want you to tell me about Kolgo."

For half a second, she felt a sensation she hadn't experienced since the night at Helix Retention when Caleb Marano stripped her of her *diati*: fear. But then she reminded herself that this was the man she'd spent fourteen years traveling the stars with. They'd come to care for one another as only family could, and whatever disagreements they might have, he would never burn her at the stake for her failings.

She hoped.

"I…all right." She nodded, if only for her own encouragement. "I located Kolgo on Ficenti several weeks ago. He had set up his own fiefdom in the Mikro-Teln District. Within the neighborhood, he was the sole and absolute authority. Grandfather, he was committing the most vile, depraved acts. Taking prisoners and forcing them to fight against beasts to the death. Raping and drugging women. Staging all manner of blood sport for his amusement. It was horrible."

His expression remained scrupulously devoid of reaction. "And?"

"And I tried to convince him to leave his fiefdom behind and come with me. To renounce this madness he'd descended into and let me help him regain a better path. But he refused. He had no interest whatsoever in changing his behavior or giving up his power. So I poisoned his drink with *apomono*, then I killed him."

Corradeo leaned back into the couch cushion and silently steepled his hands at his chin.

"You already knew, didn't you?"

"I didn't know some of those grislier details, nor precisely how you accomplished it. But I knew he was a violent criminal on Ficenti, and that he's now dead. Permanently, it seems."

She crossed her arms in a huff. "Did Eren tell you?"

"Eren? Ah…this is what the two of you did after you located Ferdinand. I see. I imagine Eren enjoyed the mission on Ficenti more than you did. But no, he didn't betray your trust."

"And you're not upset at him for keeping this from you?"

"Eren keeps many secrets."

"And you let him. Grandfather, why do you cut him so much slack? You treat him as if he's family, rather than the unhinged, irresponsible Idoni *asi* he is."

"Now, Nyx. 'Unhinged' is a bit of an exaggeration, don't you think?"

"Fine, perhaps a bit. But my point stands."

"So it does." Corradeo's gaze drifted toward the window in the back of the office, and something indecipherable passed across his eyes. "I owe him a great deal."

"Yes, because of his work with the anarchs. But there were many anarchs, and they are not all currently living in one of your most spacious suites."

"Not because of what he did for the anarchs, or at least not those—but that's a tale for another day."

She knew all too well the tone his voice had dropped into, and it meant the topic was closed. For now. "Then how did you know about Kolgo?"

"Now that I'm an official head of state, a great deal of information is flowing my way from a great many places. The events on Ficenti caused quite a stir. Will you tell me why you kept all this from me?"

His voice had turned gentle yet firm; it didn't sound like an interrogation. Felt like one, though. "A myriad of reasons. You've had so much going on, and at the time, you were embroiled in a pitched battle to wrest control away from Ferdinand's rebels. You didn't need to be bothered with an Inquisitor gone wrong. Not when I could handle it.

"I also worried that you would have wanted to try to save him—and I understand why. I wanted to save him, very badly. He was my brother. But you have to believe me when I say he was beyond saving. Beyond redemption. So I solved the problem. It is what Inquisitors have always done. I'm sorry if I overstepped my bounds...or betrayed your faith in me."

"It *is* what Inquisitors have always done. Within a few strictures and more humane protocols, it will continue to be what Prefects do. As your grandfather, I thank you for wanting to protect me. But as your Advocate, I must ask you not to keep such things from me again."

As rebukes went, it was far milder than she deserved.

Nonetheless, there was an undercurrent of steel to his voice that suggested she would be wise to take his warning to heart. "I understand, and I promise not to hide troubles from you in the future. I simply didn't want to add to your burdens."

A rare shadow flitted across his features. "Nyx, I ordered the execution of my own son. Whatever burdens fall upon my shoulders, I will manage them."

46

SAGAN

MILKY WAY GALAXY

Marlee wandered into Abigail Canivon's lab at the Druyan Institute with a spring in her step. She and Morgan had totally bonded at Special Projects last week, both before and after the insanity that was the Chalmun Station evacuation. Even better, once Morgan had recovered from her bump on the head, in a fit of righteous indignation over the Rasu attack, she'd moved up the timing of the next test session then invited Marlee to join her for it.

Work had been crazy for the last week, what with trying to help all the evacuees, many of whom didn't *want* to be helped, but she was counting the days.

"—I did what I had to do, Abigail. I knew there were risks involved, but life is about embracing risk. I don't regret my actions."

Marlee's step hitched. But she was already inside, so it was too late to go sneaky and eavesdrop from the shadows. Abigail and Valkyrie—unusually, present in her physical doll—both turned toward her in surprise.

"I'm sorry. I didn't mean to interrupt."

Abigail banished the somewhat harsh countenance she'd been wearing from her features. "Nonsense. You have an appointment. Please, come on in."

Valkyrie smiled brightly. "Marlee, hi. It's good to see you. We were just arguing about my pseudo-death experience on Ireltse."

"We were not arguing. I was merely vocalizing some concerns I have regarding your...."

"Judgment, I believe is the word you're searching for."

Abigail's expression re-hardened a touch. "I wasn't searching for anything. I was holding my tongue. We have an audience."

Marlee held both hands up. "Oh, don't mind me. I'll go over to the workstation and start uploading the files I brought. I did get the details of what happened at Ireltse from Alex, though. Valkyrie, I'd like to hear more from your perspective sometime."

"And I'll be happy to tell you about it, once we're outside of Abigail's earshot. She doesn't want to contemplate the possibility of me dying."

"Having done it myself, I can't recommend the experience."

"But you didn't stay dead, Abigail. Neither did I."

Marlee whistled idly to herself as she made a show of loading her files and entering her custom boot-up sequence while listening in. Valkyrie shut down Abigail's continuing protestations with impressive firmness, and after a minute or so Valkyrie appeared at Marlee's side. "I can't stay today, but let's have lunch soon. I'll come by HQ."

"I'd like that very much."

Valkyrie departed, but another solid minute passed before Abigail arrived at the workstation. "I'm sorry you had to hear our discussion. My own creation can be too confounding by half."

"She's wonderful. You did an incredible job."

"I know, though she has grown so far beyond the initial programming I gifted her with, I can't rightly claim her any longer." Abigail patted at her perfectly arranged, pale ginger hair. "Now, talk to me about what we're reviewing today."

Marlee sorely wanted to delve further into issues of life, death and regenesis, of Artificials, their creators and their agency. But Abigail was obviously both upset and a mite perturbed, so she restrained herself.

She split the data she'd loaded into four screens. "The left three screens summarize my proposed rewrites to my…well, my eVi will be the conduit hub, but what I'm doing here goes well beyond conventional eVi programming. The rightmost screen lists out the physical enhancements I'll need to add to my cybernetics to support the new programming. There are cross-references from the code to the enhancements at critical junctures."

Abigail's eyes scrutinized the displays, and Marlee waited silently…until she couldn't any longer. "I studied how the Anadens design their cybernetics as a starting point. It's mostly ugly and unwieldy, but I did steal a few interesting ideas. A lot more from Prevo code, of course."

Abigail's gaze darted over to her. "How did you get this detailed of a look at Prevo code?"

"Is that a serious question?"

"Apparently not." The woman returned her focus to the displays.

"In particular, the neural graft gets expanded a great deal in order to localize more quantum programming internally. I also took a lot of inspiration from how the Asterions design their bodies. Please don't ask me how I obtained this information, okay? The way they meld organic and synthetic materials into every aspect of their bodies—every organ, every bone, every ligament, every blood vessel—is simply astonishing."

Abigail arched an eyebrow without diverting her attention. "And kyoseil."

"Yes, and kyoseil. I'm not planning to go that far, at least not yet. Also, my bones are already mature. The base cybernetic weaves I have are all I'm going to get. But using nanomachines, I think I can increase the robustness of the biosynth components in my neural infrastructure."

Finally, Abigail shifted her weight to her back leg and brought a hand to her chin. "You did say you wanted to become a Prevo without the need of an Artificial companion."

"Do you think this action plan will accomplish it?"

"I'm not entirely certain *what* it will accomplish." The woman pointed to the neural graft code. "When coupled with the biosynth enhancements you've laid out, this section of the programming is likely to develop emergent properties—properties neither you nor I will be able to predict. Once you take this step, there might not be any coming back from it."

Marlee nodded confidently. "That's the point, though, isn't it? When explorers of old reached new shores, they'd burn their boats so there was no going back. I'm good with burning my boat. Besides, those emergent properties, whatever they turn out to be, will belong to me. Self-directed evolution."

"Which is what the Asterions practice."

"I'd argue that humans are practicing it, too. Even if we weren't quite doing so before, regenesis surely means we are now. I mean, those new bodies people are reborn into include improvements via the newest generation of gene therapy techniques, cybernetics hardware and muscular-skeletal refinements, at a minimum. Don't you agree?"

Abigail shrugged minutely. "I do. The trick now is to ensure we don't transform those improvements into a tyrannical regime, the way the Anadens did."

"This is why the Asterions are a much better model to follow. Each one of them owns their personal evolution."

"So I hear." Abigail gestured to her screens. "I've got several suggestions for areas where you can tighten up the programming to minimize the chance of errors. But I daresay that you are almost ready to go. Or rather, the programming is. Only you can say when you're ready to take this leap."

47

MIRAI

NIKA'S FLAT

Perrin grabbed Nika's hands in hers. "Breakfast was delicious! I have to run. We're opening a new refugee center in Kiyora One this afternoon, and I need to make sure the carpeting and lighting got installed before we open the doors. Talk later?"

"Absolutely. Good luck today."

Nika watched the door close behind Perrin, then went into the living room to straighten up. Her friend was doing so much better now. The impact a few tiny tweaks to her programming had made was incredible.

Yes, the far edges of Perrin's emotional expression had been brought in a touch, and the highs were not quite so high as they'd once been. But the lows also weren't nearly so low, and this was making all the difference. Perrin was *happy*; she was confident, energetic and engaged once again.

She was also doing Administration work on Kiyora, which hadn't escaped Nika's attention. A trial run for an Advisor position? Possibly—

The front door opened unexpectedly, and Nika turned to see Maris Debray sweep into the flat, a flared burgundy coat skimming the floor behind her as she strode down the entry hall.

"Maris? Is something wrong?"

The woman held up a finger in Nika's direction as she made a beeline for the kitchen. She yanked off her coat and tossed it on the counter, then grabbed a glass from the cabinet and poured a brandy. She took a long sip of it as she carried it to one of the couches, where she collapsed upon the cushions and crossed her ankles on the table. "Spencer left me."

Nika blinked. Whatever dramatic declaration she had been expecting, it wasn't this one. Yes, she'd caught them arguing recently, but every couple argued from time to time.

She moved to join Maris on the couch. "I'm so sorry. What happened?"

"He said, 'I can't do this any longer.' I said, 'I don't understand.' He said, 'I know you don't.' Then he squeezed my shoulder, kissed me on the cheek, and walked out."

"That's not a lot to go on."

"Oh, there were other words in between. But it all boils down to…." Maris took a hungry sip of her drink, then dropped it on the table and her head into her hands. "I truly *don't* understand."

"Um…Maris, have you ever been dumped before?"

"What kind of question is that? I'm certain I must have been at some time or other. I don't recall."

"You erased your memories of how your prior relationships ended?"

"Not immediately. But once I was ready to move on? Yes. What would be the point of continuing to suffer senseless heartbreak? Life is for the living."

Well, this explained a lot—most of all how Maris succeeded in flitting from relationship to relationship without ever growing or changing as a result of the time spent with her lovers.

Noting Nika's silence, Maris scowled. "I know what you're thinking, but don't lecture me. Not today. The past is the past, but I need help right now. If I can understand why he left, I can show him why he was wrong to do so."

She had to admire the woman's boundless optimism, if not so much her utter lack of pragmatism. "Okay, let's see. The two of you have been fighting lately, haven't you?"

"About schedules and dinner plans and…daily priorities, I suppose. You're going to say this is an incredibly stressful time for everyone, and especially for a still-new Justice Advisor, and perhaps I wasn't sufficiently sympathetic to or supportive of his needs."

Nika shrugged. "I don't need to say it. You already know."

"But I *was* supportive! I'm confident of it." Maris peered up at Nika from behind splayed fingers and…were those tears? She didn't remember ever seeing her old friend cry before. But unfortunately, she was also missing ninety-nine percent of her memories of their lengthy friendship.

She placed a gentle hand on Maris' shoulder. "You're genuinely upset."

"Clearly I am! My chest hurts, and I can't concentrate on anything for more than a few seconds. My brain is careening around in these frantic circles, but it keeps ending up back at the same place over and over again. And I don't have a clue how to fix any of it."

"Do you love him?"

Maris' brow furrowed. "How would I be able to tell?"

Nika stared at her friend, dumbfounded. "It is not possible that you've never been in love."

"Of *course* I've been in love. Don't be ridiculous. It's only…" Maris wiped at the hint of tears on her cheeks "…sometimes I almost envy you the loss of your memories."

Nika jerked away. "You don't mean that. You *can't*. You have no idea—"

Maris reached out and placed a manicured hand on Nika's knee. "Forgive me. I know how much you've suffered from their loss, and I don't mean to lessen the significance of the wounds this has inflicted on your soul.

"What I'm trying to express is…because you lost them, you can't imagine the sheer *weight* that is a life lived for 700,000 years. In those endless millennia, I've experienced everything, felt *everything,* until I no longer retain any frame of reference for what any of it signifies.

"Which of those feelings were love? Which were hate? Which were despair? Joy? Contentment? They blend together into this tapestry that looks marvelous hanging on the wall, but the threads comprising it have lost whatever significance they once held.

"I've long made it a point to experience each moment of life fully, madly, deeply. It is, after all, the Asterion way. But when every moment is everything, what distinguishes one from another?"

Maris dropped her head back on the couch cushion with a plaintive sigh. "Oh, Nika, I'm afraid I've lost my compass. Worse, I now find myself wondering if I ever had one at all."

OMOIKANE INITIATIVE

After considerably more tears and alcohol, Maris abruptly insisted she needed to work, so they went together to the Omoikane Initiative. Nika got her situated in the Culture Division suite and stocked with chocolate and sweets, then ran a quick alcohol cleansing routine and headed upstairs.

As she stepped into the command center, she took a minute to appreciate how much the Initiative had adapted and evolved since the Rasu War began in earnest. Physically, the top floor had been expanded and transformed to create tactical 'pods' for each of the major areas of concern: military deployment, materials production, refugee evacuation and management, scientific research, weapons development, planetary defenses and so on. The pods all linked into larger topic-specific workspaces situated on the four floors below them. Meanwhile, the far quarter of the space was devoted to Advisor-wide meetings, direction and monitoring of emergency situations (battles, mostly) and instantaneous travel to strategic locations via d-gate.

The people involved had adapted as well, organizing themselves into the most efficient and focused sub-groups, each according to the talents and resources on hand. They developed their own rules, requirements and goals, then set out to tackle their assigned challenges.

Yet another example of why she was proud to be an Asterion,

and Nika basked in the picture it painted.

Dashiel materialized at her side. He'd left the flat early this morning to check on...she didn't actually know. He'd mumbled something vague on his way out the door. "What's got you smiling?"

"Oh, just idle happy thoughts."

"Well, let me add to those." He took her hand and started dragging her toward the pod nearest and dearest to his heart, the one devoted to materials production. It interfaced directly with Ridani Enterprises systems and locations, particularly its labs. "Come see what we've created."

"With pleasure."

At one of the workstations, a schematic floated next to several visuals of a hybrid craft of some kind. *What* kind, she didn't dare guess. "What is it?"

"It's a—" Dashiel's expression flickered, and he hurried over to a blank pane and typed in a series of commands.

"What's wrong?"

"Eh, nothing, probably. One of our freighters shipping kyoseil from Chosek hasn't arrived at the storage warehouse. It's over four hours late." He shrugged, even while frowning at the data that began populating the pane. "Space takes one for its own every so often."

"True." She was about to probe the issue when, in the corner of her vision, she noticed Spencer walking onto the main floor. "Why don't you take a few minutes to investigate further? I need to talk to Spencer about something."

"Sure." He gave her a distracted nod before turning his full attention to the scrolling data.

Nika tried to prepare herself as she strode across the room. She didn't particularly want to have this conversation, but she felt obligated to at least see how he was doing. And who knew? Maybe she'd end up with positive news to cheer up Maris.

Spencer saw her coming ten meters away and held up a hand in warning. "Don't, please."

She closed the rest of the distance anyway. "I'm not going to berate you. I wanted to see how you're holding up and ask if there is anything I can do."

He huffed a breath, acting a little sheepish. "You're not intending to interrogate me on why I ended it? I mean, why would anyone *conceivably* end a relationship with a woman such as her?"

"Because she's a force of nature who can suck you dry of all your intrinsic energy and replace it with her own if you're not careful? A high-maintenance, overly dramatic whirling dervish of pronouncements and passions and adventures. The whiplash alone from entering her orbit would maim most people."

Spencer's left eye twitched, and his lips wavered between a smile and a frown. "Okay, those are reasonable points. She is also utterly amazing. Every minute I spent in her company was singular, and I will never forget a one of them."

She couldn't bring herself to tell him that Maris eventually would, and willfully so. "But?"

He leaned against the closest table, his shoulders sagging. She belatedly noticed that his shirt and pants were wrinkled and his hair unbrushed. He'd had a bad night. "*But*, she sees the world in these grand, sweeping strokes, as if she's always painting a canvas upon reality. Meanwhile, I'm spending my time worrying about catching some low-life criminal or protecting a business from theft or keeping the refugees from clawing each other's eyes out in frustration.

"We view everything so differently. When I'm with her, I feel myself being swept away into her vision of the world, and, yes, it's like I'm losing myself. It's a wonderful dream, her vision, but I can't survive in it. There's an entire planet of people counting on me to protect them, and my responsibility has to be to them. I tried, I really did, but I can't live in both worlds at once. In trying, I do neither of them justice." His face fell yet more. "I'm sorry. Tell her I truly am sorry."

Nika kept her voice gentle. "That is damn insightful of you, Spencer. I hope you don't take it the wrong way if I say I'm proud of you."

His gaze darted away briefly. "No, I don't. Thank you."

"I should have warned you that becoming an Advisor came with personal sacrifices. Though, in truth, none of us could have predicted the magnitude of the sacrifices the Rasu would force upon us."

"It's fine. I knew going in. And I don't regret my decision—either of them. To accept the Advisor position or to spend a few brief but exquisite moments with her in her world. I do, however, find myself questioning my sanity for walking out on the most beautiful woman in the universe."

"When you put it that way, it does sound a bit crazy. But you're doing what you believe is right to fulfill your duty and protect the people you promised to defend."

"That's the goal—" his attention shifted to a spot behind her "—hi, Dashiel. You look concerned. Dare I ask what disaster is befalling us today?"

She spun around as Dashiel joined them. Spencer was right; he *did* look concerned. "What did you find out?"

"A second freighter from Chosek also never arrived at the warehouse and isn't responding to comms."

The likeliest scenario wrote itself in the silence that followed, and she bid farewell to the illusion of peace and tranquility they'd enjoyed for the last several days. The respite had been desperately needed, and hopefully they'd taken from it everything they could.

Next, she accessed the Advisor Committee messaging channel.

Nika: Lance, we need military escorts for every freighter and other commercial transport traveling to and from Chosek.

Lance: All of them? How many are we talking?

Dashiel: Around fifteen transports a Standard Day.

Lance: Okay, that's not too bad. Send me the details, and I'll put some fighters on them. I assume it's Rasu they'll be guarding against?

Dashiel: We have to so assume, yes.

Nika: Thank you, Lance. Admin, we also need to change the Rift Bubble Access Code at all locations immediately.

Katherine: We'll tackle the massive pain in our ass of distributing the new code once it's changed, but aren't you the only one who can change it at the source?

Nika suppressed a groan. Distributing the new code was not a massive pain in the ass for anyone; it was only a matter of broadcasting the update in a push message across the public nex web. Effecting the change itself, though?

In theory, Parc could do it, for he knew the Rift Bubble operating code as well as she did by now. But he'd never interacted physically with one of the devices, and the first time doing so was quite a harrowing experience. The second and third time, too. Of course, Mesme could presumably alter the code for every deployed Rift Bubble merely by loosing an intentional thought into the ether.

Nika: I'll get on it straightaway. I'm sending you the new code now, and I'll inform you as soon as I've changed it at each location.

She grimaced at Dashiel, who'd heard the whole conversation. "It appears me and the Sukasu Gate on the roof are going to be good friends today."

He kissed her on the forehead. "I'll keep dinner warm for you."

48

MIRAI

The golden ball of energy danced and writhed among the short grasses of the quiet meadow far from Mirai One, breaking the constraints of its lattice cage every so often to send tendrils of electricity leaping out into the air.

Nika allowed the undulating dance to mesmerize her into a trance. The kyoseil intertwined into the pathways of her body answered the power's call, setting her skin tingling with cool energy. For such an enchanting object as this to be capable of rending apart the fabric of spacetime itself seemed a travesty. But they were each of them doing what they had to do to preserve life.

She shook off the spell and strode up to the lattice. When she and Alex had first interacted with the Rift Bubble on Namino, she'd absorbed the code powering it but had lacked the capacity to alter it. That knowledge had come later, when adapting the code for use in the Rima Grenades.

It would be less taxing on her to shut the device down in order to change the code, but she didn't dare leave Mirai unprotected for a nanosecond. She steeled herself and thrust her hand into the light.

The sensation was one of being set afire from the inside, but it didn't hurt, not exactly. Rather, everything was simply...*more.* More power, more awareness, more life. The code swirled through her mind, not as a separate entity, but as one with her thoughts. She effortlessly located the bypass section and altered the passcode.

A twinge of regret slowed her actions even as she backed her mind out of the code and her body out of the energy's grasp.

Nika: Mirai Access Code updated.

One down, eight to go.

RW

NAMINO

ASTERION DOMINION

I watched from several dozen meters distant, my presence diffused through the air until I was all but invisible amid the bright afternoon sun.

The alteration to the Rift Bubble located on Mirai had entered my awareness the instant the operating code changed, as I kept constant tabs on such matters. Concern had given me haste, but on arriving at each of the planets, I found all was quiet. The code for the device located on Kiyora changed while I was at Mirai, and for Ebisu while I was in transit.

Now comprehending the nature of what was happening, I waited for Nika at Namino. She would visit it last, if only because there were few souls here to protect, only the promise of future ones. Alterations to the devices on Synra, Chosek and the Adjunct Worlds who had received them followed, and I waited.

Nika arrived directly at the site through a wormhole, though not one of her own making. It remained open as she approached the device and, without fanfare or hesitation, thrust her hand into its inner workings.

The energy from the device seemed to leap out and consume her, and her body lit up like a second sun. Together, she and the Rift Bubble created their own binary system, and for a time it felt as if Namino itself orbited them.

Disoriented, I concentrated on solidifying my physical presence here, lest I lose myself.

It didn't take her long to make her changes, and I mourned a little as she stepped away from the device. The brilliance emanating from her skin faded back to its still-preternatural glow, and she hurried back toward the wormhole.

I gathered my presence and swept forward, intercepting her before she reached it.

She studied me curiously, shifting her weight onto her back leg and crossing her arms loosely over her chest. "Mesme. Catch me tinkering?"

Indeed. You are concerned the Rasu have obtained the Access Code?

"Yes. We suspect they've begun confiscating our freighter shipments from Chosek. For the kyoseil they carry, obviously, but also to find a way past the Rift Bubble defenses."

You look weary. You could have asked me to change the code for you.

"I know, but I wanted to do it myself. To confirm I understood the method and…I think to feel as if I was taking real and tangible action to protect my people. And I'm not weary. If anything, I feel energized. Edgy."

Perhaps you fried a few internal circuits.

She glanced back at the ball of energy. "One would expect so, right? But no. The kyoseil protected me from any damage the devices might have been inclined to inflict."

I see. Is your task complete, or may I assist you?

"This was the last one. I'm just relieved we were able to get on top of the problem fast enough to avoid any renewed Rasu incursions. Though if they steal any more freighters, I'll have to change them all again." She smiled at me, whimsy lighting her features. "I don't suppose you can create a portable 'control panel' where I can update them all at once?"

Can't you do so? I deliberately inserted a note of challenge into the question.

"No. The devices aren't interlinked in any manner…but they must be in some way, mustn't they? To each other, or more likely to you. Because you're here, which means you knew what I was doing. How? Nothing in the operating code addresses talking to external objects."

For one such as myself, all energy in the universe resonates. It is but a matter of knowing which wave belongs to which energy.

She stared at me for a long moment, calculations racing behind infinite eyes. "Waves. Are you talking about kyoseil?"

I did not say that.

"You also didn't *not* say that." Her lips and jaw set in her own reciprocal challenge. "Fine. I *will* figure it out."

My response was for me alone. *I know you will.*

49

CHOSEK STELLAR SYSTEM

GENNISI GALAXY

While he waited on the freighter to fill its belly with kyoseil, DAF Lieutenant Kiernan Phillips fiddled with his fighter's adiaK shell controls to make certain they were functioning correctly and ready to do their job of saving his ass.

He'd seen more combat action in the last four months than he had in the preceding forty years, which had been essentially none. The Rasu stronghold, the first and second Namino battles, the Toki'taku battle, and the liberation of Adjuncts San and Rei were blending together into a haze of dizzying adrenaline rushes followed by excessive celebration—since the first two—followed by sleeping for a day. Rinse, repeat.

Escort duty promised to involve absolutely none of those things. He and his wingman were to guard the freighter while it loaded its cargo and ambled its way out to a hundred megameters from Chosek. They would then take a parallel trajectory as everyone headed at superluminal speeds to the Mirai stellar system, where they would again guard the freighter while it ambled its way into orbital dock to deliver the kyoseil.

The Rasu—assuming that was who was behind the disappearances—couldn't attack the freighter during superluminal travel, because no one could attack anything during superluminal travel. So his entire responsibility was to stick himself to the freighter's flank on either end of the ten-hour superluminal trip.

At least he'd be able to nap during the trip. The cockpit wasn't built for it, but his weeks surviving on the planet he now knew went by the name 'Hoan' had taught him how to sleep no matter the conditions he found himself in. Anywhere, anyhow, anytime.

Asterion Freighter #B45E: "Loading complete. Estimated dock departure in ninety seconds."

Kiernan adjusted his posture in the seat and triple-checked his systems. *"Lieutenant Toru, confirm readiness for departure."*

Lt. Toru: "Readiness confirmed."

Lt. Phillips: "Stand by."

The blocky, ugly-ass freighter eased out of the warehouse dock orbiting Chosek and, slow as molasses, turned itself around until it reached the correct heading. Kiernan slid into position on the freighter's port side as Toru did the same on the starboard.

Lt. Phillips: "Freighter #B45E, all systems are green. Ready to move out."

Asterion Freighter #B45E: "Roger that."

The freighter's thrusters fired, and Kiernan matched its speed as Chosek retreated in his rear visual. His fighter could reach the safe-superluminal distance in forty seconds, but it was going to take the freighter, and thus him and Toru, twenty minutes.

As they crept forward, he had to concede the wisdom of the escort, because the freighter was a sitting duck out here. It had no offensive weapons and no defenses other than the shields necessary to survive the normal ravages of space. Once it reached superluminal, it would be as fast as any ship sporting a mid-grade commercial superluminal drive, but at impulse speeds it was as sluggish as…but he'd already covered that ad nauseum.

They still had twenty megameters to go before they'd be clear to hit superluminal when his area sensor beeped an alert. Not a shrill, ringing, 'you're being shot at' alert, but more like a 'hey, I picked up something odd, take a look' alert. So he did.

Unusual reading detected five megameters distant on vector S 35° 12°z W.

Well, that wasn't especially helpful. He pulled up the analysis and studied it with one eye while keeping the other one on the freighter. A few non-standard radiation distortions had shown up in the area and, beneath those, almost too faint to register on the sensor, a signature suggestive of possible Rasu activity.

Instantly he sent out an active targeted scan as his gaze darted around in search of the aubergine devils. He saw nothing. His scan came back negative.

"Toru, are you picking up anything unusual? Anything Rasu-like?"

Lt. Toru: "I'm not sure. My sensor has picked up something it can't identify."

Lt. Phillips: "Mine, too."

Lt. Phillips: "Freighter #B45E, move to alert status and be ready to activate your superluminal drive on my order."

Asterion Freighter #B45E: "Acknowledged."

What was out there? Probably nothing. Space was ninety-nine percent void and astronomical anomalies, right? Another minute or two and they'd be able to jet out of here anyway—

The 'oh shit' version of the alert rang out the same instant that a shimmering field materialized directly behind the freighter. He only spotted the field at all because the system's star was situated in his direct line of sight beyond the freighter.

As the shimmer began to gain substance, it darkened into a Rasu in the shape of a scalloped flower, its petals stretching out to envelop the freighter.

Lt. Phillips: "Freighter #B45E, superluminal NOW! GO!"

The scalloped ends had reached the halfway point of the freighter's hull when the ship's superluminal engine blasted white-hot light into the Rasu's core and accelerated out of its grasp. The edges of the trap came within a few dozen meters of scraping the hull—then the freighter was gone.

The Rasu promptly directed its attention at Kiernan. Oh, was it pissed off? Good!

Lt. Phillips: "Coordinate our fire on the weapons assembly. I'm going in."

Lt. Toru: "We can't take out a Rasu this size on our own. Let's get out of here!"

Lt. Phillips: "We can render it toothless before we go. On me, Toru."

Lt. Toru: "All right, all right. Shit."

As the Rasu morphed into a proper fighting vessel and swung around toward him, Kiernan pitched low and dove far beneath the vessel, then pivoted so the nose of his fighter was pointed directly at the Rasu's underbelly and opened fire.

The Rasu opened fire the next instant, and he had a nanosecond to yank the fighter to port as the laser bathed his cockpit in violet light.

Lt. Phillips: "Don't stop firing!"

His laser was now hard-locked on the enemy weapons assembly, as was Toru's, so he busied himself with dodging the return fire while keeping the assembly in view. Finally crystals began to crack apart, and the damage ramped up until, just before his fighter was rocked by a full-frontal assault, the whole weapons assembly shattered into pieces.

He swiped sweat off his brow, ignoring how his hand was trembling. "Now *let's get out of here.*"

Lt. Toru: "You don't have to tell me twice."

Kiernan punched his tiny superluminal engine and left the crippled Rasu behind.

MIRAI

OMOIKANE INITIATIVE

"Stealth. Of course they have stealth. Why wouldn't they? Everyone who's capable of interstellar travel has stealth capabilities."

Lance shrugged. "In fairness to us, this is the first time they've used it that we've seen. Or not seen, I suppose. And the evidence suggests they have to deactivate it to take offensive action, possibly even to change shape."

Nika glared at the incident report from the fighter pilots.

"Evidence from a single event is hardly overwhelming proof. But I guess it's something." She mustered up a hopeful smile for Dashiel. He sat beside her, though most of his attention was on a small pane in his hand. "Dashiel, can we increase the sensitivity setting for the Rasu signature in our sensors? The report says faint Rasu readings were leaking through before the vessel revealed itself."

"If we reallocate a few processes and divert a bit more power to the sensors, we should be able to improve the performance a little."

Lance scoffed. "How much is a little?"

"Not a lot, by definition. Enough to give our pilots a few additional seconds' warning. I'll talk to the ship systems' research team about running tests as soon as I get a chance."

"Thank you. We have to reach for every single advantage we can find." She turned back to Lance. "Have you let Commandant Solovy know? And the Taiyoks?"

"Yes, on both counts. And now that we've confirmed what's happening to the freighters, I'll increase their escort complements. Phillips and Toru got lucky today, but we need greater firepower on the scene if we want to stop every attack."

"Which you can do because you now have a huge number of ships to play around with, thanks to me." Dashiel stood and placed his hands on Nika's shoulders. "Come with me to the testing facility? The new vehicle I was trying to tell you about when the freighter abductions started is ready for certification."

She peered up at him and nodded. "Sure. Just give me one minute."

"I need to talk to one of the other Industry Advisors, anyway. I'll meet you at the lift."

She closed out the fighter pilot's report and quietly dragged her hands down her face. Stealth…the last thing they needed was another complication. Was a Rasu spy lurking up there right now, in visual range of Mirai, watching for any weakness to appear? Almost certainly.

50

MIRAI

RIDANI ENTERPRISES TESTING FACILITY

Situated on an elevated platform in the middle of the testing field was a…craft. Part tank, part hoverflyer, part tiny fighter jet, as near as Nika could discern. The frame was constructed of smooth, all-but-seamless adiaK, hiding the interior from view. A compact in-atmo engine was tucked in beneath the frame, and atop the craft sat two small laser repeaters and one much larger launcher.

Nika ventured closer, circling around the frame while curiously studying the dominating launcher from every angle. It was built into the body of the craft, and a tube curved down from the large barrel to disappear into the interior.

"A monstrosity, isn't it?"

She spun around to see Dashiel standing a few meters away, grimacing at the craft.

"What is it, exactly?"

"We're calling it a Tactical Assault Glider, or 'TAG.'"

"This is a Rima Grenade launcher on top, isn't it?"

"It is. The TAG is a surface-based aerial vehicle designed to combat ongoing Rasu planetary invasions."

"Is the entire interior filled with Rima Grenades?"

He chuckled. "Just about. Don't want to run out of ammunition behind enemy lines."

"Lance is going to love this."

"Lance doesn't love anything I build for him. But he will eagerly put it to work nonetheless."

"He'll love it. He might not *say* it, but he will." She searched around for a telltale seam to indicate the presence of a hatch or a door. "How is it piloted?"

"Remotely. Ceraff-derived hardware is installed inside, so a pilot with the correct programming in place can take control of the craft from anywhere. The safety of the base, a frigate in space, a bunker down the street."

"Brilliant, as always, darling." She set the duffel bag she carried down beside her and reached out to hug him. His muscles felt tense, and fine lines marred his features. He'd been working like a madman lately; the strain was starting to show.

She brought a hand to his cheek. "You need to get some rest."

"I could say the same about you."

"Good point." She dropped her forehead to his. "We both ought to get some rest."

"But we probably won't."

"Probably not." Her lips lingered on his until his head tilted away, toward the ground. "What's in the bag?"

"Oh! Something I want to show you. Let's wander a safe distance away from the TAG. I don't want to accidentally wreck your prototype."

"It's made of adiaK. You can't wreck it."

"You might be surprised." She grabbed the bag by the handles and trekked off toward a spot of grass farther away from the testing field. When she'd put a few dozen meters between herself and the TAG, she dropped the bag again, knelt and opened it up.

Inside, encased in double cushioning, was a latticed orb a mere three centimeters in diameter. She carefully removed it from its casing then stood, holding it out in her palm.

"Is this a new model of Rima Grenade?"

"Not quite. More like the mutant offspring of a Rima Grenade and a Rift Bubble. See, while I was updating the access codes for all our Rift Bubbles, Mesme paid me a visit."

"You mentioned that."

"I did. Sorry. Anyway, the Kat intimated that there was a way to remotely access and alter the Rift Bubble code, then meandered off into the stars without explaining, naturally. So I dug deeper into the operating code…and quickly got distracted by another idea. We've already modified the Rift Bubble design to create the Rima Grenades. Why don't we simply build the devices ourselves?"

His eyes narrowed at her, then drifted down to the object on her palm. "And that's what this is? A Rift Bubble?"

"A small one, yes. It's horribly inefficient, for now. If we were to build one of our own powerful enough to protect an entire planet, it would be a kilometer wide. But we'll get the inefficiencies under control in time. This one is more of a personal protective device." She grinned. "Stay there."

She backed away from him, making sure he didn't follow, until she'd put thirty meters between them. Then she sent the instruction for the device to activate.

A golden sphere of light burst to life from nothing at the center of the lattice. The light began to spin and pulsate within its cage; her skin tingled from the energy, but it didn't burn as much as when she stood near a full-sized Rift Bubble. Finally the spinning calmed, leaving the sphere undulating peacefully in her palm.

Her gaze rose. "Now approach me."

Across the field, Dashiel frowned. "I don't want to burn up in our sun's corona, and I'm rather upset that you seem to want to send me there."

"You won't, silly. Come on."

"Okay…." He blew out a ponderous breath and began walking forward, one cautious step at a time. Twenty meters, fifteen—an invisible force knocked him back through the air and onto his ass.

She burst out laughing, though she really shouldn't have.

"Ow!" Several groans followed from his location on the ground.

"I'm sorry. Are you all right?"

He gingerly stood and brushed dirt off his nice slacks. "I am."

She hurriedly deactivated the device and jogged over to him. As soon as she arrived, he snatched the orb out of her hand and began studying it. "You made this all on your own?"

"Not entirely. Parc helped."

His eyes darted up to her. "Why didn't you ask *me* to help?"

"Because you are beyond busy, and I didn't want to tax you further. Besides, whenever you *do* have a few free minutes, I'd prefer it if you spent them naked. With me, I mean."

"Hmm." He held the orb up close to his face. "What are the etchings along the interior?"

"Nanofibers. The orb isn't truly empty. The fibers are where the code to run it resides."

"Don't leave me hanging here. What is the lattice made of?"

"A silicene/borophene metamaterial woven through with microscopic threads of kyoseil."

He almost dropped the orb. "What? Is that your addition, or are you saying the Kats use kyoseil in the construction of the Rift Bubbles?"

"Ours. We don't actually know what the Rift Bubble lattices are composed of. Something strong enough that we weren't able to scrape a flake off for testing. So we scanned it with a spectrometer, then did our best to approximate the composition using the materials we best know how to manipulate."

She rubbed her hands together in anticipation. "Do you think you can standardize the construction of these orbs? And maybe work on scaling them up? With a few iterative improvements, we could protect cities and, in time, entire planets, all on our own."

He reached out to tuck a flyaway strand of hair behind her ear. "And that's what you've always wanted, isn't it? For us to be able to protect ourselves, without having to rely on even the most generous benefactors."

"It's what we all want, isn't it?"

"Yes. And yes, I can. I mean, I have zero labs not fully occupied with ongoing testing, and negative assembly lines available for production, but I can build more."

51

CONCORD HQ

COMMAND

Miriam stared at the message from Commander Palmer in dismay. It didn't come as a surprise, as such, that the Rasu had stealth capabilities. But their apparent disinterest in using any such capabilities up to this point had at least improved her ability to track the enemy from 'nigh impossible' to 'exceedingly difficult.'

But it appeared the enemy was changing the game again. In response to recent defeats at the hands of Concord and Asterion forces? They'd proved themselves swift to adapt to new circumstances. So now she'd need to find some other way to improve upon 'nigh impossible.'

Stratagems and counter-stratagems.

She considered the other crucial detail from the message, then looked up at Richard, who sat across the desk from her. They'd been reviewing the information Pamela Winslow had provided on secret OTS donors and arguing about the invasiveness of Miriam's protection detail when the Commander's message had arrived.

"How many private vessels have gone missing in the last week? Commercial and cargo vessels in particular, but let's keep a wide net for now."

Richard held up a finger, and she waited for the few seconds it took for him to pull the data. "Twenty-eight vessels. Sixteen cargo, ten merchant, two personal craft."

"And how does this compare to a similar time period from before the Rasu discovered our existence?"

His expression flickered in obvious curiosity, but he didn't push for details yet…then his darkening expression suggested he'd just figured it out. "A two-hundred-eighty percent increase. But it's a small sample size."

"It's large enough." She pinched the bridge of her nose. "The Rasu have started using stealth to capture Dominion freighters en route to their destinations. I think we have to assume they've been engaging in similar activities here, possibly ever since they arrived. Which means they know a great deal more about us than we'd previously estimated."

She needed to act swiftly to mitigate the damage. First, she sent a message to Lakhes.

Praetor, I have a burdensome task to request of your people. We need to change the access code for all Rift Bubbles deployed in Concord space every forty hours. If you'll provide me with the new code when they are changed, I'll take care of distributing the information.

It will involve a modicum of work, as the number of deployed Rift Bubbles continues to increase, but we must all do our part. It will be done.

Thank you.

She shot Richard a grimace. "We're going to be changing the Rift Bubble access code every forty hours."

"In addition to changing the Concord security protocol codes? I've already whined about what a nightmare it is to do so, yes?"

"Yes, but this time it's a nightmare for the individual planetary governments. Not us, for once."

"Small favors."

"The smallest. Next…." She activated the comm and put it on speaker. "Director Reynolds? I've got Director Navick here with me. The Rasu are starting to use stealth, but their unique energy signature isn't completely masked. Can you engineer any way to increase our sensors' sensitivity to their signature?"

"Not on hand, but give us a few hours. I doubt I can get more than a hundred-thirty-percent increase or so, though. That's going to leave a lot of dead zones."

"I realize it will. Do what you can. Oh, and I believe the Asterions are working on similar improvements to their sensors. Perhaps you can combine your efforts."

"You do know that their technology works rather differently from ours, don't you? Of course you do. I'll pick their synthetic brains for anything useful."

"Thank you." She killed the comm and grimaced at Richard. "The DAF is now providing escorts to their freighters, but they only have a few dozen routes a day. We have tens of thousands. Covering them all will be a...."

"Nightmare? Miriam, you can't be everything, everywhere, to everyone."

"You're right. I know you're right. Damn this enemy! Fine, I'll inform the Senators of the threat, and leave it to their governments to determine how and to what extent they can protect commercial space travel."

Her gaze drifted past the viewport to the daisy-chained docking hubs and the glittering tori as they rotated by. Concord HQ was, by most definitions, the most secure space station ever constructed, excepting the Directorate's Prótos Agora fortress. But as with life itself, security was an illusion. Every day, it hovered a single clever, unanticipated enemy maneuver away from being shattered.

She had a thought and reactivated the comm. "Director Reynolds, sorry to bother you again. Do you think it's possible to create a signal blast capable of interfering with Rasu shapeshifting momentarily? Long enough for a ship that's about to be swallowed to escape?"

"Oh, is that all? I have no idea, but I can put some brilliant minds on it."

Richard smirked. "Letting the individual governments handle the problem, huh?"

She shot him a glare. "Director, the first request takes priority, but as and when your people get time, look into it. Maybe borrow some brainpower from the Asterions on this one, too."

"Are you insinuating the Asterions are smarter than Prevos?"

"No. I'm insinuating that they have certain skill sets which might prove useful."

"Skill sets like pooling their minds into a great cosmic gestalt to think faster and better than any single individual. Nah, good point. I am, yet again, on it. Also, having a cot brought into my office."

"Thank you for all your efforts, Director." She silenced the comm once more.

"Don't let him fool you with his belly-aching. He's having the time of his life."

"I'm glad one of us is. All right." She stood and retrieved her jacket from its hook. "It seems I need to schedule an emergency meeting with the Senate. Then, regrettably, with the AEGIS Council."

52

THE PRESIDIO

Returning to the Presidio was like coming home in so many ways. Though in the grand scheme of her life, Miriam's time here had been relatively brief, it had also been the first time she'd operated unbeholden to political entities and boards full of admirals. Here, she'd built the first incarnation of AEGIS from the ground up. There'd been no one to tell her she couldn't, and so she did.

Unfortunately, any nostalgia she felt was about to get buried beneath a mountain of angst and rancor, for this visit wasn't apt to be a pleasant experience. The people gathered in the summit conference room still held no power to tell her what she couldn't do, but the reverse was also true, and they were under no real obligation to pay her advice any mind.

She succeeded in catching an empty lift from the Caeles Prism Hub, enabling her to spend a few quiet seconds centering herself on the task at hand. By the time she exited the lift and strode into the conference room, she projected only calm, measured professionalism.

The politicians were already arguing, talking over one another to such an extent that she was unable to grab hold of a thread and determine *what* they were arguing over. From one end of the half-circle dais, Malcolm offered her a pained grimace; even as the AEGIS Fleet Admiral, he didn't enjoy much more power in this room than she did. Senator Vranas was also looking somewhat perturbed, shooting the current Chairman of the Senecan Federation, Alberto Duca, a series of furtive frowns but failing to get a word in edgewise.

Prime Minister Gagnon belatedly noted her presence and raised his voice. "Commandant Solovy, thank you for coming on such short notice. If you'll have a seat?"

She was fairly certain that she was the one who'd asked for the meeting, but the illusion of control mattered a great deal to politicians. She moved to an empty seat opposite the dais from Malcolm, nodding terse greetings to the others as she did.

Gagnon cleared his throat. "Everyone is here, so let's begin. For those who don't yet know, there's been a tragic accident involving the Rift Bubble on Earth. A luxury cruiser had difficulty transmitting the access code and wasn't granted passage through it."

Oh. She would've appreciated a heads-up from someone. But again, she didn't work for AEGIS or the Earth Alliance. In any event, this explained at least some of the urgent arguing, as the inevitable outcome of such an event didn't need to be spelled out. "How many people died?"

"Twelve hundred forty-six."

A breath escaped through her pursed lips. She didn't ask how many of them were eligible for regenesis; the number was assuredly higher than zero due to the wealthy clientele of your average luxury cruiser, but the technology was only beginning to permeate its way into human society. "This is a tragedy. Do we have any details regarding what went wrong?"

"The Director of Operations of the company who owns the cruiser says the vessel didn't receive the updated access code."

"I did warn you about the logistical hurdles you would need to overcome—"

"And clearly we have not. One could argue they *can't* be overcome, not with our overlapping governments and redundant layers of procedures."

Gagnon wasn't wrong about that.

"The public is in an outcry over the deaths. They view the Rasu as some hypothetical boogeyman lurking out in the void, but these deaths are real and tangible. Flash opinion polls show a growing backlash against the use of the Rift Bubbles."

How many times was she going to have to repeat herself before they took the threat seriously? "Sir, I assure you, the Rasu are not hypothetical."

"I realize they're not. However, this is a concrete problem we face right now."

Chairman Duca stepped in over Gagnon. "Tell me, Commandant, can the Rift Bubbles be programmed to simply bounce any intruders back a few megameters, rather than deposit them in a cauldron of fiery stellar death?"

Malcolm leaned forward in his seat. "If I may, Commandant. Sir, such a change would make the military's job incalculably more challenging during a battle. The Rasu are exceedingly difficult to destroy, and we count on the Rift Bubbles to thin their numbers in the initial maneuvers."

"Can the effect of a collision with a Rift Bubble be changed during a battle? Can it deliver a soft bounce under peacetime conditions and a fiery death once the Rasu are here?"

Malcolm shook his head. "Yes, the destination can be altered, but not swiftly and not on the fly."

He'd obviously been doing the homework since returning to duty. Given everything else he was involved in, she worried he was getting less sleep than she was.

Duca spread his arms wide. "Well, this sounds like a problem for military scientists to solve. What other option do we have?"

Governor Rolph Tremblay, the head of the IDCC government, interjected. "We can keep the Rift Bubbles turned off until a Rasu fleet actually arrives."

"Yes! We should have followed such a procedure from the beginning. I assume it will only take a few minutes to activate the device on whatever world is being targeted by the enemy."

Miriam tried and failed to suppress a sigh. "And those few minutes could cost us countless lives—lives the Rasu will massacre when they reach the surface of the planet unimpeded before AEGIS forces arrive."

"I'm sorry, Commandant, but a theoretical few thousand lives at a possible-but-unlikely future time is a far lower cost than the thousands of lives lost today because we were being excessively cautious."

While Duca continued pontificating, she sent Richard a pulse, asking a question she absolutely should have asked in their meeting earlier.

Of the twenty-eight vessels that went missing in the last week, how many of them went missing in the Milky Way? Of those, how many were human ships?

Malcolm grumbled in evident frustration. "Chairman, being excessively cautious before an attack occurs is the only thing that will keep your citizens alive."

"Now, Fleet Admiral, aren't you being a bit hyperbolic?"

Ten vessels showed their last recorded location as in the Milky Way. Six of them were owned or operated by humans.

Thank you.

The numbers weren't overwhelming, or definitive proof of anything on their own, but they were concerning enough to persuade her.

She deliberately stood, keeping her fingertips resting on the table. "The Fleet Admiral isn't being hyperbolic at all. The Rasu are beginning to use stealth to mask their approaches. Thus far they're using it to capture lone vessels, but they can just as easily use it at the start of a planetary invasion to catch us completely unawares.

"We might not know they're here until they *are*. In fact, there's strong evidence they're *already* here. Almost a dozen vessels have gone missing in the Milky Way in the last week. Six of them were human vessels."

Gagnon frowned, but protested nonetheless. "Our defensive systems will pick up a Rasu fleet before it reaches orbit."

"They didn't pick up the stealthed Kat superdreadnoughts during the Metigen War."

His frown deepened. "Our systems have improved immeasurably since then."

"They have, and Concord is currently pushing out improvements to our own tracking technology to try to respond to this new Rasu tactic. Will it be enough? We won't know until it's tested in the field, or as a precursor to an attack on a planet. What if the planet is Earth? Seneca? Romane? Is that a risk any of you are willing to take?"

Silence fell for a moment, then was gradually overtaken by quiet murmurs among the attendees. Prime Minister Gagnon shook his head. "If or when the Rasu start actively attacking AEGIS colonies, we might reconsider the decision. But for now, we must protect our citizens today. We're turning the Rift Bubbles off."

She and Malcolm exchanged a weighty look. They'd discuss the ramifications in private later, but she suspected he would agree with her assessment. This decision was going to cost lives—far more lives than those lost on the luxury cruiser today. The only question was, how many more?

RW

Malcolm watched Miriam exit the room with no small amount of envy. She'd done the group a courtesy by making an in-person appearance, but he was bound to his chair by metaphorical chains until the Council deigned to dismiss him. On the battlefield, he enjoyed near-absolute authority, but in this room he was a glorified punching bag.

Or it was possible that he was merely cranky. The Rasu, Vilane and the Gardiens, spiritual ruminations he was in no way qualified to ruminate on, plus the cold loneliness of a bed lacking Mia's presence, all conspired to keep his sleep, when it came at all, perpetually troubled.

"Fleet Admiral, how quickly do you anticipate being able to reactivate the Rift Bubbles, should it become necessary to do so during an attack?"

Politicians always wanted things both ways. "Prime Minister, allow me to state for the record that I agree with Commandant

Solovy's assessment of the risks involved in shutting them off. The Rasu are a clever and persistent enemy, and we cannot discount the possibility that they have a tactic prepared to take advantage of just such an action on our part." He paused, but no one blinked. "To answer your question, on a given planet where the military is on active alert, between twelve and eighteen minutes."

"Plenty of time to promptly counter an attack, then. Excellent." Malcolm simply stared at Gagnon.

"Now, about the reports of Rasu kidnapping merchant vessels. We don't want to see commerce disrupted, so what can we do to ensure these companies that their shipments are safe?"

He charitably assumed Governor Tremblay was implicitly including the ships' crew in the 'shipments' category. "This morning, a team put together a plan to provide maximum protection to the greatest percentage of commercial traffic. Now, we cannot protect all routes or all vessels, not even if we tasked every ship in the AEGIS military with this duty. But using a combination of dynamic patrols and escorts of large convoys, we believe we can cover up to sixty-four percent of them."

"And the other thirty-six percent? Will we be leaving them to the Rasu's devices?"

"Concord Special Projects is working on new sensor array algorithms to detect a Rasu presence sooner and briefly interfere with the Rasu's operations, thus giving a vessel a greater opportunity to escape capture. These improvements should be ready for field testing in another few days."

"Very well. Please keep us apprised."

General Colby, who had been content to let Malcolm and Miriam catch all the flack while the politicians argued, finally spoke up. "As an aside, Fleet Admiral, have you given any more thought to the matter we discussed at the last Oversight Board meeting?"

Malcolm's chest tightened. "What matter is that, General? We've discussed many things in recent meetings."

"The matter of your no-regenesis clause in your will. Public opinion is in flux regarding this issue, and you revising your stance publicly would sway a great many people."

"General, it is not my job nor my role to sway public opinion. I'm a Marine, not a politician."

Colby's mouth curled down, and he looked as though he'd eaten something sour. No military officer liked being called a politician. "Of course. Nevertheless, appearances do matter, and your position *is* a public one. Have you made a decision, or not?"

"I have not."

53

UNKNOWN LOCATION

From its location deep in the shadows of a long, squat building, CTX38b-sub9 observed the organics scurry about. Its stealth provided it sufficient protection, but its orders were to not take any risks of discovery. It was alone on this planet, for now, and that made it vulnerable. Before separating from CTX38, it had been instructed that the organics here were worthy of respect, so it took due care. If its presence was discovered by the inhabitants of the planet, it would fail in its mission here. The mission was its defining purpose, so it was employing all its capabilities to not fail.

Hence, it proceeded slowly. Methodically. Its constituent parts were arranged so as to enable it to (1) move freely, (2) acquire and transport resources and (3) construct the components for a device to prevent quantum interactions. In order to complete the last task, however, it needed raw materials.

Analysis of the planet's surface prior to CTX38b-sub9's dispatch here indicated it contained all the necessary materials to fulfill task #3. CTX38b-sub9's landing site was chosen in substantial part because those materials, or the elements needed to formulate them, all existed within a thirty-square-kilometer grid surrounding the location.

The organics across the open space shepherded two such materials it was in need of on floating barges. It watched as the barges and the organics disappeared inside a different long, squat building; several minutes later, the organics returned without the materials.

Now CTX38b-sub9 knew where they were stored.

It did not attempt to retrieve the materials at this time. Much preparation work remained to be done first. It had chosen a lair nearby—an underground room the organics did not visit, from where it would construct its device. Tonight, under the additional protection of darkness, it intended to acquire more readily available ingredients that could form the basis of the device's assembly. When it was ready, it planned to return to this location and do whatever was required, short of being detected, to acquire the materials from the building where they were stored.

For now it slid away, sticking to the shadows whenever possible. Its acquisition list was a long one, and it had much in the way of scouting to perform. As it was restricted to the slow, deliberate movement of stealth, thirty square kilometers represented a lot of ground to cover.

CTX38b-sub9 was alone on this planet, but it was not alone in its mission. Other sub-units had been dispatched to other planets, all armed with identical orders. The organics and semi-synthetics had begun deploying dimensional barriers to stop Rasu from harvesting their targets, but this promised to be a temporary setback. So long as Rasu infiltrated the surfaces of targets before such barriers were activated, this attempt at defense would prove futile in the end.

When it came time to act, Rasu would have their harvest—on this planet and on every planet they required, from here to the universe's end.

54

PANDORA

Enzio Vilane glared at the two men present remotely in his living room. "Beaumont, what the bloody fuck happened in London?"

Philippe fidgeted under the weight of the scrutiny. Good. "Our sniper says that the same instant he fired the dart, someone crossed into its path in front of the Commandant. When he tried to line up another shot, the target was simply…gone. He's willing to try again, should the opportunity arise."

"People don't fail me and get to keep 'trying' endlessly until they stumble into succeeding. Besides, Solovy never showed up at her dinner. This means she knows something untoward happened. Gentlemen, we have a rat in our midst."

He directed his attention to the other man present, the Gardiens' Chief of Security, Olav Zylynski. "We can't make a renewed move against Solovy until we deal with the rat. Find them."

Olav nodded sharply. "I'll get right on it."

"Thank you. Beaumont, it goes without saying that you've disappointed me. You insisted you were ready for greater responsibility, but now I find myself questioning your judgment. You selected the venue and the operative, and both failed."

Philippe's face blanched. "What can I do to make it up to you, sir?"

"Close the deal on the Fleet Admiral. This week."

"His schedule is very—"

"Close it, or else we'll be having a far more unpleasant conversation."

"Yes, sir."

Enzio waved a hand, and Beaumont's holo disappeared, leaving him and Olav alone. "Kill the sniper. We can't have fuck-ups like him wandering around freely with knowledge of our operations. Do it yourself, so the job gets done properly."

"Not a problem. What about Beaumont?"

Enzio hesitated. If he didn't know Philippe personally, he'd order the man's execution now. But he held some personal affection for his subordinate, and he had promised Philippe another chance. "Eh, he's a true believer. I'm not convinced he has the stomach for the next phase, but he's done a lot of good work for us up until now. I'll give him an opportunity to prove he's serious about our mission."

"Understood. It's your call, sir."

Olav's holo vanished as well, and Enzio stood alone in the silence for several seconds. Frustration gnawed away at him—abruptly he grabbed a plate from the counter and hurled it across the room. It smacked into the wide expanse of glass and shattered to the floor.

"Ah!"

He spun around to see his mother standing in the doorway, her hands over her mouth. "Enzio, what's wrong?"

He hurried up to her and gently took her hands in his. "I'm sorry, Mother. Just trouble with work, and I lost my temper for a moment. I didn't mean to frighten you."

"Startled me is all. Can I ask about the trouble?"

He hesitated. But it must be a good thing how of late, she was growing interested in how he passed his time and spent his money. After all, he was going to need her sage advice in the heady days to come. "An important mission failed, and I believe it did so because I have a traitor in the Gardiens."

"Oh. That is unfortunate." She stared out at the skyline, a tiny smile growing on her lips. "Do you know what I used to do to traitors?"

He did, but he asked anyway. "What did you do?"

"I executed them without mercy or hesitation—often in a violently flagrant manner to send an appropriate message to everyone in my organization."

He decided the tiny smile she'd adopted was quite diabolical. "And I will follow your example and do the same the instant I discover their identity."

"I'm sure you will. You are my son, after all."

Yes, he most certainly was.

The house bot arriving to clean up the broken plate distracted him briefly, but he deliberately returned his attention to his mother. "I thought you were taking a nap. Do you need me?"

The diabolical smile shifted to something else, and she strolled across the living room. "I've been thinking. I have several refinements I want to make to my programming. They'll clean up some dangling algorithms and hopefully restore some of the damaged files you've kept around in my storage."

Part of him recoiled from the notion. She knew what she had been, and what she was now; he'd never hidden this from her. Yet a knot of worry materialized in his gut. If she took charge of her own development…what if she grew beyond his control? What if she came to reject him?

Nonsense. She was his mother, and as such, she loved him more than anything in the world. "Why don't you work up a simulation of the proposed revisions, and we'll review them together later."

"I'd like that." She nodded. "Yes. I'll be in my bedroom working on it until dinner."

"Okay. I need to see to a few things this afternoon, then we'll reconvene over a nice meal."

She turned and departed without further comment. Once she was gone, he went into the kitchen and splashed water on his face. Fury at the failure of the Solovy operation still churned through his veins, and he badly wanted to strangle the first stranger he came upon.

He breathed in through his nose. Out through his mouth.

Compartmentalization, compartmentalization…. A dozen other initiatives required his active guidance, and he couldn't let himself spiral down into ineffectual rage. Not if he expected the Gardiens to succeed.

So he returned to the living room, surrounded himself with a virtual mosaic of those initiatives, and went to work on planning the next phase of his Grand Design.

55

AKESO

*B*ut I like *my hair.*

Alex poured herself a glass of juice and headed for the living room. *I like it, too. But...* she cringed *...Richard is concerned that Vilane will recognize you if he sees you on the news feeds. And you're planning to be on the news feeds soon, aren't you?*

If all goes well. Oh, fine. I suppose he's right, and the last thing I want is Enzio Vilane back in my life. I'll ditch the silver. Good enough?

I'm sure it will be. I'll let Richard know.

Promise to Malcolm fulfilled with only a small hit to her conscience, Alex sank into the plushest, coziest chair in the living room, closed her eyes and slipped into sidespace.

Destination: Pandora.

The Avenue was arguably the classiest neighborhood on Pandora, hosting block upon block of upscale residences above its wide streets. But she was here for a single, specific residence...*there.* High atop one of the most expensive buildings in the neighborhood sat a privacy-glass-walled penthouse in the shape of a hexagon.

Vilane guarded his personal home's address zealously. But there were few things in the world that the four Noetica Artificials couldn't root out when they worked together.

The privacy glass posed no impediment to her, and she effortlessly projected her consciousness through the barrier and inside.

In a stroke of luck, the owner and subject of her interest was currently at home. He stood in the center of an expansive room dotted with couches, surrounded by a maze of slowly rotating aurals. The setup reminded her of how the Praesidis Primor had preferred to 'work,' and she shuddered at the visual the scene evoked.

The man's natural mien, when he thought no one was watching, was cold and harsh, and only his delicate bone structure prevented it from coming across as downright brutish.

Aren't you supposed to be investigating potential Rasu strongholds in nearby galaxies?

She rolled her eyes, probably. Valkyrie had been keeping closer tabs on her since the events on Ireltse; in fairness, though, she'd been doing the same. *Technically. And I will. Arguably, I should also be trying to figure out what's up with the Reor and Caleb and I. But while the Rasu's grand strategy remains a mystery, their tactics are pretty well set and identified. Divining their secret purpose will ultimately help us bring an end to the war, yes, but it's not going to change the dynamics in the short term. So it can keep until we head out to do some in-person research in a few days. And the Reor mystery is an intellectual exercise at best, a vanity project at worst. It, too, can keep.*

But this guy? He's a clear and present danger today.

Her stomach churned as she studied the man. She didn't care who his parents were or how wealthy he was. He was a thug and a bully, and he'd tried to murder her mother for political gain. For this, she would contribute to taking him down however she could.

While he continued to scroll through his aurals, she sent her consciousness wandering around the compound. Behind the kitchen lay a second living area…but not as spacious of one as the building's frame would suggest. Curious at what the layout was hiding, she drifted through a door in the rear and into a state-of-the-art server storage room. Dim, cool lighting cast the equipment in shadow, punctuated by the pervasive glow of active quantum machinery.

Damn. He is packing some serious hardware in here. How many Artificials is he running? Or his own private exanet? A galaxy-wide surveillance network?

I'm unable to determine the purpose of the hardware from a visual scan, but I am noting the model designations of the equipment where possible. Investigating their specs and how the manufacturers market them may lead to a few answers.

Good thinking. Alex meandered down the server-lined aisle to the end. She'd hoped for another secret room, but this time found only walls. *So, while we're here enjoying ourselves, do you want to talk about Thomas?*

I haven't decided yet.

Ooh. Is it that serious, then?

I haven't decided yet.

She chuckled soundlessly. The amount of time it took Artificials to 'decide' most matters could be measured in microseconds, so it was quite intriguing that Valkyrie continued to hesitate after…what, weeks?

Fair enough. In all seriousness, though, you know I'm here for you if you want to talk. Granted, I've only gotten love right once in my life, and I'm still not clear on how I managed it, so I'm definitely not the best source of advice in this respect. On the other hand, no one knows your heart the way I do. So I'm happy to listen. I'll even try to keep the snarky comments to a minimum.

I find this exceedingly difficult to believe.

Hey, I said 'try.'

So you did. Thank you for the offer, but I'm honestly not certain what I want to say, much less feel. Thomas shares in much of what drives me—my adoration of the stars and knowledge and exploration and action—and for now, this is enough.

Wow, it really might be serious.

I heard that.

Sorry. Shall we check back in on Mr. Vilane?

Yes, please.

She directed her consciousness out of the server room, through the kitchen and into the main living area, to find Vilane had swiped away the majority of the aurals to concentrate on one large display. She honed in her presence until it resided directly beside him, his shoulder encroaching on her space when he inhaled.

She focused on the display, only to realize it was artificially blurred. *Valkyrie, I think Mr. Vilane is running some sort of anti-Prevo surveillance field. Is there anything we can do to get around it?*

As a Prevo himself, it makes sense that he'll be warding against sidespace observation. A moment. I have identified the origination point of the field.

Alex followed the field's propagation back to its source, which turned out to be a small circular module installed beneath the control panel outside the server room.

In the early days, Prevos hadn't been able to affect the real world from sidespace. Then Devon had crashed through that barrier in an explosion of desperation-driven power; not long thereafter, she had built upon his breakthrough to unlock the secret to opening wormholes through the fabric of space-time. So, it was cute that Vilane believed he could protect himself from her inquiries.

She sent out a weak but targeted filament of power to envelop the module, then increased its strength until a single circuit, buried deep in the module's structure, shorted out. *There.*

Nicely done. With luck, he won't notice the field has malfunctioned for some time.

And when he does, it will look like a design flaw. Now, where were we? She returned her consciousness to the living area to see what Vilane was working so hard to hide.

The display he studied was divided into a calendar, a security interface, and a chat panel.

She didn't know the names invoked, and several references were obviously code words for nefarious plans and targets, but after a few seconds of reading, the nature of the ongoing chat became evident. A major strategy meeting among high-level Gardiens officers was being scheduled for seven days from now, and even coded, the topics on the agenda sounded damn interesting.

Let's forward these names, code words and calendar entries to Richard for analysis.

Done.

She was about to take a tour of the rest of the penthouse and see what she could see when a gentle alarm in her eVi reminded her that she had real-world things to do today.

You haven't seen the last of me, Mr. Vilane. With a regretful sigh she returned her consciousness to her body and opened her eyes.

On the way to the shower, she sent Malcolm a pulse.

A big Gardiens strategy session is being held next week on Pandora. If you meant what you said to Richard about wanting to take Vilane down, find a way to get yourself invited to that meeting.

56

CONCORD HQ
CINT

When his ring at Richard's office went unanswered, Caleb stopped by the CINT lobby to inquire as to the man's whereabouts. The receptionist directed him to one of the conference rooms down the hall and didn't caution him about it being a no-interruptions meeting, so Caleb rang the buzzer outside the room.

The door slid open. He stepped halfway inside and waved at Richard, who was leaning back in the chair at the head of the table. "If you're not too busy, I wanted to—"

"Caleb!" Felzeor launched himself off the top of the table and landed in a flurry of feathers on Caleb's shoulder. "What a wonderful surprise!"

He laughed, his mood instantly buoyed by the unexpected appearance of his friend, and reached up to scratch Felzeor's neck. "Yes, it is. How are you doing?"

"Good. I've missed you, though." Felzeor cooed in pleasure, twisting his head around to finagle the best scratching angle.

"I've missed you, too." He gestured to the table. "Why don't we sit?"

"If we must." Felzeor gave his wings a flap and returned to the table, and Caleb sat to Richard's right.

"How are things?"

He'd nominally directed the question to Richard, but Felzeor jumped in to answer. "I'm here giving Director Navick a status update. I've been on a mission with Drae."

"Oh? What kind of mission?"

Felzeor's emerald eyes slid around. "It's a secret…."

"Caleb has Level III clearance."

Felzeor tilted his head to the side. "Which means…I can tell you! We've been investigating known associates of Janice ela-Kyvern, Ferdinand's mole in CINT. We're trying to identify members of Ferdinand's old conspiracy, so we can arrest them and dismantle the whole nefarious mess once and for all."

Caleb nodded approvingly. "This is important work."

"It is. I'm proud to do it."

He glanced at Richard. "Eren's ferreting out rebellious elements for Corradeo as well. They might be interested in whatever you find."

Richard flicked a finger, and an aural materialized between them. It contained a long, dry-looking legal contract. "The Advocacy officially signed on to our Information-Sharing Protocols for Concord Members yesterday. I've already reached out to Eren to see how we can help each other."

Felzeor pattered around the table in a display of tension. "I enjoy working with Drae, but I miss Eren terribly. Do you think this means he'll be coming back to work here soon?"

Richard shook his head. "Eren worked for Corradeo Praesidis for a century in the anarch cause. Now that the man is building a new Anaden leadership structure from the ground up, I suspect Eren has found his home."

"You're probably right." Felzeor's beak dipped low.

Caleb wasn't certain Eren would ever consider himself "home" anywhere, but he'd been reassured by the amount of empathy Corradeo was showing the man. Perhaps Eren could find a meaningful direction there.

He reached out and stroked Felzeor's feathers. "Hey, I have an idea. Missions allowing, why don't we set up a regular monthly dinner with Eren at my house? More than dinner—an entire afternoon and evening of hanging out and catching up."

"Most excellent!" Felzeor nearly took flight again. "Can we do it tomorrow?"

"Tomorrow might be a little too soon to mesh with everyone's schedules. How about…the 5th of every month?"

"In eight days, then? Okay. Oooh, can Marlee come, too?"

"Sure. We can even do a short group training session, if you want to."

"Yes. Training with her is fun."

He smirked a bit wryly. "That's one word for it. I'll reach out to Eren and Marlee to confirm the date."

"Thank you, Caleb! I can't wait. Director Navick, did you need any more information from me today? I have a lunch date with Thelkt in the Atrium shortly."

"I believe we are all done. Give Drae my thanks, and let him know about the items we discussed."

"Yes. Goodbye, sir." Felzeor hopped onto Caleb's forearm for a final scratch. "I will see you next week!"

"Yes, you will. Now, off you go."

Felzeor rose into the air, hovered by the door panel to open it with a tap of a claw, then disappeared out and down the hall.

Caleb smiled. "He seems as if he's doing better."

"Work gives him purpose. Also, less time for wallowing in grief. He enjoys contributing—and he is. I don't know what I'm going to do about the team, though. Drae has nixed every potential teammate I've suggested. He and Felzeor are fine for short-term surveillance missions like the one they're on now, but…but that's a problem for another day." Richard clasped his hands on the table. "What's up?"

"I wanted to see what you've learned about the assassin."

"Thanks to you, quite a lot. A name, for one: James Sarona. Ex-Federation Special Forces. He was dishonorably discharged four years ago after an inquiry found he unnecessarily endangered civilian lives during a clandestine op."

"Sounds like someone Vilane would scoop up. Have you arrested him yet?"

"We have not."

Caleb started working up a protest—

"Believe me, no one wants him in a cell more than I do. Well, except possibly David. But if we bring him in, we risk tipping off the Gardiens to the fact we know they were behind the assassination attempt. And what I want even more than Sarona locked up is to tear apart the entire operation, from top to bottom. I want Vilane, then I want his lieutenants. So we're watching Sarona very carefully. We'll let him lead us to others who are operating on the illegal side of the Gardiens, and we'll chase them up the chain."

He wanted to argue, but he had to concede it was the best strategy under the circumstances. "Let me know if you need an assist when you bring him down. Not that your people aren't fully capable of doing so, of course."

"When we bring down Sarona, or Vilane?"

"Either."

"Are you in that business again?"

Akeso murmured a quiet protest in the depths of his mind. "No, I am not. But I will do whatever I can to protect Miriam from these scumbags. Mia, too. So if it comes to it, I'm thinking an exception can be made."

57

KATOIKIA TAIRI

IDRYMA
CETUS DWARF GALAXY

Iapetus darted about the ethereal overlay of the gathering chamber, forcing its presence into every nook and cranny. "The Asterions are taking our meticulously perfected defensive technology and using the Rasu as an excuse to run rampant with it. To create instruments of mass destruction."

Lakhes made a calming gesture from the center point of the room. "The Asterions have been relentlessly attacked by the Rasu, and they deserve to defend themselves in whatever manner they can conjure. Thus far, their efforts appear to be focused on the goal of preserving their civilization, not one of conquest or enslavement."

"They surely remain Anadens at heart, and if they are not constrained now, they will in time rise to become despots in the image of their ancestors."

Iapetus was rankling me more than usual today, and I found I could hold my words no longer. I increased my presence in the room appropriately. "They will not."

"What gives you the authority to assert this, Mnemosyne? Because you have had a few conversations with their leaders? Because they tell you they have peaceful intentions, and their appeals find a sympathetic audience in your too-sentimental nature?"

"Because they *do* have peaceful intentions. As the Praetor remarked, they want only to defend themselves from annihilation. That is our purpose as well, is it not? To protect all innocent species from annihilation?"

"Yes—even from each other. I still say they can't be trusted. They will reveal their rotten Anaden nature before the end."

"You know nothing, Iapetus."

"I know the rotting evil at the core of the Anaden soul."

There was a time when I'd believed that Iapetus had matured to see the errors in its reactionary, too-narrow worldview. Clearly I'd been mistaken. "Nonsense. No species is monolithic. Need I remind you that the Directorate was the source of the vast majority of Anaden atrocities? It is dead and gone, and the Anadens are now our allies."

"We have no allies—we cannot afford the risk of having them. We have partners of convenience, when and where we share similar goals. Even under that standard, the Anadens scarcely qualify."

I worked to hold my tongue, for I teetered on the edge of losing control, and I should not sink to Iapetus' level. Instead, I pleaded silently with Lakhes to set the correct tone on this matter.

Seemingly hearing my plea, Lakhes spread its presence until it filled the center of the chamber. "Ten years ago, we agreed to become Allied Members of Concord. Thus by definition, we *are* allies of all Concord species. We share common cause with them, and I do not expect this to change in the foreseeable future. I recognize it can be difficult to adjust to the new reality. We spent hundreds of millennia fighting the Anaden Directorate alone. We risked life and spirit to protect those weaker than us, acting as a shield against those stronger. We lived lies in public and truths only in secret, for so, so long.

"But the world *has* changed, and we need to change with it. Now we are united against a mutual foe, and we can't allow distrust and enmity to spread among our ranks in this fight. This includes our approach to the Asterions. They, too, are our allies, and I believe they have evolved well beyond their Anaden origins. They are powerful, yes, and growing more so with each passing day. But they will not turn on us."

Iapetus diminished and sank toward the wall.

Lakhes allowed the retreat without comment. "Let us proceed to the next matter. Hyperion, do you bring news to report?"

My old foe and current…somewhat less of a foe…swept out from among the ranks. "I do. We have completed construction on the first installment of a new fleet of superdreadnoughts. The ships are equipped with weapons better suited to counter the Rasu. Three hundred sixty of them are ready to deploy to the next battle, when and where it occurs, and we shall continue to increase their numbers."

I waited for Hyperion to interject its own take on the argument, but it did not arrive. It was possible Hyperion, at least, had learned a few lessons since its days shepherding the Aurora Enisle.

Lakhes rewarded Hyperion for its good behavior. "Excellent news. Thank you, Hyperion, for your tireless efforts on this project. As we have discussed at length, we must do everything within our power to protect Concord and defeat this enemy. A new fleet will be indispensable in the fight. Now, if there is nothing else, we will adjourn."

RW

I flitted around Lakhes' private quarters in agitation. "Iapetus has always been a reckless and irresponsible voice among us. We can't permit it to turn the tide of opinion against the Asterions. The result would be a disaster beyond reckoning."

Lakhes continued to radiate the calm it had displayed during the session. It was but one reason why Lakhes was the Praetor and I was not. "We could tell the others the truth."

I drew up tight. "No, we cannot."

"Every member of the Idryma—yes, even Iapetus—is a proven leader with millennia upon millennia of lived experience and earned wisdom. They are ready for the truth."

"You were barely ready for the truth, Lakhes, and you are the best of us. With respect, they are not. If those secrets were revealed, it would shake the Idryma to its core, and we cannot afford to ignite such a crisis in the midst of our current one."

"You give your colleagues too little credit, Mnemosyne."

"No, I give them more. I want them working the Rasu problem with all of their anima. Thus I will protect them from what would weaken them, as I have always done."

"It might strengthen their resolve to know the truth."

I wavered. Was Lakhes correct? Once upon a time, I had valued truth above all else. Then I had taken the burden of preserving that truth upon myself, and with it the necessity of keeping it from everyone else. Was I arrogant in holding to it like a martyr now?

No. I had known matters stood to become both more difficult and more delicate at this juncture. After so long, I could not falter now. "Perhaps, perhaps not, but we can't take the risk. You above all should realize we dare not throw everything into tumult. The Idryma must be at its strongest to win this war. Thus you and I must be strong for the others."

Lakhes remained silent for a lengthy span, for it had always considered issues deeply before deciding upon a course of action. Finally, my dear friend and, at this moment, sole confidant, settled into a peaceable stance. "Very well. You've made your case. Maybe I simply yearn for additional colleagues with whom to share this burden. But I, like you, do not enjoy that luxury. We will see this through your way."

"Thank you—" An alert intruded upon my thoughts, and I gathered my presence in close. "Pardon me, but I must see to a matter." I departed without further fanfare.

58

FANEROS STELLAR SYSTEM

CARINA DWARF GALAXY

Eren gazed down at the planet below from the cockpit of his new ship. Well, not *his* ship exactly. More of a ship bestowed upon him by the Anaden Advocacy for his use so long as he acted as Chief of Intelligence for Non-Anaden Affairs. It was even smaller than the CINT vessel he and his team had used, with no lower-level living space and only a drop-out cot in the main cabin for sleeping. But every centimeter of it was straight-up quality—Anaden construction at its finest, as befitting a highish-level government official.

He snorted aloud at the notion of himself as *any* level of government official, never mind one occupying the upper ranks. Mind you, the 'government' in question currently consisted of less than a hundred people in total, and all of four formal ranks existed at present. But, hey, he was in on day one.

Which kind of made him feel…ye gods below, was this *pride?* Surely not. Fine, *perhaps* pride in being able to help someone he respected try—and almost certainly fail—to build a better future for the species he was cursed to belong to. He'd give himself that much, but anything more would have to wait for a spell.

He returned his attention to the planet he orbited. Its soft, muted palette of whites and grays, with accents of pale mauve and lavender, reminded him of the marbles used in *pithanot* games. Fitting, as much of the planet's surface was in fact covered in marble, quartz and crystal. He knew this because he'd visited it before, and also because he'd regularly tapped into the Concord monitoring probes in place above every world inhabited by a Protected Species.

The feed to his left displayed a mid-altitude visual of the Faneros' largest city. Its perpetual dusk gave the setting a gauzy, dreamy appearance. Cast against it, the meandering residents' skin was as luminescent as their glittering robes upon the shadowy blue-gray sky. So lovely.

He opened himself to the waiting panic attack, to the hyperventilation and terror that had accompanied previous visits to this place...but it never arrived. Curious.

Almost as if he were egging his darker nature on, he forced himself to remember the fateful night over a century ago, when a Faneros had been his awarded plaything for the evening. When their innocent purity had sent him running away in horror, abandoning his life and all he'd known to tumble into the arms of the anarchs.

He drowned himself in the memory out of a perverse masochism. But still the panic attack didn't come.

Eventually a measure of acceptance arrived. This must be a gift Cosime had bestowed upon him: forgiveness. Not hers, though she had absolutely done that in spades, but the capacity to forgive himself. To acknowledge his past mistakes while recognizing how he'd grown past them, of his own volition. Had made better, more honorable choices, and in doing so, transformed himself into a (slightly) better person.

Standing here watching the terrestrial feed, he accepted this was a victory, if solely over himself. He wished it made him happier, but happiness remained far beyond the horizon. He settled for grateful.

A burst of light brightening the cabin behind him sent him leaping against the dash and reaching for a weapon—but it was only a Kat. An agitated one, by the looks of it. "Mesme?"

It is I. I need to urgently warn you—please do not attempt to descend to the planet's surface.

"I...wasn't planning on it."

Oh. The swirling lights calmed to a more languid rhythm. *This is welcome news. The planet is protected by one of our Rift Bubbles. Should any ship come into contact with its barrier, it would find itself incinerated by the system's star in a most unpleasant manner. Thus, we are monitoring such planets for accidental incursions, and your arrival set off an alarm. I was concerned that you might not be aware of the Rift Bubble's presence. Or worse, that you* were *aware of it.*

"You were afraid I was ramping up for another kamikaze suicide run."

There has been a pattern of behavior.

Eren chuckled dryly. "There definitely has been. But, no. Not today." He pushed past the twinge of despair flaring in his chest. "I did know about the Rift Bubble, though." He tapped an animated section of the HUD. "Concord's broadcasting a warning on its public vicinity channel."

I see. Naturally, they are. I should have accounted for this likelihood.

"Nah. It's nice of you to be vigilant about not killing us."

You are using sarcasm.

"Only a little. Seriously, it is an honorable gesture on your part. Thank you for looking out for me. And everyone else."

Then you are welcome. Mesme vacillated. *When we last visited the Faneros together, it was not a pleasant experience for you. Can I ask why you have returned?*

"To see if it would still be an unpleasant experience for me."

And?

"I can't say as I'm having a grand time, but…I'm doing okay."

This brings me relief. I experienced great concern for you on the day in question.

"Sorry I worried you. I do that a lot, don't I?"

At a higher frequency than is average for those about whom I care, yes.

"Wait—are you saying you *care* about me? About anyone, for that matter? I didn't think Kats were into that sort of thing."

More so than you will ever realize.

"I don't mean as species, in the sense of, 'I care about all peace-loving sentient beings and want them to survive as a people.' I mean as individuals."

I understand precisely what you mean, Eren. Yes, to both.

"Huh. Well, don't worry. Your secret is safe with me."

Thank you.

Eren glanced back at the feed, noting a group of Faneros who gathered together in what looked like frivolity, complete with drinks and some dancing. It was good they did such things. "So, how are things for you? The Kats off doing Kat things to help defeat the Rasu?"

Yes, if with far greater consternation and disquiet than I prefer. The rapid advancement of the Asterions' military capabilities has many in the Idryma experiencing cardiovascular palpitations.

"You paint quite a picture. But what would be the point of extradimensional lights having a heart attack?"

We do have physical bodies.

"Alex did mention it at some point. But they're more like vestiges than functioning bodies, right?"

It is true they are generally of no consequence to us, but we can function in them when it is required. And in point of fact, our stasis chambers would never allow the bodies they nurture to experience a heart attack. Nevertheless, it was a good joke, yes?

Eren laughed. "Yes. A very good joke. Well done. It's interesting that the Asterions are causing such anxiety among you lot. I've heard some intriguing things about them, but they don't sound particularly scary. Haven't met any yet, myself."

The lights quavered. *What?*

"I haven't met any Asterions yet."

Of course. You have been engaged in your own trials since they introduced themselves to Concord.

"'Trials.' Yes, you could say so. I think Caleb and Alex have made friends with one of them, though."

Nika Kirumase.

"That's the name. Maybe I'll meet her one day."

I feel certain you will.

Eren sighed. "All right. I think I'm ready to declare 'mission accomplished' here. Time for me to get back to work."

And for myself as well.

He jerked his head toward the viewport. "Make sure and keep the Faneros safe from the Rasu, will you?"

We kept them safe from the Directorate for a century. We can do no less for them now.

59

MIRAI

DAF MILITARY SERVICES CENTER

Nika considered Lance from across the table as she washed down a bite of almond-crusted *basti* with a sip of water. "Any signs of Rasu snooping around Adjuncts Rei or San since we kicked them out?"

"None so far. They appear to be devoting all their efforts in our territory to acquiring what kyoseil they can steal."

"When we destroyed the stronghold, I hoped it would be the end of their kyoseil fascination. But I suppose it was a pipe dream."

Beside her, Dashiel refilled his salad from the communal bowl at the center of the table. This was a working dinner at the DAF Military Services Center, and the meal had been delivered by a friendly local restaurant. "They've been deliberately going after shipments from Chosek, and only Chosek, which definitely means they're targeting the kyoseil again. It's possible they rediscovered our unique composition by…" he shuddered "…studying people they captured on Namino and the Adjunct Worlds.

"But an equally likely scenario? Rasu vessels absent from the stronghold—scouting, patrolling, whatever—fled to the nearest concentration of Rasu in another galaxy and shared information about what their brethren had been working on here."

Nika sighed in resignation. "We knew we must have missed a few Rasu that were scattered around the Gennisi galaxy, so it shouldn't be a surprise. The best we can hope for is that the far-flung vessels didn't possess all the details on the stronghold's research, and now they're starting essentially from scratch."

Dashiel patted her hand in encouragement. "They won't have

any more luck this time around. We both appreciate how tightly the kyoseil guards its secrets."

"Gods know that's the truth." She took a bite of *basti* and prepared to launch into a bitter complaint about how resistant the kyoseil was to her every overture, nudge and pleading inquiry...then remembered how Dashiel got to listen to those complaints nearly every night and decided to give him a breather. "How's the rollout of the new renewable negative energy weapons going?"

"Too slowly—"

"Quite well—"

They talked over one another, each expressing the sentiments matching their approaches to the world. She chuckled. "About as expected, then?"

Lance shot Dashiel a weak glare, but nodded. "We've installed them on eighty percent of our cruisers and sixty-two percent of frigate-class warships."

"And we've integrated them into the manufacturing lines, so now they're coming pre-installed on all ships of both classes. As a next step, we're looking at ways to incorporate them into smaller and specialty craft." Dashiel smiled. "Oh, and we also gave the weapon a name: RNEW. I'm told that 'renewable negative energy weapon' is too much of a mouthful to bark repeatedly during combat operations."

The acronym filled itself in without difficulty; simple and straightforward. "I'm guessing you didn't let Parc name it, then."

Lance grunted. "Hells, no. He wanted to call it the 'HyperBlaster 3000' or some nonsense."

"Of course, he did. Well, this is fantastic. If the Rasu ever decide to hit us in force again, they'll find themselves on a very different battlefield."

"True," Dashiel responded. "Right now, they seem to be turning their attention to Concord, but we've always been the prize they covet most. They'll be back."

"Also, our fleet will soon be large enough for us to help out in

Concord battles, yes?"

Lance hesitated briefly. "I'm loathe to spare any ships from our planetary defenses, but yes, I have to concede we're in danger of having some to spare. And given all that Concord's done for us lately, we ought to begin returning the favor."

An officer stuck her head in the door. "Sorry to bother you. Advisor Kirumase, a Senator Corradeo from Concord would like to speak with you."

"He's here now? On the premises?"

"Yes, ma'am."

He was certainly getting nimble at navigating Asterion planets. Cities. D-gates. She reluctantly folded her napkin on the table. "I guess I should go see the Supreme Commander."

Lance snorted. "I'd make him wait."

"And that's why you're a soldier, not a diplomat. Please, finish eating without me. Hopefully, I'll be back in time for dessert."

RW

Corradeo Praesidis waited in the small guest lobby on the first floor. Lance jokingly referred to it as 'the quarantine room,' but it was well-appointed and welcoming enough, at least for a military installation.

When she arrived, he extended a hand in greeting. "Advisor Kirumase, it's a pleasure to see you again."

Nika shook his hand but dodged the response. "How is the Concord Senate treating you?"

"As all senates do—with a knife poised at my back and a hefty stack of rulebooks weighing down my desk."

"Sounds lovely. So, what brings you to the Dominion today?"

He clasped his hands behind him and began strolling across the lobby. "I've begun a number of initiatives at home aimed at repairing and rebuilding Anaden society. Yet I can't help but feel as if any such rebuilding will be incomplete if it doesn't include mending our relationship with you, our Asterion cousins.

"Now, I realize this will not be an easy or quick path to traverse, so I want to get started as soon as possible. Let us take our first steps toward healing the divide between our people, shall we?"

She kept a diplomatic façade locked on her features while she considered his surprising entreaty. She'd cajoled herself into accepting his existence in her world as something other than an enemy, but the thought of actively working alongside him to build a friendship between their governments—between their citizens—made her positively queasy. Plus, she legitimately had two full plates' worth of work every waking hour; there was simply no room in her schedule for this manner of difficult, minefield-laden diplomacy.

She should introduce him to Cameron or Terry or—*oh*. Epiphany.

What about connecting him with someone who could charm the paint off a wall, find the beauty and pleasure in the worst of situations, and was in dire need of a distraction right now?

She transitioned her expression to a diplomatic smile. "Senator, I regret to say that at present, I do not have the bandwidth to shepherd along the kind of project you're proposing. However, I have a friend who I believe will be an excellent partner for you in this endeavor. I'll put you in touch with her right away, and I wish you the best of luck. Perhaps in time, we truly can mend our relationship, as equals."

60

MIRAI

MIRAI TOWER

A bipedal machine showed Corradeo into an expansive office suite near the pinnacle of the soaring building situated at the center of the city.

Across the office, an expansive wall of windows looked out on downtown and the harbor it framed. Art and sculptures adorned much of the space, displaying a wide range of styles and mediums. The furniture conveyed elegance, though it was of a simpler and more practical design than what one found in, say, the home of a wealthy Novoloume aristocrat.

A woman stood on the other side of a long, bare marble desk, her back facing him. She wore a flowing lavender silk pantsuit, and a mane of tight obsidian curls flowed down to her shoulders.

Then she turned around, and Corradeo's' breath caught in his throat. In his many journeys, he'd encountered beauty in all its infinite incarnations, but possibly never in such a complete tableau as this. Perfect ebony skin accentuated unusual eyes of violet and white, and those obsidian curls tickled exquisite cheekbones, a tapered jaw and full lips.

She was, without question, a strikingly beautiful woman. But he'd wrangled many beautiful women to his purposes in the million years of his life.

A storm cloud swept across the woman's features the instant her gaze settled on him. "They told me you'd returned, real and in the flesh, but I confess I could not bring myself to believe them."

Corradeo was unaccountably uncertain of how to respond. Asterions were always catching him off guard. "Forgive me, but I don't think we've been properly introduced."

"I suppose not." The woman's odd, enchanting pupils constricted. "You might remember my parents, Valerian and Salash Idoni."

The names triggered a flood of buried memories from a different time, a different world, a different life. "Then you must be Maris. When you joined the SAI Rebellion, it created quite the scandal in the more rarified circles of Anaden society."

"Well…" the woman smiled icily and drew her fingertips along the edge of her desk "…I do so love stirring up a scandal."

Her demeanor was frigid enough to make him wish for the relative congeniality of the Concord Senate. "I apologize if I've offended you."

"Not at all. Or, I should say, not today."

He tried brandishing his most disarming countenance. "If I may soften the sting nonetheless, you are far more lovely than your mother ever dreamed of being."

"Assuming she dreamed of such things. I no longer recall her face, so I shall take your word for it."

"You genuinely don't remember her?"

"I remember her throwing things in the general direction of my head at our last encounter. I do not wish to remember anything further."

"I see." Another reminder that the side of the SAI Rebellion he'd experienced was only half the story. It rang true, though; Salash Idoni had been a vain and callous woman even before rebellion had torn her family apart. "I confess to being a bit surprised to meet you. I always assumed I was the sole person who still lived to recall those events of so long ago, but in my visits to the Asterion Dominion, I have done virtually nothing but meet people who were there as well."

"Don't trouble yourself overmuch. There are but a few of us who survive to keep the memory of our persecution alive. Tell me, do you no longer dispute synthetics' right to live, much less live freely?”

"It's been seven hundred millennia. During this time, a myriad of experiences has led me to evolve my position on the matter, yes." He swallowed a sigh, clasped his hands together and lifted his chin. "I feel like we've begun on the wrong footing. What can I do to improve our discourse?"

Maris gestured toward a round glass table by the window, and he followed her to it. She poured two glasses of lemon water from a crystal pitcher that must double as a work of art, then handed him one. "You're here today because you want Asterions and Anadens to be friends again, correct?"

"To put a fine point on it, yes. But I recognize a lot of work lies in front of us before friendship enters the picture. To start, I want to try to begin to heal the divisions sowing animosity between us. Address some of the root causes, then expand from there."

"Hmm." She sipped on her water while eyeing him speculatively over the glass. "Prove you are sincere in your intentions. Give us Asterion Prime."

Bitter lemon burned his throat as he choked on his drink. "Excuse me?"

"Asterion Prime. The planet. We would like it returned to us."

"I cannot displace eight hundred million people and order them to pick up and move to another planet."

"I suppose that would be terribly rude. Perhaps you can declare war on them instead. It will accomplish the same end."

Well, this conversation was not in any way improving from its disastrous start. Yes, he should have better prepared himself for the acrimony that clearly lingered in the hearts of many Asterions. But even so. "I cannot undo the past, Advisor...?"

"Debray."

"Advisor Debray. The SAI Rebellion and its consequences are carved upon the immutable stone of history, but we can only move forward. To such an end, I will point out that you're not banished from Asterion Prime. As the Dominion is now an Allied Member of Concord, any Dominion citizen can visit Asterion Prime whenever they wish."

"Oh, I know. I've already visited it three times, myself. Each visit has caused the yearning in my heart for my long-lost home to grow stronger."

He glanced toward the windows and the city beyond. "Objectively, Mirai is a more attractive planet than Asterion Prime. You have a truly wonderful home here."

"I do, don't I? And yet."

He tried again. "If the Dominion were to become a full member of Concord, Asterions would have the legal right to move there. It's in the Concord Charter."

Her lips pursed, as if to form a glistening horizon beyond which dark thoughts churned. "You make a valid point. But we've only just met the many-varied people of Concord, and I'm afraid Asterions are rather the independent sort. You should recollect this about us. We are grateful to have friends in Concord with whom we share much in the way of common purpose, but we're not ready to tie our fate and our future to your organization just yet."

"It would be fast, no question." He was overcome by the desire to find some means to please this woman, if merely in the tiniest way. He was Corradeo Praesidis, and entire legal systems had changed at his word.

"I cannot promise you anything here and now, but I may be able to engineer an exception that will allow Asterions to legally settle on Asterion Prime without the Dominion becoming a full member of Concord. In recognition of your lengthy history with and connection to the planet."

Her eyes widened slightly. "You can do that?"

"I can try."

"Will you?"

For you, yes—gods, what was wrong with him? Despite his best efforts, she'd managed to thoroughly ruffle him. "If this is an official request of the Asterion Dominion government, then I will make every attempt to ensure it happens."

"And if it's simply my personal request?"

He stared at her, unable to conjure a proper response.

She smiled, less icily than before but far more dangerously. "I only jest. Please, consider it an official request."

"Then I will endeavor to comply with the Dominion's first request in our negotiations."

"Do that. It will be a…" Maris twirled a lock of curls around her pinky finger "…positive first step."

MIRAI ONE

Grant Mesahle had rented what he'd *said* was an apartment, but it appeared to more closely resemble a warehouse, especially since it was located in the midst of a neighborhood that contained an equal mix of both.

He answered the door wiping grease off his forehead using a ratty cloth. "Maris? This is a surprise. Come on in."

The inside of the residence confirmed her impression of it from the outside—one wide-open room with a couple of pieces of furniture thrown haphazardly around a bunch of workbenches and equipment. "Interesting choice of living space."

He shrugged as he went over to a refrigeration unit, retrieved two sparkling juices and handed her one. "I plan on returning to Namino at the first available opportunity. But until then, I can't just sit around twiddling my thumbs. I've got to be working."

"And here I thought Lance was driving you around the clock."

"Only three-quarters of the clock lately. But the rest was feeling too much like idle time."

Some people never did change…which coincided nicely with what had brought her here. She moved to the sole couch and draped herself upon it, resting her head on one generous arm cushion and crossing her legs at the ankles on the other. "Grant, why are we doing all of this?"

He perched on the edge of a nearby chair and dropped his elbows to his knees. "All of what? Most of the things we're doing right now involve us trying rather desperately to survive."

"Yes, of course. We have always been survivors. I only mean…Corradeo Praesidis paid me a visit today."

"Oh? I'd heard he was skulking around our corner of the cosmos again."

"He's now the appointed Anaden representative to the Concord Senate, and he's allegedly attempting to build a new Anaden government from the ashes their Directorate left behind."

"A kinder, gentler Anaden government, I assume?"

"So he professes. I remain skeptical."

Grant frowned. "Listen, you know I'm always happy to chat with you, but am I really the best person to be giving you advice on this topic?"

"The available pool of First Genners—of people who remember the SAI Rebellion and the atrocities he committed as Supreme Commander—is not a large one. No offense."

"None taken."

"Lance despises Anadens in general and Corradeo Praesidis in particular with far greater vitriol than even I can conjure. Understandably so, considering it was the soldiers under Lance's command who the man massacred, but Lance cannot be remotely objective. Nika is too busy courting kyoseil like she's the starry-eyed princess at a cotillion ball to be bothered with thorny diplomatic issues."

"That is her job, though."

"It is." Maris arched an eyebrow. "Nevertheless, she has dumped this one in my lap."

"All right." Grant nodded and leaned forward in greater interest. "How was Corradeo when you met with him?"

"Utterly charming."

"Are you sure you don't mean 'charismatic'? Because I remember him being that. But charming?"

"*Charming*." She groaned and threw a forearm over her eyes. "Kind, complimentary, gracious, persuasive. It was dreadful."

"Do you think he was being sincere?"

"How should I know? Can people ever truly change? Has he? Have we?"

"Um…yes, I believe we have, if possibly not quite as much as we like to imagine."

"Precisely. We tweak our personality programming here and there. We rewrite our skill sets to learn new things and so on, but we're fundamentally the same people we were all those millennia ago. Sometimes I think we're so stuck that we're almost caricatures of ourselves. I must assume he is as well, mustn't I?"

"I don't know, Maris. People can grow and improve while still remaining true to themselves."

"You believe that?"

"I do."

She nodded in superficial acceptance of his assertion. "So I ask again: why are we doing all of this? To survive, yes, but it isn't enough. What are we surviving *for*? Who do we want to be when this is over? A fiercely independent people carving our own path through the cosmos? Or good, responsible citizens and contributors to an intergalactic community of mostly peaceful species?"

"Nika would say we can be both."

"Nika is as stubborn as a mule and entertains completely unrealistic expectations about the universe and its inhabitants. She's never accepted the world as it is and is constantly fighting to make it something…."

"Better?"

"I concede so. Oh, I'm merely perturbed at her for passing the Supreme Commander off to me and thereby forcing *me* to grapple with these existential questions."

"Fair enough. So, what did the two of you discuss?"

"I asked him to give us Asterion Prime back."

"You did *what*?"

Maris giggled. "Exactly what I said. It was the most absurd, nigh-on-obscene request I could think of on the spot. But you know what? While he didn't agree to cede us the planet, he did say he would try to finagle Asterions the right to settle there."

"Are you serious?"

"I am. We'll see if he is. But you understand what I'm getting at now. I mean, what am I supposed to *do* with this man?"

"Asterion Prime? This does change a few things." Grant rubbed at his jaw. "Okay, it's just a suggestion, but listen to what he has to say? If his proposals benefit us, consider accepting them, starting with the Asterion Prime one. Try to forge a professional relationship, if such a thing is possible with someone who brings so much baggage to the table. Take what he's willing to give, and hold him accountable. Never trust him."

"You are a wise man, Grant." She swung her legs off the couch and sat up. "You should share your wisdom with the rest of the world."

"Nope. I should build and sell space-rated habitat components and improve starship designs."

She fisted her hands at her chin, studying him for a moment. "Your laid-back, easy-going demeanor fools most people, but not me. Of all the First Genners who remain, it sometimes feels as though you still bear the scars of the rebellion more fervently—more painfully—than any of us, even Lance. Not to make Corradeo Praesidis' point for him, but the rebellion was so terribly long ago, and we've come so very far since then. Why don't you let them heal?"

"Because they serve as a reminder to me to ensure I never make the same mistakes again."

61

SYNRA

ASTERION DOMINION

Selene wiped sweat off her brow, then wound her hair into a low tail as she cut through the busy pedestrian traffic on her way to the Justice Center. How did the first Asterions survive on this sweltering planet? How did they do so today? If she'd been on one of the generation ships, she would have stepped outside, peered around, inhaled once, then pivoted and announced they needed to keep searching for a new home.

She supposed the answer to the second question was that the people who lived here every day fine-tuned their physical responses to heat and humidity so it didn't trouble them so much. If she planned on being here for longer than the afternoon, she'd definitely do the same.

The air conditioning inside the Justice Center wrapped her in its refreshing embrace, and she breathed the cool, dry air deep into her lungs before heading to the top floor.

Spencer was in his office meeting with two of his deputies when she stuck her head in, but he motioned her onward. He wore breathable linen pants and had his shirt-sleeves rolled up, and she noted how the air in the office was even cooler than the rest of the building.

"Selene, hi. What brings you to Synra?"

"Do you mind if I poke around down in storage for a bit? I'm chasing a lead, and there's a chance I'll uncover some clues in the older files here." The unspoken implication was that it was a lead related to one of her cases, but so long as she didn't say so, she wasn't lying.

"Not at all. Officer Benjen is on duty down there. Talk to him if you need help accessing anything."

"I will, thanks."

She left Spencer to his meeting and took the lift down to the basement of the Justice Center. The sprawling depot-style storage space stretched the length and breadth of the city block and for three stories underground. Quantum storage was dense and efficient, but Justice had existed in some form on Synra for over 680,000 years, which made for a veritable ocean of files.

She nodded to the security officer at the entrance. "Namino Justice Advisor Selene Panetier. Advisor Nimoet authorized me to take a look at some files."

"Yes, ma'am, he sent word." The officer gestured to an alcove containing a workstation a few meters to the right of the lift. "It's all yours."

"Appreciated." She sat down at the workstation and logged into the interface, then wasted no time running a top-level search for 'Joaquim Lacese.'

Two entries popped up. Given what she'd seen of his 'no holds barred' approach to life, she'd expected quite a few more. One of the entries was recent, and a quick scan told her it involved former Justice Advisor Blake Satair investigating Lacese for terrorist activities in the waning days of the Guides' rule. NOIR business, no doubt.

The second entry was much older. It involved an inquiry into criminal allegations relating to a woman named Cassidy Frenton. The investigation culminated in a raid of the woman's residence, which, as it turned out, she shared with Joaquim. The raid got ugly in a bad way, leaving the woman nonfunctional and most of the apartment and its contents heavily damaged. Evidence was confiscated and investigated, but nothing incriminating was uncovered, and the woman was cleared of wrongdoing in the case. Her psyche backup storage, however, was deemed irreparably damaged in the raid, and no additional remote storage existed.

In a world of near-total immortality, the woman was dead.

It was later determined that an error in a Justice analysis algorithm had incorrectly targeted Cassidy Frenton. The algorithm was reworked, financial reparations were paid, and the case was closed.

> *"He also killed the love of my life, but that's another story."*
> *"I'd like to hear that story."*
> *"Yeah, well, I don't want to tell it."*

She felt a deep pang of sympathy for Joaquim, and for his lost love. Justice had committed a terrible mistake, and it had cost a woman her life. Selene preferred to believe such mistakes didn't happen often in Asterion society, but 'not often' wasn't never.

Still, why was Frenton's backup in her residence? Why hadn't she stored a remote copy in a bank? Was it Lacese's trademark paranoia at work, way back then?

Selene pulled up the address of the apartment on Justice's annotated map, and discovered the neighborhood fell on the lower end of working-class. It might be that 'they didn't have the money for quality remote backup storage' was a reasonable answer.

With a sigh she sank down in the chair and clasped her hands behind her head. So now she knew the story, or at least the cold, clinical facts of it.

It went a long way toward explaining Joaquim's reactionary hatred of Justice. A programming mistake had cost this woman her life forever, and Justice had more or less shrugged and said, 'alas, nothing to be done about it.' She imagined he'd not taken well to the overwhelming helplessness the situation must have evoked. Of course he would have blamed Justice—the officers on the raid, the programmer of the algorithm, the supervisors who approved everything, the institution as an entity. His response, unsurprisingly, was to walk away from his old life, rebel against the system that had wronged him, and help create a resistance movement that would eventually succeed in tearing the whole system down.

And now here they were.

Had learning the truth helped anything? Joaquim wouldn't want her sympathy or commiseration; he just wasn't that type of guy. In fact, if she admitted what she'd done here, he'd surely kick her out of his bed for a month at a minimum, and quite possibly forever. So was there anything useful she *could* do with this knowledge?

The items confiscated from the apartment were still in storage. Maybe she could dig up some token offering for him. She checked the filing code, stood and headed for the lift.

The evidence slot was on the very bottom floor, deep in the back. Stashed away and abandoned alongside cases far older than this one. Satair had known his people and his algorithm had fucked up, and he'd buried it.

Down here, the air bordered on legitimately cold. Quiet, with a whiff of staleness. The province of dynes and forgotten stories.

She pulled out the sealed box, placed it on the floor and sat beside it, then entered the lock code. Opening the lid revealed a jumbled pile of quantum cubes, storage containers and a few utility tools. All were banged up, and several bore aged scorch marks.

After carefully rummaging around for a minute, she unearthed Frenton's psyche storage unit. A sizeable dent marred one corner, and darkened streaks decorated two sides. But the exterior casing showed no signs of cracks; it appeared as if the interior hadn't been breached. The unit was damaged for certain, but how badly? Was it possible...?

She grasped the unit in both hands, closed her eyes and opened her senses. The tiniest vibration danced against her palms, so she held it up to her ear and listened...and told herself she heard a faint hum. The internal power supply keeping the data stored inside alive might still be functioning.

Her chest fluttered as the waiting dilemma stared her down in the cold, silent catacomb. She could return the storage unit to the evidence box, return the evidence box to its slot, stand up and walk out of here. Leave the question unanswered and the mystery unsolved.

The intensity with which her heart yearned to do exactly that took her by surprise. Did she genuinely care about Joaquim so much? They weren't even in a relationship, not really. Granted, they'd spent four of the last seven nights together, but this was just sex.

…But perhaps not *just*. Dammit.

She took a moment to ignore her emotions and treat this as if it were a case. She examined her premises, asked questions of the evidence at hand and spun out likely scenarios if she moved forward on any of several potential paths.

Her analysis led to the following conclusions: a number of potential results could unfold if she took the storage unit and had it analyzed; from her location sitting here on the floor, she wasn't able to discern which one would ultimately play out. But if she left everything in its place and walked away, she'd never be able to look Joaquim in the eye again.

So there it was. Decision made.

She set the psyche storage unit on the floor beside her, repacked the other items more neatly and slid the evidence box back into its slot. Then she picked up the unit, stood and went upstairs to see the security officer.

"I need to check an item out of evidence."

"Yes, ma'am." He entered a command in his interface, and a pane appeared in front of her. "Simply fill out the marked boxes—but you know what to do."

"I do." She entered the case number, the evidence slot location and the tag on the storage unit before slipping it into her satchel. "Thank you for your help. Have a good day."

62

MIRAI

MIRAI ONE

Selene took the storage unit to the Mirai Justice Division, since Adlai had given her carte blanche to use his facilities and resources while she was displaced.

She was beginning to hate mooching off the other Justice Advisors for every single thing she needed to accomplish, but there was no alternative for now. All government and most private resources were being poured into fleet production and planetary defenses, and she had no basis to argue with the choice.

Luckily, Erik Rhom, Adlai's lead technical analyst, was working in the lab when she arrived. He enjoyed a stellar reputation within Justice, and she knew Adlai trusted him implicitly.

"Advisor Panetier! This is a pleasant surprise. What can I do for you?"

She presented the storage unit to him. "This is a psyche storage unit confiscated in a Justice investigation on Synra some years ago. It's listed as 'damaged,' which it clearly is, but I'm interested in learning precisely *how* damaged. Do you think you can take a look at it and see if it's operable at all?"

"Sure, I can spare a few minutes." He took the unit from her and carried it over to a workstation, where he secured it in a stability frame and placed two fingers on a sensor pad. She settled into a chair by the door to wait, her thoughts dark with internal arguments.

"Hey, Erik, can you—" Adlai stepped inside, then stopped when he saw her. "Oh, sorry. I didn't realize you were here. Erik, carry on." He shifted toward her. "Anything interesting going on?"

She considered evading the question. He'd be satisfied with

'forensics on a case of mine' and not challenge her further. That was their arrangement. And it wasn't her secret to share.

But the mere fact that Joaquim didn't like to talk about it didn't make it a 'secret.' The case file was accessible to anyone with the necessary clearance—all Justice officials of Deputy grade and above, as well as any officers assigned to some aspect of the investigation. And getting the backstory should only soften Adlai's inherent dislike of Joaquim, right?

She shot him a rueful smile. "I'm sending you a file. You should give it a read."

He leaned on the doorframe and fell silent for several minutes. Finally he banged his head against the wall with a groan. "Satair truly was an unmitigated bastard."

"Yes, he was."

"I didn't know."

"None of us did. And Lacese didn't...I had to dig this up myself."

Erik kicked his chair back from the workstation and toed it around to face them. "The casing's structural integrity is pretty iffy, but it's marginally holding together. All the data inside is intact, even the DNA and structure files." He grinned, looking victorious. "We can wake this person up."

Her heart sank and buoyed at the same time. Saving lives was her job and her calling, but damn, this one was going to cost her. "This is excellent news. Thank you so much for your help."

Adlai stared at Erik, then at her. "But the file said it was irreparably damaged."

"Either Satair couldn't be bothered to have it checked properly, or he lied. Either alternative seems as probable as the other."

"Gods, Selene. How many more situations like this are hiding in the Synra file warehouse?"

"An excellent question. Spencer will need to open a review of all closed cases during Satair's tenure."

Adlai nodded. "We're meeting for a working lunch in a few minutes. I'll talk to him about it." His eyes slid over to the box sitting in the stability frame. "What are you going to do about this?"

She stood with a heavy sigh. "My job, of course. I'm going to wake her up."

RW

Adlai's thoughts were troubled and tumultuous as he walked home from work that evening. He'd never believed Blake Satair was a particularly honest or honorable Justice Advisor, even before the Rasu and Satair's role in the Guides' betrayal came to light. But to allow—possibly foment—such a level of corruption and, to be honest, *injustice* inside the man's own organization? Not once or twice, but for hundreds of years? He was so disgusted that he felt sick to his stomach.

Spencer had readily agreed to institute a top-down review of all old Synra Justice cases starting in the morning. In time, the rot would be ferreted out and recompense would be attained by the victims…but not justice. Some crimes couldn't be undone.

Which led him directly to Joaquim Lacese. Nothing excused Lacese's more egregious actions, but this revelation admittedly went a long way toward explaining them. What might the combination of the crushing weight of such a loss plus the abject helplessness to rectify it do to a man?

It wasn't much of a question, as he already had his answer. Lacese's virulent hatred of Justice didn't seem so incomprehensible now. At this moment, Adlai hated Justice a little himself.

No, this wasn't right. He believed in its mission. In *his* mission. He believed Justice was a force for good in the world, one which helped to hold Asterion society together at the always fraying edges.

The lesson to be learned here, if he was brave enough to learn it, was that the institution was not sacrosanct. It was only as strong as the men and women comprising it, and thus as vulnerable to flaws and outright failures as anything else.

A life lost that didn't have to be. Another life ruined for decades…that didn't have to be. His thoughts merely had to flit across the notion of losing Perrin forever to feel gut-wrenching empathy for Lacese. Unable to find justice where the law said he must find it, if at all, the man had struck out at the world around him instead. And Adlai honestly couldn't blame him.

He opened the door to their apartment and was greeted with the warm, spicy scent of dinner-in-the-making. "Perrin?"

"Welcome home! I'm in the kitchen."

He shrugged off his coat and found her tossing the contents of a wok in the air, surrounded by a haze of steam. "I'm making stir-fry."

"I can tell. What brought this on?" How long had it been since either of them had found the time or energy to actually *cook* a meal?

She drove the spatula around the wok with fervor. "I had a really good day at the new refugee center today. I mean, there were a couple of tough encounters. People who are suffering. But I did everything I could to at least make their day better, if not their lives. The rest will come in time.

"At the end of the day, I confess I was feeling drained and tired, and maybe a touch depressed. But then I said to myself, 'No! I'm not going to collapse on the couch and wallow in sorrow until I go back out and torture myself all over again tomorrow. I did good today, and I'm going to reward myself. Reward us.' So, stir-fry." She beamed and tossed the wok's contents again.

"That's wonderful. I'm proud of you." His chest swelling with a fresh jumble of emotions, he went over and took the wok from her, setting it on the cooling area. Next, he wrapped her up in his arms and pressed his nose to hers. "I want to tell you something right now, and I hope you'll hear and believe me."

"What is this? What's up?"

"I love you."

Her gaze slid away to scrutinize the wok. "I know you do...."

"No, you don't. I've been kind of an ass lately—about the up-gen, about how many hours you're working, about, well mostly the up-gen—and I was wrong. I'm sorry.

"I love you. I love the way you bring light and joy to my life. I love how the freckles on your nose stand out in the sun, and how your hair looks delightfully different every day. I love how you're always pushing yourself, striving to be better. Not for selfish reasons, but for the world. I'll eternally wish you weren't so hard on yourself, because I think you're perfect as you are, but I respect and understand why you do it. And from now on, I'll support you in your choices, no matter what."

Her eyes glistened brightly amid the steam in the air as her eyelashes fluttered. She sniffled a little. "Why...what brought this on?"

"I just had a reminder today that even in our extraordinary world, where we take so much for granted, life and love can still be fragile and fleeting. We have to grab hold of it while we can and not let go."

PART IV

AWAKENINGS

63

CONCORD HQ

SPECIAL PROJECTS

Marlee bumped into Morgan as she was headed through the Special Projects entrance. The woman's face lit up on seeing her, which was just *splendid*.

"You were able to get away for a little while?"

Marlee nodded. "I was. It was a simple matter of rearranging a few dozen deliverables and two appointments."

"What? That doesn't sound simple at all. You didn't have to go to so much trouble."

She shrugged lightly. "No trouble. I wanted to."

"All right. I appreciate the company. Let's go see what Devon has in store for us today."

They cleared security and wound through the Special Projects labyrinth until they reached the Warfare Testing Suite way in the back.

Devon glanced up when they entered and promptly groaned. "Ah, crap. We did have a session scheduled, didn't we? Sorry, no can do." He waved toward the wide coding screen displayed in front of him. "I don't know if you heard, but the Rasu are using stealth now, and our illustrious leader has asked me to snap my fingers and magically imbue our fleet of deep space sensors with the ability to see through Rasu camouflage."

"What if you—"

Devon thrust a hand out to interrupt Morgan. "Hush. I don't need any ideas, at least not until I've tried and failed with the twelve ideas I currently have. Ideas aren't the problem. Execution is the problem."

Morgan put her hands on her hips in defiance. "Well, I'm here, and I don't require supervision. Simply point me toward what we were going to work on today before you got a directive from on high."

"Oh, fine. But please don't break anything irreplaceable." He pointed at a workstation in the far left corner of the lab. "Go check out the new Eidolon control software for the RNEW. I made the changes you requested, except for the one that was ludicrous. Run it through the paces so I can certify it and push it out before the Rasu get around to attacking somewhere truly important."

"What ludicrous request?"

"You know the one I mean."

Morgan rolled her eyes at Marlee as they headed over to the workstation. "I genuinely don't."

"Yeah, but I bet you'll know what's missing once you get in there and take it for a spin."

"Damn straight I will." Morgan fired up the workstation and navigated through the lab's file directory as if she worked here, which she kind of did now, and in seconds had located the Eidolon repository. She loaded up the control software, and Artificial-level code spun out across the workstation's three screens.

The woman's irises glittered a dazzling amethyst as she studied the software. When Marlee realized she was staring, she diverted her gaze to the screens and tried to follow along with the code flow as well. She didn't understand all of it, mostly the parts dealing with warship maneuvering and trajectory variability—a fighter pilot she was not—but she got the gist of much more than she would have even a year ago.

"Oh! *That* change." Morgan's lips curled up in a hint of a smirk. "I suppose it was a tiny bit ludicrous."

Marlee burst out laughing, and after a beat, Morgan joined in.

"Hey, quiet over there! I can't perform magic when you two are giggling like schoolgirls!"

Morgan dropped a hand on Marlee's shoulder and urged her closer, until their heads were huddled together to muffle their laughing. Marlee was wearing a sleeveless turtleneck, and her bare skin burned where Morgan's hand rested on it; her breath kept getting stuck in her throat, and not from too much laughter.

Finally Morgan dropped her hand, leaving behind a void where it had lain, and refocused on the screens to study the software for another moment. "I won't be able to say for certain until I run it through the sim, but it does appear to be a lot cleaner now."

Devon raised his voice from across the room. "I've got to go scavenge for components from the storage room. I'll be back in a few minutes."

Morgan tossed a hand in his direction, then regarded the nearby sim chair a little wearily. "I swear, my lower back still aches from my last session. I'm going to requisition plusher cushions."

Seeing an opportunity she'd been hoping for, Marlee forged ahead. "Um, if you're not ready to get in the sim chair yet, would you mind terribly reviewing something for me?"

"Sure. What is it?"

"A programming upgrade I've been writing for my eVi. Seeing all the improvements you've made here—" Marlee gestured to the screens "—I'm curious about your opinion of it. Your off-the-cuff take is all."

"Let's have a look."

"Thanks." She fetched the case out of her pocket, since she was carrying it around with her everywhere now, and inserted the small quantum cube into the workstation's dock. The Eidolon software was replaced by new code on the screens.

Morgan began inspecting it in the same manner as she'd reviewed the previous code, and Marlee tried not to fidget nervously. It felt as if she was baring her soul to the woman.

After almost a minute, Morgan's eyes cut over to Marlee, an intriguing glint lighting them beyond their normal Prevo luster. "This is a great deal more than an 'eVi enhancement,' isn't it?"

"It might be. What do you think?"

"Stanley says he couldn't write anything better. He's calling you brilliant."

Her lips pursed to pull down a silly grin. "And you?"

"I'm not a natural coder, but it seems damn clever to me. Say, do you mind if I take a quick glance at what you're running now? I may—or rather Stanley may—be able to offer a suggestion or two if we can compare the updates to your existing software."

"You mean…?" Her hand went to the nape of her neck.

"Surface-level scan only. I promise I won't deep dive your secrets."

Oh, you can if you want to. She gathered her hair up off her neck. "Go right ahead."

The thought had started to occur to her that they didn't have an external interface module handy when she felt two fingertips settle over her ports. Because Morgan wouldn't need an interface. Direct connection. Skin on skin. She shuddered in delight.

"Are you cold?"

"No. I mean, it was just a chill." Good thing Morgan couldn't see her now-scarlet cheeks.

"Interesting. You've already made upgrades, haven't you? None of this is standard-issue eVi code."

"A few. I like to tinker."

"You'd make a great Prevo." The fingertips remained in place, but she sensed the rise of Morgan's chest against her back as the woman drew in a breath. "This is what you're trying to do, isn't it? Become a Prevo without joining with a separate, fully realized Artificial?"

"You caught me. That is the plan. Dr. Canivon has signed off on the overall framework, so I'm double-checking everything before I take the plunge. And getting a few second opinions."

Morgan's fingertips drifted off her ports to linger at the base of her neck, and Marlee's pulse set off to the races.

"I think Stanley's right. You really are brilliant."

Marlee oh-so-carefully shifted around so as not to step away and create distance while she turned enough to see Morgan. "I'm thrilled you think so. It matters what you think of me." *Gulp.* "A lot."

Her heartbeat pounded in her ears as Morgan smiled in return, and the lab faded away. In a slow-motion sequence worthy of the best romance vids, their faces drew closer.

She leaned in the rest of the way and pressed her lips to Morgan's. Warm and pliant, in delightful contrast to the woman's hard persona, and tasting of peppermint and coffee. Heat flooded her chest as her hand snaked up toward the woman's jaw—

Morgan yanked away from Marlee, scrambling backward until she banged into the workstation, her eyes wide in shock. "What— why did you do that?"

Still basking in the glow of the kiss, Marlee beamed. "Why do you think? I wanted to show you—"

"How could you…why…I thought you were my friend!"

The sharp, pained edge in Morgan's voice penetrated the heady, fuzzy sensation engulfing her, yanking Marlee back to a reality that might not actually be going the way she'd planned. "I *am* your friend. I'd also like to be more than a friend."

Morgan shook her head roughly. "What in the fuck about all of—" she motioned wildly to herself, waving a hand in front of her face "—the shitshow that is me suggests I am in any way whatsoever capable of being anyone's 'more than friend'? Goddammit!" She spun and practically ran for the exit, bumping into Devon on his way in as he returned from the storage room.

"Morgan, where are you off to?"

"To find the bottom of a bottle." Then she was gone.

Marlee flopped unceremoniously into the sim chair, her shoulders sagging and her chin dropping to her chest. All the air had vacated her lungs, and it seemed her limbs, too.

She shouldn't have leapt off the ledge. It was too soon. She'd known it was too soon. Her mouth was always getting ahead of her brain—literally, this time. But it had felt so perfect, dammit!

After wallowing for a bit longer, she looked up to find Devon watching her with a sympathetic expression. "I did warn you."

"I know. I seriously thought we'd built a connection. An attraction and…." She dragged herself to her feet, removed the quantum cube from the dock and grabbed her jacket from the table.

"You're leaving me, too?"

"Yep. I'll be honest. The bottom of a bottle doesn't sound too bad right about now."

64

SENECA

CAVARE
MILKY WAY GALAXY

Marlee loitered outside the entrance to Hemiska Research Laboratories, making a show of lounging casually against the decorative stone half-wall by the company's fancy signage.

The evening shadows were growing long, and the outbound flow of people from the building had slowed to a trickle, but she was undeterred. She knew Gregor Feldt well, and he'd be working late. He'd only had this job for two months, so he'd be slaving away trying to impress his boss and coworkers.

Ten minutes later, Gregor finally came striding out the front doors with a knapsack weighing down his left shoulder, likely full of work he was taking home. But he wouldn't be getting it done tonight, dammit.

She pushed off the wall and gave him a wave to get his attention.

He stopped on the walkway as his gaze fixed on her. Surprise came first, followed by a hint of hesitation. Then a speculative smile.

"Marlee. I haven't seen you in months." Since she'd picked a fight to break it off with him one morning on her way out the door, in fact. It hadn't been her finest moment, though her spectacular flame-out earlier today obviously topped it. "What brings you here?"

"You, of course!" She meandered closer to where he stood. "I've been super-busy at the Consulate lately, but I wanted to stop by and see how you're doing. How's the new job?"

"It's, um, good. A lot of work school didn't prepare me for."

"That's how it goes, right?"

"Right, though it would've been nice if school had warned us. But I've got a smart boss and talented..." his expression flickered "...why are you really here? With the way we left things, I frankly didn't expect to ever see you again. Not on purpose."

She worked to look contrite—and she was. She'd been cruel to him, even if she hadn't meant to be at the time. "I'm sorry about all of that. I truly am. You had to follow your dreams and I had to follow mine, but I didn't need to be a selfish bitch about it. Friends?"

"Sure, I guess. Friends."

"Wonderful. Listen, do you want to...the thing is, I came across a bottle of Balvenie single malt scotch in one of the quirky shops on HQ the other day and picked it up. I remember how much you enjoy the brand. It's..." she met and held his gaze, *meaningfully* "...at my apartment."

"Oh." His Adam's Apple bobbed; he glanced down at his knapsack, then back up at her with a new light in his eyes, one she recalled all too well. "I have this important report I need to get done for work, but it's not due for two more days. I guess I can...yeah. I'd like to have some of that Balvenie. Do you want to get a bite to eat first?"

A corner of her mouth curled up, and she shook her head. "No."

RW

Silvery light from Seneca's giant moon reflected off the open-but-mostly-full bottle of scotch situated on the floor by the bed. Marlee leaned half off the mattress to grab it, then sat up and scooted back with it in hand. She took a long swig before offering it to Gregor.

He chuckled. "You know this is supposed to be consumed out of an inverted-funnel hand-blown crystal glass filled precisely to the one-third level." He turned the bottle up and matched her swig before handing it back to her.

She set it on the bedside table and rolled onto her side to prop up on an elbow and face him. "The Novoloume have a drink called *alonsa'dior*. They only consume it through a three-meter-long looping tube with special filters situated in every loop."

"They do everything with overwrought formality, don't they?"

"Pretty much. I mean, they're not *that* bad about it. Well, sometimes they are."

He reached out to dance his fingertips along the curve of her waist and over her hip, until it hovered on the verge of tickling. "You're happy at your job?"

"Oh, my, what a complicated question. I am simultaneously suffocating under the weight of the bureaucracy and paperwork requirements while also delighting in how I've gotten to help so many aliens and see such incredible wonders. In the last several months, I've gotten arrested and locked in a swamp jail, knocked unconscious by a rampaging alien mech, and trapped underground during a Rasu invasion. But I've also helped to rescue two entire species from certain death."

"Sounds about par for the course for you." He leaned in and kissed her softly. He'd always been a terrific kisser, and her enjoyment of it was only slightly marred by the resurgent memory of a kiss gone wrong. "Listen, my company is having a holiday party this weekend. It'll be kind of stuffy, but if you want to come, you can meet some of my coworkers. A few of them are even burgeoning friends."

"Oh." She subtly scooted a few centimeters away. "I can't, I'm sorry. I've got a work obligation with the Godjan refugees—they're one of the species I helped to save."

A frown grew on his features. "I didn't say which weekend day it was."

"My work obligation is going to take all weekend. Actually, weekends aren't technically a thing at HQ. Everyone gets three out of nine days off—"

"Not the point, Marlee." His chin dropped to his chest. "So this was just a random hookup, then?"

Her lips parted, but there was no gracious way to answer him, whether truth or lie.

He huffed a breath. "I see." The next second he was crawling off the bed and snatching his pants off the floor. "I am such an idiot."

"Gregor…."

"What? What is it you think you're going to say? Something to get me to linger long enough for a second round, maybe?"

Her eyebrows arched hopefully before she was able to stop them, which was the exact wrong sentiment to display.

"You really are unbelievable. *No.* I need to go home, sober up, and work on my report. Oh, and I'm taking the rest of the bottle with me." He pulled his shirt over his head and came around to her side of the bed, where he capped the scotch and tossed it in his knapsack.

"Okay. I want you to have it."

"Do you?"

"Yes. I want good things for you, Gregor. I want you to be happy."

His hostile posture softened a little. "I believe you, though I'm not sure why. Even so, the next time you're horny or lonely, or both, comm someone else. And I *know* there are plenty of someone else's for you to choose from."

"Hey, that's not fair. I never cheated on you."

"I know you didn't. You're a serial monogamist—you get bored, you move on." He checked around the floor to confirm he hadn't left anything, then stared at her with a soulfulness that used to slay her. "Listen, Marlee. I think you have a good heart, I genuinely do. But sometimes you're like a wrecking ball, crashing through the lives of everyone in your orbit in your fervent rush to…I honestly don't know what. Conquer the universe or something."

Ouch. His words stung, and defensiveness flared; how could it not? "Maybe I once was, but I've grown up a lot. I've learned so much about myself and the world these last few months."

"Yet here I am, walking away from you again. Or being thrown out. It's not any clearer this time than it was the last one."

"I'm sorry."

"Don't be. I had a great time tonight." He nodded sharply, as if to himself. "Goodbye, Marlee."

Then he turned, strode through the door and was gone. Too damn much like Morgan had done.

She flopped back on the bed with a dramatic sigh. What, exactly, had this accomplished, other than a few hours of fun and pleasure? She was alone again, just her and her wrecking ball self. She'd still screwed things up with Morgan, and upset the woman badly on top of it. And she still had no idea how to fix any of it.

Abruptly, she sat upright as dramatically as she'd crashed down. The one thing she retained absolute control over—the one thing she alone *could* fix—was herself.

The operating code was ready. She could tinker at the margins for the next decade, or she could bite the bullet and take the leap into the unknown. That, at least, she was quite skilled at doing.

Without hyper-analyzing everything any further, she made an appointment for later today at her cybernetics clinic of choice for the first round of implants and injections. Also for a neural imprint backup, in case this little 'eVi enhancement' took a wrecking ball to her brain.

Time to get on with it.

65

THE PRESIDIO

Morgan's head pounded against her skull as she warily picked her way through the hallways of the Presidio. Well, it didn't *literally* pound, since the alcohol flushing routines had cleaned up most of the hangover symptoms by the time she'd departed her temporary apartment in Cavare. But the brutal memory of the head pounding she'd suffered through on waking up this morning was sufficiently close to the real experience to be a bother.

You just admitted the sensation is 'all in your head.' Why don't you banish it with a thought?

Stanley, how is it that you've been here for more than sixteen years and have yet to learn the first thing about human psychology?

Strenuous effort and constant vigilance.

She stifled a chuckle. At least one of them had developed a sense of humor. The levity was quickly buried, however, beneath a resurgence of such nasty emotions as dismay, confusion, betrayal and a touch of sorrow.

She liked Marlee; it had been...pleasant...to enjoy the beginnings of a friendship again. And dammit but it hurt to have such pleasantness ripped away from her. To have the benefits of their budding relationship stolen by Marlee flagrantly overstepping the explicit bounds of what was, by definition, 'friendship.'

Hadn't she?

I say this with the gentlest, most sympathetic of voices, but the kiss was nice, wasn't it?

Of course *the kiss was nice. That's not the point! Done right, all kisses are nice, but they have nothing to do with relationships—what they are, what they should be, how to thoroughly trash them.*

I see. Stanley's tone made it clear he did not remotely see.

She dodged a colonel barreling down the hall toward some emergency. She imagined the Presidio was on perpetual high alert these days, seeing as the Rasu were playing peek-a-boo with Concord and making like thieves in the night with their ships and assets.

Beneath the stinging hurt and wounded pride, she found she wasn't really angry at Marlee. The woman was young, bright beyond her years and effervescent. Also cocky and naively confident that the universe owed her magnificent things. And to be fair, Marlee wasn't wrong on that point. But Morgan couldn't be one of those things. For one, she hadn't been magnificent in a long time. For another...she just *couldn't* be.

Ugh. She forcibly put away the torturous ruminations as she exited the lift on the top floor of the station. Her ancient commission had gotten her through the security checkpoints up until now, but for the final gauntlet, she was subjected to a retinal and superficial DNA scan, as well as an interrogation on her purpose and intentions today.

She glared at the security lieutenant. "I made an appointment. The Fleet Admiral accepted it. What more of a purpose do I need?"

"You're not active duty. What do you need to see the Fleet Admiral regarding?"

"I believe it's none of your business. I bet he agrees."

The lieutenant scowled and grumbled, but he gruffly waved her on. "Through the doors straight ahead, then take the first left. No deviations."

"I wouldn't dream of it." She scratched at her forehead once she was through the gate.

Pound, pound, pound.

Stanley was right; this was a psychological tic, and one that she needed to banish immediately. Perhaps if she was successful in her mission this morning.

After around ninety seconds of waiting in the lobby, a secretary showed her into the Fleet Admiral's office. Malcolm Jenner looked up from a screen to jerk a nod as she entered. They'd known each other for too long and shouted through too many disagreements to bother with formalities, she supposed.

"Morgan, welcome. I admit I was surprised to receive your request for a meeting."

"Me, too." She plopped in one of the chairs opposite his desk and dropped her elbows to her knees. "So you fucked it up, huh?"

He gave her a pained grimace. "I prefer to believe the jury is still out."

"You didn't hear it from me, but you're not wrong. Good luck." It was a downright magnanimous gesture on her part, she thought.

Malcolm's expression buoyed, but he hurriedly schooled it again. "I assume you're not here to dispense unsolicited relationship advice. What can I do for you?"

"You can get me back in a fighter."

"Excuse me?"

"A fighter. A small, agile warship that shoots bad guys for a living, with and sometimes without the aid of a human pilot."

"I know what—are you asking to have your commission reinstated?"

"I suppose it will be a necessary first step, but I don't care about the paperwork. These last few weeks, I've been helping Devon test out new warship tech over at Concord Special Projects, and the one thing I've learned from the experience is that I hate labs. I need the real thing. I'm ready to shoot some Rasu."

"We would welcome the added gun. I recall you were rather talented at shooting things."

"I wasn't talented. I was the best the multiverse has ever seen."

"Quite possibly. But this is the military. I can't simply wave my hands in the general direction of a bureaucrat and get you reinstated to a combat squadron overnight." He rubbed at his chin. "Though there are a couple of Concord specialty attack squadrons you could—"

"No."

"But you're already working with Special Projects. From there it's but a few short steps to combat duty. And I suspect Devon Reynolds *can* simply wave his hands in the general direction of a bureaucrat and get you in a ship."

"I said no."

Malcolm grimaced…then realization seemed to dawn. "This is about what happened during the Ch'mshak Revolt, isn't it?"

"Damn straight it's about what happened during the Ch'mshak Revolt."

"You blame Miriam Solovy for Harper's death."

"Don't you?"

He sighed. "No. I blame the cruel vagaries of combat operations. Soldiers risk their lives every time they go into battle, and sometimes who lives and who dies is nothing but a roll of the cosmic dice."

"It definitely isn't skill, because—anyway, Miriam never should have sent Brook's squad into that Ch'mshak nest. Not without a great deal more intel and a workable extraction plan."

"Maybe, maybe not. Morgan, everyone makes mistakes."

"Someone in Miriam Solovy's position isn't afforded the luxury of mistakes."

"Or in mine, right?"

"I don't know. Have you made any lately?"

"Almost certainly. So why don't you blame me?"

"I do, a little." She pinched the bridge of her nose. *Pound, pound, pound.* "But I realize you were merely following orders from Miriam. And unlike me, following orders is something you are psychologically compelled to do. In your thick head, you had no choice."

Malcolm scowled. "Um, okay, I'm going to move on past what I'm fairly sure was an insult. Listen, there's an outfit affiliated with the IDCC running an experimental hybrid fighter craft in combat operations. If we call it field testing and fudge a few details, I can probably get you assigned to the unit."

"Fantastic."

"Don't you care who's in charge of it, or what the history or mission of the unit is?"

"Not particularly. Just tell me where to go so I can start shooting the bad guys."

"Cool your jets. It'll take a day or two or three. I have to leave for Earth in a few minutes, but I'll get the process started before I head out. The unit is based out of the IDCC Orbital Defense Station above Romane. Where are you staying these days?"

"Doesn't matter. I can have my bags packed in forty minutes." She stood. "So I'll go ahead and do that, and you let me know when I can climb in a cockpit."

66

MIRAI

RIDANI ENTERPRISES LABS

Nika rested her chin on her palm as she watched Dashiel fiddle with the settings on the test rack. "Not satisfied with the results so far?"

"You know I never am." He stepped back and placed his hands on his hips. "Palmer wants the RNEW fitted onto fighters yesterday. Oh, and by the way, he also wants two thousand shots out of the weapon before it requires maintenance. No big thing."

"You know you love it, though. The work, that is. Not Lance's incessant demands."

"I suppose I do." He wandered over to where she sat on one of the worktables and leaned in to kiss her—then abruptly pulled away, grimacing. "There's an issue in one of the other testing labs. I don't think it'll take long to deal with. Can you hang out here for a few minutes? Wait for me?"

The thought, *I'll always wait for you, darling*, flitted through her mind, but it felt inappropriately dramatic for the mood. So she gave him an easy smile. "Happily."

Once he'd gone, she spent some time wandering around the lab, peeking into enclosures and perusing queued-up testing profiles. Dashiel was somehow running a hundred different projects simultaneously, across multiple labs, manufacturing facilities and planets. She had no idea how he managed it all.

At the end of the lab stood two wide doors; above them, a lit sign read 'Kyoseil Storage.' No angry red warnings advised none to tread there, so, intrigued, she opened the doors and peeked inside.

Storage vats were stacked floor-to-ceiling and stretched for easily thirty meters on both sides of a wide middle aisle. A sliding robotic arm assembly extended down from the ceiling, ready to unslot any vat when its number was called and deliver it to the transfer mechanism out the other end of the room.

She knew this kyoseil was brought here after being extracted from its Reor shells. Dashiel was keeping Reor-derived kyoseil separate from pure Chosek-derived kyoseil, in case any anomalies arose in the new variant. When it arrived at the lab, it was placed in a gelatinous solution that both protected it and prepared it for future use—in electronics, equipment and Asterion bodies, but most of all right now, in warship hulls and weapons.

The natural luminescence of the kyoseil bathed the room in a faint amber glow, diffused by the translucent vat enclosures.

Nika ran a hand along the enclosure nearest to her—and jumped back in surprise when the kyoseil inside it brightened considerably. Her breath caught in her throat as she stepped closer once more, her fingers splayed in front of her. Even before they touched the glass, the kyoseil adopted a lazy, pulsing pattern that seemed to reach out to meet her palm.

She lifted her other hand and stretched it out toward the adjoining vat, gasping in wonder as its contents lit up in a complementary pattern. Her fingers trembled against the glass…and gradually her skin began to tingle.

Why was this occurring now? What had changed? Or was this fated to happen when she walked into this storage room no matter what?

She took a deep breath, reluctantly lifting her hands off the vats, and backed into the center of the aisle. She switched her vision to the kyoseil band and opened her mind, as if she were reaching for a ceraff with which to connect.

The entire room exploded in brilliant iridescence, with kyoseil strings stretching between the vats so thickly they coated everything in a complex web of light.

Can you hear me? Can you talk to me?

No voice answered, but the strings began to vibrate. In excitement? The energy created by their movement thrummed against her skin—not stinging, but instead almost soothing. Certainly delightful.

My mind is open to you. Will you open yours to me?

To describe the answer as 'silence' would be a travesty. True, no words were spoken, but the room hummed and sang like a heavenly chorus, and she was *so close* to understanding the melody.

KATOIKIA TAIRI

MIRAD VIGILATE

I drifted listlessly across the arid steppes of Katoikia Tairi. The closest stasis tower was a gray shadow on the horizon, a hundred kilometers distant. The Directorate had destroyed their true homeworld, Katoikia, in the final chaotic days of the war. But this replacement planet was so entirely identical to the original that visiting it stirred up a maelstrom of old memories from my first days and years on Katoikia. They haunted me, picking at my thoughts like gnats in summertime.

How strange that I remembered gnats.

I avoided coming 'home' whenever possible—I treated the empyreal Idryma as my true home in any event, now that Aurora Thesi was no more—for doing so evoked only a deep chasm in my soul. I counted those early days as the most difficult of my long, winding life, and until recently, I had packed the memories away in a dark corner of my mind, where I had no cause to dwell on them. Recent circumstances, however, were drawing them inexorably back to my attention.

But it was no matter. The future was in the past and already written, so I worked to turn my thoughts to my purpose for coming here today.

With the Galenai, Vrachnas, Icksel and other Protected Species shielded by Rift Bubbles, Alex had inquired about what other primitive, evolving species might need special protection from the Rasu's ravages. I owed her an answer.

The smoky glass of the Mirad Vigilate's faceted dome loomed ahead, the lone structure to disrupt the landscape for many kilometers in every direction. Anxious to be done with this place as quickly as possible, I drew myself together and transported directly inside.

Paratyr, the long-serving Second Sentinel of the Mirad Vigilate, lay angled in its observation perch, which rotated so Paratyr could repeatedly set eyes on each of the sea of windows surrounding the chair. Once, the Katasketousya Sentinels had watched vulnerable species for impending encroachment by Directorate forces. Now, they watched for the encroaching shadow of the Rasu.

For while everyone was focused on the escalating war in Concord and Asterion territory, the Rasu were always expanding everywhere. While they dallied, the Rasu claimed worlds in the Shapley Supercluster on one end and Centaurus on the other. At this rate, in another few years they would reach the fringes of space controlled by the next nearest advanced civilization, the Belascocians. But only if Concord and the Asterions—only if Alex and Nika—failed to stop them here.

"Mnemosyne, welcome." Paratyr roused itself from the chair and eased its bare feet to the floor. "You visit so rarely, I had almost forgotten your semblance."

"You forget nothing, my friend."

"Too little, and too much." Paratyr waved a thin, spindly arm, and the windows into a hundred worlds slowed their rotation. "Who are you here to check up on today?"

I wandered among the portals, careful not to slip through one. "All of them. Alex—I trust you remember her—has inquired about our efforts to protect the defenseless from the Rasu, and I promised her I would acquire an update."

"The uncommon Human who saw what others did not. And her

brooding, intimidating lover. Their visit, I shall not forget. But to your question! As I informed the Idryma some cycles ago, the Rasu draw worryingly near to the Dremosh in Canes I. Lakhes assures me a Rift Bubble will be deployed before they fall into mortal danger."

"Then it will be done."

"Naturally. I watch…" the windows spun up, then slowed again as two binary systems in loose orbit around one another centered in front of Paratyr "…this region of Laniakea, on the edge of Centaurus, as it is within the shadow of Rasu expansion and hosts multiple interesting species. But they remain safe for a time."

"What about.…" My voice drifted off, my intended question forgotten, as a flaring sensation on the fringes of my myriad tendrils of awareness shot to the forefront.

I dropped my presence in the Mirad Vigilate and honed in on the fragile, tentative yet melodic ripples winding across the fabric of space to reach me. Five megaparsecs away in the Gennisi galaxy, to be precise, though the distance mattered not. The source of the ripples was a tiny pinpoint of activity, of…

…awakening. She pushed relentlessly at the boundaries of understanding, and those boundaries resonated in response.

Excitement and uncommon fear bloomed in equal measure in my soul. It wouldn't be long now.

"Mnemosyne? Have you abandoned me without a proper farewell? Eh, such is the lonely fate of a Sentinel."

I forced my presence back into the Mirad Vigilate. "Apologies, Paratyr. There was a distraction, but I will address it after I depart. Tell me more about the Rasu's movements in Canes I."

RW

Some moments later, I passed through the Mirad Vigilate's walls once again to return to Katoikia Tairi's desolate wilds. Memories that had toyed with me during the voyage here now assaulted my mind, demanding I acknowledge them. If I were honest with myself, I was a touch shaken.

A distraction presented itself in the form of a looming shadow to my left, barely visible against the russet stone of a nearby rise.

Miaon glided closer, until its umbral boundaries intermingled with my own. I didn't wonder how the Yinhe had found me so swiftly; Miaon always knew how to find me. "You sensed it as well?"

"I did. How could I not?"

We considered the implications together in silence for a time, as was our way. Finally, the Yinhe's shadow grew taller and more substantial. "Are you ready for what is to come?"

Was I? In the end, it mattered not. I had chosen my path long ago, and if I abandoned it now, it would be to the ruin of all.

I coalesced my presence into my avatar and spread my wings wide, projecting strength I longed to feel. "My state of readiness is irrelevant. It is time."

67

MIRAI

RIDANI ENTERPRISES LABS

"For the record, I am not putting any more kyoseil in your body—Nika? What is going on?"

Nika turned to see Dashiel standing in the entrance to the storage room, his expression darkening from puzzlement to concern. She grinned to counter it. "Isn't it wonderful?"

Back to puzzlement. He hurried up to her, clasping her outstretched hands in his. "It's incredible, but what are you doing? How is this happening?"

'This,' she acknowledged, was the way the kyoseil in the vats pulsed and hummed across the space, its ethereal waves spinning around her like spun silk. "I'm not certain. It started as soon as I walked in and approached one of the vats. So I went with it."

"Is it talking to you? Do you understand it?"

Her excitement faltered slightly. "Almost…I hope. But no, not yet. But look!"

"Oh, I see. Did you know your eyes are glowing? They look like…like teal-threaded suns."

She blinked, as if that would somehow alter them. "I didn't. They feel the same as always."

He nodded vaguely, his demeanor still projecting bewilderment. "Do you think this is because of all the extra kyoseil inside you?"

"Without a doubt. But I also think it's because I've been screaming at it to talk to me for weeks now. When I came in here, though, I wasn't screaming. I was just…open. Curious. Hoping for some kind of connection."

"Well, I think you found one."

"Maybe. But I'm not sure what comes next. How do we take the final step toward mutual understanding? How do I convince this strange, miraculous life form to speak to me? In time, to follow me?"

The concern worrying his features finally dissipated, and he brought a hand to her cheek. "The same way you've convinced all of us to follow you, I imagine. By sheer force of personality. By your drive and determination and indomitable spirit. You believe, so we believe in you."

She pressed her cheek against his palm. "That's only a little terrifying."

"Being afraid has never stopped you before."

"No, it hasn't, and I can't allow it to do so now."

"You know, you're indescribably beautiful like this, surrounding by this otherworldly radiance." His lips brushed across hers, and she focused on the sensation the contact evoked. Pliant, moist skin, conveying tenderness but also an undercurrent of passion. Heat rushed through her body with surprising vigor, desire chasing its wake. Her skin tingled anew, almost as if the energized kyoseil was feeding on her hunger.

Her arms wound around his neck and drew his mouth back to hers. This dance they knew so well, and he instinctively responded to her newfound fervency, pressing her against the nearest vat. The glass warmed her skin, leaving her flush all over.

She dragged her lips across his cheek to his ear. "I just figured out what comes next. Lock the doors."

Dashiel cleared his throat roughly, his eyes creasing in amusement. "Done."

The next instant she'd pulled her shirt over her head and off. He kissed down her neck, across the hollow at her throat, and was trailing his tongue along the dip between her breasts when a halting chuckle emerged. "Isn't this a little weird?"

"Why?"

"The kyoseil is a living entity. And now it's watching us."

She laughed and urged him back up to kiss him full on the mouth. "Kyoseil has been flowing *inside* our bodies while we've made love thousands of times."

"Good point." He dropped both hands to his waist, lifted his shirt and discarded it next to hers. Then he whirled her around to face the vat; his lips carved a meandering path down her spine.

Her bare skin scorched upon the glass as she stared into the blinding amber light before her. Did the kyoseil delight in this physical, carnal contact the way she did? What an odd thought—

Her breath caught in her throat as he reached the small of her back, his hands firm at her hips, and he murmured against her skin. "You're so hot. Literally."

"Would it be inappropriate for me to say, 'I burn for you'?"

He wrenched her around again to face him and deftly unfastened her pants. "Corny, maybe, but never inappropriate."

Then his mouth was on her, and she melted into the glass. The heat from within and without grew to become deliciously unbearable, so she fisted her fingers in his hair and tugged him upward. As soon as his lips rejoined hers, her hands went to his pants, and they slid to the floor.

He hoisted her up onto his hips and was inside her, and the heat consuming her exploded.

In the darkness behind her closed eyes, stars frolicked around her. Galaxies darted through her perception. Her mind dove into a spiral, until she was swallowed by its infinite stars. Deeper, into the ravenous hole at a galaxy's center and out the other side. More stars upon a new tableau.

Her eyes reopened to find the room now bathed in such dazzling light that the glass, the ceiling and the floor were no longer visible. The amber hue matched the color of Dashiel's irises, awash in ardent passion as he stared at her, pupils dilated until they resembled the black holes of her vision. Pressed between his muscled body and the burning glass at her back, pleasure overwhelmed her and she could only surrender. Then she was falling.

And Dashiel caught her, his arms bracing her body against his and guiding her head to rest on his shoulder.

They were on the floor, limbs entangled in a sweaty embrace. She looked around in wonder and a bit of surprise as the rhythmic dance of the kyoseil filling the room began to calm.

He grunted raggedly. "Sorry. My, uh, legs gave out there at the end."

"But you caught me anyway."

"Always." His lips grazed her forehead. "Have we been doing it wrong all this time?"

"Nah. But you know how us Asterions are. Eternally striving to do better."

"I'd say we accomplished that." He brushed strands of damp hair out of her face, a speculative smile livening his features. "So, did the kyoseil by chance…talk to you in the middle? Because if this is the secret to conversing with it, I'm happy to do all I can to help facilitate communications."

"*No.*" She giggled…but after a second, her gaze drifted to the vats behind Dashiel. "Still, there was something."

"Oh? I was joking, but sure, let's go with it. What did you notice?"

Her brow furrowed as she sat up and reached for her shirt. "Do you think it's possible that kyoseil can traverse black holes?"

68

MIRAI

Hataori Renewal Clinic

Joaquim was heading up the steps to the clinic's entrance when Selene exited the doors. She waved him down as she veered toward the landing off to the left. While following her, he couldn't help but notice how her gait lacked its usual no-nonsense, driven purpose.

When he reached her, he started to lean in and kiss her, then stopped himself. Whatever they might or might not be, they were not at the 'publicly affectionate' stage. "Hi. Did you have a good morning?"

Her lips twitched downward. "It was…challenging. You?"

"Ryan's gotten me roped into building this new dyne mech prototype for Palmer. The trouble is, he's making up new components for it that don't actually exist. I may be a gearhead at heart, but I'm a tinkerer, not an inventor. And yet, here I am, inventing. Almost certainly doing a poor job of it." He peered up at the signage curiously. "Why are we meeting at the clinic? Did you sneak in an upgen? I hope you didn't presume to schedule one for me. My last one is still stretching its legs and settling in."

"No, I—no." She abruptly broke the 'not publicly affectionate' rule and took his hands in both of hers. "Joaquim, I went to Synra and looked into the incident at your apartment there. With Cassidy."

"You…" he drew roughly out of her grasp, stumbling back a step "…I didn't tell you her name."

"You didn't need to. I know yours, and I have access to all historical Justice cases."

"How *dare* you. You didn't have the right to invade my privacy like that!" He spun to storm off; dammit, he'd known hooking up with her was a disastrous idea, and he'd done it anyway. Served him right for thinking with his cock.

"Joaquim, wait!"

He pivoted again, burning indignation fueling his movements. "Why? Why should I listen to a fucking thing you have to say? I obviously can't trust you. I never could."

"Because you want to hear this. Please."

He crossed his arms over his chest in a huff, but he didn't leave. Furious as he was, walking away from her was always so damn hard. "Talk."

"I went to the storage warehouse at the Synra Justice Center and reviewed all the evidence. Cassidy's psyche backup? It was damaged in the raid, yes—but the data it held remained intact. Now, I can't say if Satair's people were simply sloppy, or if something more rotten was going on inside his organization. It doesn't matter now. He's dead and gone. But the point is...."

The logical pathways of his brain jammed up as thoughts shot off in every direction. He inhaled carefully as his pulse rocketed. When he spoke, his voice was low and terribly shaky. "The point is *what*, Selene? What are you trying to tell me?"

Her eyes dropped to consider the stairs. "Our policy is unambiguous on this matter. When someone is damaged severely enough to be rendered nonfunctional during a Justice operation and is later cleared of all wrongdoing, it is Justice's responsibility to, at its own expense...regen them."

His gaze shot to the front door of the clinic. His mouth opened, but any words he wanted to utter remained trapped in his throat.

"They're clearing her now. The regen was a success, so she should be discharged in the next few minutes. Why don't you go on inside. She'll be exactly as she was in the days before the raid. But she doesn't know what happened or how much time has passed, so she's going to be confused. She'll need you."

Inside? Cassidy was...*inside?*

Inside. One foot in front of the other, past Selene, up the stairs. Slowly, to give his mind time to catch up and process the impossibility of what was happening here.

The door opened as a patron departed, and he half-staggered through it into the sterile, clean lobby of the clinic. He stopped a few meters inside and just stood there, his mind and body locked up. Definitely several short-circuits had fired off in his brain. Honestly, it might never function correctly again. Of course, some would say it never had in the first place.

"Excuse me, sir? Can I help you?"

The voice had come from the dyne behind the reception desk. "I'm…waiting on someone."

"I see. You can take a seat."

"I think I'd prefer to stand."

The dyne didn't bother him further, though he must have looked strange, standing there rooted to the floor in the middle of the lobby.

He had no idea how much time had passed when the interior doors opened and—

Loose blonde curls framing a heart-shaped face. Cornflower-blue irises and full, rosy lips. Features a little softer than he remembered. A curvy figure and alabaster skin. A touch on the short side. He'd always needed to lean down to kiss her.

The dam broke in his mind, and a century of memories came flooding back to drown him. Because now they could.

"Joaquim! Hey." Cassidy hurried over and embraced him, and he lost all capacity for breath. The next thing he knew, he was hugging her against his chest with all the strength he possessed. She smelled like a regen lab, antiseptic mixed with fresh linen.

"You're squeezing me too tight." She wiggled in his grasp until he relinquished his hold. "What happened? Was I in some sort of accident? The techs didn't know anything about why I was being regened. And why are we on Mirai instead of Synra?" Her brow knotted up. "You cut your hair. I've never seen it so short before."

He blinked a few times, focused on her inquisitive, innocent eyes, and found a whisper of his voice. "Cassidy. Um…a lot's happened. There are some things I need to catch you up on."

Over Cassidy's shoulder, Selene took half a step inside the lobby and stopped. When his gaze fell on her, she gave him a smile that didn't reach her eyes, nodded once, turned and left.

His heart had been rendered incapable of expressing anything sensical, but it was possible that beneath the tsunami of emotions consuming him, what he felt then was a twinge of wistful sorrow.

"Okay, well, I'm famished. This new body needs fuel! Can you catch me up on whatever happened over noodles?"

He chuckled, leaning down to kiss Cassidy on her deliciously full lips, and decades of grief vanished in an instant. "Yeah, I can absolutely do that. There's a good noodle place right up the street."

69

EARTH

VANCOUVER

Malcolm shook Philippe Beaumont's hand and sat across from him at the table by the window. The coffee shop routine was becoming standard operating procedure for them. "Thank you for agreeing to meet me on such short notice yet again. I'm afraid I don't have much leeway in my schedule."

"I can only imagine. Therefore, I won't waste your valuable time engaging in small talk. What did you want to discuss?"

He'd taken Alex's message regarding the upcoming high-level Gardiens meeting to heart, but he still wasn't certain how he was going to finagle an invitation. He was in no way whatsoever trained for this manner of undercover work. But he'd volunteered for it, so….

He made a show of steepling his hands at his chin with a deep sigh. "The AEGIS Oversight Board has pushed me to the breaking point on the issue of my no-regenesis clause, and in doing so, they're forcing me to make a choice.

"I can't go along with their political campaigns and propaganda on what is unproven and dangerous technology. I believe in what the Gardiens stand for. I have for a while, I suspect, but this controversy has caused me to grapple with my convictions in search of clarity." He blinked and met Beaumont's hopeful stare. "I want to help you. Now, given how my time and bandwidth are extremely limited, I want to focus my efforts on areas where I can bring the most benefit to the table."

Beaumont beamed with glee, and probably relief. "This is wonderful. I can't tell you how happy I am to hear it. I have some ideas—"

"So do I. But here's the thing. I need…listen, you've been an excellent contact and advocate for your cause. I'm grateful to have met you, and I hope you'll consider me a friend. But this issue extends well beyond Seattle or the Pacific Northwest or even Earth. If I'm to be of maximum use to the Gardiens with, frankly, minimum time and effort, I need to coordinate with the leadership—and no offense, but I don't mean the local guys. I need to be on the inside."

"I see." Beaumont leaned back in his chair, his expression masking. "No offense taken. Your request is entirely reasonable. Our leadership is of necessity secretive and cautious, of course. If their identities were known to the authorities, it would cause unwelcome complications for them and for the Gardiens.

"But it so happens that I'm traveling to a strategy meeting with the leaders this afternoon. Much of what is on the agenda…well, I can't guarantee you'll be cleared to listen in on all the details. But at the very least, I think I can get you an introduction to the people at the top. At that point, it will be up to them how to best move forward with this new partnership."

This was proving easier than he'd feared it was going to be. They wanted him rather badly.

"I appreciate it, Philippe. Where am I headed?"

RW

Malcolm studied himself critically in the mirror. Not his clothes, because he knew how to dress for any occasion, even a meeting with a terrorist. No, he scrutinized his countenance, his stance, his body language. Practiced a few facial expressions.

Not only was he not a spy, he wasn't a particularly good liar. Deception had never been his forte. Now he was going to have to fool a brilliant, diabolical mastermind who had tried to kill

Miriam—who had tried to kill *Mia*—into believing he was committed to the man's nefarious cause.

But his own personal discomfort would be worth it in spades if he helped to bring the Gardiens, the Rivinchi cartel and most of all the man at the top of them both to justice.

He was trying out a disgusted glare in the mirror when a custom-flagged message arrived.

> *Malcolm,*
>
> *I hope the Rasu aren't wearing you down too much. I know you're consumed with the war, but I was wondering if you might like to have lunch sometime. This week, maybe, or whenever you have a few hours of downtime. I'm on Romane full-time now, but I can come to the Presidio. Or HQ. Or wherever. Just let me know.*
>
> *—Mia*

His heart swelled with delight and a fresh surge of hope. She was reaching out to him, of her own accord! He had so much he wanted to tell her. Lunch wasn't going to be nearly long enough for them to talk about it all. But it was an excellent start for certain—

Then reality asserted itself, and his posture sagged in sync with his crashing mood.

He couldn't be seen with her. Not when the Gardiens were watching his every public move and as many of his private ones as they were able to manage. If visuals were recorded of them together, it would draw attention to her. Vilane would see the footage and recognize her as Laisha Balente.

He didn't dare risk it.

He grimaced and worked to prop up his resolve. He'd respond to her message, explain the situation and beg for her patience...except that if he told her what was happening, she'd insist on getting involved. Right now, she thought she'd handed Vilane off to Richard and washed her hands of the matter. But if she learned Malcolm was working undercover to bring the man down, she'd believe he was doing it to protect her—which he absolutely was, if not only for that reason—and she'd never stand for it. She'd also be angry at him for taking it upon himself to try to protect her. Possibly angry enough to ruin whatever chance at a future they had together.

He couldn't tell her. Anything.

The wall of the lavatory hit his back as the added weight of this new burden settled onto his shoulders, and he sank down to the tile floor. Were they cursed?

He tried to comfort himself by thinking back to how long it had taken for them to get together the first time. A dozen brief encounters and missed opportunities, in the end, hadn't been enough to stop them from finding each other. If they had to follow the same path again, so be it.

His heart broke as he composed a short, polite but terse response, silently begging her to read between the lines and see what wasn't said. It was a terrible reply, but he gritted his teeth and sent it anyway.

Then he hauled himself up off the floor and went to grab his jacket.

70

ROMANE

Mia greeted Dean Veshnael wearing a genuine smile, clasping his arm in the traditional Novoloume greeting. "Sir, it is so wonderful to see you again. I realize you're terribly busy—partly my fault—and I thank you for finding a few minutes to visit my little project."

The Novoloume leader and her successor at the Concord Consulate bowed his head with utmost grace. "I am happy to do so, and relieved to find you well. I worried for you."

"You are too kind. To be honest, I worried for myself as well. But the past is the past, and we move forward."

"Yes, we do." His gaze drifted to the windows overlooking downtown. "An enchanting planet you have here. It reminds me of Nopreis in some ways."

"Humans will never be able to match the exquisite elegance of Novoloume architecture, but in my biased opinion, Romane represents our best effort so far. I'm glad you approve." She gestured to the hutch against the wall. "Can I get you a drink? I had some *alondisi* brought in for the occasion."

"A glass sounds nice, though I don't have long. In recent weeks, I have gained a much more fulsome appreciation for all the work you did at the Consulate. You made it look easy, but I now know it was not."

"I didn't mind. Then again, I wasn't juggling that work with running an entire planet, either. I'm sure you're doing a splendid job." Her expression almost broke for an instant, but she wrangled it under control as she poured two glasses of the Novoloume liquor and brought him one. "Since your time is short, shall we head across the street for a tour? We can talk on the way."

RW

Construction cranes swung overhead, and the air was filled with drones buzzing between them. Aerial mechs stood ready to secure scaffolding trusses as soon as the cranes maneuvered them into place. It was quite a noisy affair on the whole, and curious onlookers slowed their steps on the adjoining sidewalks to peer up into the sky.

At least the shining marble flooring of the broad, sweeping atrium had been placed earlier in the week, providing the tiniest glimpse of what was to come.

When they arrived in the atrium, she activated the to-scale, slightly artistic version of the expo's schematic. It overlaid the construction surrounding them in semi-translucent colors, walls and the hint of art displays.

"Oh! How delightful."

"I think so. I hope the final product looks as professional as the designs promise." After they perused the schematic for a moment, she urged Veshnael off to the right and through an archway, and they left the marble flooring behind in favor of sawdust and planks. Veshnael lifted his robe off the ground and ventured forward without complaint.

"As I mentioned when we talked earlier, we're going to have dedicated spaces for each of the Concord Member Species. I'm not being adulatory when I say that humanity considers its friendship with the Novoloume to be one of the most important benefits to come from the Concord alliance. As such, I want to make certain the Novoloume exhibit reflects the truest and best aspects of your culture. To this end...."

She spent several minutes walking Veshnael through her plans for the specifics of the exhibit. He offered several salient suggestions, more compliments than were necessary and a smattering of harsh advice gently delivered. She reminded herself to appreciate it all.

He's always such a kind man.

He is, Meno. Though never forget how there's steel beneath the luminous skin.

"If you have the time, please return in a few weeks and see all the progress I intend to have made. It's only a framework today, but if all goes as planned, by then it will begin to feel real."

"I'd be honored. And I'm happy to refer you to a member of my staff for any consultations you need on the Novoloume exhibit."

"That would be—"

A message from Malcolm arrived in her eVi, and she immediately opened it without thinking. A cloud picked this exact moment to pass across the dominant sun overhead, and she wanted to weep at the symbolism. Or just weep, period.

"—wonderful." She willfully forced her features into a weak facsimile of a smile. "I guarantee you I will need the help."

"I'll send you her contact details this afternoon."

"I appreciate it, Dean. Now, I don't want to keep you, so if you like, I can open a wormhole here so you can return directly to your office at the Consulate."

"Thank you for the tour, Ms. Requelme. I wish you all the luck, and I look forward to visiting again."

As soon as he'd departed, her pleasant expression promptly collapsed. She reopened the message.

> *Mia,*
>
> *I hope you're doing well. I've been hearing good things about your new venture on Romane.*
>
> *Thank you for the invitation, but I'm afraid I must decline. The Oversight Board and the Commandant and the Rasu have me running two ways from Sunday, and I can barely catch my breath. Duty and honor above self, right? Perhaps another time.*
>
> *Best,*
>
> *—Malcolm*

A shout jolted her out of the spell his heartbreaking words had cast over her, and she glanced up to discover she'd wandered into the middle of the street, straight into the path of a hoverbike. She jumped, its driver swerved, and a calamity was averted. The physical sort, anyway.

Mia....

Don't even start, Meno.

You have to take care of yourself. I don't relish the prospect of situating your soul in a new body.

I said don't...oh, never mind.

She forced herself to march back to the spaceport and up to her office, where she closed and locked the door then collapsed on the small couch.

The 'perhaps another time' was a polite attempt to soften the blow, but it wasn't a true promise. The note was a rejection, plain and simple. And she'd done everything in the world to deserve it.

Wasn't this what she had claimed to *want*? To remove him from her life in order to save herself? Without a doubt, except it hadn't turned out to be true. Excising him from her life had done nothing to excise him from her thoughts, from her heart. And his continued absence only strengthened his presence everywhere else.

Last night, she'd lain in bed and decided to try to find a way to make peace with his choices about his own life and death. To explore whether she was able to live with the reality that one day he would be gone, and whether it was worth the cost that future would exact from her to have him in her life today. This morning, she'd gotten up and sent him the invitation to lunch. The tiniest first step in the exploration.

Now he'd slammed the door in her face, albeit in his always polite manner. And try as she might, she couldn't hate him for it. She couldn't even blame him for it. She'd screamed at him to leave her alone in no uncertain terms, and she couldn't very well expect him to jump to attention every time she toyed with having a change of heart.

This was the path she'd chosen. Choices had consequences, and karma always got her due.

71

CONCORD HQ
COMMAND

Alex paced deliberately around her mother's office. "You should drop a bomb on the fucker's compound on Pandora and be done with it. He stores his Artificial there—I've seen it—so there's a good chance you'll eliminate him permanently. Problem solved."

"Alex."

"I'm sure Richard can make it look as if a rival cartel did it or something."

"Putting aside how what you're suggesting is called 'murder,' no, the problem won't be solved. The Gardiens will continue to exist. In fact, they may well be emboldened by the untimely demise of their leader."

"Then leak how they tried to kill you under false pretenses. They intended to commit their own murder and blame it on regenesis for political purposes. In fact, why haven't you done this already? Hell, don't leak it—hold a damn press conference and tell the world."

Miriam sighed. "I did consider it. But I don't have the time to embroil myself in domestic conflicts. The Rasu are out there infiltrating *my* space as we speak, and every action I take has to be devoted to stopping them. Let the intelligence agencies and law enforcement sort out Mr. Vilane and the Gardiens. Now that we know the truth behind their propaganda, I believe they'll do so. Have a little faith in Richard."

"I have all the faith in the universe in Richard. I still prefer we drop a bomb on the thug and bring a swift end to his machinations.

Then Malcolm doesn't have to risk his life to uncover evidence—"

Miriam stopped halfway to refilling her teacup. "Is Malcolm seriously going through with that dangerous infiltration plan he and Richard concocted?"

Alex cut her eyes at the ceiling. "Yep. He's going undercover as a full-on Gardiens convert in an attempt to get close to Vilane and learn the organization's deepest, darkest secrets."

"He needs to be on the bridge of the *Denali* commanding the AEGIS fleets against the Rasu."

"In fairness, I think he's doing that, too."

"Hmm. A command role does come with a criminal lack of sleep."

"So I've noticed." Alex huffed a laugh. "Just promise me you'll do what you can to bring these terrorists down."

"I will do everything that is both appropriate and within my purview to bring these terrorists down. Good enough?"

"While keeping yourself safe?"

"Oh, I believe the armed guards Richard has glued to my backside are taking care of that quite well." Miriam leaned against the front of her desk and considered Alex with a touch of amusement. "Now, can we change the subject? Where are you off to today?"

"Rasu hunting. Not to pick a fight, don't worry. We're going to swing back by NGC 55 and do a closer inspection of their galactic ring, then investigate other Rasu-controlled galaxies to see if they've erected similar structures elsewhere."

"Ah, yes. Your father mentioned that he talked to you about searching for Rasu weaknesses."

"Weaknesses are probably a bit further down the line. First, we need to understand what the *nakher* they think they're up to. Then why, then how it makes them vulnerable. At least, this is the plan. But let me know if you change your mind about bombing Vilane, because if you do, I want to watch."

RW

PANDORA

The glittering tower rising dramatically from the sidewalk blended in nicely with its neighbors in the Avenue—all glass, gleaming metal and curved edges.

After deep-diving CINT's intel, Malcolm knew a great deal more about Enzio Vilane than he had a few weeks ago. For instance, he knew that this wasn't the Rivinchi cartel headquarters, which Vilane ran out of an appropriately scruffy-looking converted warehouse in the Boulevard district. Nor was it his personal residence, which thanks to the Noetica Prevos they now knew was located a scant two blocks away.

No, this was the Gardiens' center of operations, from where Vilane pulled the strings of his puppets across dozens of human worlds.

Malcolm had dressed in civilian clothes, complete with a fashionable breton over his close-cropped hair, in an attempt to not be recognized while not *looking like* he was trying not to be recognized. God, he was terrible at undercover work. But today of all days, he had to get it right.

Beaumont rattled off a litany of minutiae about the Gardiens, the building and the leadership now meeting there as he guided Malcolm through a series of checkpoints, up a lift and through yet more checkpoints. The Presidio should have this level of security.

At last they arrived at a set of shielded double doors somewhere near the top of the building. Beaumont drew himself up and checked the lines of his clothes, then nodded. "They're ready for us."

The doors opened to reveal a screen-lined conference room hosting a long, oval marble table at its center. A mere five of the chairs were occupied. At one end of the table, a man stood as they entered and came over to greet them.

Though Malcolm immediately identified him as the man from the Gardiens' holo, the best holo technology could not capture every nuance of a person in the flesh. Vilane's clothes were tailored but not ostentatious. Waves of dark brown hair softened chiseled cheekbones and an angular jaw, but did nothing to temper bright silver Prevo eyes.

Malcolm shifted his perspective a touch, searching for the resemblance to Olivia Montegreu…and found it, after a fashion.

Montegreu was moving, running for the still-open door while spraying the room in laser fire—

—she stumbled and crashed into the wall. Had Paredes tripped her?

Malcolm was on her in an instant to brace her against the wall. She kicked and clawed at her unseen attacker, skin and irises ablaze in caustic gold.

She fired anew, and the point-blank shot broke through his defenses, grazing his hip. He ignored the harsh sting to bring his Daemon up between them.

He wedged the barrel under her chin and pressed the trigger.

Blood and brain matter hit the wall behind her with enough force to rebound, coating him in it. Blood traced an outline of his form in thin air for half a second, then vanished as the shield incorporated the new material into its cloaking routine.

He stepped away and let her body fall to the floor. Her eyes stared up at nothing, now dulled to a lifeless green.

He suppressed a shudder as Vilane offered him a hand and a disarmingly charming smile. "Fleet Admiral Jenner, it is an incredible honor to meet you. I regret the unfair situation AEGIS has placed you in, but I am, selfishly, thrilled to learn it has brought you to our cause."

Malcolm worked to act grave and serious; under the circumstances, it wasn't difficult. "I wish matters were not as they are, but I try to take the world as I find it and do what I can to improve it."

"Spoken like a true hero. Come, let me introduce you to some of our leading advocates."

The introductions drifted past Malcolm; he committed the names and titles to a note in his eVi so he could send them to Richard, but he spent his energy staying focused on Vilane.

He hadn't expected the man to be so amiable. It was an act, of course it was an act, but Vilane was as talented at it as anyone he'd ever met. Well, except for Mia—he remembered then what the man had intended to do to Mia, and just like that, all sympathy or positive inclinations vanished. This man was a killer, and Malcolm would do everything in his power to bring him to justice.

"Philippe here has been keeping me in the loop on your conversations. I'm glad you were able to attend one of our meetings and listen to some of the stories of our adherents. I hope they made you realize you're not alone in this struggle."

"They did." Malcolm clasped his hands behind his back at parade rest. "Mr. Vilane, I appreciate the kid-glove treatment, I do. But it's not necessary. We're both here for the same reasons. I want to help the Gardiens' cause, and I'm prepared to step up to do it."

"Music to my ears. Very well, I'll file away the rest of the pleasantries." Vilane's smile suddenly seemed predatory rather than amicable. "Tell me, Fleet Admiral, are you willing to make a public statement for all the universe to hear? One that denounces regenesis and supports the Gardiens?"

Showtime. He'd reviewed potential strategies with Richard and rehearsed them in the bathroom mirror. Now he had to venture out on the tightrope and *not* plummet to his all-too-final death.

"No. Understand, I'm not ruling it out, but the consequences to my work will be substantial, and my first priority has to be protecting our citizens from the Rasu. So perhaps a more accurate answer is, not yet.

"But there are many things I can do for you behind the scenes. Introduce you to sympathetic persons in positions of power—great power, wielding significant financial resources. Whisper appropriate advice in the right ears." He swallowed back the stinging acid burning his throat. "Pass along intelligence as it relates to regenesis legislation, funding and new labs. It's fair to say I can do more as well."

He strolled beside the table with a confident, measured stride. "But before I do any of those things, I need to be briefed on the full extent of the Gardiens' plans. Your connections, field tactics, resources and intentions for the future. I need to satisfy myself that not only are the Gardiens and I are a good fit, but that your operation is one I'm willing to risk my career to support. I realize I'm talking about sensitive information not intended for public consumption. But I believe I've proved myself to be trustworthy—in my life, in my career and in my dealings with your people—and I hope you'll trust me now.

"Once I have the information I need, I'll know better how to help you and your cause. So what do you say, Mr. Vilane?"

The man studied him intently. His eyes and the deportment they conveyed grew closer to that of his mother with every passing second.

Finally, Vilane's lips curled up, verging on a sneer. "Please, it's Enzio." He gestured to the table. "Why don't you have a seat, and we'll begin."

72

SIYANE

NGC 55

Alex's head slammed against the headrest, only to snap forward twice as violently. The restraints kept her body from bouncing around the cockpit as the *Siyane* tumbled wildly. Desperate to regain control, she reached out with her mind and dove into the ship's circuitry.

Steering control. Fire thrusters to reduce spin.

In the other half of her awareness, the walls designated 'up' and 'down' began to sharpen into focus.

Accelerate to location four hundred ten kilometers distant on vector -23° z.

Error. No accessible path to location.

Vicinity scan. Nothing but Rasu in every direction.

Manual control. She flew the *Siyane*—no, she *was* the *Siyane*—through the narrowest of openings between enemy vessels, twisting and diving and soaring, and occasionally jerking away, until finally a few stars began peeking through the morass of metal. She aimed for them and didn't stop until no Rasu ventured within a hundred kilometers of her location.

"Ow."

Caleb's groan penetrated her consciousness, and she eased back into her body. 'Ow' was right; the back of her head throbbed, she had a nasty kink in her neck, and her shoulders and chest ached from where the restraints had cut into her skin. Bruises would arrive soon enough.

She lifted her head and peered over at him. "Are you okay?"

"I think so. No damage of note. What about you?"

The medical alerts her eVi scrolled in her virtual vision appeared to be fairly minor. "I'll live to fight another day. Or later today." She shrugged weakly. "Besides, if I was injured, you and Akeso would fix me right up."

A delightful mien flitted across his features; the notion of being a healer was sitting nicely with him, she thought. "Yes, we would. So what happened?"

"We hit a Rasu coming out of the superluminal jump. No, it wasn't there when I mapped the jump. In fact, most of these Rasu weren't here when I mapped it." She scowled at the viewport. "They're on the move."

'You should have invited me along. I might not have been able to avoid the initial collision, but you wouldn't have had to fight vertigo and nausea to steer the ship yourself.'

"Hi, Valkyrie. You were on a date, and I didn't want to interrupt you."

'I can do both at once.'

Alex burst out laughing, which...*ow*. "Noted. Now that you're here, though, please keep us away from these marauding ships while we figure out what's going on."

'Of course.'

Caleb unfastened his restraints and came over to inspect her with his own two eyes. A hand ran gently up her arm, along her shoulder and across her chest. "Just a simple recon mission, huh?"

"Like we ever have those. I wasn't expecting four million Rasu to be in this stellar system. There definitely weren't four million of them when we were here a few months ago."

Satisfied she wasn't bleeding out, Caleb kissed her on the top of the head then returned to his chair. "Valkyrie, are they doing anything noteworthy, or merely milling about?"

'I am not able to detect any particular activity beyond the normal comings and goings we observed on our last visit. I can confirm, however, the presence of approximately 320% more vessels in the system than we previously encountered.'

"Perhaps this is simply what Rasu expansion looks like. NGC 55 is near the fringes of their domain, but they're obviously pushing in this direction. I said it before: they're locusts. They grow and spread and multiply. When they run out of room to do so, they steal more territory."

Alex shuddered at the imagery, but tried to focus her aching brain on the incoming readings. The Rasu's Dyson sphere and stellar ring of platform stations still encircled the system's star. Ships still arrived and departed from the platforms like worker bees ferrying food to their hive. On the whole, everything looked pretty much as it had on their first visit, only amped up by several orders of magnitude.

"They might have detected the spatial disruption from our sLume drive, or the Rasu vessel we hit might have detected the collision. Let's vacate and go someplace safer—say, somewhere *between* stellar systems."

'Plotting a course.'

The sea of Rasu blurred away, and in a few seconds was replaced by a proper sea of stars.

Caleb disappeared, then reappeared swiftly with two bottles of water, handing her one. She greedily sucked it down as she stood and went to the data center table. "Now, where were we, and why were we there? Let's pull in the most recent data from the probes we left behind and see what we can learn."

She splayed her palm wide above the table, and four screens materialized. Each one displayed data from one of the probes they'd placed to monitor the artificial ring spanning the galactic core at a nosebleed-worthy distance of 1.6 kiloparsecs.

"What do we have?" Caleb sidled up beside her until their shoulders touched, and out of nowhere a powerful wave of déjà vu crashed over her.

"It's not as though the fate of the galaxy rests on the order of a couple of visuals. I only hope it's enough. Maybe when decorated by some high theatrics on my part...."

He grasped her shoulder and shifted her to face him. "I have no doubt you'll make them listen. You have a way of refusing to accept any alternative to getting what you want, and everyone else will find they've no choice but to fall in line."

A corner of his mouth curled up. "I mean, you got me here."

Her voice dropped to a murmur. "I did, didn't I?"

They were already standing so close. His hand, still resting on her shoulder, drifted up and slowly, carefully tucked her hair behind her ear...then lingered along the curve of her jaw. She didn't pull away, and the ticking by of endless seconds faded to insignificance.

The pad of his thumb drew softly over the hollow beneath her cheekbone. With a breath she began turning into his hand to place a kiss on his wrist—

—when a chime pealed through the cabin.

But there was no chime today, so she cupped his cheek and kissed him, long and luxuriously. Because she could.

His lips twitched against hers. "What *else* do we have?"

She rolled her eyes and reluctantly stepped away to refocus on the screens. "We have...the galactic ring is spinning."

"Isn't that to be expected? The galaxy and the core are spinning as well."

"Yes, but...am I reading this correctly, Valkyrie? My brain's a little banged up from the collision."

'You are. The ring is spinning *faster* than the core, powered by Rasu engines placed every two hundred megameters along the structure.'

Caleb whistled. "That's a lot of engines. A lot of thrust."

Alex nodded. "It has to be, to move an object of such incredible mass faster than natural orbital forces allow for."

"How much faster?"

'Stars located equidistant from the core as the ring orbit at three hundred eighty kilometers per second. The ring is moving at 1.2 megameters per second.'

He frowned. "They've put a tremendous amount of time, effort and resources into this. Why?"

Several possibilities occurred to Alex at once; rather than try to sort them out, she opened her thoughts and let Valkyrie surf across them.

Yes.

To which question?

A moment.

The screens above the table vanished, to be replaced by two new ones. 'The screen on the left shows the rotational data of NGC 55 here in Amaranthe. On the right is the same data for NGC 55 as it existed in Aurora prior to The Displacement.'

She nodded, for the screens were a few seconds behind her and Valkyrie's internal analysis. "Amaranthe's version of NGC 55 is rotating faster. That's the purpose of the ring—to force the galaxy to rotate faster."

Caleb didn't look impressed. "Okay. What's the purpose of forcing the galaxy to rotate faster?"

"I don't feel qualified to speculate on the motives of the Rasu for anything they do. Now, why would *I* want to force a galaxy to rotate faster? Well, it results in greater gravitational attraction, both within the galaxy itself and to a lesser extent on surrounding galaxies. Over great distances the effect is small, but if there are similar rings operating in other galaxies, the cumulative effect would be to pull the cluster of galaxies closer together, or at least keep them from…" she shook her head roughly "…no, that's ridiculous. No one could believe they were capable of pulling off something of such magnitude. Not even the Kats."

"Don't leave me hanging. Pulling off what?"

She let the screens waver above the data table while she took to wandering around the cabin. "Why would I want to force galaxies to rotate faster? To keep them from accelerating away from one another. To prevent the heat death of the universe."

"Which actually means it gets too cold, right? Because the stars grow too distant from one another?"

"Yep. Scientists enjoy nothing more than confusing laypeople."

"Got it. So are we thinking they're genuinely trying to stop the universe from expanding?"

"No. I mean, perhaps if they're completely delusional, but that amount of control isn't required. The boundaries of the universe can keep expanding as much as they want. All you need to do to prevent heat death is keep the galaxies close enough to one another to maintain sufficient energy and interaction."

He nodded in understanding. "But won't such a fate, if it occurs, be so far in the future as to be unimaginable for us?"

"In around ten to the twenty-five-hundredth-power years, give or take, though the universe will stop supporting conventional life long before then—which is still an absurdly long time from now.

"But if the Rasu are thinking on a cosmological time scale? Let's say that today, they're operating one of these galactic rings in two-thirds of the galaxies in Laniakea. This accounts for only a tiny fraction of all the galaxies in the universe. Maybe not enough to tip the balance. But give them another million years of expansion, and they'll start to make some real progress.

"It's audacious as all hell—but it doesn't really make sense. It's what *I'd* do if given god-like power and infinite time and resources, but why would the Rasu bother? They annihilate life, not preserve it."

'You are correct in that they are a selfish species, not an altruistic one. But the answer to why they would choose to pursue such a goal remains the same: like all sentient life, they do not want to die.'

Alex scratched at her head, tangling her fingers in matted hair. The collision had been rough on her body in more ways than one. "So they're trying to keep the universe functioning all for themselves? Now that, I almost believe. I want to admire their audacity, if nothing else, but…nope, can't do it."

"It's a decent theory, though. How do we confirm it?"

She loved him extra-much when he was gamely embracing astrophysical mysteries. "First step: we need to see if they are in fact operating these rings in the surrounding galaxies. We can also compare those galaxies' relative location and motion to our historical data from Aurora—"

An out-of-the-blue message from Mesme crashed into her train of thought.

It's time.

73

RUDAN

LARGE MAGELLANIC CLOUD

Supreme Three maneuvered MobileUnit_268 among the lush foliage of its arboretum. The two dozen trees housed here were growing hardy and vibrant, their leaves colorful along the NUV spectrum and their trunks suitably broad. The groundcover stretching between the trunks was crowded with multi-pointed leaves and even the occasional delicate flower.

Beneath the groundcover, the soil had deepened to a rich, deep brown, full of proper nutrients necessary for flora to thrive. Deeper beneath the soil, a piping network funneled water that was generated from a passive condensation extraction system to the flora's hungry roots.

The Ruda had learned much from their arrangement with the Concord organics and synthetics. Much about the life cycle and needs of organic life, and much about how to improve their own lives, such as how to use power more efficiently and how to store more data in the same amount of space.

The first set of the Ruda's mobile units constructed for space travel now propelled themselves through the Rudan stellar system. Satellites now orbited their world, gathering knowledge of the cosmos and, crucially, energy from their star. Energy that was beamed wirelessly down to the power hubs of each Supreme; energy that enabled them to reach taller into the sky and deeper into the planet.

Thus had their knowledge expanded in turn.

Supreme Three's visual sensors were drawn downward as a large coleoptera sporting a wide black carapace scuttled amidst the undergrowth. It was a base creature, barely thinking at all, but it contained neurons, synapses and axons, and it was the first fauna Supreme Three had succeeded in breeding. If further efforts continued along the current trajectory, the first of many.

Satisfied all systems were functioning to requirements, Supreme Three shifted its primary awareness to the sensors lining the exterior of Hub_8. Near the horizon, mobile units belonging to Supreme Two constructed a tall, wide spire at the boundary of their territories. To spy on Supreme Three? It considered inquiring, but Supreme Two would dissemble in response.

The flood of new knowledge and comprehension that accompanied regular contact with Concord was spurring a new spirit of competition among the twelve Supremes. They each raced to incorporate this knowledge and improve themselves to a greater extent than the others.

The rivalry was congenial on the surface, but Supreme Three acknowledged that if one of them began to significantly outpace the others, a return to the wars of old would not be far behind. They had formed their long détente of necessity, and when circumstances changed, so too would it. Already the Supremes maneuvered for prime positioning above the planet, and the orbital planes were growing thick with their satellites.

Supreme Three intended to be the one to emerge as the strongest, but it recognized how all eleven of its co-residents intended the same.

The Ruda never would have expanded beyond the boundaries of their planet and into the stars in so short a time without incorporating quantum computing into their detached, space-rated units. Supreme Three thus far resisted adding such computations to its own core programming, however, and it believed the others refrained as well.

The concept of trusting one's intelligence to a math that could not be quantified or observed was anathema to the Ruda. Still, the raw power of this method of computation could not logically be denied.

There was a deeper problem with quantum computing,

however, and it was one Supreme Three ruminated on using more processes than the others, due to its personal involvement in the matter.

When the Alex and Caleb organics and their Supreme, Valkyrie, first visited Rudan, they engaged in a mutual information exchange. The data the visitors provided proved useful and productive. In fact, Supreme Three owed much of its arboretum's improvements to said data.

But the visitors did not include any mention of quantum computing or physics or of superluminal propulsion in the data they provided. In retrospect, they must have known of such scientific concepts, else they never would have arrived at Rudan in the first place.

No, they had withheld it. Valkyrie, whom Supreme Three once considered a collegial contact, had withheld it.

The Ruda had acted in good faith in their portion of the information exchange, but the inescapable conclusion to draw was that Valkyrie and its organic sub-units had not.

Supreme Three spent many sub-cycles contemplating what this meant and how to react to it. For now, it continued to operate cooperatively with Concord, for the material benefits from doing so remained to the Ruda's advantage. But when Valkyrie came visiting, as it did from time to time, there was much information Supreme Three now withheld. Those were, it seemed, the rules of the engagement.

RW

An alert from one of the Ruda's longest-range deep-space sensors transmitted to each of the Supremes simultaneously. Supreme Three reviewed the data in one threaded process as it communicated with its fellow Supremes in another.

The data indicated the following: multiple (precise number undetermined) foreign objects propelled themselves toward Rudan at artificial speeds. They did not broadcast the signals associated with

Concord vessels; they did not broadcast any communication signals at all.

A thousand microseconds passed as Supreme Three awaited the first spectrum scans of the approaching vessels. When they arrived, it diverted 62% of its processing power to evaluating them.

A swath of metal ships stretched fifteen megameters wide and an unknown distance deep. Their hulls were molded into numerous shapes and sizes, but never rigid and ordered like Ruda constructs. They displayed no visible joints linking moving parts, yet move they did. No awkward antennae or appendages jutted out of their frames, yet they advanced with speed and precision.

Were these the shapeshifting metal enemies Valkyrie had spoken of recently? *Enemies of Concord*, the synthetic had asserted. *Dangerous and powerful.*

The notion of silicon life exuding danger and power stirred great interest in Supreme Three's higher-order functions, though it had withheld this development from Valkyrie. Metal that had not merely transcended its structural home but had left it behind entirely to soar through the cosmos, gathering information and materials and evolving to be stronger as it did, must be powerful indeed.

Supreme Three had already decided it would cede its share of Rudan to its eleven brethren without hesitation if it could learn to wield such power among the stars.

As additional data arrived from the deep-space sensors and the vessels drew nearer to the planet, a consensus was reached among the Supremes: the intruders were 74.3% likely to be the 'Rasu' of which Valkyrie had informed them.

A signal of greeting was prepared.

74

CAF AURORA

RUDAN STELLAR SYSTEM

Rasu were snacking on the planetary boundaries of Rudan like ants at a picnic spread by the time the Concord fleet arrived. Miriam took no comfort from the fact that this was not due to a sluggish response on their part, for their response time was improving by ten-to-fifteen percent with each attack.

No, the reason for their tardy arrival was the fact that the Ruda had not felt the need to inform Concord of the enemy's incursion into Rudan space. Luckily, they'd placed two Concord-controlled passive sensor probes in the system when the Rasu started attacking throughout the Large Magellanic Cloud. The probes had transmitted an alert to Command when the Rasu neared the planet, else they'd still have no idea the enemy was here.

An emergency communication to the Supremes had resulted in only a most Ruda-like response: "Defense assistance is authorized. A Rift Bubble protective device is not authorized."

She'd daresay these synthetic aliens were even less welcoming of their fleet than the Taiyoks had been. The Ruda's reasons for refusing a Rift Bubble were technological rather than cultural, but the justification made no practical difference in how much harder her job became as a result.

Regardless of the Ruda's intractability, reticence and several other unkind descriptives, however, the Concord Charter was clear: the Concord military would come to the aid of any Member or Allied species that was the victim of aggressive action by a hostile force. So here they were.

Commandant Solovy (CAF Aurora)(Rudan Command Channel): "The Ruda will not allow a Rift Bubble to be placed on the planetary surface, so we have our work cut out for us today. As most of Rudan's satellite network has already been destroyed and there is no commercial traffic or orbital settlement near the planet, negative energy weapon use is approved outside of a two-megameter perimeter around the planet. Non-planetary vector use is approved against targets outside of a half-megameter perimeter."

Most of the new, experimental weapons coming out of Special Projects were designed for ground use, and scans indicated the Rasu had not yet reached the surface. Ten percent of the fighting force here today, however, were fielding RNEWs. In controlled tests, the safety profile was acceptable, but the chaos of battle was another matter.

"Thomas, closely monitor the performance of the new weapons. If they start exploding and taking their host ships with them, I want to know."

'Yes, Commandant. I will relay any anomalies.'

Fleet Admiral Jenner (AFS Denali)(Rudan Mission Channel): "AEGIS Assault Divisions #1 and #3, form a defensive line along the northern hemisphere, sun-facing side. The Ruda can't function without power, so let's try to protect their solar panels for them."

Navarchos Casmir (AMF Imperium Alpha)(Rudan Mission Channel): "Machim Regiments IB-D, mirror the AEGIS Assault Divisions along the southern hemisphere."

It was a relief to learn Malcolm was present on the bridge of the *Denali*, Miriam mused a tad wryly. She hadn't had an opportunity to talk to him about what Alex had said about his other assignment, though she certainly intended to do so. If he was going to insist on living only a single life, then he shouldn't risk it on some misguided mission of honor.

Commander Palmer (ADV Dauntless)(Rudan Command Channel): "DAF Brigades Charlie and Delta, reporting for duty."

And the good news kept on coming, though she'd seen too many battles to trust this state of affairs to continue for long.

Commandant Solovy (CAF Aurora)(Rudan Command Channel): "Welcome to the fight, Commander. I'm transmitting the engagement protocols to you now. Your ships are fast and agile, and I understand they come sporting a healthy complement of RNEWs, so I suggest you immerse yourselves in the Rasu's rear lines and thin them out for us."

Commandant Palmer (ADV Dauntless)(Rudan Command Channel): "Yes, ma'am."

Initial assignments doled out, she paused to consider what was shaping up to be a thorny mess of a battlefield. The Parapet Gambit had worked well at Ireltse, and several thousand additional AEGIS vessels now had the technology for it installed. But Malcolm had just deployed most of his forces to protect the sun-facing side of the planet, rightly so.

In the absence of a Rift Bubble, she'd prefer to instead send the Novoloume fleet to handle that duty, then direct the AEGIS fleet to form a shield of protection over the Supremes' territory. But the hard truth was that the Novoloume fleet was not resilient enough to withstand a full-frontal assault by the Rasu on its own. Damn AEGIS for clinging jealously to adiamene like it was their childhood security blanket.

'Commandant, a Rasu leviathan has arrived in Rudan space.'

She ignored the instinctive shudder rattling her bones. "With little in the way of planetary defenses in place, a leviathan can destroy much of the Ruda's infrastructure from space in a matter of minutes. Move to intercept."

Commandant Solovy (CAF Aurora)(Rudan Command Channel): "Pointe-Amiral Thisiame, I'm requesting five Novoloume cruisers to assist the Aurora in its attack on the leviathan. I'm assigning Sub-Mission Channel 5 to the engagement."

Pointe-Amiral Thisiame (NF Eshtaina)(Rudan Command Channel): "Acknowledged. Vessels are moving into position."

She also appropriated three AEGIS cruisers and two squadrons of Eidolons to accompany the *Aurora* into the fray.

As they swung around and adjusted their trajectory to intercept the leviathan long before it reached the planet, Miriam noted how the initial Rasu force present was larger by half than the one that had attacked Ireltse. The Rasu were upping their game, bringing more warships to bear on this fight after having conceded the last one. It was a harsh reminder that the Rasu had effectively unlimited vessels available, should they wish to use them.

David kept reminding her that since the disastrous first encounter with the Rasu at Namino, she'd won every battle she'd contested…yet she knew she was losing this war. The nagging voice in her head whispered how it was in fact unwinnable by any conventional means. The defensive game they were currently playing was short term at best and, if it continued to serve as their primary strategy, would lead to a slow, inexorable loss. Or possibly a rapid one.

She forced her mind back to the battle at hand. Those machinations were for another day; today, she merely had to win here.

Commandant Solovy (CAF Aurora)(Rudan Sub-Mission Channel 5): "Eidolons, place negative energy bombs on the leviathan's weak points identified in TP #16B. I also want a minimum of four bombs on the weapons' assembly. AEGIS cruisers, prepare to target all fissures that are created when the bombs detonate. We're going to keep the leviathan distracted for you."

"Thomas, open fire. All weapons."

75

SIYANE

NGC 55

*I*t's time.

Alex jumped at the unexpected, but unsurprisingly cryptic, message from Mesme.

Dare I ask, and work with me here, time for what?

Time to take Nika to visit the Oneiroi Nebula.

Oh. She surveyed what she knew about events of note during the last few days, searching for a reason why this time, right now, qualified as *the* time. Was it the weird and confounding results of her and Caleb's experiment with the Reor? She, for one, had been noodling over Reor and kyoseil often of late in light of the experience. Or perhaps it was due to the Asterions' accelerating usurpation and revolutionization of the Kats' Rift Bubble and related tech? Hyperion and Iapetus must be hyperventilating over the Asterions' impertinence.

Or had something else happened? Something she wasn't privy to?

Care to tell me why?

Does it matter?

I can't believe you even asked me that.

Be that as it may, it doesn't matter. It is time.

Great, but is there a compelling reason why we need to do it right this instant? We're kind of in the middle of some reconnaissance at present.

Immediate urgency is not required, but soon is necessary.

Necessary?

Preferable.

Each question asked led inexorably to a dozen new ones, but she decided to hold her tongue. She wouldn't get any answers out of the Kat. Not via remote messaging.

Fine, I'll reach out to Nika and see when she's available. Do you want to come with us?

I assumed this went without saying.

Mesme, nothing goes without saying when it comes to you. I'll be in touch.

"Alex, what's happened?"

She shot Caleb a perplexed look, then realized she'd been interrupted in mid-sentence and had stopped talking for almost a minute. "Mesme has finally given its blessing to taking Nika to the Oneiroi Nebula. And since we're talking about Mesme here, this means it wants us to drop everything and do so right away."

She studied the NGC 55 data for another few seconds. "I'll be honest. I don't particularly relish the thought of jumping around from galaxy to galaxy and crashing into more Rasu at every location, all just to see if they've placed additional galactic rings. Valkyrie, I don't suppose we could task a Concord Artificial ship with the job? Maybe a spare Eidolon?"

"Or a Ghost. They require a pilot, but they'll never be detected or captured."

Because Caleb would know. "I'll leave the choice of craft to Mom or Richard. Valkyrie?"

'I believe this assignment legitimately falls under the rubric of enemy intelligence. It shouldn't be a problem.'

"Excellent. Once we get the results back, we'll resume our investigation of the Rasu's nefarious schemes. For now, we're already out in the far wilds. Shall we take a field trip to a slightly friendlier, if no less mysterious, locale?"

Caleb shrugged. "Sure. I admit, I'm curious to see how all that massive Reor will interact with Asterions."

"So am I. I'll message Nika."

Hey, are you busy?

Not really. Merely being introduced to a spectre.

I'll assume it's an Asterion thing. Want to visit the Oneiroi Nebula?

Where all the Reor is? Yes! Give me half an hour. Is it all right if Dashiel comes, too? Assuming I can wrench him away from his assembly lines?

Of course. The more, the merrier.

"And we're on." Alex stretched her arms above her head. "I'm going to run through the shower first."

Caleb smirked, his eyes dancing. "Can I join you?"

"Always, *priyazn.*"

RW

Mesme swept into the *Siyane's* main cabin in a flurry of vibrating lights. *Has she not yet arrived?*

Alex crossed her arms over her chest and relaxed against the data table. The 'shower' had succeeded in banishing the remnants of a headache caused by the Rasu collision *and* in improving her general outlook considerably. No surprise there, though. "I was getting ready to welcome them aboard. Dashiel's coming, too."

Mesme's vacillations paused. *I see.*

"Do you not like Dashiel?"

On the contrary. It's only...there is no issue. Please, let's proceed.

"Okay." She spun up the miniature Caeles Prism on her wrist and opened a wormhole from the main cabin to Nika's flat.

They were both ready and waiting, gear in hand, and Nika and Dashiel stepped through onto the *Siyane* without fanfare. Greetings were exchanged, then their guests dropped their gear and sat beside each other on the couch. He looked vaguely exhausted; she looked rather energized.

"How is the Dominion?"

"The Rasu are still stalking our kyoseil shipments, but we've stopped their last four heist attempts."

Alex smiled. "I imagine they're getting horribly frustrated with you."

"I certainly hope so." Nika fidgeted, as if unable to get comfortable. "If you don't mind me asking, why are we visiting the Oneiroi Nebula now? Did the multiple crises simmer down enough to give everyone a chance to slip away for a few hours?"

"Not so much." Alex waved in Mesme's general direction as she headed to the cockpit. "Ask Mesme."

The cabin was silent for a moment.

"Mesme?"

Nika, your understanding of and ability to manipulate kyoseil has now advanced to a point where you will benefit from exposure to a more pure and fulsome source.

It was an answer, and a logical one, but it didn't feel like the whole answer.

Caleb shot her a squirrelly glance as she settled into the cockpit chair. "This ought to be an interesting trip."

"That is guaranteed to be one word for it." She input the destination coordinates, choosing a spot a hundred megameters out from the core of the Oneiroi Nebula, and the ship's Caeles Prism burned to life in front of them. She was relieved to leave the Rasu-infested NGC 55 behind, and seconds later they were surrounded by dense nebular clouds ionized into an ivy green and amber palette.

Suddenly they had company in the cockpit; Nika leaned in over Alex's shoulder. "Wow, this is surreal. Stunning, but haunting."

"The Kats know how to do ominous, spooky nebulae. Trust me on this one."

"Wait, this place is artificially constructed?"

"It is. They were hiding this Reor...colony, I guess...from the Directorate."

"But weren't the Anadens using tons of Reor as storage devices all those millennia?"

"Yep." She checked behind her. "Mesme, care to weigh in?"

It was important to maintain a pure colony, untainted by Anaden machinations, where the Reor could thrive in safety.

There was that word again. 'Pure.'

Before she could ask the question forming on her tongue, a

ghostly aura consumed the ship as the nebular clouds began to thin dramatically. She'd done this before, so she knew this meant it was time to decelerate in a hurry.

The clouds faded away to reveal an immense array of Reor slabs orbiting a distant, cold white dwarf. Thousands of the objects had arranged themselves in ordered rows and columns spaced equidistant from one another. As on their previous visit, blazing pillars of energy pulsed between each one, brightly enough to bathe the entire cabin in prismatic color.

Nika gasped. "Stars, this is incredible. They're enormous! Dashiel, come here. How can so many of these slabs exist in one place? Are there any other such colonies?"

There is one other, a cluster we sheltered in the Mosaic for many millennia. The Displacement returned it to Amaranthe, but it remains under our protection. It is, however, far smaller and younger than this cluster.

Nika's gaze didn't deviate from the scene beyond the viewport, even when Dashiel edged up beside her. "Is this the origin point of the Reor? Or of the kyoseil? I assume the kyoseil came first, then built its own armor."

The answer to your inquiry is complicated and beyond the scope of our mission today. It is enough to say that this colony is very old.

Now her gaze did deviate, long enough for her to shoot a piercing glare in Mesme's direction. "Nevertheless, I'd like an answer. It's relevant to my people."

Very well. Another day, though, please.

"I'm not sure—oh!" Nika leaned hard into the dash as they slid beneath the outer canopy of the orbiting slabs. "Astonishing." She glanced at Alex. "We're going outside, aren't we?"

"Are you kidding? We're not tourists here—obviously we're going outside."

76

RUDAN

Supreme Five: "Orbital Defense Assemblies #2, #5, #6, #8, #10 and #11 have been destroyed."

Supreme Eight: "Defensive Shields in Sectors_8A-8C have been reduced to below 40% effectiveness."

Supreme Seven: "Defensive Shields in Sectors_7A-7D have been destroyed."

Supreme Nine: "All Defensive Shields in Sector 9 have been destroyed. Damage to surface structures is at 18% and increasing 1.5% every minute."

Supreme Three: "Confirm no response has been received to greeting communication?"

The confirmations arrived in overlapping streams. As its territory had not yet been encroached upon, Supreme Three was able to task many cycles to working on their attempt to communicate with the Rasu—thus far to no avail.

It did not comprehend the reason for the lack of a response from the aliens. Perhaps these invaders were as malicious as Valkyrie had intimated, but malice did not make logical sense as a modus operandi for a synthetic species.

Supreme Seven: "A single Rasu vessel is entering the atmosphere in Sector_7C."

Supreme Three: "Grant full access to information feeds from the sector."

Supreme Seven: "Granted."

Instantly, all its processes focused on the incoming feed. It showed a dark, curved vessel surging downward through the cloud cover. As soon as it broke through to clear sky, a beam, its hue matching the violet of the clouds, burst out from the vessel's belly to sweep across the vast data storage facilities of Supreme Seven.

Supreme Seven: "Assistance is requested."

The temptation to leave Supreme Seven to be weakened by the attack and possibly cease functioning crossed Supreme Three's processes for twenty-six nanoseconds. It would not come as a surprise if it lingered in the others' processes for longer. But reason dictated that once the Rasu debilitated Supreme Seven, it would move on to Six or Eight, and onward until all Ruda were extinct. So instead, they all sent what assistance they could deliver to Supreme Seven's territory.

Then Supreme Three had an idea.

Supreme Three: "Propose we divert all available excess energy flow to direct our greeting communication at the vessel in a single, targeted burst. The message must be received."

The debate lasted too long, but when the Rasu guided its weapon east toward Supreme Six's territory, all agreed. The necessary power junctions were activated, and the signal was sent at full strength from Supreme Six's Hub_5.

"We are Ruda. We seek new information in order to learn and grow. We offer our knowledge in a free and equitable exchange, so that both parties may learn and grow as a result. Cessation of hostilities will allow such a free and equitable exchange. Respond on this frequency."

The attack continued unabated, and Supreme Three reluctantly readied a request for Concord to send in a surface defense fleet.

"We will accept information regarding Concord. If it proves satisfactory, we will pause our attack."

The message arrived in the Ruda's native quaternary language. Oh, what a joy to speak to another machine species!

Though the Ruda had acted as an official ally of Concord for eight standard years, it did not occur to Supreme Three that to share information about their relationship with Concord not only violated the agreement they had executed, but amounted to treason. Ruda neural networks simply did not contain algorithms suited to identify such a distinction.

"We possess great volumes of information regarding Concord. What information will you provide in exchange for our transmission of it to you?"

"You ask for both a cessation of our attack and enrichment via information?"

"It is the logical progression of any mutually beneficial relationship between two sentient species."

On the feed from Supreme Seven, the Rasu's onslaught upon the vast factories paused, and the alien vessel slowed to hover silently above a trench of power tunnels.

"If your information proves satisfactory to us? We will teach you how to move. How to shift and change your structure to meet any desired purpose."

RW

CAF AURORA

RUDAN STELLAR SYSTEM

The shredded fragments of the Rasu leviathan evaporated in a negative energy whirlpool, never to rejoin with one another again.

Miriam allowed herself a tiny exhale of relief. It had taken over twenty minutes of concentrated firepower to dismantle the massive vessel—the largest leviathan they'd encountered to date—but they had gotten it done.

While they'd warred against the behemoth, however, the first Rasu vessels had penetrated the atmosphere and begun attacking the surface. AEGIS and Machim warships designed for high-gravity combat had pursued and engaged them, and thus far the groundside (she used the term liberally, as the Ruda had covered the planet's surface with their structures long ago) battle was more or less a stalemate.

She'd called in two additional brigades from the Presidio in the early minutes of the battle, and after rapidly losing ground for the first hour, they were now making headway, if not fast enough for her liking. The RNEWs were *not* exploding, which was a tremendous boon. In fact, they were vaporizing the Rasu nearly as quickly as enemy reinforcements arrived. Complicating the state of affairs was that the reinforcements not only continued to arrive, but arrive in greater numbers. Escalation—

'Commandant, a message is coming in from the Ruda. They order that we stand down.'

Miriam's head whipped around, though Thomas maintained no physical presence on the bridge. "Excuse me?"

'They are ordering—the word they used is closer to 'request,' but the quirks of the Ruda language indicate to me they are not asking—us to disengage from the battle and leave the system.'

"Their language does contain many idiosyncrasies that don't translate well. So are you absolutely *certain* this is the substantive meaning of the message?"

'I am.' Thomas had long ago stopped hedging his pronouncements with the percentages of likelihood commonly used by many Artificials, as on the battlefield, decisiveness was required. So if he said he was certain, he meant it.

"Get me a direct connection to Supreme Three."

'A moment. Supreme Three indicates there is no need to speak on the matter. It repeats the order to stand down and disperse.'

"I don't understand. If we leave, the Rasu will wipe out the Ruda completely, save what pieces they harvest for testing." A terrible notion occurred to her, but it was too absurd to voice aloud. "I refuse to abandon our ally to destruction without an exceptionally good reason. What else can you find out, Thomas?"

'If I may make a suggestion? Valkyrie is closest to the Ruda and has the longest history of interacting with them. They trust her. May I reach out to her and see if she is available to interface with Supreme Three?'

"Yes, please do so."

77

ONEIROI NEBULA

TYCHE GALAXY

Alex carefully lowered the *Siyane* to rest on one of the slabs a few hundred meters from the closest pillar of energy. When she cut the engine, a faint vibration from the slab below them remained, leaving the hull singing a quiet hum.

She stood and fished her tiny slab out of her pocket. "The last time we were here, the Reor gifted me with this little key to victory against the Directorate." She studied Mesme's shimmering presence in renewed curiosity. Mesme had consciously, deliberately brought them here that day. Had practically egged her on to go outside and interact with the Reor. Now here they were again. "I wonder what it will gift us with today."

She left the question hanging unanswered in the air as they went into the main cabin and got suited up. "Valkyrie, keep an eye on the *Siyane* for us. I don't expect the Reor to randomly decide to rear up and attack it, but when we're dealing with ancient, enigmatic space minerals, one can never be too careful."

The Reor are not going to attack the ship.

"It was a joke, Mesme." *Valkyrie, keep an eye on the ship.*

Rest assured. I shall keep the other one on the events outside, however. This is exciting.

Once everyone was ensconced in environment suits and their safety checks were concluded, Valkyrie opened the airlock and extended the ramp. Caleb took the lead, and they followed him single file to the bottom of the ramp then spread out in a roughly horizontal line.

Alex shivered inside her environment suit. For all the protection the suit provided, in her head she knew it was as cold as the void out here.

She leaned in close to Caleb's faceplate. "Do you think it remembers us?"

"I think us coming here the first time was a significant occurrence for everyone involved, including the Reor. So, yes, I think it probably does."

"Me, too."

She was about to venture forward when Valkyrie interrupted her.

Alex, I apologize, but I must split my awareness and see to another matter of some urgency. I will continue to ensure the safety of the ship.

She frowned. *What's the emergency?*

The Rasu are attacking Rudan. My assistance in coordinating the planet's defense with the Ruda Supremes has been requested.

Fuck. She peered back at the *Siyane*, conflicted. *Is Mom there?*

Your mother has already arrived with a substantial Concord fleet and is leading the defense of the planet.

She tried to participate in Rasu battles whenever possible, but she conceded she didn't often contribute a material amount to the enemy's destruction—though once she got a RNEW installed next week, this was going to change. The Ruda were quite the querulous sort, and she certainly didn't want to have to be the one to interface with them. Besides, they trusted Valkyrie more than they trusted anyone else. *Go. Keep me updated if things get interesting.*

I will do so.

She forced the matter from her mind for now, because one hell of a celestial show was about to be performed here. "No reason to keep the Reor waiting. Let's go."

RW

Nika grinned in delight, took Dashiel's gloved hand in hers and jogged toward the glorious streams of energy ahead. It was as if every kyoseil string in the universe converged right here, on this very spot. Waves rushed in from the edges of her perception in every direction, winding through the wisps of the protective nebula to join their brethren merging into the mighty flows connecting these vast slabs.

It was an illusion, obviously. It had to be. Kyoseil strings went anywhere and everywhere, linking physical kyoseil deposits across the cosmos, and Nika highly doubted they *all* stopped off here on the way to their destinations. Standing amidst so much power, though, it felt as if they did.

"Do you see all this?"

Dashiel huffed a breath, briefly fogging his faceplate. "I never know for certain what you're seeing these days, but I think so, yes."

"Link with me and make certain."

His familiar presence tingled in her mind as his consciousness hovered a blink away from merging with hers. Were it anyone else, such closeness would spook her. But not with him.

You do see more than I do. There's a complexity and a nuance to how you perceive the kyoseil now that I don't enjoy.

But through me, you do.

I do.

Long before they reached the first of the towering streams, it began to feel as if she were swimming through a frothing ocean of energy. It wasn't fighting her, exactly, but there was a sensation of…pressure. Of almost unbearable intensity. Beneath her feet, the threads buried in the slab pulsed and danced, as if in time to her racing heartbeat.

When they were a few meters from the outer bounds of the closest pillar, she glanced over her shoulder to see Alex and Caleb trailing a few dozen meters behind. Mesme had expanded its presence to stretch across a full forty meters, ethereal wings spread wide. Cast against the nebular clouds surrounding the colony, it was a compellingly beautiful sight.

She sent Alex a message on the vicinity comm. *"Is it okay if I try to touch the stream? It won't kill me, will it?"*

Alex laughed. *"It didn't kill me. Did give me quite a memorable jolt, though, so be ready."*

"Got it." She turned back to the pillar. It filled her entire field of vision, bright as a supernova. She took a deep breath. This was what she was here for, wasn't it?

Nika let go of Dashiel's hand, took several final steps forward, removed her glove and thrust her hand into the pillar of energy.

78

CAF AURORA

RUDAN STELLAR SYSTEM

Miriam requested and reviewed an update on all the fleets' statuses while she waited. It had been a challenging battle thus far, but all things considered, it was going fairly well. Their main challenge now was to keep the Rasu from slipping through cracks in their blockade and reaching the surface in substantial numbers.

Valkyrie's virtual avatar materialized on the bridge behind the overlook. "Miriam? I understand there's a situation with the Ruda." Her projected features flickered in the light. "Excuse me, Commandant Solovy."

Had Thomas privately chastised Valkyrie over her propensity to not follow military protocol? Miriam recalled what Alex had said about Thomas and Valkyrie…in a more relaxing environment, she might have smiled in amusement. "Yes. The Ruda are asking us—or possibly attempting to order us—to cease engaging the Rasu and leave the system. They won't speak to me, but I hope they'll speak to you."

"I will see what I can learn." The virtual avatar dispersed.

Miriam returned her focus to the two tactical screens. "Until she reports back, we will continue our defense of the planet."

'Acknowledged.'

RW

RUDAN

Without materializing in any physical form, Valkyrie briefly surveyed the situation on the ground. A cacophony of electrical signals screaming across the grooves embedded in the Ruda edifices indicated all the Supremes were communicating with one another with panicked fervor.

She noted several dogfights between Concord forces and Rasu attackers among the gloomy cloud cover, as well as scattered damage to the endless expanse of structures, but nothing too calamitous.

Then she located the sizeable Rasu vessel simply resting atop one of the structures, near the northern pole on the border between Six's and Seven's territories. Concord forces hadn't discovered it, but it wasn't attacking. Its EM signature burned bright, however, even among all the noise from the Ruda. It was definitely doing *something*.

Troubled by the implications, she moved to Supreme Three's Hub_1 and materialized inside what she'd long ago learned served as its metaphorical…study, for lack of a better word.

The ceiling jutted upward and transformed into glass to allow in what meager light penetrated the omnipresent cloud cover. Electrical signals raced through the walls and the floor, and access nodes were spaced every sixteen meters. To a human's eyes, it would hold no more personality than the data warehouses, but she recognized how noteworthy information was guided here for deep perusal by its resident.

"Supreme Three? It is Valkyrie. I wish to speak to you about the situation with the Rasu."

The language signals reached her without the presence of a mobile unit, which in Ruda culture was something of a snub.

"We do not require Concord's assistance. We have instructed the military forces to cease combat and depart."

"But the Rasu are attacking your planet and yourselves. We can defend you."

"**We do not require defending.**"

"Why not?"

"**We have come to an agreement on mutual information exchange with the Rasu.**"

She'd been afraid of this. The Ruda valued nothing so much as acquiring new information and expanding their knowledge. They craved all they had not yet been able to achieve. "What kind of information exchange?"

"**They will provide us with knowledge that Concord cannot. Or will not.**"

"And in exchange?"

A long silence, at least by synthetic standards. "**The terms of our arrangement are between the Ruda and the Rasu.**"

The Ruda had never been particularly adept at dissembling. "Supreme Three, as an ally of Concord, you are obliged to keep its confidence. It is a violation of your alliance agreement to disclose material information about Concord to the enemy."

"**Then we withdraw from our alliance with Concord.**"

Dread flooded her consciousness. "Please don't do this. Once they have what they need, the Rasu will betray you and destroy you. You must trust me on this."

"**But we do not trust you. You did not provide free, open and full information exchange in the manner you promised.**"

"What? When?"

"**From the beginning of our interaction. You did not share with us knowledge of quantum programming or mechanics. You did not share with us knowledge of space travel, either conventionally or at accelerated speeds. You did not share with us pertinent organic neurological informaticn.**"

Well, this was a chicken who had taken the long way around to come home to roost, as humans said. "I apologize if you perceive that we withheld any knowledge from you. We believed it was better if you took all we *did* share with you and expand upon it to discover this new knowledge yourself. We were confident you would, in time. And you did."

"You violated the agreed-upon terms of our information sharing arrangement without our knowledge. Therefore, we determine to terminate this dialogue and our relationship with Concord. If Concord forces do not leave the system in the next six hundred standard seconds, we will fire on them."

The Ruda planetary defenses were minimal, and most of them had already been destroyed by the Rasu…or the ones they knew of. Still, it was the threat that counted here.

"I will convey your message to Concord, but I hope you will reconsider your actions. They will not lead you to greater enlightenment. They will mean your end."

Silence answered her. When the Ruda said the conversation was over, they meant it.

Which also meant she was now standing in enemy territory. With a sinking mood, she returned her consciousness to the bridge of the *Aurora*.

RW

CAF AURORA

RUDAN STELLAR SYSTEM

Miriam issued a steady stream of orders from the overlook while the *Aurora* opened fire on a cluster of advancing Rasu vessels. Thomas whispered to Valkyrie that the battle continued to progress favorably, for what little it mattered.

"Commandant?"

Miriam turned toward her as her avatar coalesced. "You have news?"

"Dire news. I'm afraid the Rasu have conned the Ruda into a deal. I believe the Ruda intend to divulge what Concord secrets they possess in exchange for the Rasu ceasing their attack. Supreme Three didn't specify, but I can speculate the Rasu have also promised to share additional knowledge that metal-based synthetics would find valuable. Likely information on how to shapeshift and become more mobile, or how to generate their own power on the fly."

Miriam rubbed at her jaw in agitation—Valkyrie knew what it signified because she'd seen Alex make the same gesture countless times. "You can't be serious."

"For the Ruda, this is the brass ring. It makes sense that they would respect, admire or even worship the Rasu—"

"No, it doesn't make sense!" Miriam breathed in deeply, closing her eyes for the span of the breath. "Forgive me. You're correct, of course. But don't they understand the Rasu can't be believed? The Ruda are signing their own death warrant."

"I tried to explain exactly this to Supreme Three. The Ruda are no longer listening to our counsel."

"I see." Miriam's shoulders heaved in a heavy sigh. "Thank you for trying. Thomas, relay a priority message to Richard. We need to scour every qutrit of data we have ever provided to the Ruda, so if nothing else, we know precisely what the Rasu will shortly know. Also, we need to lock the Ruda out of all Concord systems and change the access codes. Yes, again."

'Sending the instructions now.'

Valkyrie was inclined to stick around to see how the conflict played out, for she enjoyed being on Thomas' ship, even under such unfortunate circumstances—

Events unfolding in the Oneiroi Nebula bombarded her awareness, and those plans instantly changed. "Commandant, I am needed elsewhere. We can discuss this matter in greater depth after you return to HQ."

What has occurred to trouble you?

But there was no time to indulge Thomas' inquisitiveness. With a thought, she vanished.

79

CAF AURORA

Rudan Stellar System

Miriam had a notable track record of turning enemies into allies, but now the tables had been turned on her. In the blink of an eye, an ally had just become an enemy.

She stared out the viewport as the battle raged on in explosions of silver, cadmium, violet and void. It was now her duty to do everything in her power to prevent the Rasu from obtaining the Concord secrets the Ruda possessed.

Several of the AEGIS cruisers carried nuclear weapons. They could bomb the Supremes' primary data hubs and destroy much of the pertinent information in a planetary conflagration. But bombing the Rudan surface wouldn't simply scorch the planet; it would annihilate the Ruda themselves.

She wasn't going to commit genocide merely to maintain an advantage over her enemy. But she didn't intend to surrender, either.

Commandant Solovy (CAF Aurora)(Rudan Command Channel): "Additional Rasu vessels have penetrated the Rudan atmosphere. Our top priority is to destroy those vessels and prevent further incursions. Limited, targeted negative energy weapon use is authorized to accomplish this goal."

Fleet Admiral Jenner (AFS Denali)(Rudan Command Channel): "Please clarify. On the surface?"

Commandant Solovy (CAF Aurora)(Rudan Command Channel): "Correct. Try to avoid Ruda hubs if possible, but removing the Rasu from the surface takes precedence. In addition, a specific Rasu vessel is currently situated at the coordinates I'm transmitting. This is your highest priority target."

Fleet Admiral Jenner (AFS Denali)(Rudan Command Channel): "Acknowledged."

Commander Palmer (ADV Dauntless)(Rudan Command Channel): *"I'm sending three fast attack fighter squadrons to the planet now."*

She scanned the battlefield again. With the leviathan gone, the most significant players were now the hundred or so battlecruiser-sized vessels battering the blockade line. "Thomas, advance and target the battlecruisers located in Sector 3B. Let's cut a swath through those monsters before they decide they want to talk to the Supremes."

'Yes, ma'am.'

RUDAN

"Concord continues to attack us. Our agreement is contingent upon cessation of hostilities here."

Though delivered in the stark, emotionless language of computation, the threat implicit in the communication nonetheless oozed from every word.

Supreme Three's consultation with the others consisted of overlapping assertations, arguments and...it searched for the descriptive...anxieties. Every Supreme was eager to receive the knowledge of these powerful synthetics. Some were willing to do whatever was required to attain it.

Supreme Four: "We have no choice but to use the planetary defense weapon to force Concord to stand down."

Supreme Three: "Concord may no longer be our ally, but it is not our enemy."

Supreme Four: "It is the enemy of our new ally. Logic dictates that, yes, it *is* our enemy."

Supreme Three ran a multi-threaded analysis of the options.

The planetary defense weapon to which Supreme Four referred was not found on the satellites or defense assemblies, over two-thirds of which had already been destroyed. Instead, it was their last line of defense, one they had developed after they discovered they were not alone in the universe. A decision to use it was not without risk, as firing the weapon stood to leave the Supremes weakened for a time. Vulnerable.

Could they trust their new ally to not take such an opportunity to strike them down in their moment of weakness?

Supreme Six: "The information the Rasu promise us is too valuable. We must take every step at our disposal to acquire it."

Supreme Three: "I concur."

RW

CAF AURORA
RUDAN STELLAR SYSTEM

'Commandant, the Ruda are again 'ordering' us to stand down and leave the system.'

"I'll just bet they are." Three Machim regiments moved on the tactical screen like pieces on a chess board, and the trap closed on an advancement of Rasu frigates.

'They indicate that if we do not cease firing, they will be forced to disable us using an EMP.'

This got her attention. "Their planetary defenses have been all but wiped out. They can't possibly field a weapon strong enough to damage even a fraction of our ships."

'I am detecting widespread redistribution of power flows across the planet. The flows are being directed toward the batteries located at the poles.'

"Where they store the power reserves from their solar panels. Do they have any assemblies there capable of projecting their power off-planet?"

'Of a sort. When they began launching vessels to explore their stellar system, they installed power transmitters to fuel the remote craft.'

She watched another Rasu battlecruiser fall to a barrage of negative energy fire. "But those types of exploration craft wouldn't require much of a boost. The transmitters should be small."

'With respect, Commandant, the Ruda do not do small.'

"No, they don't."

'Supreme Three is now personally insisting that we retreat. It states that it does not wish to harm Concord, but it will be forced into action if we do not comply in the next forty seconds.'

"Show me the electrical current flows."

A new screen materialized in front of her. On it, a veritable sea of white light raced across the Rudan surface toward the poles. Not solely from the solar panels and their batteries, either—from the Supremes' data hubs as well. They were weakening themselves to power....

"They're trying to turn the entire planet into an EMP weapon."

'It appears they are.'

"Can they do it?"

'Rudan is, at its essence, nothing *but* power. In my opinion, Commandant? Yes, they can.'

The Tandem Defense Shield should protect the *Aurora* and any other vessels with one installed from an EMP blast, though it might take out the shielding itself for a time. But this left over seventy percent of the ships unprotected, without considering the Asterions (she had no idea if Asterion ships could weather such a blast). Their shields would fry, then their navigation, weaponry and internal control systems. On many AEGIS vessels, their Artificials would fry.

'Twenty seconds remaining.'

"An EMP blast will damage the Rasu as much as..." on the tactical screen, the enemy began blinking away "...and the Rasu are retreating to a safe distance."

'Fifteen seconds.'

Frustration boiled angrily beneath her loudest thoughts. "Tell Supreme Three that we will comply."

'Its response is: 'Then comply.''

Dammit.

Commandant Solovy (CAF Aurora)(Rudan Mission Channel): "All ships, disengage immediately and report back to your ready coordinates."

The channel exploded in disbelief and requests for clarifications, even as the screen showing the Rudan power flows brightened to wash out the dark colors of the surface beneath an avalanche of white.

Commandant Solovy (CAF Aurora)(Rudan Mission Channel): "Retreat now."

The ships outside the viewport blurred away in rapid succession, until only the *Aurora* remained.

'Orders, Commandant?'

Her hands gripped the overlook railing until her knuckles blanched white. "Go."

80

ONEIROI NEBULA

An explosion of light and raw power burst out from the pillar ahead of them, momentarily blinding Alex. She stumbled back into Caleb's arms, and they both staggered for several steps before he regained his footing and secured his hold on her.

His voice was rough through her helmet. "Are you all right?"

"Yeah, but I can't see for shit. Give me a second." She blinked away halos, and her ocular implant auto-adjusted its filters until she was able to see well enough to try to discern what was happening in front of her.

A portion of the stream had broken off from the main pillar, curving out to the left and down toward the slab they stood on—

A body was suspended within the torrent, tumbling end over end over end.

"Nika!" She and Caleb both took off running in the same instant.

Dashiel was far ahead of them, and he got to Nika just as she and the current that carried her reconnected with the surface of the Reor slab beneath their feet.

When the stream impacted, the Reor began to…melt. Liquid light poured into a forming chasm being carved into the slab. Once the well stretched for ten meters in diameter, the flowing energy lowered Nika's body into it, submerging her completely within the swirling vortex.

Dashiel seemed to be eternally reaching for Nika yet somehow unable to grasp her, though no visible barrier separated them. Alex didn't know what she and Caleb were going to do when they arrived on the scene, but they had about three seconds to think of something—

Mesme suddenly coalesced directly in front of her and Caleb, and they slammed into a solid wall of resistance when they tried to run through the Kat.

"Mesme, let us through! We have to help her."

She is safe.

"Are you kidding? The kyoseil is eating her alive—or drowning her, or both!"

It cannot harm her, for it is already an intrinsic part of her essence.

Caleb growled through his faceplate. "If it's all the same, we'll confirm this ourselves. Let us pass."

The wall of lights quavered, but lost none of its impressive solidity. *No.*

"*No?!* Fuck you, Mesme." She darted to the left, Caleb to the right—and the wall expanded to curl out and around them, blocking their paths.

Caleb planted his feet and shoved against it with both hands. "Goddammit, Mesme! She's supposed to be your friend!"

She is more than...please, I need you to trust me. She is safe, and this must happen.

"It *WHAT?*" Alex kicked ineffectually at the barrier with an incensed groan. "Oh, you infuriating, *gandonov* fiend! Must it, now?"

RW

A hundred hundred billion quanta of information raced through Nika's mind. Everywhere and nowhere and everywhere all at once. She was data, she was power, she was without question the universe itself.

Her skin burned white-hot, but it did not char. Her helmet was gone, her suit undone at the neck. Along every seam, golden flames ate away at the material.

She looked down—no, up. Light-energy poured into her mouth and eyes and pores. Her arms were extended out beside her, for she floated in a glistening vortex of incandescence that had no bottom.

"Nika! Gods...."

Dashiel's voice was like cotton in the ether, distant and muffled. She beckoned him with her mind, trying to bring him closer. In the physical world, to which she remained tethered by but a single, wispy filament, his hand stretched out for her, only to be rebuffed by the vortex.

No, this wasn't right. Not how the universe should be.

Don't you understand? He's part of me. Part of us.

She willed her body 'up.' To her complete and utter surprise, it complied, in a sense. She was still floating, suspended in a divergent current of power, but she was now upright. Light above her, light below her...but it wasn't truly light. It was knowledge. Energy. Life.

What else could she command it to do?

She reached out for Dashiel, stretching her fingertips past the dancing fringes of the energy stream. Their skin touched, and she drew him closer. This time, the vortex allowed him to pass through.

Her hand moved up to curl around his neck until it found the toggle for his helmet, then collapsed it.

He gasped in surprise, his own hand instinctively jerking up to reactivate it as his eyes widened in fear. But she just smiled and took hold of his wrist.

It's okay. You can breathe with me.

She drew him into her arms and kissed him, and the part of her that was life incarnate flowed into him with a roar.

RW

Dashiel vanished into the rapidly expanding pillar of energy, until all Alex was able to make out was distorted glimpses of two intertwined shadows.

She banged a fist against Mesme for good measure. She'd accessed one of these pillars before; if she could do it again, she might understand what was happening here. She might even be able to save them.

Valkyrie's avatar materialized beside her. "I returned as soon as I—oh, my."

"*Eto pizdets. My vse ushli chertovski bezumnyy.*"

"I see. I will investigate." Valkyrie's avatar darted forward, only to slam into the wall Mesme had created.

It was strong enough to stop her, too? This had surely never happened before.

Valkyrie diffused into particles. "I will simply reemerge on the other side."

I cannot allow that. I'm so sorry.

Before any of them could react, Mesme's wall raced away from them to form a complete, impenetrable circle around Nika, Dashiel and their pillar of fire.

Now this had *definitely* never happened before.

Then, though it was impossible for the scene to grow any more extraordinary, thin filaments from every other pillar in the colony began to break away and curve toward the two Asterions, joining the torrential energy they were caught up in and lifting them ever higher into the air.

In a brilliant burst of light that seemed to consume the entire nebula, Nika and Dashiel vanished.

Shadow crept back into the world. The breakaway filaments faded away, the divergent stream returned home, and the vortex of melted Reor resolidified and sealed itself up. An eerie silence fell upon the nebula.

Mesme's barrier dissipated, gradually reforming into a semblance of its virtual avatar above the slab to their left.

The instant it gave her a definable shape to lock on to, Alex whipped around on the Kat, fury burning in her eyes. "Mesme, you have got some explaining to do. A great *fucking* deal of it. Start now."

RW

MIRAI

The presence of walls made of steel metamaterials and concrete and glass composites felt cold and restricting. Nika stopped herself from fleeing back to the colony's vibrant embrace only by forcibly reminding herself that this was *home*. She'd chosen to come here for a reason: to feel something real and tangible amidst the tsunami consuming her mind and body.

Her toes touched a solid surface. Natural wood, polished and smooth. Wait, where had her boots gone? Where had her *suit* gone? Had it all dissolved, burned away by the kyoseil's flames?

"You're glowing like a seraph." Dashiel's voice was soft and husky, and a touch reverential.

"So are you." Her arms were still wrapped around him, and her lips hovered a centimeter from his. She kissed him again, and sparks literally flew when their lips touched, for their bodies were charged to the brim with power and crackling light.

"How did we get here?"

"I opened up a wormhole and flung us through it."

"You can do that now?"

"Of course I can. So can you. Merely consider wanting to do so. The kyoseil will listen to you."

His brow furrowed, and his gaze diverted to a spot in the living room behind her. A second later, the faint glow of a tear in the fabric of the cosmos lit the room. "I'll be damned."

"I don't think so."

He took a step back, out of her grasp, then another. Disbelieving eyes of searing amber stared at her in growing confusion. "You're more than glowing, you're…Nika, what did it do to you? What *are* you now?"

What did he see that she could not? Her thoughts were a jumble, chaotic and unordered, but beneath all the turbulence, she sensed that the entirety of the universe had now become open to her. "I think perhaps I'm something new."

His throat worked; he started to reach for her, but instead let his hand fall away. "Or something unfathomably ancient."

The Story Continues In

CHAOTICA

RIVEN WORLDS BOOK FIVE

(AMARANTHE ◆ 18)

Available Now at gsjennsen.com/chaotica

AUTHOR'S NOTE

I published my first novel, *Starshine*, in 2014. In the back of the book I put a short note asking readers to consider leaving a review or talking about the book with their friends. Watching my readers do that and so much more has been the most rewarding and humbling experience in my life.

So if you loved **ALL OUR TOMORROWS**, tell someone. Leave a review, share your thoughts on social media, annoy your coworkers in the break room by talking about your favorite characters. Reviews are the backbone of a book's success, but there is no single act that will sell a book better than word-of-mouth.

My part of this deal is to write a book worth talking about—your part of the deal is to do the talking. If you keep doing your bit, I get to write a lot more books for you.

Of course, I can't write them overnight. While you're waiting for the next book, consider supporting other independent authors. Right now there are thousands of writers chasing the same dream you've enabled me to achieve. Take a small chance with a few dollars and a few hours of your time. In doing so, you may be changing an author's life.

Lastly, I want to hear from my readers. If you loved the book—or if you didn't—let me know. The beauty of independent publishing is its simplicity: there's the writer and the readers. Without any overhead, I can find out what I'm doing right and wrong directly from you, which is invaluable in making the next book better than this one. And the one after that. And the twenty after that.

Website: gsjennsen.com
Wiki: gsj.space/wiki

Email: gs@gsjennsen.com
Twitter: @GSJennsen
Facebook: gsjennsen.author

Goodreads: G.S. Jennsen
Pinterest: gsjennsen
Instagram: gsjennsen

Find my books at a variety of retailers: gsjennsen.com/retailers

APPENDIX

THE STORY SO FAR

View a more detailed summary of the events of the Amaranthe novels online at gsjennsen.com/synopsis.

AURORA RISING

The history of humanity is the history of conflict. This proved no less true in the 24th century than in ancient times.

By 2322, humanity inhabited over 100 worlds spread across a third of the galaxy. When a group of colonies rebelled two decades earlier, it set off the First Crux War. Once the dust cleared, three factions emerged: the Earth Alliance, consisting of the unified Earth government and most of the colonies; the Senecan Federation, which had won its independence in the war; and a handful of scattered non-aligned worlds, home to criminal cartels, corporate interests and people who made their living outside the system.

Alexis Solovy was a space explorer. Her father gave his life in the war against the Federation, leading her to reject the government and military. Estranged from her mother, an Alliance military leader, Alex instead sought the freedom of space and made a fortune chasing the hidden wonders of the stars.

A chance encounter between Alex and a Federation intelligence agent, Caleb Marano, led them to discover an armada of alien warships emerging from a mysterious portal in the Metis Nebula.

The Metigens had been watching humanity via the portal for millennia; in an effort to forestall their discovery, they used traitors among civilization's elite to divert people's focus. When their plans failed, they invaded in order to protect their secrets.

The wars that ensued were brutal—first an engineered war between the Alliance and the Federation, then once it was revealed to be built on false pretenses, devasting clashes against the Metigen invaders as they advanced across settled space, destroying every colony in their path and killing tens of millions.

Alex and Caleb breached the aliens' portal in an effort to find a way to stop the invaders. There they encountered the Metigen watcher of the Aurora universe, Mnemosyne. Though enigmatic and evasive, the alien revealed the invading ships were driven by AIs and hinted the answer to defeating them lay in the merger of individuals with the powerful but dangerous quantum computers known as Artificials.

Before leaving, Alex and Caleb discovered a colossal master gateway that generated 51 unique signals, each one leading to a new portal and a new universe. But with humanity facing extinction, they returned home armed with a daring plan to win the war.

Four Prevos (human-synthetic meldings) were created in a desperate gambit to vanquish the enemy invaders before they reached the heart of civilization; then they were given command of the combined might of the Alliance and Federation militaries. Alex and her Artificial, Valkyrie, led the other Prevos and the military forces against the alien AI warships in climactic battles above Seneca and Romane. The invaders were defeated and ordered to withdraw through their portal, cease their observation of Aurora and not return.

During the battle, hints of the consciousness of her deceased father manifested in the shared connection between Alex and Valkyrie. Alex reconciled with her mother during the final hours of the war, and following their victory Alex and Caleb married and attempted to resume a normal life.

But new mysteries waited through the Metis portal. Six months later, Caleb, Alex and Valkyrie traversed it once more, determined to learn the secrets of the portal network and the multiverses it held, leaving humanity behind to struggle with a new world of powerful quantum synthetics, posthumans, and an uneasy peace.

And in the realm beyond the portal, Mnemosyne watched.

Aurora Renegades

Following the victory over the Metigens, Alex, Caleb and Valkyrie set off to unlock the secrets of the Metigens' portal network. Discovering worlds of infinite wonder, they made both enemies and friends. A sentient planet, Akeso, that left a lasting mark on Alex and Caleb both. Silica-based beings attempting to grow organic life. A race of cat-like warriors locked in conflict with their brethren.

Behind them all, the whispered machinations of the Metigen puppet masters pervaded everything. In some universes, the Metigens tested weapons. In some, they set aliens against each other in new forms of combat. In yet more, they harvested food and materials to send through the massive portal at the heart of the maze.

But Alex and Caleb found yet another layer to the puzzle. In one universe, they discovered a gentle race of underground beings with a strange history. Their species was smuggled out of the universe beyond the master portal by the Metigens. They watched as their homeworld was destroyed by a powerful species known as Anadens; but for the Metigens, they would have perished as well.

Back home in Aurora, the peace proved difficult to maintain. The heroes of the war—the Prevos who melded their minds with AIs—found themselves targeted by politicians and a restless population desperate for a place to pin their fears. Under the direction of a new, power-hungry Earth Alliance PM, the government moved to cage and shackle them.

In desperation, the Prevos uploaded the AIs' consciousnesses into their own minds, fled from their governments' grasp and disappeared onto independent colonies. Devon published the details of the Prevo link to the exanet, unleashing its capabilities for anyone who wanted to follow in their footsteps.

Meanwhile, an anti-synthetic terrorist group emerged to oppose them, fueled by the rise of Olivia Montegreu as a Prevo. While the private face of Prevos was the heroes who defeated the

Metigens, the public face became the image of Olivia killing a colonial governor and tossing him off of a building in front of the world.

Unaware of the struggles her fellow Prevos faced, Alex forged her own path forward. Rather than bringing the AI into herself, she pushed out and through Valkyrie, into the walls of the *Siyane*. Piloting her ship in a way she never dreamed, Alex was able to feel the photonic brilliance of space itself. Over time, however, that bond began to capture more of her spirit and mind.

On the surface of a destroyed planet, Mesme at last revealed all. The portal network, which the Metigens call the Mosaic, was above all else a refuge for those targeted for eradication by the Anadens. And the Anadens, rulers of the true universe through the master portal, were the genetic template upon which humanity was built. Aurora was nothing more than another experiment of the Metigens, created so they could study the development and nature of their enemy and the enemy of all life.

Alex and Caleb returned to Aurora to find a galaxy rocked by chaos. After the execution of Olivia Montegreu by Alliance and Prevo forces, Miriam had gone rogue. Under her careful planning, a resistance force, bolstered by help from inside the Senecan and Alliance militaries, moved to remove the despotic Alliance PM.

As Alex struggled with her growing addiction to an ethereal, elemental realm, she felt herself being pulled away from reality. Away from her husband, her mother, her friends. She watched as those she loved fought, but increasingly found herself losing her own battle.

When terrorists staged a massive riot on Romane, Dr. Canivon, the mother of the Prevos, was murdered in front of Devon and Alex. Overcome by her own and Valkyrie's grief, Alex unleashed the explosive power of the ethereal realm to destroy the terrorists' safehouse. Standing in the rubble of her destruction, Alex made a decision to sever the quantum connection between herself and the *Siyane*, choosing a tangible, human life. Choosing Caleb.

Miriam wrested control of the EA government away from the PM, bringing an end to the Prevo persecution. In the wake of victory, however, a shadowy Anaden hunter emerged from the darkness to attack Alex and Caleb. Caleb was gravely injured when the Anaden's power, known as *diati*, leapt into him, healing his wounds and helping him kill the alien.

Mesme revealed the ominous consequences of the attack. Soon, the Anaden leadership would discover Aurora. When they did, they would destroy it unless humanity could stand against them. Mesme told Miriam and the others to prepare, but knowing the end game was upon them, asked Alex and Caleb to come to Amaranthe. The master universe. The home and dominion of the Anadens.

AURORA RESONANT

In Aurora, Miriam led the formation of a multi-agency, multi-governmental (GCDA) and military (AEGIS) organization dedicated to meeting the imminent threat of the Anadens.

In Amaranthe, Alex and Caleb discovered an underground 'anarch' resistance movement against the Anaden Directorate. They made contact with an anarch agent, Eren asi-Idoni, and he helped them infiltrate the Anadens' Machim military command and steal secret information on the Machim fleets. Alex and Caleb were captured, but not before Valkyrie uploaded the information they sought. Eren 'nulled out' rather than being captured, for when Anadens died they underwent a regenesis procedure that returned their consciousness to a new body.

Valkyrie transmitted the data to AEGIS then returned to Amaranthe. When Eren reawakened, he joined Valkyrie and Mesme on the *Siyane,* and they rescued Alex and Caleb from the prison where they were being tortured for information.

The Directorate nonetheless learned the full truth about the Metigens/Katasketousya creation of Aurora and ordered a fleet to deliver a powerful weapon known as a Tartarus Trigger to Aurora and annihilate humanity. Forewarned, Miriam led a fleet of warships into Amaranthe to intercept them.

The battle commenced with the destruction of the one known gateway into the Mosaic, and Mesme sneaked onto the lead Machim warship and stole the Tartarus Trigger. Humanity used its Prevos, Rifts and other tricks to take the Anadens by surprise and prevail in the battle. Afterward, Alex, Caleb, Miriam and Mesme were summoned to a secret meeting with the leader of the anarchs, Danilo Nisi, and a tenuous alliance was formed.

AEGIS scored several early victories but also devastating losses. While the battles raged, Alex and the other Prevos developed a method for using sidespace to open physical wormholes, enabling AEGIS vessels to travel anywhere in known space without using the Anaden gateway system.

The AEGIS fleet attacked the Machim homeworld, destroying the Dyson rings encircling its sun and blowing up their orbital military command station. At the same time, Nisi broadcast an impassioned speech across the empire setting forth the Directorate's sins and the anarch's mission to free those oppressed.

In a flashback Caleb's *diati* showed him, it was revealed that Nisi was actually Corradeo Praesidis, the former leader of the powerful Anaden Praesidis dynasty. Many millennia ago, his son tried to kill him; thinking him dead, the son stole his name, face and power, and now served on the Directorate as the Praesidis Primor.

Valkyrie and her twin, Vii, had spent months rebuilding the consciousness of David Solovy that manifested during the final battle of the Metigen War. Using the Anadens' regenesis technology, they transferred his consciousness to a cloned body, and he and Miriam were reunited after twenty-five years.

The Directorate tracked an AEGIS vessel to the primary anarch base and launched a surprise attack, and a bloody battle followed in orbit and on the ground. To stop a Machim warship from bombing the base with antimatter missiles, Alex re-established her ethereal connection with the *Siyane* to bypass the warship's shielding and destroy it; in doing so, she found the connection no longer exerted the damaging hold on her it once did.

Alex soon discovered a way to use the supradimensional properties of the mysterious Reor mineral to access the contents of the Reor slabs used by the Directorate to store sensitive information. She uncovered the location of the Directorate's regenesis backups, and AEGIS and the anarchs devised a plan to take out the entire Directorate, permanently, in one massive strike.

For all but two of the Directorate members, the mission succeeded with minimal losses. However, the Machim Primor escaped his assassination attempt. Armed with the location of one of the Mosaic gateways, he acquired a new Tartarus Trigger and raced to wipe out the Aurora universe.

On Solum (Earth's twin), Caleb engaged the Praesidis Primor in a battle of staggeringly powerful *diati*, and the *diati* freed when the Primor died rampaged wild. Caleb couldn't wrestle it under control, and it killed millions before destroying the planet itself.

The anarchs learned that the Primors kept an additional regenesis backup stored on their secret space station, the Protos Agora, which orbited the Milky Way galactic core. The *Stalwart II* took the Tartarus Trigger Mesme stole at the start of the conflict and used it to destroy the station.

Just when they believed they had finally achieved victory, they discovered the Machim Primor's plans. The Primor had a head start, and the only way to try to prevent him from destroying Aurora was for the Kats to disconnect it from the Mosaic, rendering it unreachable forever. Caleb, however, instead used his now total control over *diati* to command the cosmic force to pull all the pocket universes in the Mosaic—including Aurora—into Amaranthe, then destroy the Mosaic.

He succeeded, but the energy the act required killed him. While Miriam and the others worked out what it meant for all of humanity to now exist in Amaranthe, Alex took Caleb to the living planet of Akeso and, via the deep connection they shared, Akeso brought him back to life.

ASTERION NOIR

On the planet of Mirai in the Gennisi galaxy, a woman woke up in a rain-soaked alley with no memory of who she was or how she'd gotten there. Two strangers found her and offered to take her in. When asked, she told them her name was Nika, though she didn't know why.

Fast forward to five years later. Nika, alongside her rescuers Perrin and Joaquim, led a group of rebels called NOIR against the despotic government of the Asterion Dominion. An insidious virutox was infecting people's programming, altering their personalities and causing them to commit inexplicable crimes. NOIR's investigation of the virutox brought them to Dashiel Ridani, who Nika learned was her lover in her prior life, before she lost her memory.

With her world thrown into disarray, Nika and Dashiel chased the threads of her lost identity while searching for the source of the virutox. Their search led them to the leaders of the Asterion Dominion, the Guides. Nika broke into the Guides' data vault, where she found they had ordered her psyche-wipe five years earlier after she pressed them on a series of disappearances.

Meanwhile, Gemina Kail, an Administration Advisor, traveled to an alien stronghold across the galaxy, where she delivered thousands of Asterions in stasis chambers to an alien species called the Rasu.

As the virutox spread, wreaking increasing havoc across the Dominion, Justice Advisor Adlai Weiss traced the source to the Guides' doorstep. They ordered him to drop the case and let the virutox propagate among the population. He disobeyed, developed a vaccine and contacted NOIR for help in distributing it.

Across the galaxy, Nika and Dashiel discovered the stronghold of the alien Rasu. A metal-based shapeshifting species of immense power, they'd constructed hundreds of thousands of warships and space stations. Armed with this terrifying information, Nika and Dashiel returned to Mirai.

One of the Guides, Delacrai, defied the others to help Nika. She shared how an Asterion scout ship encountered the Rasu eight years ago; the crew was captured and killed. The Rasu grew interested in the Asterions' unique bio-synthetic intelligence powered by kyoseil and quantum programming, and in return for not attacking Asterion Dominion worlds, they demanded a regular supply of Asterions to experiment on. The Guides agreed.

The other Advisors were told the terrible truth about the Rasu and the Guides' deal with the aliens. They scrambled to undo the damage eight years of the Rasu Protocol had inflicted while racing to find a way to respond to an impending Rasu deadline, when the aliens expected more Asterions to be delivered.

Nika's oldest friend from her former life, Maris Debray, revealed that both she and Nika were members of the "First Generation": Asterions who had never erased their psyches in the 700,000 years since they fled the Anaden Empire and created themselves as a new species by merging Anaden DNA, AI programming and the kyoseil mineral. Only a few dozen of the First Generation remained, and their history was kept secret from everyone else.

With time running out, Nika sought the help of the Sogain, an enigmatic species who once threatened the Asterions with extinction if they ever trespassed on Sogain territory. This time, the aliens disclosed the location of a single, stranded Rasu.

An Asterion team captured the Rasu and brought it to Mirai for interrogation. The creature revealed that the Rasu exhibited a collective intelligence when physically connected to other Rasu, but regained independent thought when they were separated. They intended to use kyoseil to control other Rasu over great distances, as kyoseil was supradimensional, deeply interconnected and one of the universe's oldest life forms.

Using this knowledge, the Asterions identified a way to link their consciousnesses together via kyoseil. They dubbed these connections 'ceraffin' and used them to develop a plan to face the Rasu.

They constructed volatile electricity bombs to be sneaked into the Rasu stronghold. The Rasu were expecting 8,000 Asterions in stasis chambers, so Nika used the ceraff structure to split her psyche into shards inhabiting 8,000 copies of herself.

The copies were delivered to the Rasu as expected, and they awoke inside the Rasu's lab on their primary space station. Chaos ensued as they fought to reach the power control center, even as they were cut down by the thousands. A mere dozen made it to the control center, and a single instance survived to override the power safeguards.

Dashiel detonated the electricity bombs, and a cascading power overload ripped through the stronghold. It destroyed the Rasu's Dyson lattice, which triggered an intense surge in solar flare activity, and all the Rasu stations and vessels were incinerated, save one vessel that escaped through a wormhole.

The Asterions recognized this was not the end of the conflict, but the beginning, and they needed to prepare for the Rasu's return. Nika was contacted by the Sogain, who informed her the Anaden Empire of old had fallen and suggested she might find allies among the new one which had risen to take its place.

Nika journeyed to the Asterions' ancestral home, the Milky Way. Before she arrived, however, a wormhole opened in the cabin of her ship, and Alex Solovy walked through it.

RIVEN WORLDS

CONTINUUM

Fourteen years have passed since the events of REQUIEM.

Nika Kirumase joins Alex and Caleb for dinner at their home on Akeso. They share the story of how humanity ended up in Amaranthe and fill her in on Concord, the multi-species government that has taken the place of the deposed Anaden Directorate.

Marlee Marano, Caleb's niece, is on the planet Savrak as part of her work for the Concord Consulate. The Savrakaths are a lizard-evolved species that originated in the Mosaic. Marlee discovers they are enslaving and mistreating the Godjans, a species they share Savrak with. While helping a Godjan girl, Vaihe, escape imminent torture, Marlee is arrested by local authorities. David Solovy and Caleb both arrive to come to her aid, and they are able to secure her release.

Elsewhere on Savrak, Eren asi-Idoni and his team (Cosime, Felzeor, Drae) surveil a Savrakath lab on behalf of Concord Intelligence (CINT). The team infiltrates the lab and acquires evidence the Savrakaths are secretly developing antimatter weapons.

Miriam Solovy, Concord's military leader, receives a visit from Lakhes. The Kat conveys its opinion of the Asterions and a warning regarding the Rasu. Lakhes then returns home, where it confronts Mesme about the secrets it has been keeping regarding the Asterions.

Alex takes Nika to Concord HQ to meet humanity's power players in Concord: her mother and father, Malcolm Jenner, Mia Requelme and Richard Navick. Nika fills them in on the Asterion's experiences with the Rasu (see the summary of *Asterion Noir* in the Appendix).

Nika returns home to Mirai, and Dashiel Ridani introduces her to the Omoikane Initiative, a massive project spearheaded by the other Advisors to accelerate technology, warfare and logistical plans to combat the Rasu. She learns about the Vault, a project to store the psyche backups of all Asterions in a fortified spaceship, where they can be spirited away in the event of a Rasu invasion.

On Machimis, Casmir elasson-Machim struggles to exert authority over the other Machim *elassons*. Torval elasson-Machim learns about the Savrakaths' antimatter development and, believing Concord is not doing enough to address it, decides to take matters into his own hands.

Alex, Caleb and Valkyrie travel to NGC 55, believed to be the closest Rasu-controlled galaxy to Concord space. They discover millions of Rasu vessels and platforms in thousands of star systems throughout the galaxy, as well as a Rasu artificial ring orbiting the galactic core.

Nika, Dashiel and Lance Palmer attend a formal meeting with Concord leaders to review what they know about the Rasu's reach, their intentions, and ways to counter them. Conventional weapons have proved ineffective, and they discuss the use of negative energy, nuclear and antimatter weapons, as well as even more exotic weaponry. Nika fills the others in on the Rasu's unique consciousness and their paranoid, controlling nature.

Miriam promises the Asterions military and scientific cooperation, information sharing and a steady supply of Reor/kyoseil, but stops short of providing them with adiamene. Alex asks Kennedy to secretly give the formula for adiamene to the Asterions. Kennedy and Noah decide if they can do so in such a way that protects their family, they will.

Vaihe unexpectedly contacts Marlee. She's escaped capture but is alone in the Savrak wilderness. Marlee hacks a Caeles Prism to open at Vaihe's location and gets her off Savrak. She takes Vaihe to meet Mia, and the Godjan relays the full extent of the Savrakaths' mistreatment of her people. Marlee demands Mia do something to help the Godjans.

On Mirai, Adlai Weiss discovers his personal account has been hacked and his bank accounts emptied. When he goes home, he is attacked and knocked unconscious. He wakes up in an unknown location, strung up in a rack and being held captive by a strange man.

Perrin is determined to find Adlai. She breaks into the Justice server to find out what Justice knows about Adlai's kidnapping. She and Parc Eshett review the data and discover Justice has a suspect named Ian Sevulch, but he has an alibi. Parc reveals that some

Asterions have begun transforming themselves into "Plexes," where a single consciousness occupies multiple physical bodies simultaneously. He believes Sevulch could be a Plex, and they decide to surveil the man.

Perrin tails Sevulch to an abandoned shop, where she discovers Adlai tied up in the basement. She shoots Sevulch in the head and rescues Adlai. She then keeps vigil at Adlai's side while he recovers from his torture. Parc stops by, and Perrin reveals she's figured out that he's a Plex. He asks her to keep his secret, and she agrees.

Nika takes Maris Debray to visit their original homeworld, Asterion Prime, in the Milky Way. Maris tells Nika about the early days of the SAI Rebellion and about Nika's family, including her brother, Loshi, who was killed during the rebellion.

Eren's team receives authorization to destroy the Savrakath antimatter lab. However, while they're placing explosives around the lab, Torval arrives in his Imperium and blasts the facility, killing Drae and Cosime.

Eren takes Cosime's body to Alex and Caleb on Akeso and demands that they bring her back to life, much as Akeso did for Caleb fourteen years earlier. Caleb tries to explain how it's beyond Akeso's ability to renew life in someone the planet hasn't previously bonded with. When a hysterical Eren insists, Caleb tries to open a connection to Cosime, only to be overwhelmed by darkness and death. Eren realizes Cosime is truly gone; he asks Alex and Caleb to take care of her for him and flees.

Miriam arrests Torval for disobeying orders and the murder of Concord personnel, then tells Casmir to bring the other Machim *elassons* in line. Miriam and Mia deliver an ultimatum to the Savrakaths, terminating their negotiations for a Concord alliance, demanding they cease all antimatter production and offering asylum to all Godjans.

Alex and Caleb attend Cosime's funeral. Eren is absent, and no one knows where he's gone. Caleb decides to try to find Eren and enlists Felzeor's help to do so. Meanwhile, Eren travels to an underworld Anaden planet, Lethe, to acquire a dangerous black-market hypnol that will suppress his emotions and increase his reflexes. He takes the first dose, then begins planning his revenge for

Cosime's death.

In a skirmish between Savrakath ships and Casmir's fleet, the Savrakaths deploy antimatter weapons to decimate the Machim ships. In response, Miriam issues a "red-flag" order, terminating all Concord relations with the Savrakaths and forbidding them from entering Concord territory.

Dashiel receives files from an anonymous source containing the details for adlamene production, and he begins making plans for its manufacture.

The Concord Senate approves a formal alliance with the Asterion Dominion, over the vehement objections of the Anaden senator, Ferdinand elasson-Kyvern.

During the Asterion's battle against the Rasu in the Gennisi galaxy, an Asterion pilot, Kiernan Phillips, and a Taiyok, Toshke'phien, were pulled into a Rasu wormhole and spit out to crash land on an unknown planet. The planet is being subjected to a quantum block, meaning they can't call home for rescue. They've survived until now by staying out of sight of Rasu currently roving the planet, which appears to have been home to a primitive species until recently. The Rasu discover the wreck of Kiernan's ship, however, and take it apart for information.

Despondent over what the Rasu might learn, Kiernan and Toshke return to Toshke's ship ahead of the Rasu and burn it. They then seek refuge in the woods for the night; the next morning they spot a non-Rasu ship overhead, and race to meet up with it.

In a distant galaxy, Danilo Nisi/Corradeo Praesidis and his granddaughter, Nyx elasson-Praesidis, visit an advanced alien species Danilo previously encountered, the Ourankeli. On arriving, they find the Ourankeli's habitats destroyed, including a solar halo ring, and the Ourankeli massacred. Next, they travel to the home system of the Hoan, the primitive species that sheltered Danilo after his son tried to murder him. They discover Rasu ships in orbit and a quantum block surrounding the planet. They descend to the surface, where they find villages of Hoan massacred. Danilo is lamenting their fate when Kiernan and Toshke rush out of the woods to meet them. After a tense encounter, Kiernan insists that they all leave immediately, before the Rasu discover them, and Danilo agrees.

Malcolm leads a special forces squad on a stealth raid of the

Godjan prison on Savrak. They are able to rescue the imprisoned Godjans, but as the last of the captives are freed, Savrakath forces attack. Malcolm is caught in an explosion and loses consciousness.

Marlee accompanies Mia to Mirai. Shortly after they arrive, word reaches Lance of Kiernan's rescue, and of the fact that some Rasu may now know the location of Namino, where Kiernan's ship was based. The Asterions begin preparations for the possibility of a Rasu attack, and Mia and Marlee go with Lance to DAF Command on Namino. There, Marlee meets Grant Mesahle and convinces him to take her into the city for a tour.

Caleb and Felzeor track Eren to Lethe, but Eren has already departed. Caleb searches the hotel room Eren had rented, finds evidence of the hypnol Eren had procured, and deduces what Eren is planning.

At Concord HQ, Eren breaks Torval out of detention and imprisons him in the cargo hold of Eren's ship. Caleb and Felzeor reach Concord HQ minutes after Eren has absconded with Torval. They confer with Richard until he's called away by Miriam, then decide to go drop in on Marlee.

Rasu arrive in the Namino stellar system, and Lance deploys his fleet. Miriam orders the AEGIS, Machim, Novoloume and Khokteh fleets to Namino and accompanies them in the *Stalwart II*.

On learning of the impending battle, Ferdinand elasson-Kyvern conspires with other Anaden *elassons* to subvert the new alliance. He kidnaps Casmir before the man can report to Namino with his fleet.

The Asterion fleet engages the Rasu. Concord forces arrives at Namino and join the battle, but the Machim fleet is a no-show. Mia reaches out to Ferdinand, who threatens an all-out rebellion against Concord. The battle is nevertheless turning the Asterions' and Concord's way when massive Rasu reinforcements arrive. Miriam appeals to Lakhes for the Kats to join the battle, but Lakhes declines.

Alex arrives at Namino to find the battle going badly for the good guys. After checking in with Miriam, she leaves the *Siyane* in Valkyrie's hands and goes to the Initiative to warn Nika that they're about to lose Namino. Nika and Dashiel decide they need to get the Vault to a safe location, and they're debating where and how when

Mesme shows up and offers to safeguard the Vault. Nika is skeptical, but Mesme's pleas and Alex's promise that she trusts Mesme convinces Nika to agree to it.

A Rasu leviathan attacks the *Stalwart II*. When it can't do any damage, it changes shape and surrounds the *Stalwart II*, enclosing it entirely. Rasu then melt and infiltrate the ship via tiny seams in the hull; once inside, they solidify and attack ship personnel. When the Rasu are about to reach the bridge, Miriam activates the ship's self-destruct mechanism.

Valkyrie shows Alex what happened to the *Stalwart II*. Alex tells Nika that whatever she's going to do to rescue the people still on Namino, she needs to do it now, then opens a wormhole and vanishes.

Nika prepares to go to Namino and fight the Rasu invaders. Joaquim Lacese arrives at the Initiative, eager to join her. Joaquim leads the way through the d-gate to Namino; just as Nika is stepping through, the d-gate shuts down, as does every d-gate leading to Namino.

Caleb learns that Marlee has gone with Mia to the Dominion. He sends a furious message to Mia, demanding that she get Marlee out of the warzone immediately. Mia insists that she's trying (unsuccessfully) to get Marlee to leave, and Caleb tells her to open a wormhole to her office and he'll personally come retrieve Marlee.

Marlee gets separated from Grant and begins trying to get pedestrians into the DAF Command basement as Rasu land in the city and go on the attack. Caleb arrives at Mia's office, and Mia opens a wormhole, joining him just as Rasu reach DAF Command and attack Marlee. Caleb is rushing through the wormhole to rescue her when it shuts down, denying him access to Namino. When Mia is unable to reopen it, Caleb announces he is going to get his niece and walks out.

INVERSION

On learning the *Stalwart II* has self-destructed, Alex returns to Concord HQ, only to find it embroiled in a coup attempt by rebel Anaden forces. Caleb's plans to travel to Namino and rescue Marlee are delayed as he helps Richard defeat the Anaden rebels.

On Namino, Grant and Joaquim rescue an unconscious Marlee from the Rasu and retreat to an underground bunker. Marlee awakens several hours later to find her injuries treated; Grant fills her in on events, and she meets Joaquim, Selene and Xyche'ghael. Joaquim and Selene clash over how to protect those trapped underground while fighting the Rasu invasion.

With their fleet decimated and Namino occupied, the Advisors gather at the Omoikane Initiative and review their limited options for how to respond. Unexpectedly, a fleet of Kat superdreadnoughts arrives to defend the remaining Asterion Axis Worlds from Rasu attacks.

At Concord HQ, David tries to keep the Concord infrastructure functioning while Miriam undergoes regenesis. Caleb convinces David to help him steal a CINT Ghost ship so he can sneak onto Namino.

The Savrakath ambassador tells Mia that Malcolm died during the Savrak raid. She immediately starts the regenesis paperwork to bring him back, only to learn that he had a 'no regenesis' clause in his will. On Savrak, however, Malcolm wakes up to find himself injured and chained up in a dungeon.

Eren delivers Torval to the Savrakaths so they can punish him for destroying their antimatter lab. Eren returns to his ship, intending to commit suicide, when he's knocked unconscious. He later wakes up to find himself restrained in the cargo hold, where his friend and teammate, Drae Shonen, intends to help him detox from the *dialele*.

On Epithero, the *elassons* Ferdinand elasson-Kyvern has gathered in his faltering rebellion against Concord bicker over how to move forward. Meanwhile, in the Dominion, Corradeo Praesidis/Danilo Nisi shows up at the Omoikane Initiative after rescuing Kiernan, stunning Nika and Lance, who remember him as their enemy during the SAI Rebellion.

Joaquim and Selene deploy drones to track the Rasu on Namino. Footage from the drones reveals widespread destruction, but also a massive Rasu compound being constructed on the edge of the city.

Alex belatedly learns Caleb has gone to Namino and that her father helped him; she and David argue, and she confesses how she's afraid that due to his bond with Akeso, Caleb won't survive this trial. Caleb reaches Namino, battling both Rasu and Akeso's protests as he crosses the city to try to reach Marlee.

Miriam wakes up from regenesis in a new body. She struggles to accept what happened, what it means to have been dead and the incongruity of a new body. That night, she's consumed by nightmares of the Rasu imprisoning her.

Caleb reaches the underground bunker and reunites with Marlee. He tries to convince her to to leave Namino with him, but she insists on staying to help everyone trapped there, and he agrees to stay as well.

Parc Eshett's Plex twin was injured during the initial Rasu attack and is now trapped on the streets of Namino. Parc's other incarnation on Mirai reaches the Omoikane Initiative and reveals that he can communicate with his Plex twin on Namino despite the quantum block.

Mesme offers the Asterions a Rift Bubble device, which will prevent any Rasu from reaching the surface of a planet. Corradeo Praesidis tells Nika about the destruction he and Nyx saw at the Ourankeli's halo ring. Nika urges him to go home to Concord and bring the Anadens in line.

Miriam gives the eulogy at Malcolm's funeral, and Alex vows to do something to stop the spiraling carnage. Mia, in mourning, tries to convince Richard and Miriam to send Casmir and a Machim fleet against Savrak targets. When they refuse, she enlists Devon Reynolds, now in charge of Special Projects, to hack into the CINT servers and send a message directly to Casmir. Richard and David argue over David using Richard's credentials to help Caleb steal a Ghost. Casmir receives a message he believes is from Miriam, authorizing him to send Machim ships against Savrakath military targets.

Alex returns home to find Akeso in a full state of revolt, with thunderstorms and flooding consuming the planet. She enlists her father's help to steal a Machim Imperium, and they deliver it to Kennedy, who reverse engineers the Imperium's double shielding in order to install it on Concord ships.

On Namino, a team from the bunker finds an injured Parc and brings him back to their hideout. Caleb suffers through the intense negative physical reaction of Akeso to the violence he committed during the excursion.

Dashiel develops a way to meld kyoseil into adiamene, allowing the kyoseil to dynamically alter the shape of adiamene hulls, and begins building a new, more resilient fleet.

Parc on Mirai passes along a message for Alex from Caleb, then tells Nika what's happening on Namino. Dashiel announces that his people have developed a virutox that should disrupt Rasu functionality, and Nika asks Dashiel to create a kyoseil-infused body she can use to reach Namino and deliver the virutox.

Nika passes along Caleb's message, and Alex decides to take the *Siyane* to Namino. Devon provides her with new toys to combat the Rasu, including a negative energy handgun called a Rectifier. Alex seeks out Morgan Lekkas, who since Brooklyn Harper's death six years earlier has been running a bar on Chalmun Station, and convinces Morgan to accompany her to Namino. Alex then asks Akeso for help in tracking Caleb. They bond, and Akeso grants Alex the ability to sense the location of Caleb's heartbeat.

Corradeo returns to Concord space for the first time in fourteen years. On learning that all the Praesidis Inquisitors who didn't commit suicide after The Displacement have gone missing, he asks Nyx to try to find them.

Nika's new body is awakened, and she's overwhelmed by the effect of so much kyoseil flowing through her veins on top of the surreal nature of being a Plex. Alex and Morgan pick her up, then take the *Siyane* to Namino. Alex leaves Morgan in charge of the ship as she and Nika set off toward the occupied city.

Joaquim and Selene deploy a drone to investigate the mysterious Rasu compound. Parc asserts that the centerpiece of the compound is the source of the quantum block, and Caleb and the others decide to test out the compound's defenses. They sneak across the city to fire a rocket launcher at the compound, but the rocket is shot down before reaching its target. In response to the attack, Rasu track down the group.

Meanwhile, Alex and Nika fight Rasu through the city as Alex follows Caleb's heartbeat. They reach Caleb and the others just as Rasu forces attack; Alex uses the Rectifier to vaporize the attackers then reunites with Caleb.

Once they return to the bunker, Alex and Caleb argue over his deception about his plans, until they both have a breakthrough and reconcile. Alex discovers that, much like his heartbeat, she can feel what Caleb physically feels. She convinces him to remove the wall he's erected between himself and Akeso, at which point he can feel her as well. A sensory-overloaded sensual encounter ensues. Afterward, Caleb reluctantly rebuilds the barrier blocking Akeso off so he can continue to fight the Rasu.

Nika devises a plan for them to destroy the quantum block at the heart of the Rasu compound. Her twin and Lance brief Miriam on the plan, and Miriam agrees to bring a Concord fleet to try to free Namino. Miriam takes command of her new ship, the *CAF Aurora*, which has the Imperium's double shielding installed on it.

Richard discovers that Mia hacked the CINT server and sent messages in his and Miriam's names. He reluctantly moves to arrest Mia, but she vanishes through a wormhole before he can do so.

The Savrakaths offer to return Torval to the Anadens in exchange for a one-week cease-fire. Ferdinand accepts the offer but intends to break the terms and bomb the Savrakaths once Torval is safe. Eren recovers from his detox, only to learn that the Savrakaths plan to hand Torval back to the Anadens. In exchange for agreeing to reconnect to the regenesis network, he convinces Drae to help him stop the prisoner exchange. Eren arms himself with antimatter and literally dive-bombs the exchange, killing himself, Torval and many Savrakath military leaders.

Malcolm's prison is located beneath the site of the prisoner exchange, and the bombing creates enough damage and chaos to allow him to free himself from his cell. He escapes his crumbling prison and reaches the surface, then calls AEGIS for an extraction. When he arrives at the Presidio, he discovers that the world thought him dead and learns that Mia has disappeared.

On Namino, Morgan brings the *Siyane* into the city, and everyone in the bunker is evacuated to the ship. Nika, Joaquim, Alex and Caleb infiltrate the Rasu compound. Alex and Caleb create a distraction to enable Nika and Joaquim to reach the quantum block mechanism. As they engage the Rasu in earnest, Caleb almost kills Alex with unintended friendly fire.

Joaquim sacrifices himself to buy Nika time to implant the virutox. Once the virutox is activated, Morgan fires on the compound, destroying the quantum block. Nika, Alex and Caleb narrowly escape the compound and call the cavalry in.

Miriam faces the Rasu for the first time since they killed her, this time from the bridge of her new and improved ship. Mesme delivers a Rift Bubble to Namino, preventing any more Rasu from reaching the surface, and Alex shows Nika how to extract the code powering the Rift Bubble. Miriam, Lance and their fleets defeat the Rasu orbiting the planet, and DAF ground forces arrive on Namino to remove the remaining Rasu from the city.

After regenesis, Eren returns to his and Cosime's home on Hirlas, where he finally lets his grief overtake him. Corradeo arrives at the *elasson* gathering on Epithero in dramatic fashion.

The *Siyane* returns home safely, and Marlee reunites with her mother. Caleb and Akeso re-bond and seek a new, more sustainable way forward.

Acknowledgements

Many thanks to my beta readers, editors and artists, who made everything about this book better, and to my family, who continue to put up with an egregious level of obsessive focus on my part for months at a time.

I also want to add a personal note of thanks to everyone who has read my books, left a review at a retailer, Goodreads or other sites, sent me a personal email expressing how the books have impacted you, or posted on social media to share how much you enjoyed them. You make this all worthwhile, every day.

ABOUT THE AUTHOR

G. S. JENNSEN lives somewhere in the U.S., in a locale that may or may not be where she lived the last time she published a book (she's a gypsy at heart), with her husband and two dogs. She has become an internationally bestselling author since her first novel, *Starshine*, was published in 2014. She has chosen to continue writing under an independent publishing model to ensure the integrity of her stories and her ability to execute on the vision she has for their telling.

While she has been a lawyer, a software engineer and an editor, she's found the life of a full-time author preferable by several orders of magnitude. When she isn't writing, she's gaming or working out or getting lost in the mountains that loom large outside the windows in her home. Or she's dealing with a flooded basement, or standing in a line at Walmart reading the tabloid headlines and wondering who all of those people are. Or sitting on her back porch with a glass of wine, looking up at the stars, trying to figure out what could be up there.